ALSO BY PETE HAUTMAN

Drawing Dead

SHORT MONEY

A NOVEL

Pete Hautman

SIMON &
SCHUSTER

NEW YORK
LONDON
TORONTO
SYDNEY
TOKYO
SINGAPORE

SIMON & SCHUSTER
Rockefeller Center
1230 Avenue of the Americas
New York, NY 10020

Simon & Schuster and colophon are registered
trademarks of Simon & Schuster Inc.

Designed by Pei Loi Koay

Manufactured in the United States of America

1 2 3 4 5 6 7 8 9 10

Library of Congress Cataloging-in-Publication Data
Hautman, Pete.
Short money: a novel/Pete Hautman.
p.   cm.
I. Title.
PS3558.A766S56   1995   94-47963
813'.54—dc20   CIP
ISBN 978-1-4767-4851-1

For my brothers, who hunt, and for my sisters, who don't

FELIS LEO

He hunted game in the moonshine bright,

With never a thought of harm,

But he got quite a fright when there hove in sight

Teddy, armed to the teeth with a knife and a sheath

And a rifle beneath his arm.

The colonel plugged him with a laugh,

While Kermit took his photograph.

Said he, "Those Wall Street boys would cry,

If they knew how near I'd been to die,

Oh, this country's bull, bull, bully,

I've enjoyed it full, full, fully,

For it euchres the best they can show in the West,

That's so wild and wool, wool, woolly."

—*SONG PERFORMED BY "MISS SHOOTER" FOR THE ENTERTAINMENT OF PRESIDENT THEODORE ROOSEVELT DURING THE FAMOUS ROOSEVELT EXPEDITION OF 1909*

PART ONE

You have lunch with a guy, that's good. You do a round of golf with him, that's even better—long as you don't make him look bad. But you go hunting with a guy, get out there and kill something with him, man, he's yours forever.

—RICH WICKY, DISCUSSING CLIENT RELATIONS WITH A REGISTERED REPRESENTATIVE

he open-top Hummer climbed out of the dry creekbed onto the bank, turned its blocky nose to the north, and growled up the steep side of the coulee, seeking gaps between the larger trees, rolling over the smaller saplings and herbaceous plants, flattening the mat of autumn leaves. The two men riding in the back seats gripped the padded roll bar. The Hummer lurched over a log, crushing rotted wood with its thirty-seven-inch tires.

"Feels like we're gonna tip over, Doc," said the young man in the insulated camouflage coveralls. His name was Steve Anderson, an appellation that perfectly matched his unremarkable Nordic features.

Dr. Nelson Bellweather, a pudgy, mild-looking, soft-featured, small-eyed man with thin, pale hair and smooth, polished cheeks, laughed. He wore a pink western-style shirt with silver snaps and collar points, Ralph Lauren dungarees, and ostrich-hide cowboy boots by Lucchese. His tenor laugh was practiced and frequent.

The Hummer suddenly lost purchase, skidded five feet back down the forty-five-degree slope, and stopped with its back bumper jammed against the trunk of a twisted basswood, precipitating a shower of yellow and brown leaves.

"Holy shit," said Anderson. He was sweating profusely. His new coveralls, designed to be comfortable down to zero degrees Fahrenheit, were overbuilt for this sunny October afternoon.

The doctor laughed again and brushed leaves from his lap. "Don't worry about it, Stevie. These Murphys know their business." The doctor leaned toward the front of the vehicle. "Isn't that right, Shawn?"

Shawn Murphy, the chubby ten-year-old boy in the front passenger seat, said, "Yup! We know our business, don't we, Unc?"

The driver, his narrow head in the grip of a worn, mouse-gray Stetson, nodded. He twisted the steering wheel to the right and attacked the incline from another angle. The powerful fuel-injected diesel rotated the big wheels; the Hummer resumed its climb up the leaf-littered slope. The sound of the diesel intensified with the pitch of the landscape. Anderson clung to the roll bar, staring back down the precipitous slope at a swath of crushed vegetation. The Hummer growled, lurched, and crackled its way to the ridge. At the crest, they turned onto a narrow but clearly defined track and came to a halt. The engine subsided to an almost subsonic rumble. Ricky Murphy turned to his passengers and raised a thin blond eyebrow. His sun-toasted face, framed by the worn Stetson, made him look like a famished version of the Marlboro Man.

Anderson said, "Damn, I thought we were going over backwards."

Ricky grinned. "Hell, that weren't nothin'. Didn' even need the winch." He pulled a bag of Red Man from his shirt pocket, extracted a stringy wad of tobacco, and pushed it into his mouth. He offered the bag to the boy, but when Shawn reached for it Ricky pulled it away, tucked the bag into his pocket. The boy pushed out his lower lip in an exaggerated pout, looked back at the doctor.

Dr. Bellweather grinned and gave the boy's crew cut a friendly rub.

Ricky said, "Whaddya say, Doc? You into a little cat action?"

The doctor looked at Anderson and winked. "That okay with you, Stevie? My cat first, then your buff?"

"Fine by me," Anderson said, his heart still pounding from the ascent. He'd never been hunting before. He hoped he wouldn't do something stupid. His boss at Litten Securities, Rich Wicky, had told him not to worry. "What, do you think he's gonna shoot you or something? The guy just lost a bundle; he needs some hand-holding is all. If he didn't like you he wouldn've invited you. Let him show off, whack a few beasties. Tell him he's hot shit."

Ricky dropped the Hummer into gear and followed the crest of the ridge.

Anderson's new Weatherby, which he had never fired, rested in its case in the back of the Hummer, bouncing every time Ricky hit a rock or rolled over a fallen log. He'd told the salesman at Big Don's Outfitters that he needed a buffalo gun.

"Now are you talking *buffalo* or *bison?*" the salesman had asked.

There was a difference?

"I don't know," Anderson had answered.

The salesman had sold him the Weatherby. Twenty-five hundred bucks, including the Leupold scope. The coveralls, boots, and safari hat had cost him another six bills. He hoped he could write it off.

A hundred yards up the ridge, the Hummer slowed to a crawl. "Hang on back there," Ricky said over his shoulder. He turned the wheel hard to the left, and the nose of the Hummer went down. Anderson clamped his arms around the roll bar. The hillside was no steeper than that which they had climbed, but it felt like they were going over the edge of a cliff. The Hummer bounced and skidded down the slope, taking out trees up to three inches in diameter, its tires leaving a pair of foot-wide gashes in the earth.

They landed at the edge of a flat clearing covered with the matted brown remains of the summer's vegetation. To their left, they could see the river through the trees; the land rose precipitously to their right. Anderson stood up, still keeping his grip on the roll bar. A narrow dirt road was visible at the far end of the clearing.

"How come we didn't use the road?" he asked.

Dr. Bellweather said, "The ride's part of the safari package, Stevie. This is what you call your total experience. Now you can say you rode up and down the side of a cliff in a . . . what do you call this thing, Shawn?"

"Hummer!" said Shawn.

"Same as we used to kick Saddam and the rest a them sand niggers' asses," Ricky added. He rolled his jaw and expelled a brown amoeba of mucus. "I got your cat over t'other side there." He pointed across the clearing. The outlines of a molded tan plastic cage with metal mesh sides—about the size of a large dog carrier—stood out against a rocky wall.

Ricky reached under the front seat of the Hummer and pulled out a black case slightly longer and wider than a telephone directory. He opened the case and took out an oddly shaped object that, at first, Anderson did not recognize. It looked like a power tool. He looked closer, then realized with a jolt that Ricky was holding some kind of gun, a metal box eight and one-half inches long, a little more than an inch thick, and two inches high. A short metal handle was attached at right angles to the bottom of the box, a little toward the back, just behind an oversize trigger guard. Behind the handle, an elongated loop of quarter-inch-thick steel wire, both ends attached to a pivot, was bent up and over the top of the box. A two-inch-long threaded barrel jutted from the other end of the box.

The entire device was made from dead-black metal. Anderson stared. He had never seen such a thing outside of the movies.

Ricky rotated the wire loop back, then pulled it out from the body until it snapped into place, forming an eight-inch-long stock.

"You used this baby before, right, Doc?"

Bellweather nodded. He unfolded a pair of military aviator's sunglasses and installed them on his face. Ricky handed him the gun, then produced two twelve-inch-long rectangular clips. "Thirty rounds each. Cock it, then shove that clip right up the handle there. Push it in as far as it goes."

"I know, I know." Bellweather took the clips and climbed out of the vehicle. He pulled back a knob on top of the gun, then inserted one of the long clips into the base of the handle, his manicured hands moving with precise, graceful, economical motions. Surgeon's hands. Anderson could feel his heart taking off. Was this hunting? Bellweather looked at him and grinned, his eyes obscured by dark lenses. He lifted the gun, displaying it proudly. "You ever see one of these, Stevie?"

Anderson shook his head.

"MAC-10. Forty-five caliber, full auto. George lets his best clients use it." He turned and started across the clearing, using slippery clumps of dead grass as stepping-stones.

Ricky strapped on a belt holster containing a long-barreled, large-caliber revolver. The gun looked enormous on his narrow hip. The heavy brass belt buckle, an oval four inches across, carried an inscription in raised letters: *Cowboys Do It in .45 Caliber.*

"You stay here," he said to Shawn. Ricky headed directly for the cage, his lanky body gliding easily across the uneven ground. The boy stood up and sat on the back of his seat, his arms resting along the roll bar. Anderson opened the case and took out his Weatherby. Just in case.

"Are you gonna shoot too?" Shawn asked.

Anderson shrugged. He didn't know what the hell he was going to do. This was Bellweather's scene; he was just following his client's lead.

"I shot a pheasant last month," the boy said. "Me and my dad."

"That's great," said Anderson. He wished the kid hadn't come along. He felt self-conscious playing the great white hunter. Having a ten-year-old audience made it worse. But Bellweather seemed to like the kid, and it was his show. He wondered what it would be like to grow up in a place like this, with all the guns and wild animals. The kid seemed happy enough.

Anderson shouldered his rifle and followed the doctor across the lumpy, spongy surface of the clearing. The peaty soil made sucking sounds under his new boots. A few yards from the cage, the land rose slightly. Ricky motioned for them to stop.

"You see her?"

A motionless patch of tawny fur lay flat on the floor of the container.

"How you want to do this?" Ricky asked.

"Fair chase," said the doctor. "Let it loose."

"She comes out, you want to take her right away, Doc. She gets in them woods, we're gonna have to go get the dogs."

"Don't worry about it," said Bellweather. "Everything's under control."

Anderson stepped back. His heart was hammering; he couldn't quite get a good breath. Ricky walked the final twenty paces to the cage, peered in at the captive animal. With one hand on the grip of his revolver, he unlatched the door and stepped quickly back. The cougar twisted its body around. They could see its face now, blinking yellow eyes.

The men waited.

"Might take her a minute to figure out she's cut loose," Ricky said. "She's been in there awhile, maybe got used to it."

Bellweather held the gun with both hands now, the short stock hard against his shoulder, aiming at the open end of the cage. "Come on out, kitty cat," he called.

"She's a mean one," Ricky said. He was holding his revolver loosely at his side, grinning but alert. "Eat you alive," he added.

It occurred to Anderson that he was the only one there without a loaded weapon. He fumbled with the Weatherby, then realized he had left his shells back in the Hummer.

"Kitty cat," Bellweather called. He took a few steps toward the cage. "Kitty cat!" No response. "Hey, you want to get the damn thing to come out where I can see it?"

Ricky bent forward, picked up a clod of grass and peat, hurled it at the side of the cage. It hit the wire mesh and disintegrated. The cat hissed and pressed itself against the far side of the cage.

"Shit. You want to move off to the side there, Doc. Get so she can't see you so good."

They shifted over a few yards, Bellweather keeping the MAC trained on the cage. Ricky kicked some grass aside and found a rock about the size of an egg. He drew back his arm and hurled it at the back of the cage. The stone struck with a solid thwack; the startled cougar crashed into the unlatched door and was suddenly in the open, belly to the ground, pressed against the limestone wall less than twenty yards away, black-tipped tail lashing.

Anderson stopped breathing.

The cougar hissed, ears flat. It reached out a paw and took a slow step, its side dragging against the rock wall.

"She's all yours, Doc," Ricky said, his voice low. The cougar took a step, low to the ground, moving away from the three men. "Better go for it, Doc."

The sound of thirty .45-caliber hardballs all firing within the space of two seconds sent a surge of adrenaline through Anderson's veins. For a moment, he thought the doctor's gun had exploded, but the cat went straight up, twisting in the air, a chain of red geysers erupting from its white underbelly. It hit the ground with an audible thud. Bellweather changed clips as he walked toward his prey.

Ricky said, "Hold up there, Doc. She ain't done yet."

The cat was convulsing, its tail lashing wildly. Bellweather slammed the new clip home and charged the dying cougar, firing short bursts as he ran. The sound was nothing like in the movies. Even through the ear-hammering roar of the exploding cartridges Anderson could hear the *thut thut thut* of fat leaden slugs slapping into the big cat's body. His ears rang, and the landscape seemed to be in motion.

The doctor stood over the motionless cougar, panting, the machine gun hanging empty from his hand. Ricky smiled with one side of his mouth and put his handgun away.

Anderson gulped a ragged breath, his first since the cougar had appeared. The sudden influx of oxygen hit him like a drug. He started to giggle.

Bellweather looked up, his face flushed, sun glancing off his sunglasses. "Goddamn cat almost got away," he said to Anderson. "You see it?"

Anderson nodded, a loose curve distorting his dry lips. His insides were bubbling. The Weatherby fell from his grasp. The end of the barrel dug into the muck, the rifle flopped over onto the ground.

"Kind of gets your heart going, don't it, Stevie?"

Anderson nodded, his mouth dry.

Shawn came running up to see the dead cougar. "Man oh man, you pulverized the sucker! Jeez!" Bellweather cupped a hand over the boy's shoulder.

Anderson looked down at the Weatherby, at the beautifully finished walnut stock, the four-hundred-dollar scope, the mud-covered barrel. He returned his eyes to the cougar, then to the MAC-10 in Bellweather's hand.

"Will that thing work on a buffalo?" he asked.

. . .

Two miles north of Talking Lake Ranch, Joe Crow was celebrating his thirty-third birthday sitting in one of Big River's four new Ford Crown Victoria patrol cars, parked behind a brush pile just off County Road 5. He popped open his second Leinenkugel and regarded the two fat white lines of cocaine decorating the black top of the police radio.

Thirty-three, he thought. Had he grown up yet? He didn't think so. He hadn't felt grown up at eighteen, or at twenty-one either. Real adults didn't drink beer while they were supposed to be working. Grown-ups did not spend their money on cocaine. Crow looked in the mirror, at the deep adult lines framing his mouth. Even when he pursed his wide lips, the lines were there. They would never heal. And he would never surpass his current five-foot-eight-inch height. In fact, he could probably look forward to getting shorter. Evidence of adulthood. He tore a page from a book of traffic citation blanks, rolled it into a tube, and snorted the coke into one nostril, then the other, one line for each side of his brain. He sat back and watched the early afternoon sunlight get brighter, listened to the birds singing louder, and felt like a boy again.

A car passed. His eyes flicked to the radar display. Sixty-eight. If some hot dog decided to challenge his authority by flying by at eighty-five or ninety per . . . well, he would think about chasing him down. But first he had to decide what to do with the rest of his life. Officer Crow let his mind wander.

Shortly after noon, Crow decided to quit his job with the Big River police. It was a decision to which he had come many times before. He would open a rib joint. A really great place where you could go to get some really great ribs. Better yet, he would go to Montana and play poker for a living. Buy into one of the poker clubs in Billings. Buy himself a nightclub. In Jamaica, a really cool place with reggae music and Red Stripe beer. By two-seventeen he was seriously considering learning to play bass guitar and starting the ultimate rock band. He drained the sixth can of Leinenkugel. As he laid out the last two lines of coke, he heard, faintly, a rapid series of explosions. A short burst, then a longer one.

Crow frowned. The Murphys, running another hunt. None of his business what they did, but it pissed him off anyway, the untouchable Murphy brothers running their canned hunts, blowing away everything from antelope to zebra. He'd tried to convince his chief to have a talk with George Murphy about the machine guns. It just didn't seem sporting. Orlan Johnson had listened, then told him he had to learn to mind his own "got-damn beeswax."

"You get a complaint from some citizen, Crow? I didn't think so. Listen to me. George Murphy runs a nice clean operation. The man has a class three firearms license. You just do your job, keeping the streets safe, and don't be worrying about a few got-damn zebras." Police Chief Orlan Johnson was married to George Murphy's sister.

Crow leaned over the radio and sucked the coke into his sinuses.

An hour later, his shift officially over, he was still sitting in his car, fighting the yen to drive the 150 miles into Minneapolis for another gram, thinking dark thoughts about his dead-end job, his troubled marriage, his hazy future. The rib joint now seemed like an impossibility, the rock-and-roll band another cokehead fantasy. He would grow old and fat, another small-town cop good for nothing but to provide a little sport for the local teenagers. Melinda would leave him, divorce him, marry a man with prospects.

He felt the burning again in his gut. Stomach cancer, or worse. Something rotting in there. Thirty-three years old, and his innards were dissolving from all the coke, the booze, the fried food. What did he have to look forward to? Melinda had promised him a birthday dinner, something with plenty of red meat and wine. Too bad she was such an indifferent cook, especially when it came to meat, which she wouldn't eat. They would eat dinner, drink a few glasses of wine, then she would try to start a fight—he could count on that—arguing over something trivial. He saw himself sitting there, staring wordlessly back at her as she yapped at him, numbing his brain with her New Age bullshit. Telling him something she'd seen in her tarot cards.

Or they would have what he thought of as the "feeling fight." He recalled the last one, Melinda's voice hitting a new level of stridency when she told him he was a fish. "You are so unfeeling, so flat," she'd said, "it's like you aren't really there. I get to one side of you, I can hardly see you. You don't know how to share your feelings. You've got the emotional depth of a flounder."

And maybe she was right. Certainly he didn't feel things the way she did, nor did he possess her rich emotional vocabulary. He had never cried over roadkill or felt the great bolts of joy of which she seemed capable. But he was not a flatfish. He'd said, "If I have so much trouble expressing myself, then how come you know so goddamn much about me?"

As always, the snappy comeback had failed to enrich their relationship.

Too bad he'd used up all the coke. When they were doing coke together, things usually went better. They were going through three or four grams a week lately, which was hell on the bank account but made it easier to be in the relationship. Sometimes he thought the coke was all that held their marriage intact. He knew it couldn't go on, that sooner or later they would have to give it up. Sooner or later they would bottom out.

The late afternoon sun had disappeared behind a layer of cloud, the sky gone from blue to lead; the temperature was dropping rapidly. The air felt moist and smelled like snow. Crow rolled up his window. Winter coming. He could hear the wind.

A Hummer with a camouflage paint job roared by at 78 miles per hour, 23 mph over the posted limit. That would be Ricky Murphy. Crow had never met George, the elder brother, but he'd run into Ricky too many times. The last time, Ricky had got shit-faced and started slapping some girl around outside Birdy's. Crow had intervened, given Ricky a couple slaps back, then hauled him down to the station. Ricky had spent almost an hour and a half in the lockup that time—a personal record—before the call came in from Chief Johnson, demanding that he be set free.

What the Murphys did was none of his got-damn beeswax.

A few seconds later, another car flew by—79 on the radar—a bright-pink Jaguar. Crow thought about chasing it down, but his shift was over, and besides, the last thing on earth he wanted was to meet someone who would paint a nice car like that hot pink. Opening the brown coke vial, he turned it over and tapped it against the top of the radio, hoping to dislodge a few last grains, but the vial was entirely empty.

*You want to stay in business, you got to take what busi-
ness you can get.*

—BERDETTE WILLIAMS

ack in 1946, Berdette Williams had named his joint Birdy's, but
everybody who knew him called him Berdette. Birdy's was the only decent place to get a bump and a burger between Big River and Montev-
ideo—and it wasn't all that decent. The tables were sticky, the chairs
unstable, the atmosphere a yellow mist of rancid grease, cigarettes, and
sour beer. The songs on the jukebox were ten years out of date.

Nevertheless, it remained a popular spot with the locals. Arlene,
Berdette's wife, knew how to fry up a Juicy Lucy, a beer at Birdy's was
as good as a beer anywhere, and if Berdette watered his whiskey, as
was rumored, he kept the dilution within reason. A guy could still get a
good buzz for five or ten bucks, and most nights there was a card game
going at the back table.

Dr. Nelson Bellweather loved the place. "Isn't this great, Stevie?" he
said as Berdette slid Juicy Lucy baskets in front of him and Anderson.
"First time Ricky brought me, I asked Berdette here to see the wine list."
He laughed. "He looked at me like I was from Venus—isn't that right,
Birdy?"

Berdette said, "You want another round?"

They were sitting at the big table in back, Anderson, Doc Bellweather, and Ricky Murphy, fresh from the hunt. Ollie Aamold, the taxidermist, sat shuffling a deck of cards. When Ollie wasn't up to his
elbows in the carcass of some large dead animal, he spent his hours at
Birdy's, beer in hand, lower lip distended by a wad of Copenhagen,

looking for a game of chance. Ricky Murphy, Stetson pulled low over his eyes, sipped his 7 & 7 and watched Ollie handle the deck. Neither Ricky nor Ollie had ordered food, but they both indicated with hand motions that another round would be fine.

"So I asked him," Bellweather continued, "if he had any, you know, *imported* beer. What did you say, Birdy? You remember what you said?"

Berdette shook his head wearily and walked away.

Bellweather was not offended. To him, Berdette was part of the local color. He continued his story. "So Birdy said, he said, 'What, you mean like from *Wisconsin?*'" He exploded with laughter, was dutifully joined by Anderson's hearty chuckle and a perfunctory *heh-heh* from Ricky. Ollie Aamold's features, never particularly mobile, remained inert. Grinning and red in the face, Bellweather pushed a cluster of french fries into his mouth, chewed, followed it with a pull from a Bud longneck.

Steve Anderson, famished after the drama of his first hunting experience, giddy from three Scotches and two Budweisers, took a huge bite of his Juicy Lucy. Hot cheese spurted from between the twin hamburger patties, searing his lower lip. "Yow!" he gasped, dousing the pain with a torrent of beer.

Bellweather laughed, snorting through his nose, hitting the table with his palm.

Anderson wiped his mouth with a handful of paper napkins. "Man, that's hot!" He swallowed a few more ounces of beer, then gave Bellweather a puzzled look. "Hey, Doc, I thought you were a vegetarian."

Bellweather grinned and took a cautious bite of his own Juicy Lucy. He chewed and swallowed before replying. "I am," he said. "Except when I'm on a hunting trip. Then I turn into this carnivore. It's a hormonal thing, Stevie. Can't you feel the juice? That buff started toward you, you looked so scared I bet you could've run a four-minute mile. You're still feeling a little shaky, right? Your glands pumping out that adrenaline, noradrenaline, glucagon, all kinds of neurotransmitters. Your blood is still loaded with the stuff. You need meat to replace those hormones. It's a medical fact."

Anderson took another, smaller bite of his cheese-filled burger.

The doctor went on, as if seeing it all again. "Buff coming at you, eyes popping out of your head, you got your gun. . . ." He rapped the tabletop rapidly with his knuckle. "Bapbapbapbapbap! Never knew what hit him."

Anderson shifted his eyes away from the doctor's florid features. They had driven to within fifty yards of the bison. Ricky had shown him how to load and operate the MAC-10 with the buff standing right there, watching them, about as suspicious as a pet cow. It had started trotting toward them, and Anderson had enjoyed a brief moment of fear before squeezing the trigger of the MAC. The gun had jumped in his hand, but he'd managed to get half of the thirty-round clip embedded in the bison's woolly body. The animal had stood there stupidly for several seconds before dropping, first its front legs, then its hindquarters, then tipping to the side, eyes protruding, blood-streaked gray tongue unrolling and lying motionless on the grass.

Now, with the glory of the kill fading, he was left with the suspicion that the bison had been approaching them expecting to be fed a carrot. Still, it had been a kick unlike anything he had experienced before.

"I tell you, Stevie, the way you turned that buff's face to hamburger, Ollie here is going to be patching holes for days. Right, Ollie? You going to mount up this young man's first kill?"

Ollie shrugged. "If he wants."

"Patty isn't going to let me keep the damn thing anyways," Anderson said. "I don't know why I should have it mounted."

"Got to have it mounted, Stevie. Your first kill? Got to have it mounted. I bet Ollie, here, will give you a discount. Right, Ollie?"

Ollie made a noise through his nose. "Negatory. You wanna play cards or what?"

Ricky said, "Yeah, let's play some cards."

Bellweather gave Anderson the elbow. "Whaddya say, Stevie—shall we show these country boys how we do it in the big city?"

Bellweather won the first three hands, buying the first one with a blind twenty-dollar bet and taking the other two with a pair of aces and a baby straight.

"Sheeit," Ricky muttered, throwing his cards away facedown.

Bellweather laughed, raking in the small pot. Anderson shuffled the deck and slowly dealt a hand of five-card draw. The hormones in his bloodstream were turning sour. The Juicy Lucy had settled low in his gut, swimming in a sea of Budweiser. He completed the deal, picked up his hand, and looked at three queens and two deuces—a full house before the draw. His weary adrenal gland managed to produce a few more molecules; his heart started thumping.

"Your bet," Anderson said. A full house! He was no expert, but a full boat was a powerhouse in anybody's hand.

Bellweather took a look at Anderson's flushed cheeks and pulsing carotid artery and said, "Whoa! I check! What the hell kind of hand you got there, Stevie?"

Anderson tried to hold his face still. He had always been a lousy cardplayer, ever since college. He looked at Ricky, who was the next to bet, but Ricky was looking at something up by the front door, his mouth twisted into a practiced Clint Eastwood snarl. Anderson turned and followed Ricky's stare. A cop stood leaning against the bar, watching them. His dark, rumpled hair was a couple of inches too long, and his uniform—the brown-and-tan two-tone that seemed to be the style out here on the prairie—fit him oddly, as though it had been tailored for a larger, wider man. He was not an unattractive man—women might find him interesting—but his expression seemed a bit blank, the sort of look favored by male models, military cadets, or poker players. Anderson tried to put a name on it but could only come up with "intense." The guy was intense. Intensely what, he had no idea.

The cop lifted a shot glass from the bar, poured its contents down his throat, followed it with a swallow of beer, turned away.

Anderson said to Ricky, "What's the problem—are we not supposed to be playing cards here or something?"

Ricky gave his head a snap, as if trying to flick a bead of sweat from his nose. "Don't worry about it. He ain't gonna do nothing."

"You gonna bet?" Anderson asked.

Ricky glanced at his cards, threw them away. "Fuck it." He crossed his arms and glared at the table, a small muscle at the corner of his right eye twitching repeatedly.

Ollie, who had been watching Anderson from beneath his thick, slab-like eyelids, rapped a knuckle on the table. "Check t'da powa," he muttered, his lips barely quivering.

"What?" Anderson cocked an ear and leaned closer to Ollie.

Bellweather interpreted. "He's checking, Stevie. 'Check to the power.' It's your bet."

Anderson, trying to stay cool with his big hand, bet ten dollars.

Everybody folded.

"Damn!" Anderson threw his hand down faceup, swept in the four dollars in antes.

Bellweather laughed. "Nice hand, Stevie!" He scooped up the deck, shuffled. "So, Stevie," he said, his voice taking on a new tone of forced casualness, "what's happening in the financial markets these days? You got any hot picks for me?" He dealt out the cards. "Any more of those oil stocks?"

Anderson frowned. His last hot pick, Maritime Drilling, had cost the doctor over one hundred eighty thousand dollars. Shortly after the doctor had bought in at twenty-six dollars a share, an intoxicated Maritime employee had decorated eighteen miles of the Louisiana coastline with a layer of raw, black petroleum. The stock was now so deep in the basement its share price was measured in sixty-fourths of a dollar, hardly worth the transaction cost to sell it. Dr. Bellweather had not been happy.

"That was a bad deal," Anderson said weakly. He examined his cards. Nothing. Maybe he'd wasted all his luck on that last hand.

Bellweather picked up his cards. "I'm going to be frank with you, Stevie. I need a winner. You understand? Something good this time."

Anderson understood. He'd made close to eighty grand off the doctor's account over the past year, and the guy was understandably tired of watching his small fortune get smaller. Anybody else, he'd have them mostly in mutual funds, T-bills, maybe some utilities and blue chips. But the doctor, he wasn't interested in the safe stuff. He was a thrill seeker from the word go. The only investments that got his attention were the wild ones—the Casino Magics, the Stratospheres. Bellweather was not a sophisticated investor by anyone's measure but his own. He'd even dabbled in the commodities market, but losing a hundred grand in three days had cured him of that. Still, if there wasn't a chance to quickly double or triple his money, Bellweather simply wasn't interested. Anderson wanted to tell him to jack down, let some of his money sit in some safe little fund making seven or eight percent. But he knew his client. It would be like telling a hyperactive kid to sit still and read a book—it just plain wouldn't happen. The best thing to do, Anderson had learned, was to feed the guy the little companies with sexy prospects. Maybe he'd get lucky, and maybe he wouldn't. Either way, there would be commish.

"You ever hear of BioStellar GameTech?" he asked.

"Bio . . . Stellar . . . Game . . . Tech." The doctor tasted the name, shook his head.

"Ten a'you," Ollie grumbled.

"What?"

" 'Ten bucks at you,' " Bellweather translated.

"I fold," said Anderson.

Bellweather called the ten, raised twenty, returned his attention to Anderson. "So? What about it?"

Anderson cleared his throat. "Strictly speaking, I'm not even supposed to be talking about it yet. Small California outfit, very low profile, makes virtual-reality gambling systems, IPO scheduled for early January. They've got a new-concept gambling machine that's going to make the video slots look like horse buggies. You can get in at five a share now, and I think they're going to be issuing warrants too—only thing is,

I don't know how much of it I can get my hands on. Dickie's not letting us have much of it."

"That's not good," Bellweather said, dealing three cards to Ricky, one to Ollie, and two for himself.

"Actually," Anderson said, "it *is* good. Knowing Dickie, it means he's feeding all the BioStellar he can get to his own accounts. That means it's hot. Really hot. My guess is it'll open at ten or twelve, then go ballistic from there, especially if the big casinos buy into the concept, and Dickie thinks they will. This one's going to make a lot of people rich."

Bellweather bet, was raised by Ricky. Ollie folded.

"Watch this, Stevie," Bellweather said as he raised the pot another fifty dollars.

Anderson was too far into his pitch to stop talking now. "If you're interested, I could talk to Dickie. He knows you've had a rough couple of months; I'm sure he'd be willing to work with us, maybe let us have five, ten thousand shares."

Ricky called the raise.

"Hah!" Bellweather slapped his hand down on the table. Ace high flush.

Ricky said, "Sheeit," and flipped over two pair.

Bellweather elbowed Anderson. "See what I mean? These country boys haven't got a prayer." He swept in his winnings. "So this is a good one?"

Anderson was confused. "What? The pot?"

"This BioStellar."

Anderson shrugged, watching Ollie gather up the cards.

Bellweather put his hand on Anderson's shoulder. "Look at me, Stevie."

Anderson looked. The doctor's tiny eyes were red and watery; a lump of beer foam rode the corner of his mouth.

"It's good, right? Not another Maritime, right?"

Anderson opened his mouth, not knowing how he was going to respond, when Ricky snarled, "The fuck do you want?" looking up at the cop, who was standing right there, looking at the deck of cards in Ollie's hands.

Joe Crow knew he should not be doing this. He blamed it on the pair of double Cuervos he'd just used to take the edge off the cocaine. The last thing he needed was to get into a poker game, particularly one in which Ricky Murphy was involved. He knew what Chief Johnson would say: *What the got-damn hell's a matter with you, Crow?*

"How you doing, Ollie?" he said. "Stuff any rhinos lately?"

Ollie swiveled his head back and forth. "Negatory," he said.

"You got a seat for me?"

Ollie let his head fall to his right, toward the empty chair next to the younger guy wearing the camouflage coveralls. Crow circled the table and sat down, Ricky's eyes tracking him all the way. Ollie shuffled the deck, dealt five cards to each player.

"Five-card draw?" Crow asked.

"Now what the hell you think it is, Crow?" Ricky said. "Old Maid?"

The other player, the one in the pink cowboy shirt, said, "Crow? Your name is Crow?" The man reached across the table. Crow shook his soft hand. He didn't like the way the man was looking at him, grinning like he had a secret. "I'm Dr. Nelson Bellweather." He waited, as though expecting Crow to recognize him.

Crow blinked away the tequila haze, examined Bellweather's flushed, bright-eyed face. "Let me guess," he said. "Is that pink Jag out there yours? License plate FATGONE?"

"Yes it is," said Dr. Bellweather, looking pleased.

"You were doing seventy-nine out there on County Five."

Bellweather raised his eyebrows. "Oh!" He laughed. "Were you hiding behind a billboard? Are you going to give me a ticket?"

Crow looked at his cards, focused with some effort, saw a pair of fours. "I check."

"I believe we have a common acquaintance," Bellweather said. "I mean besides Ricky here."

"Crow ain't no 'quaintance a mine," Ricky growled.

"Hey Ricky!" Berdette yelled from behind the bar. He held up a phone. "It's George."

Ricky stood up. "Keep yer hands offa my cards," he said, staring at Crow. "I'll be right back." He grabbed his drink and headed toward the bar, fighting a tendency to list to the right.

Bellweather giggled. "I guess he doesn't like you."

Crow nodded, staring at his cards, trying to turn his fours into aces. It had never worked before, but who knew? He'd rather indulge in fantasy than explore common acquaintances with a guy who'd painted a Jaguar pink.

Bellweather persisted. "I know your brother-in-law. Dave Getter, right?"

Crow's head snapped up.

Bellweather flashed a victory grin. "My lawyer. Dave is my lawyer. When I told him I hunted out here, he told me his wife's brother was a

Big River cop. John Crow, right? I always remember names. That's you, right? How many John Crows can there be?"

"It's Joe," said Crow. He did not like this Dr. Bellweather.

Bellweather waved away the correction. "John, Joe—what's the difference? You're the same guy, right?"

Crow sighed. His stomach was hurting again. In a prick contest, this guy would give his brother-in-law some serious competition. It made sense that they had found each other.

"Dave's a good man," Bellweather said.

"Dave's an asshole," said Crow. He was about to enlarge on this observation when he looked up and saw Ricky Murphy charging across the room, straight at him, brandishing one of Berdette's wooden barstools, holding it high over his head like a bludgeon.

The image had a cartoonish, unreal quality about it. Ricky's movements seemed slowed down, but then so were Crow's reactions. He tried to stand up, his thighs hit the edge of the table, bottles of beer tipped, foam gushed over cards. Crow twisted, got his legs free. Ricky was still coming, his face red and distorted with fury. Crow took a step back and crouched, hands extended clawlike to meet the assault.

But Ricky had someone else in mind. He brought the stool down hard across Dr. Bellweather's back. The legs of the stool splintered. Bellweather collapsed to the floor, air squeaking from his astonished lungs. Ricky's momentum carried him crashing into the card table, stumbling over it, directly at Crow, who, without conscious thought, landed a perfect right jab on the point of Ricky Murphy's jaw. Ricky went down hard, facefirst on the floor, and remained still, his Stetson rocking gently on its crown beside him.

Crow shook out his hand, which had gone numb.

Dr. Bellweather had managed to get up on his hands and knees. The young man in camouflage helped him stand. The doctor looked dazed and in pain, his eyes not quite focused.

"You okay?"

Bellweather nodded uncertainly.

Crow asked, "What was that about?"

The doctor shook his head, bewildered. "I . . . I can't imagine." He gripped his friend's arm, not quite able to stand up straight.

Ricky was stirring, limbs twitching in anticipation of consciousness.

Crow said, "If I were you, I'd get out of here."

"Are you going to arrest him?" the doctor said.

Crow shook his head. "Best thing would be if you'd get in that pink car of yours and go."

Bellweather opened his mouth to object, then clamped it shut. Ricky raised his head, muttering and cursing. "You're dead, cocksucker," he growled, his eyes on the doctor.

Crow dropped a knee onto the small of Ricky's back, grabbed him by the hair, put his mouth near Ricky's ear. "Stay," he said, his voice tight and low. "One move and your head's a basketball. Understand?"

"You better get the fuck offa me, Crow."

Crow pulled up on Ricky's head, bounced it once on the linoleum tile.

Ricky groaned and went limp. Crow turned to the doctor. "Get out of here," he said. "Now."

The camouflaged man said, "C'mon, Doc. Let's get going." He steered the stunned doctor toward the door.

Crow watched them leave. He thought, This is not good. He could feel Ricky's breathing, the rise and fall of his rib cage against his knee, the tense muscles of his back. The world had grown small again, and darker. The sounds of excited conversation grated on Crow's ears, a distant roar. Berdette was coming across the room, shaking his head, holding the old shotgun he kept under the bar. A wave of something awful swept through Crow's body. It wasn't nausea, or pain, or anger, or sorrow. The fight had taken something out of him. Something was missing, as if he had a hole, a cavity inside, as though he had misplaced some essential part of his being. He struggled to identify it.

Berdette said, "Joe? You okay?"

Of course. He knew now what he needed.

He said, "Berdette, how about you bring me another double Cuervo."

Anderson cleared his throat. "So what happened back there, Doc?"

Bellweather shook his head, both hands gripping the steering wheel, his back rigid. He hadn't said a word since they'd left Birdy's.

"Is he crazy or something?"

Bellweather nodded.

"What are you going to do?"

Bellweather shrugged, shook his head, shivered.

Maybe I better shut up, Anderson thought. They rode in silence for a few miles. It was getting dark, and a few snowflakes flashed across the headlight beams. The beer and the Juicy Lucy had finally merged to form a comfortable warm mass behind his navel. He let his head fall back against the headrest and closed his eyes. He had been asleep only seconds, it seemed, when Bellweather finally said something.

"What?" Anderson shook his head to clear it. The snow was getting heavier.

"I said I want in. That BioStellar. What have I got sitting in my account, Stevie?"

"Cash?"

"Altogether."

"I don't know. A little over two hundred thousand. About two twenty."

Bellweather nodded sadly. A year ago it had been six times that. "I've got a situation with the feds, you know."

"You've mentioned it."

"Right. Well, I've been fighting with those bastards for over a year now. You think Ricky Murphy clobbered me? That's nothing. The IRS, they're the ones that're killing me. They're going to take every last dime I've got. If I want to have anything left over, I'm going to have to make a play. I want you to put me in all the way, Stevie. I need to get back up into the seven-figure range, you understand?"

Anderson stared out through the windshield. It would be irresponsible to put all of the doctor's money into one security, especially something as speculative as BioStellar.

"Uh, Doc, you know, there is an element of risk here."

"I don't want to hear about it. Life is too short. If this baby doesn't take off, I'm screwed anyways. I can play the market or take my money out to Vegas and put it all on a number."

Anderson hesitated, thought a moment. "You don't want to go to Vegas," he said.

It is a card of profound significance, but all the significance is veiled.

—Arthur E. Waite, The Pictorial Key to the Tarot

Melinda sat on the sofa, facing east, legs shrouded by her black cotton bathrobe. She heard the key in the front door but did not look away from the tarot cards laid out on the coffee table before her. There was a problem with the number three card, which represented the best that could be expected. The card was Death, and it had appeared upside down, a promise that something would be taken from her, something she had no right to possess. The door opened; a river of chilly air slithered into the room, carrying with it a few flakes of snow. Melinda shivered, lifted her eyes to watch him enter. She could tell by the way he closed the door, overcareful and deliberate, that he'd had a lot to drink. She lifted her wineglass in her hand, sipped. So had she.

"Hi," he said.

Melinda smiled, nodded. They weren't the sort of drunks who would scream and throw furniture. Their conflict occurred on nonphysical planes, his intellectual, hers emotional. But it was just as real. If she was drunk enough, she wouldn't feel the pain until later, when she would see it in the cards.

Joe Crow removed his coat, hung it on a hook by the door.

"Winter," he said. He unbuckled his belt and holster, hung it beside the coat, sat down heavily in the Queen Anne chair on the other side of the coffee table.

"Happy birthday," Melinda said.

"Sorry I'm late. I ran into a little problem. Ricky Murphy again."

"Do you want some wine? There's a bottle on the kitchen table." There was only a glass or so left. She hoped he wouldn't drink it. She thought she might need it to get to sleep.

He shook his head. "Is there anything to eat?"

Melinda said, "Bread, ham, pickles, sour cream, ketchup, bananas." She closed her eyes, visualizing the refrigerator in greater detail. "Eggs, lettuce, jalapeño peppers, stale tortillas, apple juice . . ."

He looked disappointed. "What happened to that birthday dinner you were going to make me?"

"You were late."

"What if I'd been on time?"

She shook her head. "You weren't going to be." She said it as though she'd had special knowledge, as though the future had been laid out for her, and in part she believed it. In part she was the Queen of Wands. A more pragmatic Melinda, however, knew that she'd spent the afternoon and early evening chipping away at the little rock she'd bought for his birthday present, shaving off a little hit here, a little hit there, reading the cards, delaying the planned dinner ten minutes at a time until it became clear that Joe was late. She stared down at her obstacle card, the nine of wands: *delay, suspension, adjournment.* She'd done the last of the coke an hour ago.

Joe nodded, signifying not understanding but acceptance. As always, he would refuse to engage her.

"What happened with Ricky Murphy?" Melinda sipped her wine, a dark-red Bordeaux that Joe would have enjoyed with the steak she had planned to serve but had never gotten around to buying. She let her eyes rest on the tarot layout, listened to her husband talk about his day. It wasn't very interesting—he said he'd spent most of his shift sitting in his car, waiting for speeders. Joe's significator card, the King of Swords, had not appeared in any of her layouts. She listened, hearing a few key words, but most of her attention remained on the cards. Their message was disturbing. Every layout she'd spread that night had delivered the same message, had confirmed what her pragmatic mind had been telling her for months. Joe's voice receded to a drone, then something caught her ear, a familiar name.

"Who did you say?"

"This Dr. Bellweather. I don't know what kind of doctor he is. He's not a local. I got the impression he works out of Minneapolis. He knows Dave Getter, so I'm sure it's something sleazy. The next thing I know, Ricky is trying to kill the guy with a barstool, and I had to step in."

"Is he okay?"

"The doctor? As far as I know."

"Why did Ricky attack him?"

"I have no idea. I asked, but all I got from Ricky was 'Fuck you, Crow.' It was very strange. One minute they were playing cards, then Ricky gets a phone call, and a minute later he's trying to break the guy's skull. After I got the doctor out of there I had to do something with Ricky, so I cuffed him to his Hummer."

"His what?"

"That thing he drives. Haven't you ever seen it?"

"Cars all look the same."

"You'd remember this one. Anyway, one thing led to another, and I had a few drinks with some of the guys. So that's how come I'm late." He looked at the tarot cards. A sarcastic note entered his voice. "But you probably could see all that in your cards."

"That's right, it's all here." And more, she thought, as her eyes were drawn back to the final card, the sign of things to come: the Empress, reversed.

"He's still there, as far as I know."

"What?"

"Ricky. He's still handcuffed to his Hummer." He laughed. "It's proba- bly the longest he's ever been locked up."

"Do you think that was a good idea?"

"What difference does it make? Ricky already hates my guts, and Or- lan Johnson thinks I'm his prize fuckup. What's he gonna do, fire me? Arrest me?"

"He could."

"Ask me if I give a shit."

Melinda looked back at the Empress. "Do you give a shit?" she said quietly.

Joe leaned toward her. "What?"

The Empress sat before the trees, behind the wheat, elegant in her poppy-studded gown, her stellar diadem, judging with her accusatory, pitiless gaze. *Alienation. Domestic upheaval. A relationship in chaos.*

"What's wrong?" she heard him ask.

She felt tears on her face. She hadn't planned it this way, but there was no more waiting left in her. She hadn't planned to give him this for his birthday.

"What?" he asked. She could hear the fear in his voice, as clear as the message in the cards.

• • •

Mrs. Orlan Johnson, née Hillary Murphy, let the telephone ring. She was reading one of the sexy bits in this week's historical romance novel. The ringing phone could not compete with the contessa's heaving bosom as it pressed hungrily against the broad, firm pectorals of Raban, the outlaw prince. As his hard lips sought the tender spot at the base of her throat, Hillary heard a voice calling her name.

"Hill!"

Ring!

"Hill! You want to get that?"

Hillary pressed her lips together and looked up from her book.

Ring!

Why didn't he get it himself? And where was he yelling from anyway? She could hardly hear him.

Ring!

"Got-damn it, Hill, I'm sitting on the got-damn pot!"

Ring!

Hillary set the book on the end table, levered herself up from the chintz sofa, crossed the room to the ringing phone.

"Hello?"

It was her brother George. Who else would let the phone ring fifteen or twenty times? Anybody but George would have given up a dozen rings ago. As usual, he wanted to talk to Orlan.

"He's busy," Hillary said. "Do you want him to call you back later?"

"Busy? Tell him to get his ass off the shitter and get on the phone, Sis."

"George, it's after ten o'clock at night. We're getting ready for bed." She didn't like to see her husband jump to attention every time George snapped his fingers, even though she could see why it had to be that way. Left on his own, Orlan would never get anything done. Still, she wished he would stand up to George now and then, show her brother he wasn't just a flunky in uniform, even if he was.

"Who is it?" Orlan shouted from the bathroom.

She put her palm over the mouthpiece. "It's George, honey. Do you want to call him back later?"

"I'll talk to him." She heard the toilet flush, the door opening, and her husband's thumping progress down the stairs. As always, after she'd spent an hour with Raban, the outlaw prince, it came as a nasty dose of reality to see her husband, especially bare-chested. His pectorals were soft and swollen, almost like a woman's breasts. Below them, a pale, flaccid abdomen drooped over unbuttoned trousers. Everything about him was soft and gelatinous. She handed him the telephone receiver and went back to reading her novel.

The conversation was brief and one-sided. Thirty seconds later, Orlan Johnson hung up the phone, sighed, and sank into the sofa beside his wife.

Hillary lowered her book and said, "So what did George have to say?"

"He called to complain about that Joe Crow."

"Who?"

"One of my men."

"Have I met him?"

"Yeah. At the department picnic. I remember you told me he looked like a Celtic rogue, whatever the hell that is."

Hillary frowned and tried to remember. "Oh, yes. The one with the dark eyes. The brooding one. A very attractive young man. With the pretty blond wife. The weaver."

"Yeah. Well, he's been bothering your brother Ricky again. Handcuffed him to his Hummer. I guess Ricky was pretty upset."

"Why did he do that?"

"Knowing Ricky, I'm sure Crow had his reasons, but . . . well, I can't have my officers doing that sort of thing. If the kid's being a little rambunctious, then fine, jack him down a notch, but Crow has this thing about Ricky, keeps wanting to lock him up."

"That's not good."

"I know. I talked to Crow about it before, but he's stubborn. Too much got-damn Irish in him. George thinks I should get rid of him."

Hillary said, "Well, then, I expect George is right. He has to go."

Orlan Johnson sighed. "I suppose. It's too bad, though. I kind of liked the little guy."

Crow sat in the dark living room, savoring the moments of numbness that came and went, punctuating longer bouts of pain. He held a bottle filled with green Chartreuse, a thick, sweet liqueur with a medicinal taste, made by monks from an ancient recipe. It was the only alcohol they had left in the house. He took a large sip, shuddered, wedged the bottle between his legs, picked up a tarot card. He couldn't see its image in the dark. He tore it in half, then in half again. He tore each quarter into smaller pieces, let them flutter to the carpet with the rest of the tarot confetti. He heard a rustling and a moan from upstairs. Melinda, tossing in bed. How could she sleep?

Trial separation, she called it.

What a lousy birthday.

He swallowed some more Chartreuse. The pale-green liquid hung in his throat, crept toward his stomach. He thought, Is this what it feels like to hit bottom? Is this as bad as it gets?

The worst thing was that he suspected Melinda was right. Moving from Minneapolis to Big River, searching for the good life, fleeing the temptations of the unclean city—it hadn't worked. Their four years in a small town had only intensified the negative. Perhaps it was right that they should separate, that they should try to live their lives apart.

He took another hit off the Chartreuse, held the fluid in his mouth. What a piece of shit you are, he thought, sitting in the dark with a mouth full of fluorescent green monk juice. He stood, made his way toward the kitchen, whacked his shoulder on the doorjamb, spat the Chartreuse into the dish-filled sink. This had to be it. Anybody who tries to get drunk on Chartreuse has got to be sitting at the bottom of the shaft, with no way to go but up.

The realization produced a moment of euphoria, of freedom. He thought, I don't have to do this anymore. I don't have to be a cokehead, a drunk. He took a deep breath, flooded his lungs with more air. It was true. He had a choice. This must be what they call an epiphany, he thought. This must be what it feels like when your life changes, when you shrug off your past, when the future opens up and you are free to live your life.

He heard a car pull up in front of the house. Red flashing lights filtered through the curtains. Voices. Banging on the door.

I was wrong, he thought. He hadn't hit bottom after all.

He was free, all right, but he was still falling.

PART TWO

Professional men, they have no cares;
whatever happens, they get theirs.

—OGDEN NASH

ice view," Joe Crow said.

David Getter nodded, not looking up from his desk, making notes on a thick, densely typewritten document. His crisp white sleeves were fastened at his wrists with initialed cloisonné cuff links; a complicated-looking burgundy necktie was precisely centered and snug at the base of his throat. His black-and-gold Mont Blanc fountain pen hovered over the page, darting in and out of the text. Holding his mouth in a small, tight oval, Getter clicked his tongue after each hasty scribble.

Crow turned back to the seven-foot-high window. He could see the frozen Mississippi to the east, the Minnesota River valley to the south and, beyond, bisected by a pillar of steam from the Black Dog power plant, the gray late-November horizon. Looking down past his feet, he identified Marquette Avenue forty-three stories below. Downtown Minneapolis, dotted with piles of snow and crisscrossed with skyways, surrounded the IDS tower. The height made him feel loose in his stomach. He reached out a hand and pressed his palm against the cool glass.

"Everybody does that."

Crow jerked his hand back; a steamy print remained on the window.

Getter had cleared his polished desk and was leaning back in his chair. His mouth had relaxed. "I can tell how many new visitors I've had by counting handprints at the end of the day." The mouth became a broad, practiced smile. "Sorry to have kept you waiting." He pointed with his pen toward the document. "I had to take care of that while it was still fresh in my mind. How have you been, Joe?"

Crow lowered himself into one of the two identical upholstered chairs in front of Getter's desk. The chair, which looked luxuriously comfortable, felt awkward and lumpy. Crow wasn't surprised. He crossed his legs, uncrossed them, shifted his weight from one hip to the other.

"I've been fine," he said. "How have *you* been, *Dave?*"

"Great. We're great." With Getter, it was always *we*. "Mary says to give you her love."

Crow nodded. Mary, his sister, sending her love via David Getter. Like using a pit bull to deliver a valentine.

"You said you had some work for me," Crow said, wanting to get down to business, be out of there before Getter started with the head games.

"Just a little job, Joe. Give you a chance to pick up a few dollars. How's the apartment working out for you?"

Too late. Head games were in session.

For the past month Crow had been living in a sterile, cheaply furnished efficiency in Lakeview Court, a suburban apartment building owned by Getter. Broke, jobless, credit card maxed out, separated from Melinda, Crow appreciated the fact that Getter was letting him slide for a month or two on the rent. Looking now at the lawyer's face, at the phony patina of compassion and concern, he wondered whether he might be better off wrapping himself in newspapers and Hefty bags and sleeping under a bridge. He pushed back in the chair, then twisted his hips. Every position he tried felt worse.

"The apartment's fine," he said. "Everything's fine."

"How are things going with you and Melinda?"

He knows damn well how things are going, Crow thought. "Doesn't Mary keep you posted? She talks to Mel every damn day." He clamped his mouth shut, not wanting Getter to see him hurting. His marriage was disintegrating, but Melinda's friendship with his sister Mary was still going strong. It felt like betrayal. "We're still separated, but still talking," he finally said. "Anyway, *I'm* talking."

Getter nodded. "Good for you, Joe."

"Good for me," Crow said, staring at Getter's tie. What had looked like a detailed geometric design he now recognized as a flock of embroidered ducks, all exactly the same, their wings interlocked in a pattern, flying from the vicinity of Getter's liver toward his left shoulder. Getter probably thought they were pigeons. Mary must have bought it for him—Minnesota chic.

Getter's features moved into a new configuration. "I ran into our friend Orlan Johnson last week."

Crow's diaphragm spasmed. "Oh? Was he in town?"

"I had to drive out to Big River. He seemed embarrassed to see me. I think he feels bad about what happened."

"I doubt it. What were you doing in Big River?"

Getter flicked off Crow's question with a hand motion. "Joe, before we talk about this job, I have to ask you something," he said. The catalog of unconvincing expressions he was able to produce was remarkable. No doubt he sat in front of a mirror and practiced. The one he wore now was probably called Grave Concern with Traces of Pity.

Crow waited for the shot.

"Are you staying clean?" There it was. Getter steepled his fingers.

"I'm doing fine," Crow said. "I've got my four-week plastic medallion and everything."

"Sorry. I had to ask, you know."

Like hell you did, Crow thought.

"I mean, if I'm recommending you for this position. Did I tell you what you'll be doing, Joe?"

"You haven't told me a damn thing, *Dave*."

"You see, it's not like I'm just asking you to serve some papers or something. You won't be working for me. I'm acting as a go-between here, as a favor to you and to my client. Do you understand?"

"Not yet. What's the job?"

"You'll be providing personal protection for a gentleman who feels his life is in danger."

"Bodyguard, in other words."

"Yes. You can see the reason for my concern. He knows something of your history, and I had to assure him that you're solidly on the wagon. I needed to hear it from you."

Crow sighed. This was getting old.

Getter stared across his desk, lips pressed together, tapping his chin with his pen. Another phony expression: Agonizing over the Big Decision.

Crow said, "You know, these chairs are incredibly uncomfortable."

Getter sat back and grinned, showing nearly all of his neatly arranged teeth. It was the first completely natural look Crow had seen on him that day.

"Milo!" Crow listened for an answer. He shook the box of Meow Mix and called again. "Milo!" He waited another minute, hugging himself, holding the glass door open with his shoulder. It was five degrees below zero, twenty-two below wind chill—what the TV weatherman called "bitter cold"—and he was standing outside in a T-shirt, sweat pants, and slippers. Stupid damn cat. He went back into the lobby, walked down the carpeted hall, identified his apartment by the number on the door. The walls had recently been painted a neutral grayish-cream color; the odor of latex paint lingered. As Crow returned the Meow Mix to its place above the refrigerator, the only cupboard Milo had so far failed to penetrate without human assistance, he told himself that the cat had disappeared before, told himself that Milo would show up when he was good and ready. Probably got himself locked in a garage someplace. Or charmed his way into some lonely old lady's apartment. Dining on smoked oysters and whipping cream.

It was five o'clock in the evening and already dark out. Crow had grudgingly agreed to meet his prospective employer—whoever the hell he was—at nine. Every time he remembered Getter's smirking refusal to tell him the client's name, he had to repress the urge to get on the phone and bow out of the deal. The problem was, he didn't think he could refuse a job when he couldn't even afford to pay rent on the apartment. Also, he owed Getter for extracting him from the Big River jail.

After his arrest for aggravated assault and unlawful restraint, Crow had used his one phone call to contact his brother-in-law, who, being a relative, he had hoped might represent him pro bono. Getter had hopped into his Mercedes, driven halfway across the state to Big River, thrown some aggressive-sounding legal jargon at Orlan Johnson, and had him back on the street by noon, less than nine hours behind the gate. So far so good. All it took was for Crow to agree to quit his job with the police department, an easy call under the circumstances. In a way, it had worked out for everybody. Orlan Johnson got rid of Crow, Crow got rid of his job, and Getter got Crow for three hundred thirty dollars. He'd waived the legal fees but billed him for mileage to and from Big River at one dollar per mile. So much for pro bono.

The hundred bucks a day he was being offered for this bodyguard gig was not exactly Fat City, but it beat driving all over town serving papers in the middle of winter.

Crow unfolded the sofa bed, revealing the same tangled mass of sheets and blankets he had crawled out of that morning. He sat on the edge of the mattress. A couple hours of sleep would be nice. He thought about Milo, the way Milo would tuck his feet under his black furry body and wrap his tail around his toes and let his head sink down between his shoulders and close his yellow eyes. Milo could sleep anywhere, and usually did. Crow lay back and stared up at the textured

ceiling, trying to convince himself that he was sleepy, thinking about
the way it feels when you are very tired and can't keep your eyes open.
He tried to remember a good dream, something he could replay, something that would lead him into unconsciousness. He thought about how
it had been with Melinda, her body radiating heat, the sound of her
sleeping, breathing through her mouth, making little sounds with her
lips. He sat up, picked up the phone, and dialed. One hundred fifty-
three miles to the west, in the small house they had bought together in
Big River, Melinda Crow answered her phone on the sixth ring.

"Hi," he said. "Are we still married?"

"I don't know. Who is this?"

"I couldn't sleep."

She laughed then, a throaty laugh that threatened to awaken a painful
cascade of memories. "Is that why you called? I'm supposed to put you
to sleep?"

Now that they were separated, their conversations were always
friendly, a kind of light, teasing banter that insulated them from whatever it was they were going through.

"Milo took off again. He's been gone since last night."

"He's probably got himself a girlfriend."

"He doesn't do that anymore. I made him give it up. All he does now
is slink around and act dangerous."

"Sort of like you. How come you want to go to sleep at this hour?"

"I got a job. I'm supposed to meet the guy tonight at nine."

"Oh! That's right! Dave found a job for you. Mary told me about it
yesterday. I had lunch with her at the Blue Point."

Everybody knew what was going on in his life except him. Why did
that bother him so much? And if Melinda had driven all the way to the
cities and then had lunch with Mary, why hadn't she called him? He was
afraid to ask.

Melinda correctly interpreted his silence. "I had some business in
town. I would have called you, but I had a ton of errands to do."

Weak, but at least she acknowledged the oversight. They were supposed to be working on opening the lines of communication. Was this
progress?

"So how is my favorite sister?" he asked. "Still smiling all the time?
Was she wearing her crystals?"

"Just a few. You shouldn't give her such a hard time, Joe. She's trying
to find herself. Like the rest of us."

"She's not going to find herself in all that New Age bullshit."

Melinda didn't reply at once. Crow realized he'd put his foot in it again, using the descriptive terms "New Age" and "bullshit" in the same sentence. His tarot-card-reading, organic-vitamin-popping, seaweed-eating wife owned a few quartz crystals of her own. During their last few months together, the things had been popping up all over the house, multiplying like Tribbles.

"It's not all bullshit, Joe." Her voice was cool. "One day you'll see. But I don't expect you to believe that. You think you've got it all figured out, that what you see is what you get. It's the things you can't see that guide your life, you know."

Crow closed his eyes and took a deep breath. "Sorry," he lied.

"That's okay," she said, but he could tell it wasn't.

"I just called to tell you I got a job. But you knew that already."

"It sounds exciting. Mary said you were going to be a bodyguard for a friend of theirs."

"Right." He opened the nightstand drawer and picked up his Taurus, a .38 snubby that he'd bought during his rookie year with the Big River police. The checkered plastic grip was cracked; he'd wrapped it with silver duct tape. "Dave wouldn't even tell me who the guy is. He lives out on the lake, not far from Dave and Mary's. All I got's an address."

"Well, as long as you know how to get there."

"If I wasn't so damn broke I'd tell him to shove it. You know the only reason he's doing this is he's hoping I turn into a paying tenant. Also, it's another opportunity for him to remind me he got me out of jail." Crow pointed the .38 at a magnet on the refrigerator door and squeezed the trigger. The hammer came back a quarter of an inch. Crow released the pressure, and the hammer settled back down.

"At least you'll have some money coming in."

"Yeah. I thought about joining the homeless, but it's pretty cold out."

"It's supposed to get colder," she said. "Below zero the rest of the week."

You could always talk about the weather. They could talk about the weather all winter long, and in the spring they could talk about it some more. Crow filled his lungs with new air. "So how have you been?"

"I'm doing okay, Joe."

Crow waited, then said, "I'm doing okay too."

"That's nice."

Their conversations always came to this. They would talk for a few minutes, search for a painless topic of mutual interest, then drift into empty pleasantries. Sometimes he thought that Melinda would forget who she was talking to, or that she found it impossible to care. He always wondered if she was high. Usually he could tell, but not always.

He pictured her sitting at the kitchen table, holding the telephone against her shoulder, using one hand to arrange two lines of cocaine on the Formica surface with a single-edge razor blade, brushing back a wisp of fine blond hair with the back of her other hand.

He pictured her sitting in the leather chair in the living room, sipping cognac, leaving a faint lip print on the rim of the snifter.

He pictured her in bed, propped up against the mahogany head-board, watching the TV with the sound turned off, touching up her short nails with an emery board, a decanter of raspberry liqueur resting atop the clock radio.

"Where are you?" he asked.

"In the kitchen."

"What are you doing?"

"Talking to you. Standing at the stove heating up some milk for hot chocolate."

Crow liked that. He filed away the other images and concentrated on seeing her at the stove, watching the gas flame heat a saucepan full of milk. He blinked, and his own apartment came back into view. Cardboard moving cartons piled against the far wall, still unopened. While the boxes remained untouched it was as though the remains of their marriage would be preserved, as though the bond could endure, for a while, without its human components. What I need, he thought, is some lonely lady to make my bed, unpack my boxes, and feed me smoked oysters and cream. Or hot chocolate.

After a time Melinda said, "How are we doing? Are you sleepy yet?"

Crow said, "No."

The Cocaine Anonymous meeting at the Golden Valley Community Center ran like a tape loop from three P.M. until one A.M., a ten-hour coffee and cigarette orgy with a formal twelve-step session commencing every two hours. Crow parked his Rabbit between an old rusted-out Honda and a custom-painted gold Cadillac Eldorado with all the trimmings. After his conversation with Melinda he'd tossed and turned in bed for an hour, finally decided the hell with it, got dressed, and drove over to the CA meeting.

For the past month, Crow had been making it to CA meetings two or three times a week. He preferred the CA groups to the AA groups—they were darker, funnier, faster, and more colorful. AA people, by comparison, struck him as gloomy and sluggish.

The meetings seemed to help. Not that he had trouble staying

sober—since his episode with the green Chartreuse he'd felt no real desire to get high again. It was more a matter of having trouble *being*
sober. Once he'd made his decision to get clean, Johnny Yen had
booked. The monk juice had chased him right out of town. There were
no intense cravings, no overwhelming urges to run out and score a
gram or a bottle. Still, he attended the meetings dutifully, sitting quietly
during the proceedings and participating as little as possible. He always
felt a little bit better when he left—less empty and not so alone.

Crow walked in late to the seven o'clock session. The group leader, a
former pro basketball player named Chuckles, was addressing a wildly
diverse group of sixteen cokeheads, telling them about his personal relationship with God. They were on step three that night—the one
where they were supposed to hand over the reins to "God as we understand him"—not one of Crow's favorites.

"It was the hardest thing I ever did, axing The Man to take the
wheel," Chuckles said, his cavernous voice filling the classroom. Chuckles, who owned the customized gold Caddy, was heavy into vehicular
imagery. He was in his mid-fifties, had skin the color and texture of a
Brazil nut, and a wandering left eye. Chuckles had been clean, he
claimed, for three years. Crow took a seat near the back and listened to
the big man's rap, letting the words melt together, trying to clear his
mind of Melinda.

"A man axes for a lot of things in his life," said Chuckles. "Only thing
is, we so busy axin' for things make us feel good, you know what I
mean, we cruisin' down the highway, we forget to get us some help
from The Man Upstairs. You know what I mean?"

Someone on the other side of the room snorted. Chuckles jerked his
head up, scanned the room with his good eye, landed it on a woman
with spiky blond hair, a furious slash of lipstick, and a black leather
jacket carrying enough zippers and chains to befuddle Houdini. He put
a long finger beside his nose and nodded. "And I include you ladies in
that too," he said.

As always, the CA participants were a twitchy lot. Virtually all of
them were smoking and drinking coffee from paper cups. Some were
hunched forward, listening intently to Chuckles' discourse on step
three; others had their minds turned inward, observing an internal dialogue, waiting to break up into smaller groups so they could spew it
all out. The group was predominantly male, about a third white, a
third black, and a third other. The three women in the group represented three extremes: a young, angry-looking, eggplant-colored,
three-hundred-pound woman in an orange muumuu; an extremely

tense, dandruff-ridden redhead in a navy-blue suit, whose pink nails were bitten far beyond the help of any manicurist; and the blond woman with the chains and the rock-and-roll hair. The men in the room displayed variations of similar breadth and intensity.

Chuckles finished his talk with a prayer, which made Crow uncomfortable, as always. He chose to visualize his own "higher power" as a mean-spirited, grinning gnome running an enormous factory, dashing frantically from room to room, shouting nonsensical instructions to uncaring workers, throwing switches and pressing buttons at random. Crow would acknowledge a higher power, but that didn't mean he had to like it, and he was damned if he was going to turn his life over to the little despot. Maybe he had an attitude problem—as many had suggested—but at least he was staying sober.

The large group broke down into three smaller groups. Crow wound up with an ex-gang-banger named Jellybean, whom Crow had met before; an emaciated kid with a head full of proto-dreadlocks; the muumuu woman; and the rock-and-roller with the spiky hair. They all exchanged first names. The kid with the locks called himself Vince. The muumuu woman said her name was "Vogue, like the magazine." The rock-and-roller's name was Debrowski.

"Say what?" said Jellybean.

"Da-*brow*-ski," said Debrowski. "Like the fucking magazine." She had a nice voice, deep and clear.

Jellybean sat back. "Hey, it's cool. Da. Bra. Ski. I got it." He turned to Vince. "You got that, brotha?"

Vince muttered, "Hey, I just be bein' here."

Jellybean took another run at it. "Duh-*bra*-ski."

"Close enough, Bean," Debrowski said. She looked at Crow. "So what's your story? I haven't seen you here before."

Crow said, "I don't have a story." At least not one he cared to share. A black-and-red button on Debrowski's motorcycle jacket read *Bitch + Attitude.*

She raised her eyebrows. "Like hell," she said. "So what do you do when you're not hanging out with us losers? I bet you sell shoes or something. That what you do? I bet you used to get a snootful and sell those shoes like a demon. Used to be number one with a shoehorn, I bet."

"That's right," said Crow. It didn't pay to argue with some people. Obviously, this woman didn't play by the rules. "I sell shoes. I'm this wizard with a shoehorn."

Debrowski laughed.

Crow repressed a smile. Strangely enough, he liked her. At least she wasn't moping around and feeling sorry for herself. He figured her for a newcomer, maybe on her third or fourth meeting. She would never make it past step one. He found himself wondering what she would be like with a few drinks in her.

Debrowski winked at him, as though she'd scanned his thoughts, then turned to the voluminous Vogue, whose large lips were knotted into something resembling the terminus of her digestive system.

"So what are you looking so pissed off about? You're not the only one can't go out and get fucked up tonight."

Vogue glared.

Jellybean muttered, "No shit."

Crow hid a smile. This was not going to be one of your peaceful gatherings, but it promised to be interesting.

V

Work ain't about making money, son. It's about spending time, and you only got so much of it you can afford to shell out.

—SAM O'GARA

S tanding in front of his dresser, David Getter centered his tie and snugged it up.

"Why do you have to go?" Mary Getter looked at his reflection in her vanity mirror. She was applying a layer of AromaVedic Restorative to her face, carefully spreading the oily cream over the fine lines at the corners of her eyes.

"I have to go introduce him to his new boss."

"You have to be there for that? Joe can't introduce himself?" She replaced the jar in its pyramid. As usual, she felt a comforting warmth as her fingers entered the twelve-inch-tall, open-sided copper structure. The pitch of its sides exactly matched that of the pyramid at Giza.

"It'll be better if I'm there."

"I don't see why you have to go out there in this cold. It's below zero."

He shrugged into his suit coat. "It's just over on the other side of the bay, Mary. I won't be gone long."

"I don't see why you have to get all dressed up."

"I always get dressed for business meetings."

"This is business? I thought you were just doing Joe a favor."

"A business favor."

"And you have to be there?"

He slipped his wallet into his inside jacket pocket. "I want to be there."

Mary watched her husband make a final check for lint on his shoulders and sleeves. She took a deep, cleansing breath, forcing the negativity out of her body, seeking a critical mass of positive thought. David was so fastidious. Always looked good, smelled good, kept his fingernails clean. It was good of him to have found Joe a job. Surprising, but good. She knew that Joe and her husband didn't get along, but that didn't stop David from doing the right thing. He's a good man, she told herself. He tries so hard.

A brass plaque on the stone arch read: ORCHARD ESTATES. Crow guided his Rabbit through the arch, entering a tangle of neatly plowed streets named after fruits and berries. He followed Cherry Curve to Appletree Drive, then explored Blueberry Street, Circle, and Lane before locating Blueberry Trail. The homes of Orchard Estates were set well back from the winding streets, each home well isolated from its neighbors by heavily wooded borders and a minimum lot size that must have run five or ten acres. From the little he could see from the street, all the homes appeared to be large and expensive, and no two the same. Still, Crow had the sense that all had been designed by one architectural firm. He suspected that clones of each one of these homes existed elsewhere, on other lakes, in other "exclusive estates."

Blueberry Trail, a short street that quickly dead-ended, was buried deep in the maze. The last house, number 17380, was a split-level mock Tudor on a large lot, secluded from the neighbors by a couple acres of woods on each side. A three-foot-high bank of carefully plowed snow defined the outer perimeter of a circular driveway. He recognized Getter's Mercedes parked near the front door and pulled his Rabbit in behind it. An aging Dodge station wagon was parked at the far end of the driveway. White deicing pebbles dotted the brick walk that led to the front door. Checking his watch, Crow noted that he was late by twenty minutes—roughly equivalent to the amount of sleep he had gotten. It was going to be a long night. He pressed the illuminated doorbell button.

He was about to press it again, when a tinny voice said, "Yes?"

Crow looked for the speaker, found it set into the stucco to the right of the door.

"My name's Crow," he said. "I'm here to—" He remembered he didn't know the name of his prospective client. "I'm supposed to meet Dave Getter here."

The door opened, and a cloud of warm, moist, rich-smelling air poured out into the night. A mild-featured man in a rumpled gray sweater and rimless eyeglasses, about Crow's size but older and softer around the cheeks, motioned him to enter. Crow stamped the snow off his feet and stepped into the vestibule. What was that smell? Something strong and organic, but not unpleasant. He shrugged out of his trench coat, an eighty-nine-dollar poly-cotton knockoff of the Burberry classic, and held it out to the man who had answered the door. The man frowned at the coat.

"I am not a butler," the man said. "Mr. Getter and my brother are back in his office." He turned and walked into a spacious, severely formal parlor. The upholstered furnishings were done in white and ivory damask, the matching glass-topped end tables supported by a fragile framework of white oak. A cut-glass chandelier sent spatters of light across patterned white satin wall covering and an eggshell-colored carpet. The room had a cold, sterile feeling. No one would want to *be* in this room. No one would ever be offered a glass of red wine or a cup of coffee here. It was a room to be photographed, or a room to walk through, being careful not to brush against anything. Crow stopped at the perimeter of the carpet, aware of his snow-caked, salt-rimed wing tips.

The man said, without turning back, "Don't worry about it."

Crow noticed a faint gray path across the carpet, evidence of many feet passing since the last cleaning. The glass tabletops supported a patina of dust. Crow followed the man who was not a butler through the parlor and into a formal dining room that carried over the same sterile theme. The floral arrangement on the table had been dead for weeks, or longer. They walked down a short hallway. The man rapped twice on the door at the end. "My brother's office," he said laconically as he turned and walked back down the hall.

A moment later, Dave Getter opened the door. "Car trouble?" he asked, raising his eyebrows.

Crow jerked his head from side to side. The odor that he had noticed before was much stronger here.

Getter ran his eyes down Crow's well-worn brown herringbone sport coat, black cotton turtleneck, and faded twill pants. He stared for a moment at the beat-up wing tips, then took it all in again in reverse.

"Looking sharp, Joe."

"Thanks, Dave." He looked past Getter. "Oh," he said, recognizing the smell at last—the smell of leather and bone.

The "office" was as large as the living room but had been decorated after a somewhat different aesthetic. Grayish pink suede wallpaper was sandwiched between the oak wainscoting and a picture rail, from which a collection of elaborately framed wildlife paintings—a bull elk, a herd of bison, a stalking mountain lion, a flock of Canada geese— hung on braided maroon cords. A chandelier made from bleached deer antlers and wrought iron hung to within seven feet of a grizzly bear rug that lay in ambush in the center of the room. A gas flame flickered in a fieldstone fireplace at the far end of the room. Above the mantel, a mounted bison head was flanked on one side by an eight-point white- tail and on the other by a four-foot-long elephant tusk mounted on a teak plaque. A snarling leopard, seven feet from nose to tail, crouched against one wall, frozen in time. The rest of the room was crowded with furnishings that appeared to have been constructed exclusively from the hides, antlers, horns, and bones of large dead animals. A sofa and a love seat—pale leather accented with zebra hide—looked almost sedate beside an uncomfortable-looking but cleverly designed chair made from moose antlers and woven strips of dark leather. Crow felt as if he were in the belly of a great beast, about to be drenched by stom- ach acids, surrounded by the indigestible parts of previous victims.

A man wearing professionally faded jeans, an ornately embroidered red rodeo shirt, and a deep suntan stood with his hip resting on the corner of an antique mahogany desk, the only piece of furniture in the room that did not include parts from dead animals. When he saw that he had Crow's attention, he walked across the grizzly bear's flattened back, holding out his hand.

"Thanks for coming, Joe," he said, flashing a wide, white smile. "Dr. Nelson Bellweather. Good to have you on board!" He stood about five- nine in his ostrich-hide cowboy boots, giving him a couple of inches over Crow. He raised his chin, took Crow's hand in a firm, precise, ephemeral grip—long fingers clasped and released and were gone. Tip- ping his head back a few more degrees, he looked at Crow expectantly, waiting for a response. Getter followed the encounter with the intensity of a dog on point. Crow examined Bellweather's face: soft, smooth, regular features. Narrow lips. Gray eyes, wispy blond hair. Somewhere between forty and fifty. Dr. Nelson Bellweather looked like his brother the nonbutler, but younger and with more attitude. He kept his head tipped back. Crow's eyes fixed on the small, perfect ovals formed by his nostrils.

"Nice place," Crow said. "You shoot all this furniture yourself?"

Bellweather cocked his hip and hooked a thumb in his belt. It looked utterly artificial, like a pose he had seen a bad guy strike in a fifties horse opera. He laughed, a little too loud. "Some. You remember me, don't you?"

Crow hadn't, but suddenly he did. "I remember you," he said. He felt as though someone had shoved a long, rusty pin into his likeness. "The pink Jag, right?"

Bellweather grinned, showing most of his teeth. "I loved the way you handled Ricky."

Crow felt no pleasure at the compliment. The episode had cost him far too much. He looked at Getter.

"You having a good time there, Dave?"

Getter squelched a smile and held out his empty palms as if to say, Who, me? Crow gave him a blank stare, the same expression he had found so useful as a cop, and held it until Getter looked away, finding something fascinating about the wallpaper. Crow turned back to the doctor. "What's going on here?"

Bellweather turned up his smile. "Joe, I can't tell you how pleased I was when David told me you had agreed to work for me."

Crow raised his eyebrows. "I didn't know that I had agreed to anything," he said.

Bellweather tipped his head back another five degrees and swiveled it toward Getter. "David?"

Getter jerked his head around. "Yes? What?"

"Didn't you tell me that Joe was on board?"

"That was my understanding. I told Dr. Bellweather he could count on having you, Joe."

"I don't remember saying anybody could 'have' me, Dave," Crow said. "I want to know what's going on here before I agree to anything." The last time he'd felt like this was when a friend—now an ex-friend—had invited him over for a beer and he'd found himself in the midst of an Amway recruiting seminar.

Getter reached out and put a hand on Crow's shoulder. "Joe—" he began. Crow twitched his upper body, and Getter's arm bounced off him as if repelled by a magnetic field. Getter backed off a step. "Now listen, Joe, this is exactly the kind of attitude that gets you in trouble. Dr. Bellweather has offered you a good job here, and I've gone to a lot of trouble—"

Bellweather interrupted. "Why don't you let me and Joe talk, David. I'm sure we can work this out. He has some very legitimate concerns, and I'm confident that I can satisfy him. You've done your part, and I thank you for it. Mary must be waiting up for you."

Getter looked from Crow to Bellweather. "You sure?"

"Quite sure."

Getter shrugged and left the room.

"You don't like him," Bellweather said. "I don't blame you. David is a good lawyer, but he likes to make people uncomfortable. It was never my intention to take you by surprise. David is like that. He likes to blindside people, catch them off guard, make them uncomfortable. It's part of his power trip."

Crow looked again at the mounted leopard.

Bellweather followed his glance and laughed. "I guess we all have our power trips. Do you hunt, Joe?"

"Just birds. I like duck hunting. So what's this all about? Why do you think you need protection?"

"Because I've been threatened. So you're a hunter then? I should take you out sometime. We could go duck hunting, if that's what you like. Me, I like every kind of hunting."

Crow looked from the leopard to the bison head to the elephant tusk, thinking that a day in a duck blind with this man would be enough to make him give up hunting forever.

"I'm living here alone now, as David may have mentioned. My wife left me a few months ago."

"Dave didn't mention anything. I still don't know what I'm doing here."

"It was no big deal, getting the divorce, except it cost me a lot of money. We were married only a year and a half. Just long enough for her to spend a fortune decorating this place. What did you think of the front parlor?" He read Crow's expression and laughed. "It's pretty awful, isn't it?"

"So you're being threatened by your ex-wife?"

Bellweather frowned. "I don't believe I said anything like that."

"You haven't said anything at all."

"David warned me you were feisty. Did he ever tell you how he came to represent me?"

"He didn't even tell me who you *were*."

"Oh—of course. We just went over that, didn't we? Well, when my wife decided to divorce me, I didn't have a lawyer I liked. The guy I was using was a wimp. So, on a whim, I dialed U-N-H-I-T-C-H."

"I always wondered what kind of clients he gets off those billboard ads."

"I drive past David's outdoor advertising every day on the way to the clinic. It works—what can I say? Have you seen *my* ads?"

Crow shook his head. Other than their brief meeting at Birdy's, he'd never heard of Dr. Nelson Bellweather.

"I got the idea from David. Every Sunday. 'Fed up with dieting? Dial F-A-T-G-O-N-E.' You wouldn't believe how many calls I get."

A light came on. He'd seen the doctor's ads after all. "You're the one in the *TV Week*."

"That's me!" said the doctor. "West End Clinic—Plastic and Reconstructive Surgeons."

"You do nose jobs, silicone breasts, things like that?"

"We offer a full range of services. Tomorrow I'm seeing Mrs. Archer Pillsbury-Cargill. We're going to take a little subcutaneous fat off her hips."

Crow recalled the printed advertisements. " 'Liposuction our specialty'?"

"That's right." Bellweather pursed his lips. "In this business, it pays to specialize."

Crow swallowed, then wished he hadn't. Something tasted awful. Better he should have walked into another Amway meeting. How did these people find their way into his life? Were they attracted to him the way a cat is attracted to the one person in the room who hates cats?

The doctor was talking again.

"My brother Nate—you met Nate?"

"More or less."

Bellweather gave him a quizzical look, then continued. "Nate stayed with me last night and this evening, but he has a regular job, and *his* wife hasn't left him yet. That's why I asked David to track you down, Joe. Did he tell you anything at all?"

"He told me you were looking for a bodyguard. Look, I don't know what your situation is, and apparently you aren't interested in telling me. I'm sorry if Dave gave you the wrong impression, but I really don't think I'm the right person for this job. There are companies that specialize in this sort of thing—"

"I'm not interested in some tough-guy bodybuilder type, Joe. I saw you handle Ricky Murphy. That's what I want."

"I was drunk, and so was he."

"Think how good you'll be sober."

"Let me give this one more try. Why do you think you need a bodyguard?"

Bellweather stood up and walked toward the fireplace. He looked up at the bison mount, straight into its flared nostrils. "You saw it. The Murphys. You heard Ricky threaten to kill me."

Crow shook his head. "Ricky's just a hothead. Besides, that was weeks ago. If Ricky was really trying to kill you, he's had plenty of time to do it. Why do you all of a sudden think you need protection?"

"I've been gone. After he attacked me in that bar, there were phone calls. I decided to take a vacation. I've been staying with a friend in Costa Rica. I just got back the night before last."

That explained the suntan. "What set him off that night?"

"I have no idea. And I thought, like you said, that whatever it was that caused him to go off on me like that, he'd have calmed down after six weeks, but I was wrong. Last night he made another attempt on my life," Bellweather said. He added, "It was unsuccessful."

VI

Now Ricky, he's got a temper on him, and I got the brains, but the one you got to watch out for is my mom.

— GEORGE WASHINGTON MURPHY

row sat in the moose-antler chair. After testing all the furniture, he had found it to be the most comfortable. Bellweather had retired an hour earlier, and the house was dead quiet. He stared dully at the rug, at the grizzly bear's open mouth. Crow yawned. He could feel himself fading. Less than three hours since he'd walked into this job, and he was already bored comatose.

He was having trouble taking his new employer's concerns seriously. True, he had seen Ricky attack the doctor at Birdy's, but that was nearly two months ago. Bellweather claimed that Ricky had taken a shot at him two nights ago as he was driving home from the clinic. It sounded unlikely, though not impossible. Ricky had driven up behind him, the doctor claimed, as he was cruising west on I-394. Right there in rush hour traffic, he'd leaned out the window of his Hummer and started blasting away with a revolver.

Bellweather had gripped an imaginary steering wheel as he told his story, reliving the experience. "If I hadn't managed to get a truck between us and then get off the freeway, who knows?" He steered to the right, then dropped his hands onto his lap. "He might've killed me. He gets in that Hummer of his, has a few drinks, he'll do anything. He's crazy, you know."

Some of Crow's doubt must have crept onto his face, because Bellweather had insisted on taking him into the attached garage to show him the bullet holes in his car.

"Can I ask you something?" Crow asked. "Why did you paint it pink?" He opened the passenger door. "Jesus, it's pink inside too." Pink leather upholstery, pink-wrapped steering wheel, pink sun visor . . . Even the gearshift—a manual transmission, to his surprise—was topped by a pink knob. It was enough to make him blush.

"I bought it for my wife. She was a Mary Kay distributor when I met her."

"You're kidding."

"All custom paint and leather, cost me a fortune, and she hated it. When we split up, she got the Mercedes. You see this hole? This is where the bullet came through."

Crow put his finger in the hole. "You sure it wasn't a rock?"

"In the rear window? The slug was buried in the back of the passenger seat. There's another hole in the trunk lid. I found the bullet rattling around in here." He lifted a hinged, leather-upholstered lid to reveal a large, empty compartment in place of the back seats.

"I thought these new Jags were four-seaters."

"I had them pull out the back seats—too small to sit in anyway—and build a storage compartment. Room for my hunting equipment. The trunk in this thing is barely large enough for the spare."

"And you think it was Ricky shooting at you?"

"How many camouflage Hummers do you think there are in this state?"

"Did you call the police?"

"Sure I did. I gave them Ricky's name, told them where they could find him. But guess what? Ricky was playing cards all night with Orlan Johnson and a bunch of his buddies. I don't know why I bothered. What I need is a guy like you, Joe."

It was just as well. He'd already decided to take the job. He really did need the money. Even if the doctor was only enjoying a paranoid fantasy, he seemed to be able to afford it.

After Bellweather retired, secure in the knowledge that the ever vigilant Joe Crow was keeping him safe from the predations of the Murphy clan, Crow wandered the first floor, inspecting Bellweather's various possessions and trying to guess what each item had cost. The white living room gave him the creeps. In its own way, it was scarier than Bellweather's trophy room. True, the office was full of dead animal parts—but in the living room, nothing had ever been alive.

The more he looked around, the more neglected the place looked. Dust balls gathered in the corners, faint gray trails crossed the carpeted floors. The few plants were dead or dying. The place needed a housekeeper. The guy had plenty of money—why didn't he hire a cleaning service?

A door off the kitchen led downstairs into a finished basement, complete with game room, bar, and workshop. The shop tools all had come from the same store, probably all bought on the same day. The table saw blade still had a label glued to it. All the hand tools were shiny and appeared to be unused. It looked as though Bellweather had bought himself a complete home workshop on a whim, had it installed, forgotten about it.

The billiard table had seen some use, but not much. Crow made a few shots but found the game uninteresting without pockets to shoot for. Like squash, billiards had an aristocratic tang to it that made him uncomfortable. He wandered back upstairs into the kitchen and stared at the floor for a few minutes. Crow was no expert, but this was one beautiful tile job. Every tile was slightly different, each had the sort of character that usually came only with great age and use. Must have cost a fortune. Apparently there was money to be made in the liposuction business.

Behind the kitchen, a set of French doors led into a large room that featured the same white carpeting as the front parlor, but this room had been stripped of its furniture—only a few dents in the carpet and an ugly floor lamp remained. It was too bad, because it had the nicest view in the house. One entire wall was windowed, looking out over a long, snow-covered backyard that led down to the frozen lake, gray and still in the moonless night, crisscrossed by the darker lines of snowmobile trails, dotted with black icehouses. Crow stood staring out past his reflection, imagining how it would look in the summer, with sunlight and boats and warm breezes and jumping fish.

Amanda Murphy had not slept well since the night of Sean's first heart attack, back in '74. After his second coronary, three years later, when the Good Lord finally took him, she had thought, even in her grief, that the one good thing was that now he was gone she could get a good night's sleep, not be clinging fitfully to awareness all night long, listening to him respire, hearing every wheezy breath as though it were his last. But Sean's death had changed nothing. The awareness that immortality had passed her family by was enough to ruin her sleep every night for the rest of her life. Her dreams became more vivid and disturbing with every birthday. Thank the Good Lord she was pushing seventy-five and would not have too many more nights of lying awake alone in bed. She hoped she would go before any of her three children.

Amanda sat up in bed and looked out the window of her room. The sky was low and dark, her view of the woods a study in tangled charcoal against the paler gray of snow-covered earth. Winters were the worst. The nights were so long. She could see the three Talking Lake Ranch snowmobiles lined up outside the lodge, and the old Ford pickup truck with the plow. Ricky's Hummer was gone. Now where would that boy be, middle of the night? Out chasing some waitress, no doubt. She wasn't going to think about it. Whatever he did, the Good Lord would forgive him. Boys will be boys. She felt for her slippers, wiggled her toes into their fuzzy interior, and shuffled down the hall toward the kitchen, to heat a cup of cider. Maybe have a shot of Jim Beam with it, which would put her down for an hour or two, at least. Get her closer to the dawn.

George, her elder son, was sitting at the kitchen table in his plaid flannel nightshirt, eating Skippy peanut butter straight from the jar. He looked up as she entered, loaded up his tablespoon, inserted it into his mouth. The thick smell of peanut butter hung in the air.

"You're gonna get fat," Amanda said. She would have preferred to have the kitchen to herself. With George there, she would have to skip the Jim Beam. George had this idea that old women shouldn't drink. Not that he could stop her, but there would be a scene. Hot cider would have to do.

" 'M already fad," mumbled George.

Amanda opened the refrigerator and took out a plastic jug of apple cider, filled a mug, and put it in the microwave for two minutes. She distrusted microwave ovens on general principles, but George's wife—thank the Good Lord *she* was finally gone—had bought one, and Amanda now found herself using it daily. While her cider was heating, she watched her peanut-butter-eating son. George was right; he *was* getting fat. Strong, healthy, and only forty-nine years old, but definitely carrying a few extra pounds around the middle. Not rail thin and nail hard like his daddy. Still, it wasn't like him to be eating straight peanut butter at three A.M. George usually slept like a bear. Something was bothering him.

The microwave dinged. Amanda took her steaming mug and sat down across from him. She blew across the hot surface of the cider, took a cautious sip. It was very hot, but it smelled wonderful. George screwed the top back onto the peanut butter jar. She watched his cheeks writhe as he worked his tongue around in his mouth, cleaning his teeth. He was a good-looking boy, she decided. Fat as a prize hog, but strong, and he had his father's eyes.

"Trouble sleepin'?" he asked.

Amanda snorted. She always had trouble sleeping, as he well knew. She had complained about it every single morning for the past two decades.

"I ain't the only one sitting here in the middle of the God-blest night," she snapped.

Her words set him back a few inches. It still amazed her, the effect she could have on her boys. Ninety-four pounds to his three hundred, and she could still knock him off his chair with a few sharp words.

"Sorry, Mandy," he said. He sounded like a boy again. Only difference was, over the past four decades the title *Mommy* had evolved into *Mandy*. "Ricky's took off. I'm worried he's gonna get himself in trouble. Nelly Bell is back, you know."

"Ricky told me."

"I was hoping he'd just disappear."

"He's an evil man."

"I know, Mandy, but he's a long ways away. He won't bother us again. We oughta just forget about him."

"He's laid a taint on our family. Who will punish him? Who will do the Good Lord's work?"

George shook his head. "It better not be Ricky. I don't know how many times old Orlan will be able to cover for him. Besides, it's not going to make a goddamn bit of difference to Shawn. What's done is done."

Amanda pressed her lips together so hard she could feel them buzz. "The doctor laid a taint. Ricky is a good son."

"He's a goddamn fool," George said.

She grabbed the spoon out of George's hand and whacked him on the forehead.

"Ow! Mandy, that hurt!"

"I won't have language like that in my kitchen George Washington Murphy. You can't sleep, that's fine by me but I'll be buttered and toasted if you think I'm going to sit here, three o'clock in the God-blest morning, and listen to your cussing!"

George leaned back, pressing his hand against his forehead.

"I'm gonna have a big lump, right in the middle of my forehead."

"Boy, you're gonna have more'n that if you don't learn to talk better." Now *she* was all het up. She stood and got the bottle of Jim Beam out of the cupboard next to the sink, poured two fingers into a water glass, brought it to the table, took an angry sip. "Don't you say a word," she said.

George looked at the glass of whiskey, gave his head a slow shake, and opened the peanut butter jar.

Crow jerked his head up and popped his eyelids open. He was sitting at the kitchen counter. Had he been asleep? He blinked; his eyes felt stiff and dry. His watch read 3:47. Something had startled him—the creak of tires on cold snow. He stood and listened. A thrumming, the low sound of a large engine. A snowplow? It sounded close, as if it was right outside. Crow walked quickly to one of the front windows, peered past the edge of the curtain. A Hummer with a camouflage paint job sat parked in the driveway, idling. He could see a man in the driver's seat, Ricky Murphy, staring fixedly at the door. Crow felt under his jacket for his gun, snug in its worn shoulder holster. The familiar grip felt good in his palm. The smooth texture of duct tape. He looked again through the window. Ricky was still sitting there, not doing anything yet, just looking.

What did he think he was going to do? Crow watched for a minute. Ricky lifted something to his mouth, tipped his head back. Drinking a beer. Crow considered his options. He could simply wait and see what happened. Or he could call the cops, let them deal with it. That would be the smart thing to do.

He moved away from the window, walked back through the house to the kitchen, picked up the phone. His hand hovered over the keypad. What would happen if he called the cops? Not much. If they showed up while Ricky was still there, what would they do? Give him a ticket for the open can of beer? It didn't seem sufficient. Would they act on Bellweather's earlier complaint? Probably not, seeing as Ricky had a solid alibi, vouched for by the chief of the Big River police. He put down the phone and let himself out through the back door. The deep snow immediately filled his shoes. He circled the house, trudging through knee-deep snow, and approached the drive, shielded by a low hedge. The faint silhouette of Ricky's hat shadowed the frosted rear window of the convertible top. Hoping his attention would remain on the front door, Crow climbed over the snowbank and approached the Hummer from the rear. He crept up to the back bumper, came around the driver's side. Taking a slow, deep breath, he jerked the door open, grabbed Ricky's collar, and pulled him out of the Hummer.

"Hey!" Ricky hit the ground with his shoulder. The Hummer lurched forward. Ricky rolled, grabbed for the revolver in his belt holster. Crow kicked as the revolver cleared the holster, hitting him in the elbow. The gun flew from Ricky's hand, skidded across the icy driveway. Crow ran for the gun, scooped it up, and turned it on Ricky. It weighed about twice as much as his little Taurus.

Ricky climbed to his feet. "Crow?" Crow found the astonishment on his weasely face to be immensely gratifying. Ricky bent over, picked up his hat, wedged it back on his head. "The fuck you doin' here, Crow?"

"Shut up." He glanced back at the Hummer, which was still moving. Its wheels had been turned into the snowbank, which it climbed easily. Crow expected it to stall out at any moment, but the Hummer showed no sign of slowing. The driverless machine rolled easily through the two feet of snow, heading toward the other side of the circular driveway.

"That your car over there, Crow? I'd move it if I was you."

It was on a collision course with his Rabbit. Crow ran after the possessed Hummer, which was picking up speed. He was still ten feet behind it when the three-ton vehicle ground into the Rabbit's front bumper, pushing the smaller vehicle aside, then came to rest with its steel brush guard against the trunk of a three-foot-diameter elm tree. The engine coughed, died.

Crow stopped, his wing tips sliding on the icy driveway, turned back toward Ricky, who was right behind him, too close. Crow jabbed the barrel of the confiscated revolver into Ricky's midsection.

"Oof." A mist of beery breath filled the space between them. Ricky stumbled back, doubled over. He raised his head and said something Crow couldn't understand, something not nice.

"Shut up," Crow said. He held the gun out, looking down its long barrel. He couldn't believe this. He'd had an accident, smashed up his car, and no one had been driving.

"Real fuckin' swift, Crow," Ricky wheezed. He stood up straight, breathing better now. "Musta knocked 'er inta gear when you pulled me outta there. I always knew you was a dumb shit."

"I said shut up." Crow held the gun trained on Ricky's midsection. The trigger, a cold, insistent band of metal, pressed against the pad of his forefinger. He felt the blood gathering in his face, felt it swelling. He imagined doing it. Just letting it happen.

Ricky's expression became uncertain. "Hey-y-y." He took a step back. "Take it easy now, Crow. I was just sitting here having myself a little brewski. You gonna shoot me for that?"

"What are you doing here?" Crow heard the words coming out, level and clear, calmer than he felt. He shifted his stance, standing up straighter. His gun hand relaxed slightly.

Ricky rolled his shoulders and curled his upper lip. "Just thought I'd drop by and see how you cocksuckers live, Crow. I didn't know you was hanging with old Nelly Bell. You and him got a little thing, hey, that's your business."

"What's your problem with Dr. Bellweather?"

Ricky laughed. Crow cocked the revolver; it made a loud click, just like in the movies, but Ricky was not impressed. Whatever he had seen earlier in Crow's face was gone. "I got no problems, Crow. You're the one's got problems." Ricky turned up the collar of his parka and buried his hands in his pockets.

Crow became aware that he was standing outside, no hat or gloves, and it had to be ten or fifteen below zero. The gun metal sucked the heat from his fingers, his toes were numb, he began to shiver. One more try.

"Talk to me, Ricky. Why are you harassing this man?" He strained for an authoritative note, but his shivering carried through to his voice.

"Ha-*rass*-ing? That what you call it, Crow? You're more fucked up than he is." Ricky started toward the Hummer.

"Hold it right there," Crow ordered.

"Screw you, Crow. It's too fucking cold for this." He stopped. "You gonna give me my gun back?"

Crow kept the big revolver trained on him. Ricky spat on the driveway, climbed into the Hummer, backed it away from the elm tree. He grinned through the window, flipped a left-handed bird, and rolled off down the driveway. Crow watched until the taillights turned onto Blueberry Trail and disappeared.

The front door was locked.

He had started back around the house, when the door opened. Bellweather in his flannel pajamas, cradling a shotgun, a pricey-looking double-barreled job with a carved stock and a gold-plated rib. "For a minute there I thought you were going to shoot him," he said.

"It wasn't necessary," said Crow. He stomped the snow off his feet, slammed the door shut.

"Next time, it might be."

Bellweather was trying to act cool, like it was no big deal that Ricky Murphy had shown up in his driveway. Crow didn't buy the act. The doctor's voice sounded different, and there were new lines on each side of his mouth. The man was scared. Crow tried to think of something reassuring to say but could only come up with, "Well, he's gone now."

Bellweather's eyes drifted, looking for purchase. They settled on the gun hanging in Crow's hand. "Nice gun," he said. "What is it, a forty-four?"

"I don't know." All he knew for sure was that it was big, heavy, and cold.

"May I see it?"

Crow hesitated, then handed Bellweather the gun.

The doctor swung open the cylinder. "Forty-one mag Ruger. You'd've gone right through him with this baby." He went through a rapid, confident ritual—unloading, dry firing to check the action, spinning the cylinder, showing Crow he knew his way around firearms, showing him he could handle it. He replaced the six long rounds in the cylinder, snapped it shut, returned the gun to Crow.

"Good weapon," he said, pushing out his jaw. "Seven-inch barrel, plenty of stopping power. You going to keep it?"

"I'm sure as hell not going to give it back to him."

A car drove by, a flash of headlights through the trees. Bellweather stiffened, grabbed his shotgun.

"Easy, Nels," Crow said. "It's just a car. Ricky's gone."

Bellweather licked his lips, smiled, and lowered his weapon. He took a breath and let it hiss out through his nose. "You believe me now, don't you," he said.

Crow nodded. "Yeah, I believe you. But I still don't understand why they're riding you."

Bellweather regarded Crow with an undecided expression. "Neither do I," he said. "And I'd prefer you did not call me that."

"Call you what? Nels?"

"Yes. You will call me *Doctor* Bellweather."

Crow took a long breath. Just when he was starting to feel all right about working for the guy, he punches another button.

VII

Colonel Roosevelt's son, Kermit, it seems, showed more enthusiasm than caution in the pursuit of African big game.

—HUNTING BIG GAME IN THE WILDS OF AFRICA—
THRILLING ADVENTURES OF THE FAMOUS ROOSEVELT
EXPEDITION

The Ruger felt heavy and too large in his hand. Crow sat in Bellweather's office and played with Ricky's gun, aiming at the bison and the antelopes, making quiet popping sounds with his lips. The trigger was stiff and hard to pull. He aimed the unloaded gun at the bison's snout, squeezed the trigger. The sharp, loud snap was absorbed by the suede walls.

"Kapow," he whispered. Ricky Murphy's visit had given Crow a second wind; he was wide-eyed and full of nervous energy. Bellweather had gone back to bed. Crow loaded the gun and pushed it into his belt. Why hadn't he thought to confiscate Ricky's holster while he was at it? For the third time that hour, he patrolled the first floor of the house. With a part of his mind he watched himself acting out, amused and somewhat embarrassed. Soon, he knew, he would crash. Fatigue poisons would reach critical mass in his bloodstream, and this jittery euphoria would give way to irritation, anger, or sleep. The digital clock on the kitchen stove read 4:54. In three more hours he would be escorting *Doctor* Bellweather to his clinic.

He peered, again, through the front window. Nothing but snow and darkness. No Hummer. No Ricky Murphy.

He replayed the night in his memory. What he remembered most intensely was the way his finger had felt on the trigger, Ricky Murphy's skinny, cowboy-hatted head in his sights. The memory had an edge to it, a metallic, cocaine bite that turned his teeth numb.

Crow pushed away from the door. The gun in his belt was digging at his groin. He pulled it out, sat down on one of the ice-white living room chairs, and set the Ruger on the end table. That felt better. He leaned back in the chair and examined the ornate chandelier. It was, after all, a very nice thing to look at, he decided. He closed his eyes, opened them to a galaxy of sparkles, closed them again.

The sound of running water awakened him. Shafts of early sunlight blasted past the curtains and caromed from the white walls; light from the chandelier now appeared dim and yellow. Crow leaned forward and let his head hang between his legs. He could hear padding sounds coming from upstairs. The brush of slippers on thick carpet. The muted howl of a hand-held hair dryer. He looked at his watch—eight o'clock. He went to the downstairs bathroom, sat on the toilet for what turned out to be no reason at all, washed his face, rubbed his teeth with his index finger, pushed his hair back behind his ears. It could be shorter, he thought. And cleaner. He would have to remember to bring a comb next time, and a toothbrush. Maybe even a change of clothes.

Bellweather's idea of breakfast was a tall glass of orange-brown effluent that oozed noisily from his Juiceman 3000. Crow hadn't paid much attention to what had gone into the machine, not understanding at the time that he would be forced to ingest it in liquid form. Now it was too late. He remembered that there had been a few carrots and something that looked like red lettuce.

"You don't have any coffee?" he asked, glaring suspiciously at the thick fluid. It seemed to be moving in the glass, changing to a deeper shade of umber.

Bellweather took a heavy slug of juice. "Ahh," he said. "Try it, Joe. This stuff'll give you more energy than a whole pot of espresso."

"I don't think I want that much energy." What the hell. He took a sip and quickly swallowed, like a child taking medicine. Tentatively, he tasted the coating that had remained on his tongue. It wasn't bad, but he wasn't going to admit it. He sipped his breakfast, staring down at the deep reddish brown ceramic floor tiles, which had far more character and beauty than Bellweather ever would.

"You like the tiles?"

"Yes, I do," said Crow, happy to be able to give a straight answer for once.

"Spanish. My ex got them out of an old *finca,* over two hundred years old. Cost me thirty-six bucks a tile. That woman could spend money like the government." He finished his juice. "Drink up. I have to get to the clinic. I have a nine-thirty." He left the kitchen and returned a few seconds later wearing a heavy gray wool overcoat with a white fur collar. He pulled on a pair of matching gray driving gloves. "You ready?"

They backed out of the garage into cold, clear daylight. Crow's Rabbit, its right quarter panel crushed into the wheel well, sparkled with new frost. Bellweather stared at it for several seconds, then said, "When we get to the clinic, I'll have my receptionist call and get somebody out here to pull that metal away from your tire. I think you'll be able to drive it then." Shifting into first gear, he spun the wheels, fishtailed out onto Blueberry Trail, guided the Jaguar out of the Orchard Estates complex. He turned onto County Road 40 and accelerated, the twelve cylinders bringing the Jag quickly up to seventy. Icy, exhaust-scented wind sucked in through the hole in the rear window.

Crow sat back and watched the traffic. They followed the county road to I-394, merged with the eastbound traffic. Bellweather drove the Jaguar jerkily, accelerating or braking, shifting lanes at every opportunity but to no purpose. He started to hum "Lara's Theme" from *Dr. Zhivago*. Crow tried to tune it out but failed.

"I have a problem," Crow said.

The doctor stopped humming. "What?"

"I feel like you're not telling me something."

Bellweather pushed out a wet lower lip and raised his brows, but kept his eyes on the road. The humming resumed. Crow crossed his arms and waited.

A few seconds later, Bellweather asked, "What do you think I'm not telling you?"

"I'm having a hard time believing that you have no idea why Ricky Murphy is so interested in you."

The doctor nodded. "I don't blame you." He downshifted to fourth gear and accelerated, backing off only when he was about to mount the bumper of a green minivan. "I'm having a difficult time with it myself. That altercation at Birdy's last month, at first I was thinking it was a fluke, just Ricky having one of his psychotic episodes. Even the next day, when he called me on the phone, saying he was going to feed me my own testicles, I attributed it to some sort of chemical imbalance. I offered to write him a Prozac prescription, but he wasn't interested. So I tried to call George, you know, thinking that he might be able to calm his little brother."

"What did he say?"

"Amanda, the old lady, answered the phone, and when I identified myself . . . well, it was astonishing, actually."

"Oh?"

"She launched into a tirade, all fire and brimstone and I would die in agony in the ashes of Gomorrah. Screeching. I had to hold the phone away from my ear. I couldn't make any sense of it, and she wouldn't put George on. The old lady's crazy, you know, and that's a medical opinion."

"You never talked to George?"

"I called him a few times, but it was always Amanda who picked up. Believe me, it's not just Ricky. It's all of them. I even had David call out there. He was able to get through to George, but George said he had no idea what I was talking about. The whole family is disturbed, in my opinion."

"Do you owe them any money?"

"A little, but I don't think that's the problem. I owe money to a lot of people. None of the others have started shooting at me." He took a breath, let it hiss out from between compressed lips. "At least not yet."

"How much do you owe them?"

"Not much. Ten, twenty thousand. He hasn't even sent me a bill for that last hunt, the one where Ricky interrupted our little celebration by attacking me. It's not the money, Joe. It's something else. I'd like to know what it is as much as you do."

Bellweather exited the freeway. He rolled through the stop sign at the end of the ramp, turned right.

Crow still suspected that Bellweather was withholding something. He said, thinking to test this theory, "You want me to look into it? See what I can find out?"

Bellweather said, "It's not in your job description, Joe, but if you can learn something I'd appreciate it. Maybe some of your friends with the police in Big River will know something. If you want to put in a couple hours on it, make a few calls, just keep track of your time and I'll take care of you."

"I'll ask around," said Crow. "By the way, we haven't talked about when I get paid."

Bellweather turned into a parking lot. The building was small but with a pricey-looking marble facade. The only signage was a two-foot-wide brass plaque to the right of the double front doors: WEST END CLINIC • PLASTIC AND RECONSTRUCTIVE SURGEONS.

"Would Wednesdays be all right? Your check will be issued through the clinic, and that's our usual payday."

Crow nodded, frowning. It would be a stretch, but as long as he knew the money was coming, he could make it.

"Good," said Bellweather. "I'll arrange to have your car put back in working order. You can take the Jaguar. I'll have Nate pick me up later. Call me if you learn anything." He opened the door and climbed out. "See you tonight?"

"Nine o'clock." Crow got out, circled the car, slid behind the wheel.

Shawn Murphy propped the barrel of his single-shot .22 in the crook of a small branch that jutted shoulder high off the side of a naked basswood sapling. It fit perfectly. He pulled the butt of the rifle against his shoulder and lowered his head to the sights, aiming the rifle directly at a windfall ten yards away. He waited, trying to take his mind off the cold that penetrated his gloves. The thermometer had read ten degrees when he left the house half an hour ago. He couldn't stay out too long—Grandy would be mad as hell if he frostbit his cheeks again.

The cottontail would come out soon. He had scared it up a few yards back, followed its zigzagging flight, and seen it duck into the windfall, a tangle of dead trees and brush. If he waited long enough it might poke its head out, give him a clear shot. It was the only game he'd seen all morning, and he was determined to bag it. So what if it was cold—he was a good hunter, and he wasn't a wuss. He could beat the crap out of any kid in his class.

Shawn thought about Jimmy Svengaard, who had called him a fat-ass. Shawn had caught him and tackled him and sat on top of him until he started crying, and Mr. Lantermann had pulled him off and sent him home. He didn't care. Shawn hated school anyway. None of the kids liked him, and he didn't like them. He would rather go hunting. The only thing was, Grandy got really mad when he got kicked out, and his dad acted weird too, like he had done something stupid, which Shawn didn't understand because his dad was fat too, and if somebody had called his dad a fat-ass they would *for sure* get knocked down and sat on—or worse.

Five minutes later, the rabbit had not yet appeared. Shawn's hands were getting colder, and his cheeks had that heavy feeling, like slabs of ice. The heck with it. Shawn picked up a stick and heaved it at the windfall. His throw fell short, but the cottontail burst from cover, ran along the base of the chain-link fence, then ducked back into the woods before he could get his sights on it.

Shawn slapped a hand against his hip. This had to be the worst hunt ever. It was too cold. All the animals were holed up, waiting for warmer weather. He considered pursuing the rabbit. If he was very quiet, if he walked softly, he might be able to walk up on it, get a shot. He took a step, and then another, his Sorels riding atop the crusted snow. It was easy walking, as long as he could stay on the crust, but because of his weight he often broke through. He wished his dad would get him a pair of snowshoes. Better yet, a snowmobile of his own. His dad could be a real jerk sometimes. Shawn followed the nine-foot chain-link fence for fifty feet before his left foot broke through the crust and he was in snow up to his thighs. "Shit," Shawn muttered. Once you broke through, it was hard to get back on top. He grabbed the fence to pull himself up, then he saw something large and dark a few yards in front of him and froze.

A bear, he thought. His heart tried to scramble up his ribs, and he stopped breathing. Was it a bear? Too big. It was on the other side of the fence, which enclosed the north quarter, the four-hundred-forty-acre spread where they kept the main elk herd and a few volunteer whitetail. Shawn relaxed. It was just a big damn elk was all, lying on its side.

"Hey, elk!" he shouted. The dark mass stirred and rose up. "I'm gonna get you, elk!" He crashed through the crust, trying to scare the animal into flight. The elk took a few steps away from the fence, and Shawn had his first good look at it. A bull, its enormous antlers reaching higher than the top of the fence. It was the biggest elk Shawn had ever seen.

"Number One!" he breathed.

Number One, the biggest, most elusive, most spectacularly antlered elk on Talking Lake Ranch. He was the trophy everyone wanted, but Number One could simply disappear when he wanted to. He'd heard Ricky and his dad talking about it, about how Number One knew when he was being hunted, how he could just melt away, disappear into the bogs, and nobody would see him for weeks. Shawn stared in awe at the legendary creature—only fifty feet and a few yards of galvanized steel wire between them—just standing there staring back. According to his uncle Ricky, Number One was a world-class specimen, the biggest ever seen east of the Rockies, and maybe the biggest in the U.S. of A.

Shawn forgot about the rabbit, about his stiff fingers and freezing cheeks, about everything but Number One. He raised his .22 and pushed the barrel through the chain links, centered the sights on the elk's massive body. Number One snorted and did a dance to the side, one fist-size eye fixed on the boy.

Shawn pulled the trigger. He heard the sharp crack of the exploding cartridge but didn't notice the small rifle's modest kick. Number One jerked, but stayed where he was. Shawn could see his nostrils jetting steam. Had he missed? He cracked the rifle open and fumbled in his jacket pocket for another round. His hands were so cold he could hardly feel the shells, but he got hold of one and managed to get it into the chamber and close the rifle. Number One had moved a few yards farther away. Shawn took careful aim on the elk's midsection and fired. This time the elk took off running.

"Gotcha!" Shawn shouted.

Shaking with excitement, he reloaded again, but the elk was no longer in sight. Shawn wiped his nose on his sleeve.

"God!" he said. "Number One!" Suddenly the need to tell someone what he had done overwhelmed him, and he started the one-mile trek back home. He crashed through the crust for fifty yards until he reached a hard-packed snowmobile trail. "Number One!" he said, again and again, imagining himself at school, telling the other kids. They · wouldn't laugh at him then. They wouldn't care that he was fat. He was almost home when it occurred to him that his dad might not appreciate his shooting Talking Lake's prize elk.

VIII

> *Do you like TSE-TSE FLIES, POISONOUS SNAKES, and UNSAFE WATER? Are you willing to spend FORTY OR FIFTY THOUSAND DOLLARS for the chance to bag your trophy? Can you handle DISAPPOINTMENT, DYSENTERY, and HARASSMENT by U.S. Customs officials? If the answer is yes, then you should go to Africa for your next big game hunt.*
> *But if you want a COMFORTABLE, GUARANTEED, HASSLE-FREE HUNTING EXPERIENCE, consider TALKING LAKE RANCH.*
>
> —TALKING LAKE RANCH BROCHURE

his Bellweather, he's a trophy hunter. You should see his house. Stuffed animal heads all over the walls. He has a chair made out of antlers." Pressing the phone against his ear, Crow sat back on the cheap sofa bed that had come with his apartment. It wasn't nearly as comfortable as Bellweather's moose-antler chair.

"Sounds like your kind of place," Melinda said.

"What d'you mean?"

"You hunt. You used to go out every fall and shoot ducks. I used to have to cook them for you."

"That's different. Duck hunting is different. This doctor doesn't even eat what he shoots. I think he's a vegetarian. You should see what he has for breakfast."

Melinda laughed. The memory of her cool hand stroked his spine. Crow leaned forward eagerly and ground the phone against his ear. He imagined Melinda at her phone. She would be dressed in jeans, probably, and a sweater, with her straight, pale-blond hair piled on top of and behind her head, held in place with one or more of her curious barrettes. Melinda liked animal shapes—snakes, pigs, butterflies—and she had assembled an impressive menagerie of hair-control devices, none of which was altogether effective in taming her wandering tresses. Six weeks after moving out of their home, Crow still found the fine blond hairs on his clothing and, once, on his pizza. He imagined her now—sitting at the kitchen table holding the telephone in her left hand and curling a lock of hair around her right forefinger, the way she did when she was bored. Or she would be working the crossword puzzle, filling in the blanks with whatever words occurred to her, ignoring the clues, which she said were usually wrong anyway, filling in the empty spaces with whatever was on her mind. She would be wearing pink lipstick to match the chipped and abraded polish on her nails.

"Are you doing the crossword?" he asked.

"I'm brushing Felix," she said.

Crow nodded to himself and let it take form. He could see her brushing Felix, white cat hairs drifting off in every direction. He took a breath and flattened the image.

"Milo is still gone."

"He'll be back."

Crow didn't want to think about it. He said, "So anyway, this doctor thinks the Murphys are out to get him, but he doesn't know why. You remember the Murphys?"

"The Murphys? The ones you had the troubles with?"

"Yeah. Ricky and his brother George. I'm thinking about driving out there this afternoon to talk to them." Actually, it hadn't occurred to him to actually drive out to Big River until he heard himself say it. "Maybe I can find out why he's making trouble for my client." I could stop by, he mouthed silently. "You should see the car this doctor has. It's a pink Jaguar." I could show it to you. We could go for a ride. Talk.

When Melinda did not immediately reply, he said, "It probably won't take long." A few miles from her house.

"Why don't you just phone him?"

Wrong. Wrong. Wrong.

Crow cleared his throat. "I want a face-to-face. I want to just drop in on him, ask him what's going on." He could hear his breath striking the mouthpiece, he could smell the warm plastic.

"That doesn't sound very smart," Melinda said. Her voice sounded as though she was holding the phone away from her mouth, as far as her arm could reach.

There were four black cats at the Humane Society. One, a long-haired, yellow-eyed tom, looked a lot like Milo, but he lacked Milo's stylish notched ears and confident bearing. The other three weren't even close. Crow spent a few minutes playing with an orange kitten, sticking his finger into the cage and letting the kitten bat at it.

A tired-looking woman who seemed to be in charge listened politely as Crow described his missing cat. She took his phone number and promised to call if a black cat matching Milo's description showed up, but strongly suggested that he stop back every day because, as she put it, "We see a lot of cats."

Crow got back into Bellweather's Jaguar. Melinda appeared, again, in his mind. He forced his thoughts to turn, pushed them in other directions. Bellweather. Ricky Murphy. Big River. He was tired, but not sleepy. He started the car. I'll just go for a drive, he told himself, turning west on Highway 12. A few miles later, he stopped, bought a roll of clear packing tape from a hardware store, and covered the hole in the rear window. When he reached the outer suburb of Maple Plain he turned south, taking one of the small county roads down to Highway 7. It wasn't the most direct route to Big River, but it would feel less like he was going home.

When Shawn burst into the kitchen, Grandy was standing at the stove, stirring something in a pot.

"You want a bowl of hot soup, boy?" she demanded. Grandy never called him Shawn. She said that was Grandpa's name. Except Grandpa's name was spelled S-e-a-n, which was the *real* way to spell it. Shawn had never met his grandfather, but according to Grandy, old Sean Murphy had been a great man. Thin as a rail and tough as a nail.

Shawn said, "Sure, Grandy."

His grandmother scowled at the diminution of her name, but Shawn knew she secretly liked it. If she didn't, she'd have come after him with the spoon. Instead she peered closely at his cheeks.

"You get yourself frostbit again, boy?" Grandy always called him "boy."

Shawn shook his head. His thawing cheeks burned like slabs of hot lead. Grandy glared at him, her lips pulled into a wrinkled knot. For a moment, he was afraid she was going to get mad. Grandy was nice, mostly, but she could get scary mad in a second. More than once, she had whacked him for no reason. Or for no reason he could figure out at the time. Shawn kept his eyes on the ladle in her hand.

Grandy shrugged, and her mouth relaxed. She turned back to the stove. "You just take that coat off and sit down, boy. How was school?"

"Okay," Shawn said. Sooner or later she would find out that he had been kicked out, but he was no way going to be the one to tell her. After getting his shot at Number One, he had spent the rest of the day in the barns, feeding things to the animals, teasing the bobcat with a stick, and carving his initials in several interesting places. He wanted to tell someone about Number One. He would explode if he didn't say something, even though he knew it might get him in trouble. He felt the words tumble from his mouth.

"I saw Number One, Grandy. He came right up to the fence!"

"Eh?" She put a wide bowl full of soup on the table. "You mean that big old elk? Must be the size of a house by now."

"He's pretty big."

Shawn tasted the soup. It had plenty of noodles in it, and he liked that. He liked that Grandy hadn't asked him what he had been doing out by the north quarter when he should have been in school. Sometimes she missed stuff. He ate steadily, spooning the broth into his mouth as quickly as he could swallow. He was starving! Grandy watched him eat, her small mouth pulsing with each swallow the boy took. Shawn wondered what she was thinking. With Grandy, you couldn't tell.

Shawn finished the soup and held up the bowl.

"Can I have some more?"

Grandy shook her head. "Not until dinnertime."

"How about can I have a cookie?" Grandy made great chocolate chip cookies.

She shook her head. "You're getting fat, boy. You get much fatter, and we'll have to call you a girl."

Shawn blinked. A girl? What was she talking about?

"I'm still hungry!" It was not a sensation he was accustomed to ignoring. Grandy had never before refused to feed him.

"A boy gets too fat, he turns into a girl," Grandy said. "You get any fatter, I'll have to put you in one of my dresses."

Shawn gaped, then understanding flashed in his mind. She was fooling with him. He laughed and said, "Oh, Grandy, that's stupid! Dad's fat, and he's not a girl!"

Shawn realized in an instant that he had made a mistake. Before he could move, Grandy's sharp claws dug into his shoulders and pinned him to his chair. Her face filled his vision, and her old-lady breath rained down on him.

"Don't you talk about your father that way, boy." She cuffed him on his frostbitten ear. "You're half girl already. You hear me? Half girl!" She reached down and grabbed his crotch, squeezing. Shawn gasped as a balloon of pain filled his gut.

"You know what this is for, little boy?" she hissed.

Shawn shook his head, terrified.

"It's for going pee-pee and for making babies. You do anything else with it, you'll turn into a girl. You understand me?"

Agonized, Shawn nodded. He thought he was going to puke up his soup. As quickly as she had grabbed him, Grandy unclenched her claws, stood back, and crossed her arms.

"You go see your father now. He's in the lodge. You go tell him how you saw his big elk today. Tell him how you were out looking at the animals when you were supposed to be in school."

Shawn pushed his chair back and fled the kitchen, a conduit of pain pulsing from his groin to his frostbitten cheeks.

IX

Actually, he's good for business. The rest of my cus-tomers, they look at him and tell themselves that com-pared to Harley, they got it all under control.

—BERDETTE WILLIAMS

The coffee was black, bitter, and at least four hours old. It reminded him of the coffee at CA meetings. Adding sugar only produced another unpleasant sensation: now it was too sweet. Berdette walked by and eyed Crow's cup, looking for something to do. Crow shook his head, lifted the cup to his mouth, let his upper lip disturb the black, oily surface, set it back on the bar. Berdette's wife, Arlene, sat slumped in one of the booths, reading the *Big River Herald*. It was a few minutes before noon.

Berdette's only other customer, Harley Pike, was hunched over the far end of the bar, clad in his usual greasy jeans and motorcycle jacket, scowling at the remaining half inch of beer in his glass. Bits of foam clung to his scraggly gray-and-blond beard. Harley was the nearest thing Big River had to a town drunk—Crow had picked him up off the street dozens of times. Sometimes Harley had been cooperative, happy to sleep it off on a jailhouse cot. Other times he had been having too much fun to let anybody interfere, and Crow had been compelled to use force. He wondered whether Harley remembered him.

"Hey Berdette," Crow called.

Berdette turned and pointed at the coffeepot, looked at Crow, and raised his eyebrows. A column of horizontal wrinkles climbed nearly to the peak of his hairless head.

"No, not that, please."

Berdette looked hurt. Crow didn't feel sorry for him. He figured Berdette owed him something back for all the money he'd spent there during his years as a Big River cop, when he'd ended every shift with a few shots of Berdette's watered-down Cuervo.

"What do you hear from the Murphys these days, Berdette?"

Berdette's eyes narrowed, and his cheeks inflated. "Nothing much new. But if that Ricky sets foot in here one more time, I kick his ass." Berdette was close to eighty years old, shorter than Crow, maybe a hundred fifteen pounds, but if Ricky had walked in the door at that moment, Crow might have put his money down on Berdette.

"What about the rest of them?"

Berdette said, "That what you're doing back here? You got something going with those boys?"

"Not *with* them," Crow replied.

Berdette nodded. "They been trouble ever since George took over from his daddy. Actually, his daddy was trouble too. What do you want to know, Joe?"

"Anything you can tell me."

Berdette's eyes went into a distant stare. "Well, now," he said, "that ain't much. I see George and Ricky and their mama at Saint Luke's every Sunday, but that's about it. They pretty much keep to themselves, except when Ricky gets a few under his belt."

"You remember the last time I was in here?"

"Not likely to forget."

"You remember that guy Ricky clobbered?"

"Sure I do. Doctor something, from the cities."

"You know why Ricky went after him that way?"

Berdette shook his head. "I don't never wonder why Ricky does what he does, some of the shit he does."

"Fucker!"

Startled, Crow looked down the bar at Harley Pike, who had lifted his glare from his beer glass and fixed it on some invisible object floating above the bar, a few inches in front of his face. "Goddamn motherfucker," Harley snarled.

Berdette said, "You need another one, H.?"

Harley blinked and looked back at his glass—which was now empty—his vision forgotten for the moment. He fingered the small pile of coins on the bar, pushed forward three quarters and an assortment of smaller change. Berdette refilled Harley's glass, letting the beer flow down its side, bringing the amber fluid right up to the rim, a no-foam, no-bullshit beer. He took the coins, rang them into the register. Harley clasped his battered hands around his beer glass and fixed his moist eyes on the fullness of it.

Berdette added an unwanted splash of hot coffee to Crow's cup. "H. gets testy when he's on empty."

"Testy when he's full too," Crow said.

"Couple more beers, he'll mellow out just fine. I oughta kick him out of here, but I don't know what he'd do with himself. Puss'll be out to pick him up pretty soon. She knows how to handle H. when he's got a bellyful. Anyways, he's mostly mouth these days. Not like that Ricky Murphy—who knows why he does what he does?"

"So you haven't heard anything, like the doctor did something to make Ricky mad? Or something different going on with the Murphys?"

Berdette shook his head. "Far as I know it's been just business as usual. George is still sellin' them canned hunts a his. It's got to where you want to shoot a rhinoceros or some damn thing, George'll go out and find one for you, if you got the loot. You ever been out to their place?"

"Never had reason to."

"You know, they got close to four thousand acres out there. Mostly river bottom and coulee, but it's a hell of a chunk of land. Damn shame what they do with it, but I guess they got a right. I hear they even got a real live tiger for sale. Forty thousand bucks, you can go shoot yourself a tiger. Hell, for forty thousand bucks I'd let you shoot Arlene."

Arlene heard her name and looked up from her newspaper.

Berdette told her, "Never mind, sugar." He lowered his voice. "I'd let her go for twenty in the off-season."

"He's really got a tiger out there?" Crow asked.

"Wouldn' surprise me he had a tyrannosaurus."

"So who lives out there now?"

"Just the three of 'em—George, Ricky, and Amanda. And George's kid. George's wife took off on him a few years back, but the kid still lives with George. A course, the daughter, Hillary, she married your old boss Orlan. I ain't telling you nothing you don't know. They still live in that big yellow house up on Front Street."

"What kind of a guy is George?"

Berdette grunted. "You never met him? He's a big guy, sort of goofy looking. But don't be surprised if you like him."

"Y'wanna fight?"

Crow turned his head and looked at Harley Pike, who had climbed off his stool and was standing a few feet away, bowed legs spread, fists clenched white, eyes red and half closed.

"You think yer tough?" Harley demanded.

Crow, keeping his face carefully neutral, said, "No, Harley, I'm not tough."

Harley stood his ground, feet anchored to the floor, the top half of his body swaying as if he were standing in a small boat on a choppy lake.

"You wanna fight?" he said again, advancing a step, projecting an aroma of alcohol and dental decay.

Crow shook his head, breathing shallowly. "No, thanks, Harley. No fight left in me today."

"Cuz I'll fightcha, goddammit. Punch yer lights out." He lowered his brow and glared.

Crow nodded. "I know. You want a beer, Harley?"

Harley's expression softened. "You buyin'?" he asked suspiciously.

"Sure. You want to get the man a beer, Berdette?"

Berdette was already pouring.

Crow waited for Harley to get settled with his replenished glass, then slid off his stool and laid three dollars on the bar. "Thanks, Berdette."

"I didn't tell you anything you didn't already know. You gonna tell me what's going on?"

"I would if I could, Berdette, but the truth is, I'm as much in the dark as old Harley there. I just haven't got a clue."

George Murphy didn't think his little pair of deuces was going to cut it. Orlan was probably sitting on jacks or better. Murphy sighed and considered calling the bet anyway. For one dollar, he could afford to see what his brother-in-law had that was worth a double raise. And so what if he lost? If Orlan was willing to put up with Hillary, the least George could do in return would be to drop a few bucks at the card table.

Still, he hated to lose. Especially to a guy like Orlan. Even a dollar. Even fifty cents.

Another strategy occurred to him. He could raise another dollar, maybe bluff his way into a pot. Better yet, he could raise it up two dollars. The limit was supposed to be one, but what the hell? It would give Orlan something to think about. George fished in his pile of change, counting out quarters. He heard the door that led into the house open and close. A shadow fell across his arm. George turned his head and looked into his son's face.

"Dad?"

George felt a pang in his chest, an oleo of irritation, tenderness, disgust, and love. The boy looked so soft and vulnerable. He smelled like chicken soup. His nose ran and his eyes watered. George looked around the lodge, a room sixty feet long and thirty feet wide. The single ridge beam, thirty inches in circumference, had come from a white pine that he and Ricky had taken down to make room for the lodge. A fire crackled in the fireplace at one end, a potbellied wood stove stood near the entrance. At the far end of the room, his Bengal tiger lay in an orange-black-and-white pile, watching the cardplayers through slitted eyes. The five picture windows looked out over the river valley, a spectacular panorama to which he had long since grown accustomed. This was his favorite room, the hub of Talking Lake Ranch. During the fall, when the urge to hunt was strong, there would be five or six hunting parties on any given day, Mandy would be bustling around the lodge making sandwiches and drinks, George and Ricky would be taking one group after another out to hunt. During peak season he'd have outside guides bringing in clients, and sometimes he'd have to hire a few of the locals to help out.

He didn't have much time for the kid when he was busy like that. Maybe that was why the boy had done what he'd done. Maybe it was his own fault.

Now, except for Orlan and the three off-season duck hunters from Sioux Falls, the big room was empty—the other three tables held only a few old hunting magazines and the duck hunters' cased shotguns. Mandy was nowhere in sight. He wished she hadn't walked into Shawn's room that day. He wished she hadn't told Ricky, hadn't got him all excited. He wished he could forget about it, put it out of his mind. Now that he had time, maybe he could get to know his kid a little better, take him out to shoot a deer or something. The kid was getting big, maybe big enough to handle the 30.06. He put a hand on Shawn's shoulder and squeezed affectionately. Shawn winced and twisted away. George gaped at his son, embarrassed—he had hardly touched him.

"Grandy said I got to talk to you," Shawn said, rubbing his shoulder.

Orlan Johnson, the belly of his two-tone uniform pressing against the edge of the card table, sipped a vodka tonic and drummed his fingers on the table, waiting for George to make his move. The other men, all nursing their Budweisers, watched, bored, waiting for the next deal. They had shot and paid for twenty-four mallards and eight woodies that morning. The hunting was over for the day, the fireplace was putting out the Btu's, and everybody felt a little sleepy.

"Not now, Shawn," George said. "Your daddy's about to clean these fellas' clocks. You can pull up a chair and watch if you want." He slid a handful of quarters toward the center of the table and watched Orlan's lower lip slide out and down.

"Thought it was a dollar limit," Orlan complained.

George raised his eyebrows. "Can't handle my action, Orlan?" He heard Shawn dragging a chair from one of the other tables, felt him settle at his elbow.

Orlan sighed and examined his cards intently. He snorted and threw them into the pot. "Christ, you're lucky," he said. "What did you have?"

George grinned and threw his cards away, facedown. Let him wonder.

The outside door opened, and Ricky stepped into the lodge. An invisible whirlwind of icy air filled the room. Ricky closed the door, and the cold air settled, pooling around their feet. George swept in the pile of change. Orlan Johnson shuffled, getting ready to deal the next hand. Ricky took off his cowboy hat, shook off a few flakes of snow.

"Colder'n a Fargo whore out there," he said. "Hey, Orlan. How you doin'?" He replaced his hat on his head, then nodded to the three duck hunters, whom he hadn't met.

"You want in?" Orlan asked, holding up the deck of cards.

Ricky shook his head and turned to George. "I was just up on the north quarter, checking out the fences. Saw Number One crossing the creek just above the coulee."

George said, "No kidding? I haven't caught sight of that monster since September. How's the old boy looking?"

"Not so good. He was walking sort of funny. I tried to follow him, but he took off on me, and I didn't want to spook him any worse than he was. He's sick."

George's face fell. He had been growing Number One for fifteen years. He said, "How sick?"

"He don't look good at all. He's kind of hunched up, like he's got a problem in his gut. You think we should run a special on him?"

George's jaw pulsed. The cardplayers were all looking at him nervously. Screw them, he thought. Fifteen years he'd had Number One, an elk so big, so fast, and so smart it had survived three guided hunts over the past two years. George had been getting a couple hundred a day in guide fees just to give hunters a chance at Number One, plus another thirty thousand if they bagged him. So far, no one had even come close. Number One somehow knew when he was being hunted, got himself down in the bottoms, down in the bogs, where nobody could get a shot at him. You could bugle all day and not get a rise out of him.

So far, every hunter who had pursued the big bull had been forced to settle for a lesser trophy.

And now he was sick; maybe dying. If somebody was going to bag him, they'd have to do it pretty damn quick. A shadow of mourning swept over him. He'd had that damn elk longer than he'd had his only son. George turned to look at Shawn, but the boy had disappeared.

Of all wild beasts, a boy is the most difficult to manage.

—*PLATO*

The private road leading into Talking Lake Ranch wound a treacherous, rutted, sloping path through maple woods, a tangled gray-and-white winter landscape that gave the eye nothing distinct on which to focus. Bellweather's Jaguar, surefooted on pavement, skittered uncertainly down the icy track. Half a mile in, Crow began to think that he had turned down the wrong road. He slowed to a crawl and looked for a place to turn around, but the woods rose steeply on his right and dropped into a shallow ravine on his left, and the road was barely as wide as his car. He stopped and shifted into reverse. The rear wheels spun and the back of the car slid sideways, nearly dropping off the edge of the elongated ice rink he was using for a road.

"How come I let you talk me into this?" he said to himself. He continued down the hill in first gear. Minutes later, he arrived at a gate made from wooden poles. A metal sign on the gate read TALKING LAKE RANCH—MEMBERS ONLY. The hasp was secured by a large, round padlock. The driveway, however, did not pass through the gate but rather made a jog around it. Apparently, getting out of a vehicle to open the gate was too much trouble—especially in the winter—so the Murphys and their visitors simply drove around it in their 4 x 4s. Crow followed the short detour, wincing as the low-slung Jag bottomed out twice on the ridged path.

Two hundred yards past the gate, a long, sprawling complex of mismatched buildings emerged from the woods. The largest structure, a log building about the size of four triple garages placed end to end, began with a prominent stone chimney, topped by a ragged plume of wood smoke, and ended in a short covered walkway leading to a fawn-colored clapboard house, two story, matching patterned curtains in all the windows. The Murphy residence, he guessed. Beyond the house, a series of three identical low metal-sided barns filled a clearing in the woods.

The entrance to the log building, a pair of oversize double doors, was marked by a carved wooden sign: THE LODGE.

Three 4 x 4s and two snowmobiles clustered near the entrance. Crow looked for, but did not see, Ricky's Hummer. Good. He parked the Jaguar alongside a black Toyota 4-Runner and shut down the engine.

The silence inside the car pressed against his ears. Good ideas, he reflected, do not always travel well. He climbed out into the crisp winter air and pushed his ungloved hands deep down in his pockets. The muffled sound of dogs barking came from within, or behind, one of the metal-sided barns. The only other sound was the faint hiss and creak of wind on frozen gray branches.

To his right, the driveway led to a sagging metal Butler building. Maybe the Hummer was in there. Crow banished the thought. Ricky would be here, or he would not. Up the hill from the garage he could see two cottages built back into the woods. Guest cottages, he suspected. He started back toward the lodge, paused, decided to look around a bit. He circled the house, following a trampled path that led between the house and the barns. His wing tips, absurd in this woodland setting, creaked on the packed snow. As he came in view of the kennel behind the barn, the dogs stopped barking and began to wag their tails, three hounds with their noses pressed up against the chain-link fence of their kennel, staring at him.

Crow said, "Nice dogs."

At the sound of his voice, the barking resumed with renewed vigor. Crow shook his head. He should know better than to talk to animals.

The land behind the lodge dropped away quickly. He could see the river through the trees; wide white shelves of snow-covered ice sandwiched a leaden ribbon of water. He wondered if he could throw a rock that far. The distance seemed to shift—as he watched, the river receded. A wet wind rolled up the bluff; Crow turned up the collar of his trench coat and buttoned the storm flap. Looking back at the lodge, he discovered a bank of five picture windows above him, running most of the length of the log building. It would be a great view from inside. He glanced back at the house, noticed something moving behind the glass.

Someone—it looked like an old woman—was watching him from an upstairs window. Crow lifted a hand and smiled. The old woman backed away from the glass. He turned toward the river again, shivered, then retraced his steps, sending the kenneled dogs into a new level of frenzied barking.

The old woman was waiting for him at the side door. She was not quite five feet tall, and pink scalp showed through her white hair. She stood in the open doorway wearing a housedress, little pink flowers on white cotton, her veiny, sinewy arms crossed, staring up at Crow with eyes the color of bitter chocolate, frowning in a way that made her mouth disappear in a whorl of wrinkles. A few seconds into an awkward silence, Crow realized that she was not going to speak.

"Afternoon," he said.

The old woman nodded, confirming his statement.

"Is George around?" he asked. He felt like a little boy asking if George could come out to play.

"Who the devil are you," the old woman asked, "making them dogs bark themselves silly?"

"My name's Crow."

"What kind of name is that? You a Indian?"

Crow shook his head. "I'm looking for George Murphy. Are you Mrs. Murphy?"

Mrs. Murphy nodded, studying him. "Crow," she said, pushing out a small, surprisingly pink lower lip. "You're a friend of Ricky's, aren't you? I've heard him mention your name."

I bet you have, Crow thought. He tipped his head to the side and smiled, striving for neutrality. "I know Ricky." He wished the dogs would stop barking. His toes were freezing, and his ears were going numb. Mrs. Murphy didn't seem to be bothered by the cold.

"Shaddup!" she bellowed, frightening both Crow and the dogs into silence. She returned her attention to Crow, looking at him as if he had suddenly materialized before her. "Is there something I can help you with?" she asked.

Crow shook his head. "It's a private matter."

Her eyes shifted to the sky. "Private? His daddy Sean was the most private man I ever knew. Never knew what he was thinking. Never let on nothing till the day he learned he was going to die. Oh, how he hated to die."

"I'm sorry," said Crow, feeling uncomfortable. The old lady was batty.

"Don't be," Mrs. Murphy commanded. "He's been dead fifteen long years now, God rest his soul, though we mostly only miss him on holy days now. He was pure Irish, you know, and liquor was poison to him. Of course, you being a Indian, I'm not telling you anything you don't know about liquor. Is there something I can do for you?"

Crow was mostly Irish—no Native American ancestors that he knew of—but he understood that bit about liquor being poison. "I'd like to talk to George," he said.

"Ricky's not here. He's took off someplace in that truck of his."

"George. I'm looking for George."

"George? I thought you said you were looking for Ricky. You can go look for him in the lodge." She stepped back and slammed the door.

Crow walked around the house to the lodge, pulled open one of the double doors, and stepped inside, relaxing his shoulders and letting the warmth penetrate. The air held a rich animal smell.

The lodge, he discovered, consisted of a single open room. Directly opposite the entrance were the picture windows he had seen from outside. The view of the river valley *was* even more impressive from inside, filling the entire bank of windows. He let his eyes rest briefly on the panorama, then turned his attention to the room itself. Several bulky club chairs and a long sofa upholstered in burgundy leather faced the windows, looking out over the trees across the river. A collection of mismatched wooden chairs were ranged at tables on and around a fifteen-by-thirty-foot Oriental rug that was centered on the polished wood floor. To his left, the wrinkled, determined-looking head of a rhinoceros jutted out into the room from above a huge fieldstone fireplace. On each side of the fireplace hung a collection of trophies, including an elk, three black bears, a cougar, a leopard, and a pair of boars. Below the rhino head, an octagonal green felt card table was surrounded by four men, intent on a hand of cards. Three of the men he did not recognize. The fourth man, the one dressed in a police uniform, was Orlan Johnson.

Crow looked toward the other end of the room. At first, his mind refused to process the image. Then he remembered what Berdette Williams had told him. Yes, the Murphys did indeed have a tiger. The animal was reclined on its belly, examining him through unblinking eyes. The primate in Crow wanted very badly to climb the nearest tree. Fortunately, since no trees were available, the more evolved portions of his mind recognized the heavy chain leading from a collar around the tiger's thick neck to a substantial-looking steel ring bolted to the wall. The floor was covered with straw—from the way it was scattered, it appeared that the tiger's territory was strictly limited to a half circle about fifteen feet in diameter. A large jointed bone—the leg of some sizable creature—lay near the perimeter of the circle. The bone was scarred; shreds of meat and gristle still clung to the joint. The animal smell he had noticed upon entering sorted itself out in his mind: straw, tiger piss, and aging meat.

"Is that who I think it is?"

Crow turned and looked at the cardplayers. Orlan Johnson was grinning at him.

"I'll be got-damned. It *is* Joe Crow! What the hell are *you* doing here?"

Crow crossed the room to stand a few feet from the table. He wished his heart would slow down. He could still feel the tiger tasting him with its feline mind. That, plus being in the same room with his old boss, a guy who had had him arrested, then forced him to resign, was playing hell with his glands. He forced himself to speak calmly.

"How you doing, Orlan?"

"I'm doin' fine." A loose smile crawled across Orlan Johnson's wide face. A cigar with a plastic mouthpiece jutted from between his teeth. "You wanna play? Play a little stud?" He was drunk. A tall glass filled with ice cubes, carbonated fluid, and a lime rested at his elbow. That would be a vodka tonic, Crow recalled. Johnson never drank anything but vodka tonics, which he believed were less detectable on his breath.

"I'm looking for George," Crow said.

"He just left. He's all upset because his elk got sick." Johnson laughed through his nose, blowing ashes on his uniform.

"You just missed him," said the sandy-haired man to Johnson's left.

Johnson said, "George likes to feed his beasts when he gets upset. You still play poker, don't you, Crow?"

Crow ignored Johnson and addressed himself to the sandy-haired man. "Any idea where he went?"

Johnson said, "Jus' a frien'ly game, Joe. Dollar limit."

One of the other men, a nondescript but well-groomed fellow wearing a red chamois shirt and an expensive watch, stood up and introduced himself and the other two men. Crow shook their hands and instantly forgot their names. All three men, he noticed, were drinking Budweisers. Their identical grips were firm, dry, and practiced. Executives of some sort, probably worked for some corporation large enough to have sent them to handshaking school.

"You know," one of the men said, "George didn't walk out of here but a couple minutes ago. You might want to check out by the barns."

Johnson said, "Why don't you sit down, Crow? Four makes for a lousy card game. George'll be back sometime. Might as well win some of our money while you're waiting. You want a beer?"

Crow shook his head, staring at his former boss, imagining how it would feel to step around the table and grind the heel of his right hand into that bulbous nose. Rage swept through him, then was gone, leaving only a shaky nausea in its wake. The air in the lodge was stale and heavy and warm. The sweet smell of Johnson's cigar combined with the yeasty, alcoholic aroma of the beer and settled low in Crow's gut. He had to get out of there. "No, thanks," he mumbled, heading for the door.

A large, pear-shaped man in a baby-blue snowmobile suit was standing beside Bellweather's Jaguar, staring down at it. He turned his head and looked at Crow, blinking. Framed by the blue hood, his face had the rubbery, slack look of the mentally impaired. He pointed a mittened hand at the car and lifted reddish eyebrows over mud-brown eyes.

Crow smiled and nodded, half expecting the man to clap his hands together and giggle.

The man did not return his smile, but said, "Don't you feel like a jerk, driving that thing?" There was no trace of arrested development in the clear, deep voice.

Crow made a rapid mental adjustment. "Are you George Murphy?" he asked.

The man pushed back his hood. His hair, red shot with gray, covered most of his protruding ears. He had a swollen red spot in the center of his forehead. "That's right. Is Nelly Bell here?"

Nelly Bell? Crow repressed a smile. "If you mean Dr. Bellweather, no, he's not here."

George Murphy took three swift, fluid steps, bringing him to within arm's reach of Crow, who had to strain to keep himself from backpedaling. The man could move, considering his size. At closer range, his eyes did not appear so much muddy as opaque. Murphy lowered his head, tipped it twenty degrees, and peered into Crow's face like a curious gorilla looking into a camera.

"You are Officer Crow," he said. Steamy breath crossed the space between them. It smelled of peppermint. "Ricky said you was working for that son-of-a-bitch. I thought we were rid of you." He paused and pressed his lips together. "I see I was mistaken."

Murphy's face went through several mutations as he spoke, as if small animals were scurrying about just beneath his skin. The effect was both comic and alarming. His language also seemed inconsistent, like that of an intelligent but uneducated man trying to speak with unaccustomed formality.

Crow said, "It's a small world."

"Like hell it is. What do you want, Officer Crow?"

"I want to talk. You mind if we go inside? It's cold out here."

Murphy snorted and turned away, walking toward the barns. Crow hesitated. Was this a summons or a dismissal? He decided to take it as an invitation, pushed his hands into his coat pockets, and started after the lumbering Murphy. He looked up at the house as they passed and caught the old woman watching him through one of the upstairs windows. Crow waved, and once again she backed away from the glass. Murphy unlatched and opened the door leading into the first barn, stepped inside. The smell hit Crow hard; his nostrils clamped shut at the organic intensity of it.

The long metal building was illuminated by three bare, low wattage yellow light bulbs hanging from cords seven feet off the straw-matted floor. The left-hand side of the barn was divided into stalls. Breathing shallowly, he followed Murphy into the dimly lit interior. The first three stalls were vacant, but the fourth was occupied by an ugly, barrel-shaped creature that pushed its snout through the metal bars of the gate and snorted steam. It was a pig, but uglier and meaner looking than any pig Crow had ever seen—coarse speckled gray-and-black hair, long legs, and a hunched back. Murphy stopped, pried the top off a plastic garbage can, scooped out a handful of corn, and tossed it into the stall. The hog produced a hoarse squeal and proceeded to vacuum up the kernels. It paused in its feeding and raised its head, showing a pair of six-inch-long tusks jutting from its lower jaw. Crow met the tiny, glittering eyes, shuddered.

"A little treat," Murphy said. He grabbed a small metal bucket from a nail on the wall, filled it with corn, moved on to the next stall, which contained a smaller, reddish version of the same species. He tossed out another scoop of corn, then looked back at Crow, a demented grin filling his face.

"I like to feed them."

"I can see that," Crow said. "What kind of pig is that?"

"Russian boar. We got twenty, thirty razorbacks running wild down on the bottoms, but I like to keep the Russians penned up here until we need them. Sometimes they don't mix so good with the native stock."

"They sure are ugly."

"Eye of the beholder, Officer Crow. I hear you have climbed on the water wagon. I respect that. More people should try it."

"Who'd you hear that from?" he asked.

Murphy laughed. "It's a small world."

The next few stalls were empty, but a larger stall at the far end of the barn held a mottled gray-and-white ram with horns corkscrewing out eighteen inches from the sides of its head. The ram stood chewing something, apparently oblivious to their presence. Murphy threw it some corn, but the animal showed no interest.

"He's not happy," Murphy said. "These exotics don't last long in our climate, even if you keep them indoors."

"Then why keep them?"

Murphy looked surprised. "Why, to *hunt*, Officer Crow. Aren't you a hunter?"

"That depends on what you call hunting."

"Do you shoot wild animals?"

"I've been duck hunting."

"Then you're a hunter. We hunt ducks here ten months a year. You should try us. We'll fix you up in one of our deluxe blinds, guarantee you all the shooting you want."

"I'm not sure I'd call what you do 'hunting.' "

"Really?" Murphy smiled. "What would you call it?"

"What do you call it when chickens are killed at a slaughterhouse?"

"I would call that profit taking. You've never hunted on a preserve, have you? If you had, you wouldn't compare it to killing chickens."

"Slaughtering cattle, then. What I wouldn't call it is *hunting*."

Murphy regarded Crow mildly. "You don't know what you're talking about," he said. "You should keep your mouth shut, you don't know what you're talking about."

Crow did not want to debate the ethics of preserve hunting. "Let's talk about Dr. Bellweather," he said.

Murphy frowned and shook his head, refusing to be diverted from his topic. "We've got four thousand acres of some of the toughest terrain you ever saw, and some damn fine trophies on the hoof. And don't you let anybody tell you a preserve-raised animal is any different from a wild one. Let me tell you. We got this one old elk, he's gonna go in the Boone and Crockett record book, rack the size of a Volkswagen. I personally guided three hunts on him, and he's survived every one. Smart as a damn cat. We got a hundred twenty miles of trails through woods, scrub, field, and bog. You could spend a month chasing after old Number One and never see the old bull. You hunt Talking Lake, you got yourself a real challenge. Maybe you get your game, maybe you don't. And we can make it as hard as you want. You want a real

challenge, you ought to try going after one of our Russians. You go after one with a handgun, you got yourself a real hunt."

"How about I go after them with a machine gun?"

Murphy shrugged, looking disappointed. "You could do that if you
wanted to," he said. "We cater to all styles of hunting."

"How about if I want to shoot myself a tiger?"

Murphy smiled, his lips tightening across his teeth, then curling back.
"I doubt you can afford it. Now what was it you wanted to talk about?"

"Dr. Bellweather. I understand you're trying to kill him."

Murphy chuckled. It was a fine, chesty laugh that seemed at odds
with his rubbery, mobile features. "The man is obviously paranoid. I'm
in the business of hunting animals, not men. Why would I want to kill
Nelly Bell?"

"I don't know. Why did Ricky pay him a visit last night?"

"Did he? Well now that's pretty strange, seeing as Ricky was here all
night reading his Bible." Murphy turned and started back down the row
of stalls, stopping in front of the gray Russian boar. "Let me tell you.
You maybe won't believe this, but I respect you, Officer Crow. When
you had your troubles with Ricky? Hell, I knew he was asking for it.
Fact is, a couple hours cuffed to the Hummer actually seemed to improve his personality." He paused, smiling with narrowed eyes. "A
course, I had to ask Orlan to get rid of you, but you had my respect. I
didn't respect you, I'd pick you up right now and feed you to the goddamn hogs. And don't think they wouldn't eat you. They eat anything."

Crow stared into the rubbery face, thankful for the Ruger in the
waistband of his pants, the Taurus in his coat pocket. It could easily go
down that way. Somebody getting shot. Or fed to the hogs. If Murphy
thought of Joe Crow as a serious threat, he wouldn't think twice about
eliminating him. Crow had no doubt that George, like his brother Ricky,
was capable of killing people as well as animals. His eyes kept returning to the red spot on Murphy's forehead, glowing like a third eye. For
too long, George Murphy had been a bugaboo of his mind. Now that
he had met the man, the bugaboo was real. A shudder rolled up his
spine. The moment passed.

"Somebody once told me I'd probably like you," Crow said.

Murphy laughed loudly, throwing his head back. "Who told you
that?"

"It doesn't matter. He was wrong."

"Of course he was." Murphy frowned and bit his upper lip. His bottom teeth were short, white, and widely spaced. "It wasn't Nelly Bell,
was it? I didn't think so. Is there anything else I can do for you?"

"You haven't answered my question."

Murphy threw the rest of the corn into the gray hog's stall, hung the bucket back on the wall.

"Let me tell you, Crow. You want to know what it is? It's none of your goddamn business is what it is. It's family business is what it is. It's nothing to do with you. My advice to you: Next time you see Ricky? Leave him do what he has to do."

"Just let him take out the doctor? I don't think so."

Murphy shrugged. "That's too bad."

"Ricky's a good boy."

Both men turned. Amanda Murphy had materialized a few feet behind them, still in her cream-and-pink cotton housedress, stark white legs planted in a pair of oversize green rubber Sorels, veiny arms crossed tightly over pendulous breasts.

George said, "Mandy, what are you—"

"Ricky does what he's told."

George moved to his mother, took her arm. "Mandy, let's go back inside. You'll catch cold out here."

"The doctor has laid a taint on us."

"A *taint?*" Crow asked. "What's that?"

In the next barn, Shawn Murphy stood staring into a metal cage at a two-year-old black bear, a young sow. The bear was asleep at the far end of her cage. Shawn threw a few pieces of food at her but got no response beyond an irritated twitch of her heavy winter coat. Once, he had poked her in the ear with a long branch and she had charged at him, crashing into the side of her mesh cage, hot spit hitting him right in the face. That had been exciting. But today the old sow refused to be provoked. Bored, Shawn went to look in on the cougar cubs. The two cats were curled up in the corner of their cage, sleeping. All the animals seemed sluggish today.

Maybe Ricky and his dad wouldn't find Number One. Maybe the elk would die in a boggy thicket and no one would ever know he had been shot. Or maybe he'd heal up and get better.

Shawn kicked the side of the cage. One of the cubs opened its eyes, glared at him dully.

His dad was going to kill him. They would find Number One, and they would know who had shot him. What would he do? It was too awful to think about. After the way Grandy and his dad had reacted when he'd told them about Doc Bellweather, Shawn was scared. He hadn't thought it was any big deal. He wished he hadn't said anything. Doc was his buddy, and a good customer for his dad. He'd thought if he'd said it was Doc's idea, then his dad wouldn't be mad anymore. Everything would be okay. But then Grandy had found out, and she'd flipped. Everybody started acting crazy. And now this thing with Number One. Shawn shivered. Who knew what was going to happen?

He could run away. The problem was, he had nowhere to run to. If it was summer, he could run away to become a woodsman, or a hobo, but it was winter and it was cold.

He was hungry. Maybe Grandy was napping. Maybe he could find something to eat. He could grab some cookies, or a loaf of bread, take it up to his room and keep it there. His mouth began to water. He left the barn and headed for the house. Suddenly the solution to his problems appeared before him.

"Doc," he breathed, staring at the pink Jaguar parked in front of the lodge.

Amanda Murphy turned the full intensity of her gaze on Crow. "You are barren?" she said. "You have no children?"

Crow shook his head.

"There are evil men among us, who prey upon the children, who seek to soil their innocent souls, to lay a taint. The child is marked forever and must suffer mightily to regain his place at God's table. What can one do? Revenge is thine, sayeth the Lord. The Hand of God is the Will of the Faithful."

Crow said, "What are we talking about here?" He looked at Murphy, whose face had gone leaden and still.

"Suppose you had a kid," Murphy said slowly. "Suppose you had a little boy. Suppose you found out some son-of-a-bitch had been playing doctor with him. Telling him things. What would you think about that?" Murphy's voice had gone smooth and quiet. His eyes shone with excess moisture. "Think what you would do."

Crow thought, Is he saying what I think he's saying? He felt a sharp pain in his shin, realized the old lady had kicked him and was about to kick him again. He backed away. Amanda's face was contorted into a tangle of folds and fissures. She lashed out with her right Sorel, grazing his kneecap. Crow reached into his coat, felt the big grip of the Ruger. He looked at George, hoping he would do something to stop the old woman. George let her take another kick at him, then cupped his hands around her narrow shoulders and held her in place.

"Mandy, we have to let the man go."

"He is the scion of the doctor. Set the hounds on him."

Murphy shook his head, his jaw clamped tight enough to crumble most men's teeth. He indicated with a jerk of his head that Crow should leave.

It sounded like a reasonable suggestion to Crow. The old woman spat at him as he sidled past her.

"Can you smell the taint?" she hissed. "It hangs on him. Like stink on a wet dog."

He pushed through the barn door and limped toward his car, anxious to make his departure. The dogs were barking at him again. He picked up his pace, imagining the trio of rangy hounds charging at him across the expanse of packed snow, red-eyed and slobbering. His shin throbbed where the old lady had kicked him. He wouldn't feel safe until he was back on the highway, landscape flashing past. He reached the Jaguar, looked behind him. No charging pack of hounds; just George Murphy and his mother, standing in the doorway, staring at him with American Gothic intensity. Crow opened the door, climbed in, fitted the key into the ignition. The car started. He backed up, shifted into first gear, and headed up the long, slippery driveway.

A few inches behind Joe Crow, Shawn Murphy pushed his head up against the storage compartment lid and peeked out. He didn't recognize the man driving, but this was definitely Doc's car. Shawn concentrated on breathing silently. The guy must be a friend of Doc's, otherwise he wouldn't be using his car. If he was quiet, if the guy didn't know he was there, everything would be all right. Sooner or later, they would get to Doc's house. Shawn would live there with him in his big house in the city. He would go to a new school, where the kids didn't know him. His dad would never find him. He thought about how mad his dad was gonna be, and how Grandy was gonna be even madder. But if he was gone, what would it matter? Doc would hide him. He would have to, because they were mad at Doc too. And besides, weren't they friends? Didn't they have fun together?

XI

A multi-dimensional cornucopia of proven state-of-the-art Subtle Energy Electromagnetic and Sacred Light Geometry Technologies for all issues of emotional, mental, and physical well-being. One Solution to All Problems. FREE information.

—Classified ad in Sedona: Journal of Emergence!

he quiet, spacey sounds of Enya meandered through the house, softened by the curtains and weavings, reflected from hanging crystals, amplified by the glass pyramid displayed on the mantel above the gas fireplace. Candles, tall white tapers, burned in every room. On the right front burner of the gas stove, a kettle of potpourri simmered; the air was moist and rich with spicy aromas of cinnamon and clove.

It was three-thirty in the afternoon. Sunlight pressed against drawn curtains; thin bars of yellow light crept up the walls and across the hardwood floors.

Melinda Crow danced, eyes nearly closed, in the center of the four-by-six-foot blue cotton rug she had woven from strips of recycled denim, her arms sweeping from left to right and back again, her hips performing a languid figure eight, long blond hair swinging from breast to back to breast. These movements caused her to turn slowly, each revolution taking several seconds.

Although the outdoor temperature was below zero, it was warm inside the house, and she wore only a light sundress of soft, unbleached cotton—the one dress that let her move freely without bearing down on her shoulders, chafing her nipples. The music flowing from the stereo was quiet and gentle, and she could hear herself breathing. She could smell the cinnamon. Flickering candles filtered through her short, pale lashes.

The portrait mirror that usually hung by the staircase now lay flat on the kitchen table. As Melinda performed each slow rotation, her eyes widened slightly as they swept across the doorway that led into the kitchen. She could see the mirror and the parallel white lines that cut across its breadth.

The song ended, and in the silent seconds before the next cut began, the sound of her bare feet on the denim rug raked her eardrums, her breathing became harsh, her nipples recoiled from the raw cotton. Melinda stopped moving and pulled the fabric away from her breasts. The next song, a faster, more upbeat tune, began.

Melinda said, "Shit." She stepped off the rug, feeling grit between her feet and the hardwood floorboards. Crossing the room to the stereo, she turned it off. A faint ringing persisted in her ears. She sat down on the futon sofa, stood up, crossed her arms, made a fist with her right hand, and struck herself on the hip. She examined the magazines on the coffee table, flipped through a recent copy of *Sedona,* skimmed an article about a woman whose unhappy cat, Spark, was processing her irritable bowel syndrome. The woman's problems with her lower intestinal tract, it turned out, had resulted from her running over a cat with her car several months earlier. Spark's purpose, according to unnamed sources channeled through veterinarian Dr. Kuhan Lightbody, was to help the woman through her period of mourning by helping her process her irritable bowel. Melinda skipped to the end of the article. It turned out that Spark was channeling the dead cat, who wished the woman to know that he forgave her and that he hoped she would drive more carefully in the future. After several months of hypnotic age regression therapy, the woman and her cat made a full recovery.

Melinda closed the magazine. Hypnotic age regression. Was that the solution, the way to begin again? She sat still for a full ten seconds, hands resting on her thighs, eyes moving jerkily, seeing nothing, her mouth open, passing air. She licked her lips. Her eyes returned to a focused state.

"Now what?" she said, her voice flat.

When there was no response, she shrugged and went into the kitchen, where she took her seat at the mirror. She pulled a purple elastic band from her wrist and used it to tie her hair back, picked up a short gold-plated tube. There were four thick lines left, each about four inches long. Melinda considered, then used the edge of a gold-plated single-edge razor blade to divide each fat line into two thinner lines. She arranged the lines neatly, in pairs. The final result looked like four white equal signs. She then went over the entire surface of the mirror carefully, seeking out every stray grain of cocaine and incorporating it into the design. When all was perfect, she brought the gold-plated tube to her left nostril, leaned forward, and made one of the lines disappear. She moved the tube to her right nostril and snorted the other half of the equal sign, then sat back, a gentle smile on her lips, staring down into the mirror. Within moments, she became disturbed by the fact that there was an odd number of equal signs on the mirror, and she proceeded to consume two more lines.

The light cotton dress pressed in on her. She slipped it over her head, let it fall to the floor. Suddenly it occurred to her that she had not heard the Beatles song "For the Benefit of Mr. Kite" in *years*. Which album was it on? She could not decide between *Sgt. Pepper* and *Magical Mystery Tour*. Where were all her old records? She and Joe had retired all their record albums when they bought the CD player, but she was sure they had not thrown them out. In her mind, she thought she could see the box on the top shelf of the closet in the spare bedroom.

Felix had commandeered the bed. Over the past months he had created a depression, lined with his shed white fur, in the exact center of the bedspread. He greeted Melinda with a green stare and a twitch of his tail. Melinda sat on the edge of the bed and stroked him, an activity that Felix tolerated but did not seem to enjoy. He had never been a friendly or a particularly wonderful, wonderful cat. Was he channeling a dead relative? Was he processing for her?

"Felix? Are you feeling my pain?"

The cat jumped off the bed, ran out of the room.

Melinda remembered why she had come into this room. She opened the closet door. The air inside smelled old and dry. The old record albums would be in a cardboard box. Digging through the closet, she came across her high school yearbook. A treasure! She sat on the floor and opened the black-and-red cloth-covered volume.

Some unmeasured time later, she stared in wonder at a picture of herself, the Melinda Lee Connor of fifteen years past. She stood and looked at her body in the full-length mirror on the closet door. Her face was not so bad. Her eyes dropped to her breasts. Still good, though a couple of inches lower now. She looked at her thighs.

Her thighs. Larger now, decidedly so, and dimpled with cellulite. Awful. Disgusting. A lump formed at the base of her throat. All the evil in her life—the bad thoughts, the drugs, the wasted years, the Fritos—had gathered on her legs, shaming her. She went to the bathroom cabinet and found her jar of Mountain Dove Fat Burner, which drew fat energy directly through the skin and radiated it in the form of pure light energy. Sitting on the edge of the bathtub, she slapped a glob of the golden, rosemary-scented cream onto her right thigh and began massaging it into her skin, pressing it through the pores. Methodically, using all her strength, she kneaded every square inch of her burgeoning thighs. A film of perspiration grew on her body. She could hear her own breathing, a loud huffing, echoing from the bathroom walls. Ten minutes later she stood before the mirror, staring in horror at her throbbing, burning thighs, thunder thighs, bigger than ever, now glowing bright red and reeking of rosemary. She wanted to cut them off, grow a new pair.

Or she could do what Mary Getter had done. What she had been thinking about. A way to start over. She would have to call Mary, get the number of that clinic. What was it? She thought she should remember.

The doorbell rang. Melinda sucked in her breath, held it. She peeked out the bathroom window. A pink car in the driveway. No one she knew drove a pink car. A Mary Kay saleswoman? Good. She wouldn't have to answer the door. The doorbell rang again. Something she was forgetting. Yes. Joe had said something about a pink car. She moved to the far right edge of the window, looking through the glass at an angle, trying to see who was standing on the front doorstep, but the edge of the chimney blocked her view. The doorbell rang again. She was sure it was Joe.

She heard his key slide into the lock, heard the dead bolt click open, heard the doorknob turn, the bang of the door against the chain. She imagined him standing pressed against the door, glaring angrily at the two-inch gap. He had installed the chain himself.

"Melinda? It's me, Joe." His voice echoed.

"Go away," she whispered, letting her head fall back to rest against the wall. She wasn't ready for him, if she ever had been.

He called out again. After a time, she heard the door close, heard a car start. She looked again, saw the car back out of the driveway. The license plate jumped out at her: FATGONE.

That was it. The doctor's phone number. Of course. She wondered how much it would cost. He had told her not to worry, that they could work something out.

She watched the pink car pull away and suddenly regretted not answering the door. What was it about Joe? What was it that made her afraid? She looked again at her thighs, the red now fading to pink, and thought about how it would feel to have all the fat sucked out of them. She imagined a sound, a whooshing sound like a vacuum cleaner, or a toilet flushing. She imagined it would be like blowing her nose, a sudden ejection of superfluous matter. She wondered what Joe would say.

Would he notice? Would he care? Married the better part of a decade, and she still had no idea what went on in his head. Maybe that was it. Maybe that was what scared her.

Crow tried to think about what he had learned at Talking Lake Ranch. Or had he learned anything? The ramblings of a crazy old lady, and the veiled accusation by her corpulent son, might add up to nothing. He tried to imagine Bellweather and a young boy, together. The image was foggy and unconvincing. A semi came up behind him, honked, and moved out to pass. Crow looked at the speedometer. Forty-five. He let the truck pass and pull in front of him, then sped up to match its pace. He tried to get his mind back on the Murphys, but thoughts of Melinda had taken over. He was angry. He was sure she had been at home. The door had been chained, and besides, he could tell. The house—*his* house—had felt occupied. He turned on the radio and proceeded to review all the things he had ever done for her, all the little sacrifices he'd made, all the troubles he'd endured, all the efforts he'd made to save their marriage. And the bitch wouldn't even answer the door. Angrily, he punched the buttons on the radio until he found a country station. He was no country music fan, but there was a time for everything.

As he was passing through Dassel, Crow's anger began to subside, and his memories suddenly expanded to include Melinda's noble acts, sacrifices, generosities, and efforts performed on his behalf. Like the sweater she had made for him for his birthday, thick as a quilt; must have taken her two hundred hours. He recalled a time when he had been able to talk to her and when he had cared enough for her to listen. Aided by the sad sounds of Clint Black, Crow's thoughts soon turned to his mistakes, foolish acts, and irritating behavioral quirks, trying to understand what it was he had done, how he had lost her. As he approached the cities, the sky clouded over and a fine, misty snow created a haze in the air. His thoughts darkened with the sky, and he arrived at Orchard Estates—the Jaguar slipping and spinning its tires on half an inch of fresh snow—filled with ambient, undirected anger. He was almost disappointed to see that his Rabbit had been roughly repaired, the fender pried away from the wheel as promised. He triggered the automatic opener clipped to the visor, waited for the garage door to roll up, drove the Jaguar inside, then went out and checked the ignition of his Rabbit. No keys. He had hoped to simply switch vehicles, head straight back to his apartment, and catch a few hours' sleep, but it looked as though he was going to have to see Bellweather after all. Walking up to the front door, he felt his anger establishing a new direction. During the three-hour drive from Talking Lake Ranch, he'd had trouble seeing Bellweather as a child molester. Now, as he stood on the doorstep, it crashed to the front of his mind. He could see it.

Nate Bellweather opened the door. Crow held up the keys to the Jaguar. "I need my keys," he said, stepping inside.

Nate closed the door. "You'll have to ask my brother about that."

"Where is he?" Crow asked.

"Watching movies." Nate pointed toward the back of the house.

Dr. Nelson Bellweather, his ostrich-hide boots propped on his desk, sat watching a large-screen television set into the wall. Crow noticed that the doctor looked different to him now. Smaller and softer. More like a pederast than a surgeon.

"Joe!" he said. "Aren't you a little early?"

"I came to pick up my car." Crow lifted a hip onto the edge of the desk and looked at the picture on the TV screen. A zebra, grazing in a field. The sound of wind. A nature show? Bellweather pointed a remote control and turned off the sound. Something was wrong with the picture: behind the zebra, a row of pine trees defined the edge of the field. Pine trees on the African veld? The zebra suddenly staggered to the side, fell to its front knees. A line of red blots appeared across its abdomen. The zebra regained its feet and took off running, but it went back down after only a few yards, this time hitting the ground facefirst and remaining motionless. A man's jacketed back appeared, running toward the fallen creature. The man looked back over his shoulder and grinned at the cameraman. Bellweather. The image froze. Bellweather put down the remote control.

"You know, Joe, there's always hope. One day you're looking at disaster, the next thing you know, you're the smartest guy in the world." He thumped himself on the chest.

"Oh?" Crow had no idea what this was about.

"You ever hear of a little company called BioStellar GameTech?"

Crow shook his head.

"Well, neither had anybody else!" Bellweather laughed, always an unpleasant sound. "Except me and a few other brilliant investors. You want to know what it closed at, first day of trading?"

"Not particularly."

"Thirteen!" Bellweather slapped his thigh. "I'm going to ride the son-of-a-bitch to the *moon,* Joe!" His eyes were wet, his lips loose.

Crow had never seen this giddy, nearly hysterical side of Bellweather.

It made him wonder about his other extremes of behavior. When he was around ten-year-old boys, for instance.

"I take it that's good," he said.

Bellweather nodded vigorously.

"Well, congratulations. By the way, I drove out to visit your friend George Murphy this morning."

Bellweather's mouth fell open. He blinked, and the light seemed to leave his eyes. "You what?"

"I helped him feed the pigs," Crow added.

Bellweather let his head fall back, took a breath, and blew out his cheeks. He shook his head as if he could not quite believe what he had heard, let the air hiss out between tightly held lips. "I hope I don't have any more holes in my car," he said. He pulled his booted feet off the desk.

"Your car is fine."

"I thought you were just going to make a few calls, talk to your friends." Crow shrugged.

"I hired you as a bodyguard, not an investigator. You could have gotten yourself killed. Then where would I be?"

Crow said, "Is it true?"

Bellweather looked puzzled. "Is what true?"

"About George's kid."

Bellweather frowned and shook his head. "What about him?"

Crow thought, Is it possible that he doesn't know? More specifically, that he doesn't know that George Murphy knows? He said, watching the doctor's face, "He thinks you've been playing doctor. With his son."

Bellweather's mouth fell open. "What's that supposed to mean? Is that all he said?" If he was acting, he was damn good at it.

Crow cleared his throat and looked away, toward the frozen video of the dying zebra. He shifted his gaze to the fireplace, to the bison head above the mantel, to the elephant tusk. Someone was putting on a show for him. Bellweather's bewilderment was convincing, but so had been George Murphy's painful anger and his mother's rage. Had they invented the molestation of his boy for Crow's benefit? It seemed farfetched.

Crow asked, "So you know the boy?"

"Shawn? Sure I know him. He's a nice kid. Says he wants to be a doctor when he grows up. What did George say? Does he think I did something to Shawn?"

"He implied that you molested him."

Bellweather gaped, then burst into a nervous giggle. "Mo-*lest*-ed?" He

stood up and paced the room, shaking his head, the heels of his cowboy boots striking the floor sharply with each step. "Mo. Less. Ted. Mo-
lessssted." Repeating it, trying it different ways. He pointed a long finger
at Crow. "What did he say?" His voice rose. "What *exactly* did he say?"

"He said you'd been playing doctor with his boy. Did you?"

"No! Of course not. George told you that? Why did you go out there
anyway? You think you can believe anything he says? He wants you to
quit, leave me unprotected, that's what he wants. It's not true. What exactly did he say? What did he say I did?"

"He wasn't specific."

Bellweather shook his head. "George knows I didn't do anything.
Sure, I got along good with the kid. Shawn used to hang around the
lodge. I taught him how to play gin rummy. Christ, I can't believe
George told you that. I can't believe you listened to him. What did I tell
you? What did I say to you? I told you he was crazy, didn't I? Playing
doctor. You want to know what that was all about? I'll tell you. Shawn
says he wants to be a doctor when he grows up, so I'm telling him
stuff. The hipbone is connected to the leg bone. Colds are caused by
viruses. Hair is dead but skin is alive. George was there, hell, the whole
time. Playing pinochle with Orlan. Right there in the lodge. The kid
wants to be a doctor. You want to know what I think? I'll tell you. The
kid likes me, but he's scared of his old man. Who wouldn't be, a guy
like George?" Bellweather abruptly stopped pacing. "That's what it
was," he said. "The kid likes me. George can't handle it."

"He gave me the impression that it was a lot more than that."

Bellweather's face was getting darker.

Crow went on. "Why would he make something like that up?"

The doctor was quivering, his fine hands knotted into fists, his
cheeks blotchy. Crow observed this clinically, not knowing who, if anyone, was custodian of the truth here. What had really happened between Bellweather and the boy? He might never know. Did it matter?
Five minutes ago, he'd been convinced he was working for a child molester. Now he wasn't so sure. He still thought it possible, perhaps even
probable, but he wasn't sure. Could he work for a *suspected* pederast?
A few hours' sleep—something he hadn't had much of lately—would
help him to sort and clarify. Crow started for the door.

"Where are you going?"

"I'm going home. Where are my car keys?"

"You don't believe him, do you?"

"I don't know what to believe. Where are my keys?"

"George Murphy is psychotic. You can't believe anything he says."

Crow shrugged, thinking the same could easily be true of Bell-weather.

"Keys," he said.

"They're in your car, under the floor mat. You're coming back tonight, aren't you?"

"I'll be back." He remembered a question he had been meaning to ask. "By the way, that tiger, is it a pet? Or are the Murphys planning to sell it to some trophy hunter?"

Bellweather crossed his arms. The question seemed to calm him. He liked to talk about hunting. "Actually, the Bengal was supposed to be mine. George got it for me. I suppose he'll be selling it to somebody else now."

"You were going to shoot it?"

Bellweather nodded. "Fair chase. That's the only way I'll hunt. They release the animal, and it's just you and the cat, one on one. Same as hunting in the wild, except you know the game is out there. I was jaguar hunting down in Costa Rica last month. Took me three days in that damn jungle before I even caught sight of one, and another week to get a clean shot. Cost me a fortune. Then I try to bring it home, and the U.S. Fish and Wildlife people grab it at the border. A shame. It was a beautiful cat. Those game wardens are worse than the IRS."

"You sound like George. I thought jaguars were an endangered species."

"That's what the Fish and Wildlife people claim, but try and tell them that down in Central America when some little kid gets hauled off into the jungle and devoured."

"Does that ever happen?"

Bellweather shrugged. "There are stories. You ever see one of those cats up close, you believe it. The fact is, there are a lot of jaguars in the jungle, more than anybody knows. Those Fish and Wildlife people are a bunch of self-important, overzealous bureaucrats who have nothing better to do than harass legitimate sportsmen. These so-called endan-gered species—you know you're not even supposed to shoot one that's been raised in captivity?"

"Shoot one what?"

"Doesn't matter. Tiger, rhino, leopard, jaguar, you name it. If it's on their list and they catch you, you could go to jail. These are domestic animals we're talking about here. Next thing you know, they'll be pros-ecuting ranchers for sending cattle to the slaughterhouse."

"I didn't think cattle were endangered."

"That's exactly my point," said Bellweather. "That tiger George got for me, it's just an old female, way past her breeding years. Do you think the species is going to be hurt when she dies? Hardly. No real reason not to take her. She's a gorgeous cat, isn't she?"

Crow turned away from Bellweather and walked out of his office. He passed through the dining room. Nate Bellweather was sitting on the white sofa in the living room, reading a copy of *House Beautiful*. The concept of the canned tiger hunt hung on Crow like a fog, cold and clammy. Did it offend him more deeply than the thought of Bellweather playing doctor with a ten-year-old boy? Perhaps.

The world had become very quiet and dark. Shawn waited, counting his breaths. He counted to two hundred, then sat up and pushed the blanket aside. He felt like he'd been hiding for days. When he climbed into the Jaguar, he'd expected to remain hidden for only a few minutes. He had expected to surprise Doc as soon as they were off the ranch, but when the driver turned out to be this other man, a stranger, Shawn hadn't known what to do except stay quiet and wait. Now the man was gone, and it was dark. The engine popped and hissed, cooling. Shawn climbed over the seat and fumbled for the door latch. He remembered that Doc's car had a funny kind of door handle. There. The door opened, and the inside light came on. It wasn't much of a light, but he could see that he was in a garage. Was it Doc's garage?

He hoped Doc would be glad to see him. During the long ride, he'd been thinking about what had happened several weeks before. When his dad had walked into his bedroom and caught him *doing* it. He remembered the awful feeling, holding his boner, his pants around his ankles, looking up at his dad's big red face. Shawn had instantly known that he was in some kind of trouble.

"What are you doing?" his father roared. "Put your pants on, god-dammit!"

Shawn yanked his jeans up so hard it hurt. He was scared. How bad a thing had he done? He didn't know, but it must've been pretty bad the way his dad was breathing, the way his face was all red and splotchy. He shoved his stiff penis into his jeans and zipped them up.

His dad had his mouth clamped shut, breathing through his nose like one of the buffaloes. "Where'd you learn that?" he asked in a gravelly voice. "A boy your age."

Shawn gaped at his father, watching his face display a series of tics and minor convulsions, waiting for the next eruption. For several seconds, they stood without moving, the only sound that of air rushing in and out of his dad's lungs. He seemed to be calming down. For the first time, Shawn dared to hope that he wasn't going to get hit. "Where'd you learn that?" George repeated in a softer voice.

Shawn saw an opportunity to deflect his father's anger. "Doc showed me how," he said, thinking that invoking Doc Bellweather's name would make it legitimate. Doc was an important client. He thought that his dad would say something like, "Oh, well, if Doc told you it was okay, then never mind."

Wrong.

Right after he'd said that about Doc was when he saw Grandy, standing right there behind his dad, her face all twisted up the way it got when she was about to hit him, only this time she didn't. She fell down on her knees and just started screaming. It scared his dad even worse than it did Shawn, on account of he hadn't even known she was standing there at all. George had jumped about six inches off the ground, which was a lot for a guy as big as he was.

But he hadn't got hit, at least. Just locked in his room for what seemed like days but was really only a few hours. And then for about a week they were all acting real weird around him, not talking much. He hadn't seen Doc since. He knew that he had gotten Doc in trouble. His uncle Ricky told him flat out that he was going to shoot the doctor "right in the fuckin' nuts." Of course, Grandy wasn't around when he'd said that, or she'd've popped him one.

He hoped the doc wouldn't be mad. He thought about it. Yeah, Doc would probably be mad. But Shawn would take a mad Doc Bellweather over a mad George any day, and when his dad found he'd shot his prize elk, he was gonna be boiling.

He heard the muted sound of an engine turning over just outside the garage door. The engine caught. Shawn remained still, listening. He heard the engine sound deepen, then the creak of tires rolling across packed snow. He pulled and twisted several knobs on the dashboard until the headlights flared bright on the back wall. He was definitely in a garage. He climbed out of the car. There were two doors, the large overhead door through which the car had entered and a normal, people-size door. Shawn went to the smaller door, turned the handle. The door opened directly into a kitchen, which reminded him that he was hungry. He could hear faint voices. He stepped inside and took a breath. He decided to go for it.

"Hello?" he called.

The voices ceased.

"Anybody here?"

He heard quiet footsteps. He took a few more steps into the kitchen. One doorway led to a hallway, a second doorway opened into a dining room. Shawn started for the dining room. He had taken only two steps when a figure dove through the door, hit the floor, rolled, and came up into a kneeling shooter's stance, pointing a gun right at Shawn's face. Shawn froze, mesmerized by the black hole in the end of the long barrel. For a moment, he thought he was about to be shot, but things had happened so fast he had no time to become frightened. Would he feel anything? One full second crawled by. He noticed that the hole in the end of the gun barrel was moving, jerking from side to side. He looked past the gun and saw the two hands wrapped around the grip, pale-knuckled and shaking. The man attached to the hands had sweat oozing from his forehead. His mouth was squeezed shut so hard his lips were white. As Shawn watched, the man's mouth opened and made a croaking sound. He cleared his throat and tried again.

"Nels, it's some kid!" he shouted.

Shawn heard footsteps approaching, and Doc Bellweather appeared, holding a double-barreled shotgun. He looked at Shawn, shook his head as if he couldn't quite believe what he was seeing, let the barrel of the gun drop toward the tile floor.

Shawn grinned. "What's up, Doc?"

But Doc didn't laugh like he usually did.

Shawn thought, Uh-oh.

Nobody said anything for a few seconds. Doc took a deep breath and started shaking his head again.

He finally said, "What did you tell your dad about me, Shawn?"

Shawn shrugged. "Nothin'."

"Right. I'd ask what you're doing here, but I'm afraid you'd tell me you've run away from home. Please don't tell me that—although I don't know *what* you could tell me that I want to hear."

Obviously, the truth wasn't going to get him anywhere with Doc. He was going to have to make up something good. He said, "My dad was going to beat me. He was gonna tie me up and beat me till I got all bloody." He gave that a second, but Doc didn't give him much back. "Because I shot his elk. Number One?"

That got a reaction.

"You shot Number One?" Doc almost smiled, but mostly he looked like he was going to be sick. "You're kidding me."

"Uh-uh. They were gonna tie me up and beat me, him and Ricky both, but then they just decided to kick me out. He said I should come live with you."

XII

You got to forget about that cat and get yourself a real animal. Like a dog. A big dog.

—SAM O'GARA

ilo was still missing. There were no pawprints in the fresh snow. Crow shook the cat food box and called, but it had been three Minnesota winter days now, putting Milo's return in the possible-but-doubtful category. He still hoped Milo had inveigled himself into the lap of some kindly old lady, but he feared that the kindly old lady was another personal myth. He returned the Meow Mix to its place above the refrigerator and started work on his own supper. It was looking like frozen pepperoni pizza and an overripe banana. Frozen pizza, banana, a glass of warm milk, if the milk hadn't soured, then sleep. He turned on the oven and put in the pizza. The package directions always said to preheat the oven, but in Crow's experience it didn't make much of a difference. Either way, it was going to taste like a frozen pizza.

He ate the banana and waited for the pizza to cook.

The telephone rang. Crow touched the handset. It rang again and he felt the vibration. He remembered Melinda doing that, claiming she knew by the feel who was calling. Sometimes she was right. He lifted the handset with no idea who would be on the other end.

"Hello?"

"Joe? Hi, it's me!"

"Melinda?"

"How are you doing?" She sounded too bright, too loud—but she was there, she was talking.

"I'm okay," he said, feeling unexpected relief, as if a weight had left him. His anger at her that afternoon . . . now he realized he had been worried. Concerned. Angry with himself for not just busting into her—his—their house to see that she was all right. Not twisted in cocaine-induced convulsions. Not lying dead on the bathroom floor. "How are you?" he asked.

"I'm fine. How did your trip go?"

"Good. I met George Murphy. We fed the pigs." He paused. "I stopped by the house," he said.

"Really? When was that?"

"A few hours ago."

"I guess I must have been sleeping."

She was lying.

"I guess so," he said.

"I just called to say hi."

"Uh-huh." Something in her voice convinced him that she was high. Sitting in the kitchen in front of the mirror, doing lines and making phone calls. He wanted to ask, but he knew whatever she told him he would not be able to believe.

"And I wanted to invite you to dinner."

Crow felt his heart beating. He was unable to reply.

"Joe?"

"Dinner? When?"

"Oh, I don't know. Tomorrow? About seven?"

After weeks of closing him out, she was opening a door. What had happened? Best not to ask. With Melinda, it could be anything—her horoscope, her analyst, a channeled communication from the Pleiades. Maybe she just missed him.

"That would be fine," he said in a wooden voice. He would have to tell Bellweather that he'd be late tomorrow night. See how he took it. He could smell his pizza cooking.

"See you then?"

"Okay." He hung up the phone, feeling scared. Replaying the conversation in his head as he pulled the pizza from the oven, he wondered whether her call had been nothing more than a coke-induced impulse. Would she phone again tomorrow and call it off? Or worse, would he drive all the way out to Big River tomorrow night to find the house empty and dark? Was the invitation from the real Melinda or one of the other Melindas? The cokehead Melinda. The space case Melinda. The cold, withdrawn Melinda. His thoughts skittered around the question and finally fell into a reminiscence about the days when all the Melindas had occupied the present. He ate the pizza quickly, without tasting

it, trying to focus on memories of her slim body, her fine blond hair, the
sound of her breath, hot in his ear.

He look like he been gut-shot, bro," Ricky shouted over the pop
and buzz of his Thundercat. He twisted the key, shut down the snowmobile, and walked back to the sled. The spotlight above the lodge entrance draped a cone of yellow light over the scene.

George Murphy stared down at the dead elk. The frozen body of
Number One was strapped to the plywood game sled. He and Ricky
had hauled in bison, whitetail, antelope, and more than a few elk, but
somehow George was not quite prepared for the demise of Number
One. The eight-by-eight monarch had been a symbol, a figurehead, a
living testament to Talking Lake's status as a world-class operation.

Number One had also been a sort of living savings account. An easy
twenty-five thousand—maybe even more, to the right party—plus
whatever other services he could add on. Most important, the elk's
mythic reputation had brought in a lot of business over the past few
years. But in its current condition—dead—the beast was just a few
thousand bucks' worth of antler, meat, and hide. The caked blood
looked black under the yellow yard light.

"Look at that rack, would you?" Ricky grabbed one of the elk's sixteen spikes. "I bet you shit to gold brick he runs over four twenty
points. Record book for sure."

George squatted and pressed his finger to the small entrance wound
just in front of the elk's left rear leg. If not for the frozen river of blood
that caked the animal's flank, the wound might have been hard to find.
Such a small hole. A gut shot. Probably took it hours, maybe even days,
to die. He asked, pointing at the wound, "Is this all?"

Ricky shook his head. "He's got one more hole on his leg; couldn't
see nothin' else. Looks like somebody shot him with a twenny-two or
somethin'. Slug's prob'ly still in there. I suppose it could be he speared
hisself somehow, only I don't know on what, bro."

George did not know either. He was certain the wound had been
caused by a lead slug. He experienced an unwelcome image of his son
Shawn's little single-shot .22 rifle. Where was that boy? It was almost
suppertime, and he hadn't seen the kid since he'd interrupted the
poker game.

"You had any groups out that way? Some asshole packing a little
handgun, maybe?"

"Nope. I ain't run a hunt up that way in three weeks."

A thin, jangling sound of metal on metal came from the direction of the house.

"Dinnertime," George said.

"What you want to do with him?"

George opened his mouth to tell Ricky to just butcher the damn thing. Cut it up for meat and send the head off to Ollie Aamold to have it mounted. Since it was sure to be a record-book elk, he might get a few thousand for the mount alone. Old Number One would pay for his feed if nothing else. But a partially formed idea floated into his mind, and he hesitated, not quite sure that what he was thinking was possible. The idea persisted. He said, "Hey, you remember Rudolph?"

Ricky said, "Huh?"

"You remember that stuffed deer the game wardens were using last fall? They were setting it up, this stuffed deer they called Rudolph, setting it out in a field at night, using it to catch shiners. End of the season, Rudolph had so damn many holes in him they had to tie boards to his legs to get him to stand up straight. Shiners didn't know the difference. They just kept shooting the thing. Coulda been a cardboard cutout, they'd still have shot it up."

Ricky looked puzzled.

George smiled. Yes, he was definitely having an idea. It was getting more solid by the minute. "What say we get this guy into the barn, keep him nice and clean. I'm having an idea."

The hot dish was ready. Hot and ready and sitting on the cast-iron trivet in the middle of the table. Four plates on the table, and four glasses. One glass filled with milk, two with apple cider, the fourth with Pepsi. Alone, Amanda Murphy sat at one end of the table. She had said her prayers; now she was doing a slow burn. She took a sip of her Pepsi. The double shot of Jim Beam she had added improved its flavor immensely. She could hear the rumble of a snowmobile outside. They would say they hadn't heard the bell. Sooner or later they would get hungry, and they would sit down with her, and the hot dish would be cold, but God bless it if she was going to eat alone.

She was on her second Pepsi when George and Ricky came in through the kitchen door, talking and laughing. When they caught sight of her sitting alone at the table, their grins faded away.

"You ring that bell?" Ricky asked, peeling down his black nylon snowmobile suit.

"I runged it," Amanda said darkly.

George and Ricky arranged themselves at the table.

"Where's that boy?" George asked.

"I thought he was with you."

George shook his head. "I ain't seen him since this afternoon. You seen him, Ricky?"

Ricky, loading his plate with hot dish, shook his head. George frowned and stood up. "I'll go see if he's in his room." He clomped up the stairs. A minute later, he was back, holding Shawn Murphy's single-shot .22 rifle in his fist. He pushed the gun at Ricky, who opened the breech and sniffed, then made a sour face.

"He's not up there?" Amanda asked.

George shook his head. Ricky set the rifle on the floor and pushed a forkful of hot dish into his mouth. George remained standing.

Ricky said, his mouth full, "Prob'ly hidin' out in the barns, bro."

"Either that or he's been taken," Amanda said.

"Taken?" George said.

"That stranger this afternoon. He was up to no good, I could tell."

George stood up. "I'm going to check the barns." He started for the door.

"What stranger, Mandy?" Ricky asked.

"That Crow," Amanda said.

"Crow?" Ricky looked wildly at George. "You hear that?"

"I heard it," said George. "I talked to him. He didn't take the boy."

"You *talked* to him? Christ, why didn't you keep him around till I got back? I owe him, goddammit."

George's face darkened. "Don't you 'goddammit' me, goddammit."

Amanda said, "Language, boys."

"Just 'cause you didn't see him take Shawn don't mean it didn't happen," Ricky said. "He's working for Bellweather."

"I know that." George opened the door. "I'm going to look in the barns."

"It won't do any good," Amanda said. "I can feel it in my bones. The boy has been taken."

George closed the door behind him.

"That son-of-a-bitch!" Ricky slapped his hand on the tabletop. Amanda Murphy brought a serving spoon down sharply on his knuckles. "Oww!"

"Watch that mouth! Don't you be talking about your brother that way."

Ricky brought both hands under the table and glared. "I was talking about Crow."

"He's gone." Amanda swallowed the last of her drink, then coughed. "Can't you feel it?" Her eyes watered. "The boy is gone."

The Minnetonka cokeheads were more subdued, more suburban than the Golden Valley crowd, but it was the only meeting he could find on Saturday night. The old Minnetonka Mills Middle School, now abandoned by its faculty and students, provided space to a wide range of community groups, from the various twelve-step programs to the Beautiful Boulevards Floral Club. Crow didn't know anybody there, and when it was his turn to introduce himself, he smiled and shook his head. He knew he wasn't doing himself any good by sitting there silently, feeling superior to the young white male upper-middle-class drug addicts that made up the rest of the participants, but it was the best he could do. It beat tossing and turning in bed, beset by flickering Murphys and Melindas.

A man who looked like he sold BMWs for a living was talking about step eleven. Crow had long since decided that he would never make it to step eleven. He wished he hadn't come. When they broke down into smaller groups, Crow left the room, went out into the hallway, sat on a bench, and listened to the building. Other groups, in other rooms, produced a low, throbbing sound. To Crow, it sounded like a prolonged moan. He knew he should go back to his apartment and try again to sleep, but he didn't feel like moving.

A door opened down the hall, and a group of people trickled out, moved slowly toward him, toward the front entrance. Mostly men, a little older than the group he had just abandoned. Juicers, Crow decided. AA. Again he felt superior. As if it was somehow smarter for him to have destroyed his life with cocaine. Never mind that he had nearly always begun his cocaine binges with a drink and invariably had drunk himself to a stupor when the coke was gone. Intellectually, Crow knew that he was as much a drunk as he was a cokehead, but he identified more readily with the CA people. The myth that cocaine was a civilized, refined, and exclusive pleasure still had power over him.

He clasped his hands together and stared at the worn linoleum floor, waiting for the AA crowd to pass by.

A pair of leather jeans tucked into motorcycle boots stopped directly in front of him.

"Hey, what do you know? The shoe salesman." A cloud of smoke drifted toward the floor.

Crow lifted his head, his eyes passing a metal-encrusted black leather jacket, landing on a small, heavily made-up face framed by a spiky halo of pale hair. Debrowski, the wild card from last night's meeting, grinned and took another drag off her cigarette.

Crow said, "What do you know, it's the bitch with the attitude. You missed the CA meeting."

Debrowski fired two jets of smoke from her small nostrils, looked down at the black-and-red button on her jacket, removed it, and put it in one of her numerous zipper pockets. "I'm in AA mode tonight, Shoe. I do the whole show. AA, NA, CA, Triple A. Sort of a holistic approach to installing clean mental software. I got to tell you, though, this recovery routine gets old."

Crow nodded. "I know what you mean."

"I bet you do." She sat down beside him on the bench. "So how come you're sitting out here? You in a zone or something?"

"I couldn't handle the scene." Crow gestured toward the room where the CA meeting was still in progress.

"Let me guess." Debrowski put a forefinger to her chin. Her nails were short but not bitten. "Too suburban for a big-city boy like you, right?"

Crow grinned and shook his head. "Actually, I'm a small-town boy."

"Yeah? They still talk about you back in Lake Podunk, I bet. Local boy makes it big in the shoe business. How am I doing, Shoe?"

"I'll make you a deal," Crow said. "You quit calling me Shoe, and I'll buy you a slice of pie."

"This a date, or are you just hungry?"

"Hungry," Crow said.

Debrowski nodded. "So what am I supposed to call you?"

"Call me Crow."

"Like the bird?"

"Yes. Crow like the bird."

XIII

BioStellar GameTech President, CFO Indicted—
SEC Investigators Allege Massive Fraud

—WALL STREET JOURNAL

aking calls at home was part of the job, and for the most part Anderson didn't mind. With all the trading happening on the overseas exchanges, a lot of his customers had gone on-line with their home computers, numbers junkies sitting in front of the screen all night, watching their digits flicker. He'd lost a few clients to the automated trading systems, but a lot of them stayed with him for the hand-holding, which was turning out to be a twenty-four-hour, seven-days-a-week job. He just wished they wouldn't call during *Seinfeld*.

"Let the machine get it," he said to Patty as she moved to answer the phone. Jerry Seinfeld and Elaine were fighting over a piece of cheesecake. He heard his answering machine pick up, heard his own recorded message, a beep, then a familiar and most unwelcome voice.

"Stevie? This is Dr. Bellweather. You home? I have to talk to you. I'm going to have to sell a chunk of that BioStellar a little ahead of schedule. I need a little cash, you know? Call me . . . ahh . . . *soon*, okay? Bye."

Anderson groaned and let his head flop back.

"What's the matter?" Patty asked, hitting the mute button on the remote.

"I'm going to have a very unhappy client. You remember that Dr. Bellweather?"

Patty frowned and looked up over the mantel at the enormous mounted bison head that had invaded their household. "What about him?"

"Remember I told you he took this huge position with BioStellar?"

She shrugged. Patty didn't have much interest in shoptalk. Aside from the money, which she liked, and the bison head, which she did not, her husband's activities were not of great interest to her.

"Well, he did. I don't think he knows yet what happened. I couldn't bring myself to call him when the news broke this afternoon. They stopped trading it this afternoon, you know. Dickie got all his guys out of it yesterday and this morning, but I didn't hear about it till it was too late. I never got around to calling the doctor." He shook his head. "He's not going to be a happy camper."

"That's too bad."

"He's a child molester, you know. It serves him right."

"How do you know he's a child molester?" Patty was interested in scandal.

"George Murphy told me. Remember last month, I was telling you that our guide at the hunt club attacked the doctor?"

Patty nodded.

"George called me up a few days later and apologized, offered me a free duck hunt. He told me that Bellweather had tried some funny business with his kid. I always had a funny feeling about that doctor."

"So he lost a lot of money?"

"He lost it all. And then some."

"It's inspirational," Debrowski said, puffing on her Camel between bites of cherry pie. "I see these young guys, want to make it big in the music biz, killing themselves every way they know how. I've had two bands flame out on me in the past six months."

"Drugs?"

"Drugs, egos, and girlfriends—the three death knells for a rock band. Most of 'em use and abuse all three. I know I did. Damn near lost my business." Debrowski was in the process of rebuilding her one-woman business, organizing tours for up-and-coming rock bands.

"You abused your girlfriend?"

"Don't take me so goddamn literally, Crow-like-the-bird. Let's talk about you a minute. So you don't sell shoes? How do you survive?"

"I'm . . . ah . . . I'm working for this doctor." This child-abusing lipo-suctionist, he thought.

"You're a nurse?"

"Sort of. I'm a bodyguard."

Debrowski laughed, then quickly stifled it when she saw his face color. "Hey, sorry! It's just that that's almost like being a cop. You don't look like the type."

"Too short?"

"Not what I meant."

"I used to be a cop."

"No shit? I'd never have guessed."

The waitress topped off their coffees.

"Thank you," said Crow to the waitress.

"You're welcome," said Debrowski. "So how come you're not a cop anymore?"

Crow smiled, pressed a forefinger against his right nostril, sniffed.

Debrowski said, "Ah."

"Actually, they got rid of me for other reasons, but the coke was there, making it happen. Like what I did to get fired wasn't worth getting fired for, but I felt like such a piece of shit 'cause of all the dope I was doing, I just didn't have the guts to fight it. On some level I figured I deserved it, you know? We balance our own set of scales."

"No shit."

Outside, a light snow had begun to coat the parking lot. Baker's Square customers came and went. Crow and Debrowski ate pie and traded lives. At one point Crow asked her how long she'd been clean.

"I'm not clean. I still smoke cigarettes and listen to nasty music."

Crow waited for more. He was guessing it was days, weeks at most. Her eyes were too tight, her words too sharp. She stubbed out her cigarette.

"I made it through today," she said. "That is all ye know on earth, and all ye need to know."

Crow closed his eyes, opened them. Debrowski was intently tearing the cellophane off a fresh pack of Camels. "Is that a quote or something?" he asked. It sounded familiar.

She smiled, not looking at him. "It's from a thing by this Brit dude. Died when he was twenty-six."

"Drugs, ego, or love?"

"All three, Crow." She lit a cigarette. "It's like I was telling you: they go together."

The digital clock on his dashboard read 9:49. Late again. The Rabbit started, reluctantly. Crow sat huddled over the steering wheel, shivering, waiting for the temperature gauge to show signs of life. Until the needle moved, he had discovered, the car would not. Put it in gear too soon, the thing would die and maybe not start again. He watched Debrowski pull away in her rusted yellow Honda, watched her taillights disappear.

In a few minutes he would be back at Orchard Estates, making life safe for a zebra-shooting, fat-sucking possible pederast. Instead of eight hours of sleep, he was running on five cups of coffee supplemented by a slice of French silk pie and a couple hours of conversation with Debrowski, first name Laura, fellow recovering dope fiend. He felt as if he'd had his first real conversation in months, maybe years.

The idling engine settled into a smooth roar. Crow put the Rabbit in gear and headed out of the parking lot, sliding a bit as he hit the street. The snow felt greasy under his tires, and the steering wheel was a few degrees off center, courtesy of Ricky Murphy's Hummer. He drove carefully through the frosted streets, pulled up in front of Bellweather's house a few minutes after nine. The windows were dark, and there was no sign of Nate's beat-up Dodge wagon. It didn't look as though anyone was home. Had Bellweather and his brother gone out? What was he supposed to do, sit outside and wait for them to return? Leaving the car running, Crow walked up to the front door and rang the doorbell. Thirty seconds later, he pressed the button again, repeatedly, then returned to his car and waited, inventing reasonable explanations for Bellweather's absence. He decided to wait until ten-thirty. He let his mind replay bits of conversation with Debrowski.

At one point, while he was finishing his third or fourth cup of coffee, Crow had mentioned that he was married. Without missing a beat, Debrowski had said, "That means we can both relax now, right?" It had been a good moment. Crow needed a friend, not a lover, and apparently Debrowski was riding a parallel track.

At ten-twenty, gazing idly at the dark house, Crow noticed the window. The juniper bushes that wrapped around the corner of the house obscured most of it, but when he looked directly at the window he could see that it was open. Crow felt his heart rate increasing, followed by numbness and a sense of unreality. He had felt this way often as a cop. He recognized fear. Don't think about it. Go through the motions. He buttoned his coat and got out of the car. A set of footprints he had not noticed before led from the driveway across the front lawn to the window. The glass pane had been shattered, the window unlocked and raised. Crow peered inside. He brushed a few shards of glass from the sill, then boosted himself up and into the small guest room next to Bellweather's office. The door was closed. Crow stood without moving for a full minute, listening. He could hear nothing. Easing the door open, he let himself out into the hallway and stood for another minute, listening.

Nothing.

Crow explored the house. Bellweather's office had been slightly trashed. The bison head had been ripped off the wall, a chair was kicked over, a framed print lay shattered on the antique desk. It didn't look as if the office had been searched but appeared more as if someone had had a temper tantrum. It had that Ricky Murphy feel to it. Crow reached under his armpit and touched the Taurus, turned his back on the office, and started up the stairs.

Bellweather's bedroom looked like a decorator's attempt to create a hypermasculine decor—everything was covered with ducks, dogs, lions, bears, and horses, from the framed reproductions of British fox-hunting scenes on the walls to the mallards embroidered on the pillows and bed skirts. Even the bedposts terminated in stylized lion heads. A row of bullets had shattered the ornately carved ebony headboard and ripped into the mattress. No blood. Crow stared at the perforated headboard, trying to make out the complex bas relief. A safari, he finally decided. A great white hunter, a file of native bearers, giraffes in the background. He went back downstairs and checked the garage. It was empty, the Jaguar gone.

One muscle at a time, he began to relax. He picked up the kitchen telephone, searched his mind for a number, punched it in.

The phone rang eight times before his sister Mary answered with a husky "Hello?"

"This is Joe." He waited three seconds.

"Joe?"

"Joe your brother," he said. "I need to talk to your husband."

A minute later, Dave Getter came on the line. "What is it, Joe?" He cleared his throat. "What's wrong?"

"Why would something be wrong?"

Getter took a moment to reply. "I was asleep."

"Your friend has disappeared."

"What friend? What are you talking about?"

"I'm at Bellweather's. He's gone. Nobody's home, and there's a broken window."

"Why are you telling me this? Why don't you just call the cops?"

"Do you know where he is?"

"No. Are you saying somebody broke in? What are you saying?"

"Somebody broke in, but I think Bellweather had already left. He hasn't paid me a dime, you know."

"I'm sure he'll be back, Joe. In any case, this has nothing to do with me. All I did was introduce you two."

Crow squeezed the phone. "What do you know about this guy?"

"Nothing. I've done some legal work for him. Look, if it's not working out, I'm sorry. Maybe I can find you something else."

"No, thanks. Tell me something, Dave. Does Bellweather have a taste for young boys?"

"What? No. Really?"

"According to George Murphy, Bellweather molested his son."

"Well . . . you know how that goes. One wild accusation, and everybody goes nuts."

"What kind of work did you do for him? Has he been in trouble before? Anything to do with little boys?"

Getter hesitated. "Uh, not to my knowledge. Our business had nothing to do with little boys. In any case, I don't generally concern myself with my clients' sexual preferences. Besides, don't you think . . ." He paused, then began again in a deeper voice. "Looking at it logically, Joe, it seems to me that if that were true, he would have gotten into some other area of medicine."

Crow was not tracking. "What are you talking about?"

"You have to look at the big picture, Joe. Your theory doesn't stand up. In the first place, I just can't see Dr. Bellweather as a child molester. And even if he was, wouldn't he have gone into pediatrics or child psychology? Or become a minister, or a gym teacher? Something like that. He is, after all, an intelligent man. If he liked young boys, he would be in a profession that gave him access to kids. I mean, if you had a foot fetish, you'd open a shoe store, don't you agree?"

Crow held out the telephone receiver, wrinkling his nose as though it had given off a noxious odor. Where was all this shoe store shit coming from? He hung up the phone, wondering why he had made the call in the first place.

He let himself out through the front door, got back in his car. The windows were already starting to frost over. He started the engine, put the car in gear, and took off. If Bellweather was still alive, he would be in touch. If he was dead, then Crow was out of a job. Either way, there was nothing he could do. He decided to go home. He would take a long shower, then go back to bed. If he was very deliberate about it, if he lay perfectly still, if he did not allow his imagination to stray, he might even get some sleep.

• • •

Crow opened the door to his apartment, turned on the light, and surveyed its bleak interior. The unfolded sofa bed, blankets a tangled mess, clothing piled on the floor. The cardboard moving boxes, fragments of his former life. Bare walls. The persistent smell of latex paint. He remembered that in another eighteen hours he would be going back to his home in Big River. Dinner with Melinda. The thought frightened him, but it was the only thing happening in his life with a hint of positive spin. He threw his trench coat on the bed and kicked off his shoes. The apartment felt cold.

He might be out of a job, but at least he had Ricky's Ruger. He tugged the gun from his belt and examined it. Probably worth five or six hundred bucks. He could always sell it. That made him feel better. He laid the gun on the thin mattress, shrugged out of his coat, let it fall to the floor, unfastened his shoulder holster with the Taurus, let it drop onto the coat. He sat on the edge of the mattress and peeled off his socks. Toenails needed trimming. He took off the rest of his clothes, piled them on top of his coat and gun, went into the tiny bathless bathroom, stepped into the shower, and turned the water on, as hot as he could stand.

Twenty minutes later, he turned off the water and opened the plastic shower door. He knew immediately, without knowing how he knew, that something had gone wrong. He grabbed a towel and dried himself, keeping his eyes on the bathroom door. It was standing open a few inches, just the way he had left it. Had he heard something? No. It was a smell. Like wet leaves. He wrapped the towel around his waist, put a hand on the cool, wet doorknob, and pulled.

The smell was stronger. Crow leaned out the open doorway and looked across the sofa bed to the left, toward the kitchenette.

George Murphy was standing in front of the open refrigerator, perusing Crow's collection of condiments, sour milk, and petrified pizza. He swiveled his head toward Crow and unleashed a demented grin.

"You don't eat so good, Officer Crow," he said. His blue baseball cap had a bright-yellow corn cob embroidered on the front.

Ricky Murphy stood against the wall, just on the other side of the bed. He was wearing a black canvas duster, the leather-lined collar turned up, his Stetson riding low on his forehead. A wad of tobacco distended his left cheek. The familiar-looking Ruger in his left hand was pointed in Crow's general direction. Crow locked eyes with him for an instant, then looked back at George.

"There's some ice cream in the freezer," Crow said. "Help yourself." Moving slowly, he stepped out of the bathroom. He wished he had a pair of pants on. His faded navy-blue twills were there on the bed, only a few inches away. He imagined himself reaching for them, saw himself die. He sensed that any sudden movement could get him killed. Ricky would twitch, and it would be all over. Under the circumstances, he decided to be a statue.

George had the freezer open. "Looks like you got a couple pizzas in here too." He came out with a cylindrical container. "Chocolate. My favorite. Where are your spoons?"

"Look in the sink," Crow said.

George found a spoon, wiped it on his coat, sat down at the short counter that served as a dining area, pried off the top of the ice cream carton. He winked at Crow, spooned a mound of ice cream into his mouth, rolled it around with his tongue until it softened, and swallowed.

"This is good ice cream." He held up the carton, reading the label. "Haygun Days? I never heard of it. Ricky, you ever hear of Haygun Days?"

Ricky shook his head, his eyes never leaving Crow. A stringy glob of tobacco-laden spittle arced from his mouth and landed on the pillow. Crow noticed another glob nearby, soaking into the sheets. That was what he had smelled. Wet leaves. Ricky shifted the wad of tobacco to his other cheek with a deft contortion of his tongue. Crow looked away.

George treated himself to another spoonful of ice cream. "Take it easy, Crow. Why don't you come on over here, have a seat? Let's talk. You like to talk, right?" He pointed the spoon toward the stool on the other side of the counter.

Moving slowly, Crow walked around the bed, stepping on his pile of clothing, dragging his bare foot across it to feel for the Taurus. His toe hit something heavy. The gun was there, under his shirt, still in its holster. Not that it would do him any good. He noticed that the door leading into the hallway was undamaged. "How'd you get in?" he asked, not expecting an answer. The locks in this apartment building were so cheap they'd probably slipped it with a credit card. He sat down across from George, who smiled, his mouth full of chocolate ice cream. Crow heard Ricky moving, felt him come in close behind him. He decided that the best plan, if you could call it that, would be to ignore the gun bearer and focus on the ice cream eater.

"What can I do for you?" he asked.

George examined Crow's face. "I'm looking for my son," he said.

"Here?" Crow asked. "I don't get it." The words had hardly left his lips when Ricky jammed the barrel of his revolver, all his speed and weight behind it, into Crow's lower back. His kidney exploded with pain, his body snapped back, his shins cracked against the underside of the counter, the stool flew off to the side, and Crow hit the floor with his shoulder. He felt the pain slicing up through his abdomen, striking the base of his skull with audible force. The small fragment of his mind that was still working thought that he had been shot. He could hear voices.

"That wasn't necessary, Ricky."

"Bullshit. The son-of-a-bitch has it coming, and more."

"Well now you just ease off there. Let's talk to the man, see what he has to say, okay?"

Crow heard the words, decoded them. All he could think was, If I've been shot, how come my ears aren't ringing? He opened his eyes and saw greenish gray carpeting. The pain was rapidly localizing. He reached back, expecting the hot liquid feel of blood. Nothing. He realized that he had just taken a kidney punch, a blood pisser for sure, but knowing that he wasn't carrying a slug of lead in his abdomen made the pain tolerable. He pushed himself onto his hands and knees, looked up at George.

"Are you all right?" George asked. He sounded genuinely concerned. "Can you stand up?"

Crow straightened his back, turned and looked at Ricky.

"He gets excited sometimes," George said. "Don't worry about it. Pick up that stool and sit down. I just need to ask you a few questions."

Crow climbed to his feet, his abdomen twisted to the left. Keeping Ricky in his field of vision, he picked up the stool and sat, the wooden seat ice cold on his bare buttocks. His towel had fallen off, but it no longer seemed important.

George leaned across the counter and spoke, his large lips squeezing out the words. "All I want is my son. I want to know where he is."

"I don't know where he is," Crow said, watching Ricky.

"I want him back."

"Look, I don't know anything about this." Crow pronounced the words carefully, wanting to be absolutely clear. "I've never seen your boy. All I know about him is what you told me."

George reached back and pulled out a wallet, flipped it open, and pointed a thick finger at a small color photo of a chubby, dark-haired boy. "Shawn," he said.

Crow shook his head.

George sat back, picked up the ice cream, spooned another ounce into his mouth. His eyes got smaller. "Then tell me where I can find Nelly Bell."

"I have no idea," Crow said. "I was supposed to see him tonight, but when I got there he was gone. Someone had broken in. A window was broken."

"Yes, he has better locks on his doors than you do. Where is he?"

"I don't know."

"He has Shawn."

"It's news to me. What makes you think he's got him?"

"We found his Vikings cap. Right on Nelly Bell's kitchen counter. Where is he, Crow? Where is Bellweather?"

Crow hated to repeat himself. "I told you," he said, shaking his head, "I don't—" He saw Ricky moving and brought his arm up, this time catching the gun butt on his left triceps, a hard blow that spun him off the stool and numbed his arm. Ricky swung again, a vicious backhand that clipped Crow on the chin as he staggered back, then he connected with his boot, a perfect Tony Lama shot to Crow's dangling testicles. Crow doubled up and hit the floor with his face. Ricky followed through with a series of nasty kicks to the gut and ribs, which Crow hardly noticed—for the moment, his universe began and ended with his balls.

"That's enough, Ricky. Leave him alone."

"I say we pop 'im."

"Get out! Now! Let me and him talk, okay? The important thing is we find Shawn. You kill him, it ain't gonna do us any good."

Crow heard the shuffle of boots on carpet, heard the door open and close. He wanted to throw up, but that would hurt too. Every muscle in his body had gone rigid; he could feel his heart pulsing waves of pain up his abdomen and down every limb. He heard George Murphy's voice.

"I'm really sorry about that, Officer Crow. Ricky's upset about his nephew, as I'm sure you can imagine. Would you like some ice cream? A glass of water?"

Days or seconds later, Crow opened his eyes and acquired a sitting position. He looked down at his crotch. Things were still attached, but the pain filled his lower abdomen. He lifted his head. Out of focus. He squeezed his eyes closed, which hurt, then opened them, which also hurt. George Murphy's face—friendly, solicitous, caring—hung before him.

"Are you all right?"

Crow looked around. His apartment appeared normal. The walls weren't covered with blood. For some reason this surprised him. The only thing out of place was the big man sitting in his kitchen.

"Ricky's gone," George said.

Crow touched his chin. It felt pulpy and tender. Ricky gone? His mind, churning, produced a moment of regret. How could he kill a man who was gone?

"Are you sure you don't want some ice cream?" George was holding out a spoon. Ice cream dripped on the countertop. Crow fixed his gaze on the spoon but did not move or reply. Murphy shrugged and ate the ice cream. "Let me ask you something," he said. "Are you still working for Nelly Bell?"

Crow shook his head slowly. He opened and closed his jaw. It seemed to be working. "I don't think so," he said. It was a true and—more important—a safe response. His voice sounded and felt awful, like bubbles rising through sand.

"Then you need a job, right?"

"No."

"I want you to find my son."

"I don't know where your son is," Crow said.

"I believe you. I really do. If I didn't, I would have let Ricky keep kicking you. Ricky gets excited. You have to understand that about him. He's convinced that you took Shawn. I personally don't believe it. I don't think you would do a thing like that. Besides, when I watched you drive away you were alone." Murphy paused, his brow contracted. "Maybe you don't know where he is, but I think you can find him. You do that sort of thing, right? You find people."

"Call the cops," Crow suggested. "They do that sort of thing too." His left arm was hurting now, a sharper sensation that cut through the throbbing in his gut. He stood up, grabbing the counter for support.

"Take it easy now," George said, standing and reaching out a hand to steady him. Crow brushed it away. George shook his head sadly. "Look, I don't want the police involved here. It's nothing we can't take care of—me, you, and Ricky. I'll pay you for your time, of course."

"That's what Bellweather said."

"Really? He hasn't paid you? Then you'll be looking for him anyway, won't you? That's good. Let me know when you find him." Murphy grinned and clapped him on the shoulder. Crow almost collapsed. "Tell you what," Murphy said, his hand on the doorknob. "If I find him first, I'll collect your money for you. How much does he owe you?"

Crow staggered toward the sofa bed, lowered himself to the mattress. "Two hundred dollars."

"Two hundred? You must work cheap."

Crow bent forward, as if he was about to vomit, slipped his hand into the pile of clothing, came out with the Taurus. He aimed it at Murphy's belly.

"Fuck you," he said. Not brilliant, but to the point.

Murphy laughed. "I can tell you're upset. We'll talk about this again tomorrow." He opened the door. "I have to get going. Let me know if you find anything, okay?"

"Fuck you," Crow said again. It felt good to say it, even if he was repeating himself.

Murphy said, "Good night, Officer Crow." He closed the door.

She's got eyes in the back of my head.

—*SEAN MURPHY'S JOURNAL*

manda made the best pancakes. Thick, tasty, and about a quarter pound each. A couple of them would keep a man moving till lunchtime, and if his bowels were sluggish, they'd move those too. George Murphy cut his stack into wedges, applied a half cup of Log Cabin syrup, and loaded them methodically into his mouth. Ricky cut his with the edge of his fork, a bite at a time, butter and a sprinkle of sugar, but no syrup. Amanda stood at the stove and watched. She liked to watch the boys eat. When they had both finished devouring their stacks, she quietly poured them another round of hot coffee.

George was in one of his moods.

Everybody knew that Ricky had a short fuse, and people had said the same thing about her. But George had his moods too. Ever since he was a little kid, good-natured most of the time, he did what she told him, worked hard—but there was a devil inside him. Amanda had learned to leave him alone when he was like this. Let him stew, and he'd get over it. Don't ask him any questions; don't try to tell him what to do.

She knew he was worried. Last night they'd come home late, without the boy. So far, neither George nor Ricky had seen fit to let her know what they had learned. She watched George sipping his coffee, glaring down at his syrup-covered plate. He didn't look like he was going to talk anytime soon, so she addressed her question to Ricky.

"How'd it go last night?" she asked.

"Nelly Bell's got Shawn. We found his cap," Ricky said.

George lowered his chin; his jaw pulsed. He dipped his finger in the pool of syrup remaining on his plate, licked it. Amanda could see the warning signs. This was not the same peanut-butter-eating George Murphy she had whacked across the forehead with a spoon. She tried something like that now, he might bust her one. Still, she persisted.

"You talk to that friend of yours? That Crow man?"

"He ain't my friend," Ricky said. "And he didn't tell us nothing."

"He doesn't know anything," George growled.

"Bullshit," Ricky muttered.

George dropped his coffee, and his arm shot out. The back of his fingers raked audibly across Ricky's cheek, the coffee cup hit the edge of his plate and shattered.

Ricky shouted something unintelligible, jumped up, and backed away, holding a hand to his face. His chair crashed to the floor. Amanda reached back and grabbed her spatula. Ricky took his hand from his face, looked at it.

"You oughta cut those nails, bro."

George blinked at the mess on the table as though its origin were a complete mystery.

Amanda watched the coffee drip off the edge of the table. Her momentary fear turned to anger. "You want that boy to grow up a man, you better find him quick, George Washington Murphy," she said. "You got that fat son-in-law of mine out lookin'?"

"Orlan? What good would that do? Nelly Bell's in Minneapolis or someplace. He ain't even in Orlan's county."

"So send him to Minneapolis."

"We send Orlan to the cities, who knows what kind of trouble he'd get hisself into."

"Least he'd be out lookin'." Amanda, her chin raised, gripped the spatula. George reached out and took it from his mother's hand.

"We'll find him, Mandy. We'll find them both." He put a hand on his mother's forearm and squeezed gently. "I've got that fellow Crow working on it. Might be he's found the boy already."

Amanda said, "Well, if you won't call him, I will. What's the use of having a cop in the family if you don't use him?"

"Call him if you want, for all the good it'll do. Meantime, I got a dead elk to sell." George turned and lumbered out of the kitchen. She heard him walk down the hall, slam the door to his office.

"What's his problem?" Ricky dabbed at the scratch on his cheek with a napkin.

Amanda shook her head and set about cleaning up the broken coffee cup. "I don't know for sure," she said. "Only I think I better cook him up a batch of prunes, just to be on the safe side."

On the third ring, Crow awakened. He counted the rings without moving, without opening his eyes. The phone rang eight times. After the echoes faded, Crow slowly opened his mouth and worked his jaw from side to side. Yes, it hurt. He opened his eyes and blinked at the ceiling until the texture came into focus, rolled his eyes from side to side. He turned his head to the left, toward the kitchenette. No Murphys there. Sunlight glared through the window over the sink. He lifted his head and looked at the locked and chained door. He looked to the right. Nothing. Nobody here but Joe Crow. He looked down his body. His right arm ended in a hand, in the hand was a revolver, the Taurus, his index finger on the trigger. He pulled his finger out of the trigger guard and let his head fall back. He was lucky he hadn't shot himself in the foot during the night. He imagined what it would be like to wake up that way, two or three toes suddenly blown to hamburger and bone chips.

He didn't want to move. To move would hurt. It would probably hurt a lot.

The telephone started to ring again. This time he turned his head and watched it, two feet away on the end table. It looked exactly the same ringing as it did silent. It persisted for ten rings. Crow closed his eyes.

Inevitably, boredom overcame inertia. He rolled onto his side, swung his feet out past the edge of the mattress, and sat up. The pain from his injuries was not as great as he had feared, but a wave of nausea caught him by surprise. He staggered into the bathroom and vomited a few paltry ounces of bile into the toilet.

The telephone rang. Crow sat naked on the cold floor, fascinated by the patterns he saw in the bathroom tiles, listening.

Sally Jessy had found two couples who had been married over ten years without ever consummating their marriage. Somehow, they had felt the need to go before a national television audience to defend their lifestyles. The two men did not have a lot to say. Uniformly wooden-faced, they both said, in so many words, that they simply were not interested in sex. They wanted a friend, a cook, and a companion. The wives both took somewhat more complicated positions. They claimed to be *interested* in sex but not in having intercourse. They claimed to like to "cuddle," whatever that was, and they wished their husbands would do more of it. One of the women was an avid reader of romance novels, the other a family counselor.

The studio audience was aghast. The spectacle of four married middle-aged virgins brought forth a tide of concern. Had they consulted physicians? Didn't they want children? Were they saying that sex was bad? The two couples became defensive and angry. Sally Jessy looked tired.

Hillary Johnson did not understand what all the fuss was about. She understood completely. And so did Orlan, for the most part, although in the early years of their marriage things had not been so clear. Perhaps if she had laid down the law, so to speak, on their wedding night, their marriage would have had fewer difficult moments. Even now, even after her change of life, she occasionally found it necessary to rebuff his drunken probes. She envied these television couples the purity of their relationships. There was something holy about it.

Conveniently, Sally Jessy went to a commercial just as the telephone rang. Hillary hit the mute button on the remote and picked up the phone. It was her mother.

"I don't know about that, George. I mean, I appreciate you calling me, but—" Steve Anderson, the phone pressed to his ear, nodded, then nodded again. "Uh-huh. Uh-huh. It's really that big? Jeez, where would I put it? Just a minute. Hold on." He punched the hold button on his phone and sat back to think a moment. An eight-by-eight elk, guaranteed over 400 Boone and Crockett points, his name in the Records of North American Big Game. He pictured it, the seven-foot-wide rack, hanging over his fireplace. How would Patty deal with *that?* He smiled and looked around his new office, with its window. He could see the frozen Mississippi winding through downtown Minneapolis. It had been a good year. If he kept on pulling in the big checks, Patty would deal with it just fine. The mounted bison head had been a tough sell, but once he got it into the house she didn't mind it so much. It wasn't as though he was asking her to put the damn thing in their bedroom. She even seemed to enjoy it when he told dinner guests how he'd bagged it with a single well-placed shot, right to the heart, from three hundred yards. Ollie, the taxidermist, had done a terrific job of concealing the thirteen bullet holes the MAC-10 had left in the buff's face.

That first hunt had hooked him, despite its strange aftermath when

Dr. Bellweather got clobbered by Ricky Murphy. Anderson had returned to Talking Lake Ranch to hunt pheasant and duck, this time as the host, with one of his other clients. That had been fun, but nothing like shooting something really big, something you could hang on your wall, something really impressive. He'd been thinking for weeks about arranging another big game hunt, thinking along the lines of a Russian boar, which was available for under a thousand bucks, but this elk sounded like a onetime opportunity, get his name in the record book and everything.

Of course, it would all be a write-off. He'd find time to talk a little business, maybe lay a sales pitch on George or Ricky.

It was too damn bad about Doc Bellweather, what had happened to his account. Anderson felt awful about the whole sorry mess. The only good thing was the eighty grand in commish he'd netted.

The telephone beeped, telling him his call had been on hold for sixty seconds. Anderson punched the blinking button.

"George? Sorry about that. Okay, you said you wanted how much? Ouch! I know, I know. You were asking thirty before, I remember. Uh, you want to tell me how come the discount? Uh-huh. So you need to get it on the books by next week. . . . Oh! You mean the safari club books. Okay, I get it. That's great. You need an answer right now, or can I call you back tomorrow? Yeah, I'm pretty sure. Uh-huh. Okay, I'm your man. Just let me call you back tonight to confirm it, and I'll let you know when I can be there for the hunt. This is guaranteed, right? We don't get the elk, I don't pay, right? Good. Thanks for thinking of me! Bye now!"

Anderson disconnected, enjoying the breathless thrill a man gets who has just spent twenty thousand dollars on an ego trip. He'd felt this way when he'd signed the sales agreement for his 7-series BMW. Of course, he wouldn't be able to drive a dead elk. On the other hand, he couldn't shoot his Beamer.

George hung up the phone and settled back into his pigskin chair and waited for the warm, bubbly feeling that usually accompanied the closing of a good sale. He shifted his butt around, looking for the good spot. The crudely fashioned chair, made by his father, was not altogether comfortable. He was having trouble getting settled. The lumps in the chair seemed sharper and more insistent than usual, and he had the distinct sensation that little bugs were flitting around his head, just out of sight.

He had sold an already dead elk for twenty thousand dollars. He should be feeling good, but he wasn't. It was Shawn and that doctor. George squeezed his eyes closed and tried to imagine where they were and what they were doing. Shawn's face appeared for an instant, then the doctor's superior little smile, then all was obliterated by rage, a bright-yellow light tinged red at the edges. George forced his mind back to neutral and made a conscious effort to think.

What would his old man have done? Suppose he, George Murphy, had been kidnapped as a child. What would old Sean have done about it? George tried to imagine his father's rage, but all he could see was the old man tipping back his quart bottle of Cabin Still, wiping his mouth on his shoulder, blinking his squinty eyes, maybe taking a swat at him. What his old man would have done, before he did anything else, was he would have gotten shit-faced. Maybe driven over to Birdy's and bragged about it, like having his boy kidnapped made him a big man in Big River.

George tightened, then relaxed, at the thought. At least he was a better man than his father. He had that.

He still half expected the kid to show up at any moment, come walking in out of the woods. Or maybe he'd get a call from Orlan Johnson. "Yeah, George, we found 'im walking down the highway. He's fine, just a little cold and scared. . . ." Shawn's disappearance seemed unreal. As unreal as when Shawn had been born, and when the child had spoken his first words. George had never entirely believed that the boy existed—now he was supposed to believe the boy was gone.

Shawn had run away. George could appreciate that. He had run away himself at that age, two or three times. Kids did things like that. But why had he run to Bellweather? The thought of his boy running to see the doctor made the bright light come back. What would he do when Shawn returned? When George had run away as a boy, he had always returned home to a whipping from his old man, a hot meal from Mandy, and then life would go on. Why did he keep thinking about his father? His father had been a drunk, lazy and irresponsible, and had spent his entire life half broke. George hadn't respected him as a child; why did he keep thinking about him now?

Because he didn't know what to do next. He had actually considered going to the Minneapolis cops, but what would he say to them? My son has run away with this faggot doctor? And what if they found the doctor and arrested him? Bellweather, being a doctor and all, would probably claim that he had rescued the boy from an abusive environment.

George wrenched his thoughts away from Bellweather and thought

again about the twenty thousand dollars he would be getting from
Steve Anderson. He opened his eyes and looked out across his desk at
Louise, the pedestal-mounted Russian boar his father had shot back in
'44. He remembered old Sean, even more shit-faced than usual, telling
him that Louise would be his one day. "M'legacy t'you, Georgie. Fuggin'
Louise." He remembered his father showing him the safe built into the
stuffed pig's hollowed-out interior. "Yer m'oldes' boy, Georgie. She's all
gonna be yers. Ever' las' fugging dime. Secret, you an' me. E'en yer
mama don' know boudit."

After old Sean died, his skin yellow, abdomen distended with diseased liver, his heart a sack of collapsed muscle, it had taken George
three hours to find the combination to the safe. He'd finally discovered
the magic numbers in an envelope taped to the bottom of a desk
drawer. He remembered his excitement, locking the door to his father's office, his hands shaking as he pulled the hog away from the
wall, dialed in the combination.

George's mouth turned down at the memory.

His father's legacy: a half-filled pint bottle of Cabin Still, an IOU for
ten dollars from somebody named Fred, and a handful of pennies,
nickels, and dimes—no quarters—that added up to one dollar and nine
cents. A notebook half filled with largely illegible entries. His father's
precious thoughts. George recalled the first thing he had read in that
journal:

*Today I got a buck off the lick in the south 1/4. He was a 6-pointer,
and big. Later on I smacked Georgie on account of the little shit would
not shut up. Amanda blew her stack on account of I knocked off a tooth,
but it was just a baby tooth. The problem with women is, they will get upset over anything. A boy needs to be hit sometimes.*

George remembered that day. Did Shawn need to be hit? Perhaps,
but until he came home, there was no point in thinking about it. The
next scrawled entry, covering most of the page and nearly impossible
to read: *If God didn't mean for a man to drink, he wouldn't of invented
Amanda.*

In a few places, Sean Murphy had tried his hand at poetry.

> *Once was a gal name a Mandy*
> *Use to be sweet as candy*
> *And when she got old*
> *All wrinkled and cold*
> *Mandy was still pretty randy*

George found such observations about his mother disturbing. He still kept the notebook in the safe. From time to time, he would pull it out and force himself to read a few more lines, but it never made him feel better. The only part of his hog-encased "legacy" that George had got any use out of was the safe itself. The idea of a giant, hairy piggy bank amused him, as it had his father. He still used it to store his ready cash. In this business, you had to have cash money on hand. You never knew when you'd get a chance to pick up a good animal.

The tiger, for instance.

If he hadn't had cash on hand the day Jack Wild's Wild Animal Show had passed through Alexandria, he'd never have got it. Jack Wild, the proprietor of the small traveling circus, had called George the morning his troupe of misfits were loading up their beasts and props into two beat-up semitrailers, getting ready to leave for a show in Wisconsin.

"Hear you're looking for a big stripy cat," Jack had said.

Of course, George had been interested. He'd been trying to get his hands on a tiger for months. Dr. Nelson Bellweather—at that time one of his best customers—had been calling him up every couple weeks, asking when he was going to get a tiger. Nelly Bell had a hard-on for the big cats. Wanted one of each. George had been putting him off—there just weren't that many tigers around.

"What do you got?" he'd asked Jack.

"I got an old female, good looking but mean as hell. She fucked up one of my guys last night, caught a claw in his arm and ripped the sucker open. Cost me a hundred eighty bucks to get him stitched up. Nobody wants to work with her."

"How much?"

"You get a truck and a cage out here in the next couple hours, she's yours for ten."

George did some quick math in his head. He'd told the doctor a tiger would run him about forty K. To make his standard endangered-species markup, he would have to get the price down.

"I can go eight," he said.

Jack waited a few seconds before replying. "You bring me cash and get up here before eleven, you got yourself a cat."

Having a pile of cash around the house was more than a matter of convenience. It was a business necessity. Of course, Ricky didn't know about the safe. George told him that all the family money was tied up in investments and property. Ricky was an idiot when it came to money—if he knew about the safe, he'd be asking for money constantly.

Other than George, the only family member who knew about Louise was Shawn, who had been hiding under the desk a few years ago, playing some six-year-old game, when George pulled the pig out from the wall and made a deposit.

Shawn. The kid was always getting himself in trouble. The day Shawn had discovered the existence of the safe, George had smacked him a good one for spying on him—then immediately regretted his action. He'd had to calm the kid down, promise him a Popsicle or something, then show him how the safe worked.

"You just lift up this flap, and there's the door, see?"

"How do you open it?"

"You have to have the secret combination."

"What's that?"

"It's a secret. But one day, when I'm gone, you'll have it. Then it will be your secret. Everything will be yours."

By two-thirty in the afternoon, Crow had showered, dressed, eaten half a pizza, and let seven phone calls ring unanswered. He had stripped away the tobacco-soiled bedding and taken it downstairs to the laundry room. He was sitting on the folded sofa bed, wearing the Taurus in its shoulder holster, thinking about calling Melinda, wishing he felt a little better—or a little worse. How sick was he? Too sick to attempt a reconciliation with his wife? Sick enough to check into a hospital? Mortally wounded?

The truth was, after taking a few aspirin, he didn't feel so bad. There had been no visible blood in his urine. His ribs were sore but lacked the stabbing pains associated with shattered bone. Even his genitals seemed to be recovering.

He wished he felt just a little bit better.

He kept thinking about George Murphy. Not Ricky, but George. Eating his "Haygun Days." Each time the thought intruded, a shiver traveled down his body, briefly visiting his wounds as it passed. When he thought about Melinda, the same shiver plucked at other wounds.

He had been sitting on the sofa for over an hour when the intercom buzzed. The telephone calls had been easy to ignore. Someone at the door, however, was a more immediate issue. He got up and pressed the button on the intercom.

"Yeah?"

"Crow? Are you okay?"

"Who is this?"

"Debrowski."

Crow stared at the intercom.

"You gonna buzz me in?"

Crow hesitated. He hardly knew this woman. He didn't want her to see him in this condition.

"Crow?"

He buzzed her in. When he opened his door, it took her a few seconds to absorb his battered appearance.

"I tried to call you," she said. "No answer. I was in your neighborhood, so I thought I'd stop by. So what the hell happened to you?"

Crow shook his head. "What are you doing here?" he asked.

"That's right, Crow, make me feel welcome. You're doing great so far."

"Sorry. I'm a little confused."

"Then quit trying to think. I had a feeling is all."

"A feeling?"

"Yeah. You know. Woman's intuition." She fired up a Camel. "Mind if I smoke?"

"Yes," said Crow.

"I'll just finish this one up, then."

"Fine." Actually, it smelled pretty good. Crow sat down on the sofa. "Have a seat."

Debrowski remained standing, puffing on her cigarette. A pillar of blue smoke drifted toward the ceiling. "So I'll tell you what. I was thinking about you this morning, and I had this feeling that you were, you know, fucking up or something." She squinted her eyes against the smoke and crossed her arms.

"And?"

"It was just a feeling. Sometimes I think . . . sometimes I make things up in my head that I know are probably wrong, but I can't stop thinking them. You know what I mean? Anyways, I decided to call just to say hi, see how you were doing. You didn't answer the phone. I thought maybe you were still at work, so I called again later. Then I was out driving around and I thought, what the hell, I'd stop by. You got any coffee?"

"I'm not fucking up," Crow said. "Not that it's any of your business."

Debrowski nodded. "I know what you mean."

"Good."

"So what happened to your face, Crow?"

"Ran into a door. You want some coffee?"

"Said I did."

Crow stood, keeping his face frozen to conceal the bolt of pain that ran up his back, and put a kettle of water on the stove. Debrowski followed him into the kitchenette. She noticed the bowl of cat food on the floor.

"You got a kitty cat?"

"I did. He ran away."

"Really? When? What's his name?"

"Milo. Haven't seen him in four days."

Debrowski nodded. "I used to have a cat. You check the Humane Society?"

"Yesterday."

"You should check again. You put up any signs?"

Crow shook his head.

"You should put up some signs, Crow. You got yourself a good cat, you don't want to lose it."

"I know. I've been busy." Actually, it hadn't occurred to him. He'd always thought of Milo as the self-sufficient type.

"He'll probably come back. That's how you tell a friend, you know. No matter what kind of shit you pull, they keep coming back."

Crow said, "Are we still talking about my cat?"

"What's he look like?"

"Black. Big and black." Crow put a paper filter in the Melitta coffeepot, added three scoops of stale Folger's. "Yellow eyes."

The intercom buzzed.

Crow poured a stream of boiling water onto the grounds.

The intercom buzzed again.

"You going to answer that?" Debrowski asked.

Crow shrugged, put down the teakettle, looked out the kitchen window into the parking lot. A familiar-looking police car was parked directly in front of the entrance. He poured coffee into two plastic mugs. The intercom buzzed repeatedly. Debrowski went to the window to see what he was looking at.

"You got a police problem?"

"I don't know. I got some kind of problem." Crow tried to think of a reason why the Big River police would be visiting. He couldn't think of one. He pressed his lips together and handed Debrowski her coffee.

She sniffed, took a cautious sip.

"You want to talk about it?"

"Not really."

The intercom gave off one final blast, then fell silent. Debrowski lit another cigarette. A moment later, they watched Orlan Johnson return to his squad car and spin his way out of the icy parking lot.

"You going to group tonight?"

Crow stared into his coffee. "I don't think so. I'm having dinner with my wife."

"Oh. I thought you were separated."

"We are."

"Oh." She lifted her coffee. Crow could hear the crinkling of her leather jacket. "Well, listen, how about if you do something for me?"

"What's that?"

"You want to talk or something, give me a call, okay?"

When good things happen, sometimes all that happens is they make the bad times seem worse.

—JOE CROW

f he wouldn't answer the door, then he wouldn't answer the got-damn door. And if he wouldn't answer the got-damn door, then what the hell was a guy supposed to do? Who was he s'pose to be, Dirty Harry? Break the got-damn thing down?

Anyways, he didn't believe it. Why would little Joe Crow go and steal a got-damn kid for anyways? If George Murphy couldn't keep track of his own got-damn kid, then how the hell was anybody else supposed to find the little son-of-a-bitch? Damn, he hated politics.

Got-damn Murphys.

Christ sakes, what did they expect him to do? Just because a guy gets to be chief of the got-damn police doesn't mean he can snap his fingers and the kid comes like a got-damn dog. Wise-ass little son-of-a-bitch anyways. Bunch a assholes.

Christ sakes, what a drive! Damn near three hours just to ring a guy's doorbell so he could say he tried. Now he had to drive all the way back again.

Got-damn Hillary.

He pulled into a liquor store in Cokato, bought a half pint of peppermint schnapps and a couple cans of Bud.

The beers got him to Litchfield. He stopped at a gas station to take a leak, got back in his squad car, cracked the seal on the schnapps.

Half an hour later, Orlan Johnson wrenched the wheel of the patrol car, bringing it back into the approximate vicinity of the right-hand lane.

Got-damn curvy roads.

A green sign flashed by. Big River—24 miles. Johnson took a last pull off the schnapps, rolled down his window, tossed the dead soldier into the ditch. He felt in his pocket for an El Producto. Hill hated it when he came home reeking of cheap tobacco, but there was a chance that if he smelled bad enough she wouldn't notice the booze. He lit the cigar and puffed furiously.

It didn't work. He wasn't in the house more than two minutes when Hillary figured it out.

"Well?" she asked, before he hardly even got his got-damn coat the hell off.

"Well what?"

"What did you find out? Did you talk to that Officer Crow, like I told you?" She was carrying one of her books. One of the hardcover ones, cost a fortune, couldn't wait for the got-damn paperback. She crossed her arms, hugging it.

Johnson glared at her, giving her his best chief-of-police stare. Some sort of misguided schnapps-driven intelligence inspired him to reply, "He isn't an *officer* anymore, Hill. I fired his got-damn ass."

Hillary stepped closer, wrinkled her nose. "You didn't even talk to him, did you?"

"I couldn't find him, got-dammit." He had intended to get right in her face with that one, but her angry eyes forced him to look away. "Wasted the whole got-damn day looking for your nephew. Least you could do is cut me a little slack."

"What about his wife?"

"Who? Whose wife?"

"Joe Crow's wife. Maybe he's staying with his wife."

Johnson wasn't following this line of thought. "You don't know what you're talking about. They got separated."

"She might know where he is. I want you to go see her."

"The hell I will."

"The hell you won't," she said. "First thing tomorrow, after you've sobered up."

Johnson drew himself up, gaining a good three inches. He thought hard, seeking a witty response, but all he could come up with was the old favorite: "What the hell's that s'pose to mean?"

"You're drunker than a skunk. And you smell like a cigar."

"Like hell!"

That was when she hit him with the got-damn book. Damn near broke his got-damn nose.

•   •   •

Crow thought of it as *the house.* Not *their house,* for he had moved out over a month ago, and certainly not *Melinda's house,* because he still owned half of it, but *the house.* Sometimes, talking with Melinda, he referred to it by the address. "How are things at 3410?" he would say.

It felt odd to be ringing the bell, waiting on the front steps. He almost hoped that she wouldn't be there. That she'd forgotten, or had chosen to forget, that she'd invited him for dinner. What was the occasion? He preferred not to speculate.

She opened the door and stepped back, giving him plenty of space.

A few things had changed since his last visit. The sofa, which had been against the south wall, now sat in the center of the living room, facing the fireplace. A framed lithograph of penguins leaping into an Antarctic sea was propped on the mantel beside a copper-and-glass pyramid. Finchley, one of a pair of finches they had bought, together, at the Bird Barn, was missing from his cage. Finchster, the other finch, had died a year ago. Otherwise, the house looked much the same—it was easy to remember living there. The wallpaper was the same, and the weavings. The furniture they had bought together—cheap stuff, most of it purchased from Wicke's or Sears. He remembered painting the ceiling, getting paint in his eye.

Melinda had bound her long, pale hair in a casual twist that looked as if it was about to unravel. Two picks, looked like chopsticks, held it in place. No makeup, at least not that he could detect. Maybe a little something on the lips. She was covered with a great deal of fabric—a long, loose wraparound skirt the color of raw pine, one of her own handwoven fabric belts, a ribbed rust-colored turtleneck, and over all an absurdly long off-white cotton cardigan—must have had twenty buttons—that hung like a duster past her knees. Her feet were tied into a pair of fabric creations that looked like a cross between slippers and hunting boots. Crow wondered whether she was wearing leather these days. A three-inch-long quartz crystal caged in sterling silver vines hung between her breasts. He decided to ignore it.

He would have preferred her in jeans and a T-shirt—wholesome, casual, and accessible—but he supposed that this outfit was something special, something she had put on for his benefit. Either that or she was feeling fat again, a delusion that came and went like the weather, accompanied at times by bouts of bulimia that she would not acknowledge.

"You look nice," he said.

"Thank you," she said with a faint smile, her soft blue eyes sliding away.

He had been there for—what?—nearly a minute? And they hadn't touched. He hadn't hugged her, an easy and natural thing to do fifty-nine seconds ago, but the moment—had there been a moment?—had passed. Crow crossed the room and lowered himself into a chair, his chair, wincing at the sensation in his gut. His body hurt, but not as bad as it had a few hours ago.

"Are you all right?" she said, looking at his swollen jaw, reaching up to brush her own cheek with her fingertips.

"A little sore, but I'll be okay."

"What happened?" She crossed her arms, uncrossed them, took a half step back.

"I ran into a door." He didn't want to talk about the Murphys.

Melinda bit her lower lip and headed for the kitchen. "Can I get you something to drink?" she called over her shoulder.

"Juice. Something like that."

He sat down. To keep his mind occupied, he counted the candles burning in the room. Sixteen. No doubt a number of great significance.

Melinda returned with a glass of apple cider for him, a glass of white wine for herself. Crow tried not to look at the wine, not because he wanted any but so that no disapproval would show on his face. Melinda pulled out a side chair and sat in front of him.

"Cheers," she said, candlelight flashing from her eyes, her wineglass, her crystal pendant.

By the time the lasagna was on the table, they had talked about the neighbors, Melinda's latest weaving, and national politics. Somehow that led to Big River politics, which led to Talking Lake Ranch, and Crow found himself back on the subject of preserve hunting versus "real" hunting. Melinda had had only the one glass of wine, but she was loosening up.

"It's all about killing animals, Joe," Melinda said as she cut through layers of cheese and pasta. "The animals don't know the difference. Either way, they die in a state of terror."

"It's different," said Crow. "In the wild, animals are free. They live each day knowing they have to struggle to stay alive. There is a balance there, between freedom and risk. Hunters are a part of the picture. It's been going on for millions of years. It's the most natural thing there is. But what the Murphys are doing is completely unnatural. They buy and sell domesticated wild animals. It's not sport. You go duck hunting there, they have ducks that are trained to fly over you. It's like a shooting gallery. It's like hunting chickens on a chicken farm."

He waited for her response. Melinda could be fierce in defense of helpless animals. He loved the passionate Melinda. When she was angry, she was alive.

"I don't see the difference," Melinda said, sounding more weary than fierce. "A dead duck tame is just as dead as a dead duck wild."

She had another glass of wine with dinner. An Australian chardonnay. The lasagna was wonderful. Caesar salad, the real thing, dressing made with organic eggs, Spanish anchovies, homemade croutons. Real butter. Melinda the vegetarian had no problem with animals held in bondage—just don't kill them for meat. She made a special exception for anchovies. Crow wanted to ask her why she had invited him for dinner, but the conversation was flowing in other directions. Movies neither of them had seen but about which they both had opinions. Books. Family. She asked him about his dad, and Crow realized he hadn't seen the old man since August. She told him that his sister Mary had taken up pottery.

"She has a real feel for it, Joe. She's making coffee mugs."

"Good for her." Crow hadn't seen much of his sister since she had married Dave Getter. He would never get used to the concept of Getter as a brother-in-law—he resented his sister for marrying the jerk—and he resented that her friendship with Melinda was so close, so solid. It bothered him to imagine them together, but he did not understand why.

"So what's the occasion?" he blurted.

Melinda looked as if she'd been slapped. "What do you mean?"

"I mean, how come you invited me to dinner?"

Melinda shrugged and stood up. "I thought it would be nice," she said. "Isn't it nice?" She went into the kitchen. "Do you still like spumoni?"

It *was* nice. Crow shifted in his chair. A minor twist of pain from his groin came and went, making him realize that he had forgotten about his injuries for almost an hour. He decided to try to enjoy himself, go with the current.

"It's nice," he said quietly. He looked back through the kitchen door. Melinda was opening an ice cream carton. Crow raised his voice. "It's nice," he said.

Melinda nodded, digging into the carton with an aluminum scoop.

• • •

"You were so cute," Melinda said, laughing, eyes bright with memory. "We had a lot of fun, didn't we? We had some really good times." Her face, flushed from wine and recollection, glowed in the firelight.

She had thrown a pine log on the fire. The spitting, crackling resin made a miniature fireworks display in the fireplace. He had told her— how many times—not to use pine. It was bad for the fireplace. It coated the chimney with resin. She had never listened to him before, and on this night, his eyes full of Melinda, he said nothing, choosing instead to bask in her capacity for joy. Melinda was capable of great bouts of happiness. In such moments, Crow would plunge unguarded into the effervescent soup of her emotion.

Crow opened his eyes. Something hanging over him in the half light. He blinked, brought it into focus, remembered. Copper tubes; a four-foot-wide pyramid-shaped framework suspended from the ceiling with a coil of tubing at its apex. He sat up and pushed the feather comforter forward, drew his feet back and swung them out over the side of the bed. His body hurt. Whatever powers the pyramid held, it had not repaired his aching body. Oh well. It seemed unimportant now, a minor aberration, charming in its own way. If she wanted to believe in such things, why should he argue? He would tell her how much better he felt.

He was in their old bedroom; he was in Melinda's bedroom. The door was open a few inches, and he could hear one of Melinda's spacey New Age tapes playing on the stereo downstairs. He opened and closed his mouth, frowning at the taste. His lips were swollen, unaccustomed to long, hungry kisses. He closed his eyes and listened to the music, imagined Melinda on the sofa in her bathrobe, her feet tucked under her body, reading a book. It would be one of her books about channeling or the tarot, something to go with the music. He felt tired and sore, but relaxed. Maybe sleeping under a pyramid had some therapeutic effect after all.

He stood up carefully, letting his tissues stretch, replaying the evening in his mind. The memories arrived with a warm, rosy tint. Melinda making dinner, his favorite, more relaxed than he had seen her in months, smiling, talking, listening, laughing. Sitting in front of the fire after dinner, surrounded by candles, and she had drunk a third glass of wine—but that was okay. The bottle, still half full, sat quietly on the dining room table while they made love first in the living room in front of the fire, then again, slowly, on her soft bed. How had it happened? He wasn't sure. They were talking, and then a moment had come and this time he had touched her, felt her soft hair on his palm for the first time in . . . it seemed like years. He remembered laughing with her, saying whatever came into his mind. Remembering the good times. Something good had happened. He looked down at his body, at his muscular and compact torso. He felt taller, as if his shoulders had come out of a perpetual hunch. In the bathroom mirror, his face looked younger—the bruise on his jaw seemed a minor, youthful blemish. He frowned at the stubble on his jaw, ran a sinkful of hot water, and shaved using Melinda's razor, careful because the blade was meant for legs, not faces, and had not been sharp for a long time; he did not cut himself once. He brushed his teeth with Melinda's toothbrush, then rinsed it several times and tapped it dry on the edge of the sink. Looking at himself in the mirror, he smiled. I'm not such a bad guy, he thought.

Sitting on the edge of the bed again, he thought of things to say to her. He remembered she had asked him to look at her body, her lips quivering. He had told her she was perfect, and so she had appeared. She'd said her thighs were getting fat. He'd told her no, your thighs are beautiful. He stood up, imagining himself walking down the carpeted stairs, moving quietly to the sofa, where he would interrupt her reading with a soft kiss. He thought of the things he would say to her: that he loved her, that he missed her, that he wanted her. That he wanted to remain her husband. That he wanted to start over, try harder, make it right. He took a deep breath, smelling the last wisps of their lovemaking. Melinda's terry-cloth robe hung on a hook by the door. Crow put it on. The sleeves were short, but it felt good.

He noticed, first, that the wine bottle on the dining room table was empty. Then he saw Melinda in the kitchen, sitting at the table, leaning forward, her eyes on him, her chin raised—elated, defiant, and determined—staring at him with brittle, merciless clarity. He saw the big mirror that belonged on the wall by the staircase, now on its back covering most of the kitchen table; four long white powder lines, perfectly parallel, were spread across it like the clawmarks of a frost giant. Melinda was naked, her hard nipples resting on the edge of the table, tiny blue veins showing through the translucent flesh of her breasts. She was holding a gold-plated single-edge razor blade in one hand, a matching gold-plated tube in the other: his gift to her two Christmases ago.

• • •

Crow found his clothing scattered before the fireplace. He found his coat draped over the back of the upholstered side chair by the front door. He let himself out into the bitter night air and, after three tries, started the Rabbit. He observed himself driving south through town, then pulling out onto the highway, driving perfectly, flawlessly, precisely, holding his hands at the ten and two positions on the steering wheel, breathing in, breathing out.

he room was smaller than most third world jail cells, and far colder. Windowless; unfinished plywood walls; translucent corrugated-plastic roof. A tiny kerosene heater cranked out the Btu's, but with the outside air temperature hovering around twelve degrees Fahrenheit, it was never quite warm enough. The floor was a solid sheet of ice, about twelve inches thick.

"Son, you got to pretend you is one," croaked Sam O'Gara, his voice shredded after two days of kerosene fumes, cold feet, and Pall Malls. His diminutive, wiry, gaunt frame was sealed into a pair of lumpy, greasy coveralls stuffed with an assortment of undergarments. He wore a mottled corduroy cap with turned-up earflaps. Several days' growth of white-and-gray whiskers gave his wrinkled features a silvery sheen; his button eyes penetrated a veil of blue smoke from his cigarette.

"I don't have to pretend, Sam." Crow had met Sam O'Gara, his natural father, for the first time at the age of eighteen. Since then, they'd had friendly if sporadic contact. Crow liked Sam. But they just didn't have a lot in common. He looked down into his fishing hole through the clear winter water. He could see the rocky bottom of the lake nine feet below. He moved his short jigging rod up and down, looking to see that his minnow was still on the line. Not that he gave a damn if he caught anything. He already had more frozen walleye and crappie than he could fit in his freezer.

For the past forty-eight hours, his world had been restricted to a rented cabin on the southwestern shore of Lake Mille Lacs and this six-by-eight-foot ice-fishing house, a half mile offshore. The first day had been interesting for about three hours. He had never spent much time with Sam, not in such close quarters. The old guy had started to repeat himself. Crow figured that was due to the half pint of Jack Daniel's the old man had sucked down. By midafternoon, the conversation had become solid reruns. Even his questions were the same.

"Getting any nibbles, son?"

"Nope."

"Got to stick with it. Fuckers'll be bitin' soon."

"Hope so."

"You betcha."

"Uh-huh."

"I lost another goddamn minnow . . . you getting any nibbles?"

The same short conversational loops, over and over. Sam kept forgetting about the status of Crow's marriage. Kept going back to it.

"So how's that little gal you was with, that Melinda?"

"She's fine, Sam. We're separated."

"I figured. Too damn bad."

"I know."

"They ain't worth chasin' twice."

"Uh-huh."

"Your mama couldn't stand havin' me around, y'know. Persnickety as all get-out."

"Uh-huh."

"I say hell with'm all."

They must have had that exchange half a dozen times. Crow couldn't decide whether Sam was drunk, senile, or trying to make a point. Another favorite exchange went something like this:

"Y'know, son, I got no regrets."

"Uh-huh."

"Not that a guy wants it all carved on his rock, understand."

"I bet."

"Never let 'em push me around."

"Uh-huh."

"Always swung back."

"Right, Sam."

"Goddamn bastards. I got no regrets."

The ice-fishing trip had been Sam's idea. After his evening with Melinda, Crow had returned to his apartment and spent a long, fitful night, never really sleeping, all his energy going to stanch the flow of images flooding his mind. When the phone rang at seven-fifteen in the morning, he had answered it. Sam's shredded voice had been a welcome distraction.

"Son!"

"Hi, Sam."

"How come you don't never call me?"

Crow had sat up in his bed, moving slowly, feeling twangs, stabs, and thuds throughout his body. "Uh," he said.

"Hell, I ain't seen you in so long I can't remember what you look like, son! I'm thinking about making a run up to Milly today, do some fishing. You want to come?"

Every year, Sam invited him to go ice fishing. And every year, Crow declined. Ice fishing? A sport that served only to get the feebleminded off the streets for three months a year. Much to his own astonishment, Crow had agreed to go. Why not? What else was he going to do?

Now here he was, sitting out on the ice holding a line and staring down through a hole in the ice, listening to a wrinkled, chain-smoking, whiskey-drinking gnome tell him that he had to pretend to be a damn fish.

Sometime during the morning of their second day on the ice, Sam stopped talking. At first, Crow was relieved. They had a run of action and landed three small walleye each, then endured a long silence punctuated only by the sounds of Sam lighting his Pall Malls and unscrewing the cap to his Jack Daniel's. Crow leaned close over the hole and stared into the dark, fluid world. His minnow, impaled on the hook, hung motionless near the bottom of the lake. The silence grew in length and breadth. Crow raised his head. Sam was quietly smoking, staring down at his hole. A layer of thin blue haze, about two feet thick, cut across his chest. Crow felt a numbness in his ears and wondered whether he was losing his hearing. He cleared his throat, producing a faraway, muffled sound. Suddenly he needed to hear his own voice. He began to speak. He started by telling Sam about the doctor. He spoke slowly, enjoying the way his voice echoed off the corrugated-plastic roof. Sam listened, nodding and grunting at appropriate moments. Crow told him about Ricky Murphy, about feeding the pigs with George Murphy. Told him about Melinda, and about the beating he had taken from Ricky Murphy. Sam sat sipping his whiskey and smoking his Pall Malls, making no comment. After what seemed like a long time, Crow ran out of things to say. He felt as if he'd been pissing for hours and had no fluids left in his body. He looked down through his hole. His minnow twitched. How do they stay alive for so long? he wondered. He tried to imagine himself hanging from a giant hook. How long would he survive? Five minutes? Ten? The giant hook was vivid in his mind, so he put a few other people on it, just to see how they'd look. Bellweather, Ricky Murphy, and Orlan Johnson all expired within seconds, but George Murphy just looked pissed off.

His thoughts drifted, and before he could catch himself he'd slipped back a decade and a half. At the age of nineteen he had devoted himself—briefly—to the study of Zen Buddhism. It took him an entire three weeks to grow impatient with the leisurely pace of Eastern philosophies and opt instead for the more dramatic results available through the magic of the purple microdot. One hit of LSD, and Zen Buddhism came to seem irrelevant. Some of the stories, however, had stayed with him. He recalled one in particular, about a young Japanese student who, seeking enlightenment, sought out a teacher deep in the wilderness. He found the teacher sweeping leaves in the forest, apparently oblivious to the young man's presence. The young man tried speaking to the teacher but was completely ignored. Eventually, the student went to another part of the forest and began sweeping leaves himself. Years later, he was enlightened. He ran back through the forest to the teacher and said, "Thank you!"

Crow lifted his gaze from the hole in the ice and regarded his father, who appeared to be transfixed by the sight of his fishing line entering the icy water.

No way, he decided.

Something tugged at his line. Crow gave it a yank. No resistance. He reeled in the line. No minnow.

"Got a nibble there, son?"

"Did have." Crow scooped another minnow from the galvanized bucket and affixed it to his hook.

Sam pulled in his own line and examined his despondent minnow. He lowered it back into the icy water and watched it sink. "That George Murphy fellow, ain't he the one got you arrested?"

So Sam had been listening after all.

Crow said, "It was Johnson who busted me, but Murphy was behind it. The whole thing was just a way to get back at me for messing with Ricky. I always knew that it was George pulling the strings, but I never met him till a few days ago." A few days? It seemed like weeks. "When I think back on it, it was just as well. If George and Orlan hadn't nailed me, I'd've done it to myself."

"So you ain't still mad about it?"

Crow considered. "Oh, yeah. I'm still mad," he said. "The worst part of it was having to ask that son-of-a-bitch Getter for help."

Sam grinned, showing a set of long yellow teeth. "Don't like ol' Dave much, eh?"

Crow shook his head.

"Sort of a priss-butt, ain't he?"

"Something like that."

"That doctor fellow. You think he took that kid?"

Crow said, "I don't know if he *took* him, but my guess is he has him. Murphy said that they found the boy's hat at Bellweather's place. I don't know why he'd lie about something like that."

"Don't make sense to me. Even if the guy is a goddamn pre-vert it don't make sense. There's kids all over the place. Why grab one could get you killed?"

"I don't know."

"Where you think he went to?"

"I figure he's left town."

"Don't make sense. You say he's rich?"

"He sure acts like it."

"You think so? Seems to me, rich guys don't just disappear. They own too goddamn much stuff. It's like they got a leash on 'em."

"You sound like Debrowski."

"Who?"

"A friend of mine."

"What is he, Polish?"

"I don't know."

"Sounds Polish. I bet he's a hairy mother." Sam had an enormous collection of such gems. Poles are hairy. Finns always carry knives. Scots are inveterate liars. Crow steered the conversation back to Bellweather.

"Something must've happened that scared that doctor, Sam. He must've grabbed the boy and took off. Maybe he thinks the kid will buy him some kind of insurance. Maybe he thinks he can cut a deal with George Murphy. Whatever it is, it's not my concern. I'm out of it."

Sam nodded and reentered his ice-fishing trance. After a few minutes, he lifted his stubbly chin and asked, "You playing much cards these days?"

"Not much, Sam. You need money for that."

"That a fact? I ever tell you the time I won a bundle offa Amarillo Slim?"

"I thought it was Johnny Moss you won the bundle off of."

"Yeah, well, I played 'em both."

Sam claimed to have been a high-stakes player in his younger days. Claimed to have won millions playing no-limit poker from roadhouses in Brownsville, Texas, to the card clubs of Gardena, California. Crow believed maybe ten percent of it, sometimes less. Sam said he'd had to give up the road because of his stomach. "One thing you got to have, you want to sit in those games, you got to have an iron gut. Mine got rusted out. I play a few close hands, I get all twisted up inside. Poker's for you young fellows." Crow thought that the whiskey and cigarettes might have had something to do with his father's stomach problems, but he knew better than to argue.

"Down in Tulsa, must've been about nineteen hundred sixty-two, we was playing lowball back of a truck stop, me and Slim and a couple of the local ranchers, plus the old guy owned the truck stop. I can still see it, five guys sitting around with these big hats on. We always use to wear our Stetsons down there. Everybody wanted to be a damn Texan. Anyways, this trucker hears there's a game going, and he comes on back and wants us to deal him a hand. Only thing is, we're playing with a fifty-dollar ante—understand, that was big money in those days—and this boy only had three hundred dollars in his pocket, wants to sit in a few hands. Course, I don't want no part of that, but Slim says, Hell, boy, I'll take your three bills. Slim never could say no. So I say to the trucker, Fine, you just sit right down here and play. I'm going to take a walk. And that's what I did, goddamn it."

Sam jogged his line up and down, lit a cigarette. Was the story over? Crow couldn't be sure. Sam's stories often just trailed off without making a point. Crow unscrewed the top of his thermos and poured the last of the coffee into a plastic cup. It was still slightly warmer than body temperature. A few minutes later, as if a button had been pressed, Sam resumed his story.

"So I come back an hour later, and wouldn't you know it, the trucker'd got lucky and was sitting back of the biggest stack on the table. Ol' Slim is down to the ones, pulling bills off his roll looking like a dentist made to yank his own choppers. So I sat down and got back in the game. I busted that boy in about an hour."

"Slim?"

"No. The trucker. He had so goddamn much fresh money he didn't know what he was doing. See, one thing you always got to know is, who's got the money? Ol' Slim, he finally came back, but he didn't win a dime offa me. I took down close to twenty G's that game."

"That's great, Sam."

"Only reason I won was, I knew not to play against short money. A guy like that sits down at your table, what reason have you got to play against him? What do you think you're gonna win? He's got nothing to lose, and you're sitting there trying to protect your big stack. You might take his three hundred bucks nine times out of ten, but the tenth time he's going to rob you."

"Are you trying to tell me something?"

"Thing is, a guy that's got nothing to lose, he can afford to stir things up. Never know what a guy might turn up."

"A guy might turn up dead."

Sam shrugged. "You feelin' better today, son?"

Crow considered the question seriously. Physically, only a faint aching in his side remained. And he was having periods measured in minutes when he did not think about the Murphys, Bellweather, or Melinda. He thought he was feeling pretty good, considering that he had no resources, no money, and no hopes. Actually, that was no more true than it had ever been. He still had his VW, twenty pounds of frozen walleye, fifty-some bucks in cash, and the hope that his cat would come home. He'd left a bowl of food out on his apartment balcony.

"I feel fine, Sam."

"Like hell you do. You felt fine, you wouldn't be sitting in a damn ice-house with your old man. You'd get in the goddamn game. And if you're playing against a New Yorker, watch out he don't short the pot." Sam fixed him with a glare, daring him to agree—or disagree.

Crow reeled in his line. "Okay, Sam." He smiled, remembering a poem written by a Japanese monk who, after years of study, had attained his spiritual goal:

Now that I'm enlightened
I'm just as miserable as ever.

PART THREE

XVII

Never give a client advice regarding a decision he has already made for himself.

—RICH WICKY

eorge Murphy handed him a beer. "Get you loosened up for the hunt. You know what they say. One steadies the eye." He laughed. "Two, you're good looking. You ever hear that one?"

Anderson said, "Heard what one?"

"Three beers, I'm brilliant. Four, I'm bulletproof." Murphy tipped his head, his fleshy face sliding toward his left ear, and grinned. "Five, I'm invisible."

Anderson laughed politely and sipped the beer. It tasted sweet and wasn't quite cold enough, but he planned to drink it quickly. Midafternoon, only a couple hours of light left, and he wanted to get on with the hunt.

Murphy, however, seemed to be in no hurry. He leaned his butt against the edge of his desk, his muddy eyes fixed on Anderson.

Anderson held the opaque gaze for two seconds, then let his eyes slide away. Murphy seemed like a nice enough guy, but he made him uncomfortable. He looked around the office, which managed to be both spartan and cluttered at the same time. Other than the old desk, the homemade leather chair, a few hundred old magazines, potato chip bags, empty coffee cups, and a gun cabinet, the only notable feature in the room was an enormous stuffed pig.

"That's a big pig," Anderson said.

"Those are the real tusks. Six-inchers."

"So you think this elk is going to run over four hundred points?" Anderson asked.

"I guarantee it." That was when the interrogation began. "So what do you hear from your friend the doctor?" Murphy asked.

Anderson looked confused.

"Bellweather," Murphy prompted.

"Oh!" He had been trying to forget Dr. Bellweather altogether, put him out of mind.

"You talk to him lately?" Murphy had a funny look on his face.

Anderson said, "Not for a few days."

"You sure?" Murphy crossed his arms.

Anderson blinked. What was going on here? There was a distinct edge to Murphy's voice. He said, "I'm sure. We aren't doing business any longer."

"Oh? Why's that?"

The conversation was getting very uncomfortable. Anderson took a long swallow of beer. He had come here to hunt, not to talk about Dr. Bellweather. The beer foamed in his belly.

"He take his business to somebody else?" George said.

Anderson shook his head, not in answer to Murphy's question but in an effort to avoid it.

"I don't know," he said, ending his statement with a belch. "Excuse me."

Murphy said, "That's okay, Steve. Just us boys here. So what happened with you two? You have a falling-out? He make a pass at you or something?"

Anderson hunched his shoulders. He wasn't enjoying this conversation. Not good to be passing out information about a client, even if Bellweather *was* a child molester, as Murphy had claimed. Also, his parting of ways with the doctor had not been amicable. It did not reflect positively on his skills as a stock picker. The value of the doctor's account had nose-dived after the SEC seized the BioStellar corporate records, dropping the value of his account six figures into the nether zone, necessitating a margin call, which the doctor refused to honor. A very sticky affair, and still very much unresolved. Besides which, it was none of Murphy's goddamn business. Anderson decided to play a safety.

"It's history, George. Dr. Bellweather and Litten Securities are no longer doing business together, and I am not at liberty to discuss the particulars."

"You know where I can find him? He's not at home or at his clinic. I've been trying to get in touch with him."

Anderson shrugged. "Sorry."

"It's important," Murphy said, his voice flat. "You know what kind of guy he is, right?"

"I know what you told me. Look, I came out here to hunt elk, not talk shop."

Murphy leaned forward. "Let me tell you something you don't know. He has something that belongs to me."

"I'm sorry, George. My tongue is tied."

"He has my son, Shawn."

Anderson cleared his throat. Holding the beer bottle in both hands, he said, "Your son?"

"That's right."

"I don't understand."

"It's what I said. He has my son. You met him, didn't you? Shawn. A good kid."

"Jesus! Look, I don't know where he is. If I did, I'd tell you."

"So you don't know where he is?"

"I said I didn't."

Murphy held up his hands. "Okay, okay, I believe you. I was just asking, Steve. You don't want to tell me, that's okay. I understand."

"It's not a matter of what I want to tell you. I really don't know where he is." He looked at the beer bottle in his hand, set it on the desk among the coffee cups and back issues of *Outdoor Life*.

Murphy turned his head to look out his window, but his gaze was blunted by the frosted surface. "What's it like out there? Still snowing?"

"It's snowing."

Murphy nodded. "Good for hunting elk. They can't see you coming."

"Did you call the police?"

"They can't find him. Think about what he might do to my boy, Steve. You sure you can't think of where he might be?"

Anderson shook his head, trying to remember what the Murphy kid looked like.

"You know any of his friends? People he might stay with?"

Anderson considered. "Well," he said, "he has a brother."

"Ah. His name?"

"Well, it's Bellweather. Ned, I think. Or Nate."

Murphy leaned forward so far Anderson thought he was going to fall on his face. "Where's this Ned or Nate live?"

Anderson tipped his head back, gripping the arms of his chair. "It's Nate. Somewhere in Minneapolis, I think."

The office door opened, and Ricky walked in. His face was red, his Stetson studded with melting clumps of snow. He clapped his gloved hands, nodded at Anderson, then said to George, "Best get on with it, bro. She's gettin' thick out there."

"I've never seen a kid could eat like that, Nels. I've got to loosen my belt just to watch him."

Shawn pushed the last piece of cheese pizza into his mouth and pretended not to hear. He thought it was stupid the way Nate talked about him—like he wasn't even there. Like he was a dog or something.

Doc Bellweather said, "He's a growing boy, Nate. He needs his calories—don't you, Shawn?"

Shawn looked up and nodded, took another cheesy bite. No sausage, pepperoni, mushrooms, or any of that stuff. Shawn liked plain cheese, and lots of it.

"You sure polished off that pizza," Doc said. "You want some dessert?"

Shawn nodded, his mouth full. It was weird, spending all this time with Doc. Sometimes he acted really pissed, and then he would act really nice, like now.

"Why don't we all have some dessert, then. You've got cookies or something, don't you, Nate?"

Nate shouted, "Hey, Ginny! We got any cookies?"

Nate's wife, a pinch-faced woman wearing stretchy violet slacks and a beaded sweatshirt, appeared in the kitchen door.

"We got any cookies?" Nate repeated.

Ginny glared at each of them, then opened a cupboard door, pulled out a plastic tray of Oreos, slapped it on the table.

"I need you to help me with something," she said to Nate, her voice flat.

"Can't it wait, honey?"

"No."

Nate shrugged and followed his wife into the living room. Shawn twisted apart an Oreo, scraped the filling off with his front teeth before eating the black cookie part. He was on his sixth Oreo when Nate returned, his face a shade darker.

"So how long you planning on staying, Nels?" he asked.

"You having a little domestic problem, Nate?"

"Look, this was supposed to be just for one night. You've been here three days now. Ginny's getting perturbed. She doesn't like the idea of keeping . . ." He inclined his head toward Shawn. "You know. And the idea of those guys looking for us. I mean, you can't blame her for being worried."

Doc rolled his eyes, looked at Shawn, and winked. "Women," he said.

"I have to agree with her, Nels. What if they come looking for you here?"

"George doesn't even know I have a brother. He doesn't know you exist."

"Why don't you take a vacation. Maybe you could disappear for a while till this thing blows over."

"What, I'm supposed to grow a beard and sell watches to the tourists? It's not going to 'blow over,' Nate. If I have to disappear, I'm not going to do it broke."

"I still can't believe it. All the money you've made, and you don't have *anything?*"

"I explained this to you, Nate. My property has been seized. You know what that means?"

"I don't see why you can't just declare bankruptcy. Don't you get to keep your house? Don't the courts protect you from your creditors?"

"Not from the IRS they don't. And not from George Murphy. Look. In the last three years I've gotten divorced, which cost me a fortune. I've been hit with a few big malpractice suits that I had to settle for cash. And then the feds go back five years and disallow close to half a million dollars in legitimate deductions."

Nate rolled his eyes. "Imagine that. They wouldn't let you deduct your hunting trips."

"I used those trips to promote my practice. And to observe medical techniques used by surgeons in other nations. You wouldn't believe the size of the boob implants they're using down in Buenos Aires. Anyway, I could've handled the tax bill until that twerp Anderson, who's supposed to be *earning* money for me, manages to lose every last dime I had on the market. I miss my deadline with the feds, and the next thing you know, I'm sleeping on my brother's couch."

Shawn wasn't following much of this, but he liked the part about the boob implants. Doc looked about as mad as he'd ever seen him. Nate was mad too. When Ricky and his dad would have their arguments, or when Grandy got pissed off, that was scary. But watching Doc fight with his brother, that was kind of funny.

"Yeah, well, you don't have to sleep on it anymore."

"Oh, really? You want me to get killed?"

"I just don't see you staying here with this kid, that's all."

The doctor sat back in his chair and drummed his fingertips on the table. "Look, all I've got to do is come up with enough money to get me out of the country, get myself set up in Guttmann's clinic."

"Guttmann?"

"That doctor I met when I was hunting jaguar down in Costa Rica. He has a cosmetic-surgery practice in San José, does eyelids and chins for every rich bitch from Guatemala to the Panama Canal. He's just getting started in liposuction and as much as told me I could buy into his clinic."

Nate crossed his arms. "I told you, I don't have any money to spare."

The doctor shook his head. "I'd need about a hundred grand, plus money to live on till I get my own practice going. It's not cheap down there. I'll need money to make it work. Look, I just need a day or two to work it out, okay? Maybe I can coax a loan from some of the guys I went to school with."

"You haven't used them all up already?"

"I suppose I have." He sighed.

Shawn didn't get it. Doc kept insisting he was broke, but he had a whole house full of *stuff*. "I thought you were rich," he said.

"Sorry to disappoint you, kid." He tapped his chin with a forefinger, gave him a funny sort of stare. "Actually," he said slowly, "I do have one thing that might be worth something."

"What's that? Your car?"

Doc laughed and rubbed Shawn's back. "Oh, yeah," he said. "I've got that too."

Shawn grabbed another handful of cookies, looked up, and caught Nate staring at the depleted Oreo package, the corners of his mouth turned down. Shawn grinned, his teeth coated with black-and-white cookie.

Dr. Nelson Bellweather's house showed no sign of occupation. A light dusting of snow lay undisturbed on the walk. An official-looking white notice was tacked to the front door. Crow got out of his car, walked up the steps, and read it.

He returned to his car, drove out of Orchard Estates, and took the shore road around Maxwell Bay and across a narrow isthmus. After several wrong turns, he found Applewood Curve and followed it to a low, sprawling house that looked out over Stubbs Bay. He parked in the meticulously plowed driveway and sat for a minute, trying to imagine living in such a place. There was something cold about it, reminding him of Bellweather's living room. Pale-gray stone, flat white trim, acres of glass over white-on-white drapery. The snowbound landscaping displayed a painful symmetry. Crow took a breath and got out of the car. The flagstone walk was dotted with deicing pellets. Minnesota safe.

Brass script on the white lintel spelled out the house number: One Thousand Eighty-Seven. Two matching four-foot-tall urns, featureless, white, and empty, flanked the door. Crow pressed the doorbell.

Mary Getter opened the door and smiled. "Joe! What a surprise!" It wasn't a bad smile, although a little crinkling around the eyes would have improved it. "Come in. I wasn't expecting you. How are you?"

"I'm fine, Mary." Crow stepped in through the front door. As always, the interior of the Getter residence was ready for a *House Beautiful* photo session. The Suburban Sterile look. He was suddenly conscious of his own appearance, which the Lake Mille Lacs fishing trip had not improved. Beard, jeans, and jacket, all going on three days. His hands reeked of fish, even after a thorough scrubbing at the Amoco station in Garrison. Maybe he should have gone back to his apartment first, changed clothes. The hell with it. She was his sister. She'd seen him in worse shape than this.

"How are you?" he asked.

"We're fine," she said.

"Is Dave home?"

Mary shook her head. "He's at work."

"Good. I wanted to talk to you."

"Oh?" She grimaced bravely, stretching her mouth out in a parody of her usual smile. He imagined he could hear the inner gates slamming shut.

"Do you have any coffee on?"

"I can make some."

"That's okay. Don't bother."

Mary took a step back, pirouetted, and headed toward the rear of the house. "It's no trouble."

Crow followed her into a spacious kitchen that looked as though food were not permitted within its sterile confines.

"I've been fishing," he said. She wouldn't ask him what he was doing there, or why he reeked of sweat, kerosene fumes, cigarettes, and dead walleye. She wouldn't even ask him about the fading bruise on his jaw. He could show up wearing a burlap sack and a top hat, and she still wouldn't ask. Nevertheless, he felt the need to explain. "I went up to Mille Lacs with Sam."

"Oh?" she said. Mary did not care for Sam. Their mother, Virginia Crow, had raised them without a father. Shortly after her death—Joe was eighteen, Mary two years older—Sam O'Gara had appeared, claiming to have sired them. Joe believed it, Mary would not. He couldn't be her father, no matter what he claimed.

"We were ice fishing."

Mary nodded, filled the coffeemaker, turned it on, then flipped on the exhaust fan over the stove. A quiet hum filled the air. Mary stood beside the coffeemaker and waited, holding her hands in a knot. Ignoring her discomfort, Crow examined his sister. Thirty-five years old, she dressed and carried herself like a well-preserved forty-five. Her pale hair was cut short and expensive, with nicely done golden highlights that would look natural come August. Loose, cream-colored twill slacks, an expensive-looking, oversize taupe cardigan, gray-on-ecru loafers—it should have been a study in home-alone casual, an outfit Martha Stewart might wear to entertain the neighbor's Persian cat, but his sister was cursed with an inner tension, emitting a jangle of concern, uncertainty, fear, and disapproval. The overall effect was as if she was channeling a mildly hysterical June Cleaver. Crow might have suggested this possibility to her, but he was sure she'd have informed him that June Cleaver was a fictional character and not available for channeling. Mary's sense of humor had atrophied over the years.

She hadn't always been that way. Mary had once had a quick wit, an infectious laugh, and a tough, practical core. After picking up a Studio Arts degree at the U, she'd spent her twenties working a variety of jobs, running with a diverse collection of artists, musicians, poets, and other shaggy, earringed, disaffected sorts, trying new things, having a good time. She'd survived a succession of interesting boyfriends, maintained a studio in a decaying warehouse on the fringes of downtown Minneapolis, and she'd even sold a few of the quirky painted wooden assemblages that she constructed in the small-morning hours.

Crow had liked his big sister. They'd gotten along great back then, going out to hear live music whenever he was in town, having a few drinks, comparing notes on their ever tumultuous love lives.

But in her late twenties Mary began to change. At first, Crow thought it was a temporary thing, a love affair gone wrong, money troubles, something fixable. Her laugh lines became worry lines, her wide, curious eyes narrowed. She became sadder and slower and intolerant of her friends' laissez-faire attitudes. A cloud of desperation settled over her. One day, sitting in the New French Bar drinking beer, she'd said to him, "Joe, I'm thirty years old. I want to be a grown-up. I want to live in a real house. I want a baby."

Crow, who had never wanted any of those things, had said, "You're nuts. What do you want a kid for? You aren't even married."

Stupid damn thing to say. Next thing he knew, she'd given up her studio, joined a Unitarian church, and begun to dress more conservatively—letting her hair revert to its natural color, ordering new clothing, none of it black, from Lands' End and L. L. Bean. The new Mary met Dave Getter at a church-sponsored singles night. A few weeks later, she went to work for him in his office, and within three months they were married.

Crow had tried to like his new brother-in-law but failed utterly.

As Getter's law practice grew more profitable, Mary continued to evolve. She started highlighting her hair and buying her clothing from Saks and Cedric's, creating a more expensive Mary. Her face became more masklike, her mutated laugh lines disappearing from lack of use. She became a grown-up and got her house, but she showed no signs of fertility. Apparently she or Dave had a problem, but Mary never spoke of it and Crow didn't ask. He suspected that her failure to conceive had triggered the latest phase in her evolution—she had discovered the New Age.

Crow did not know whether it was Mary or Melinda who first discovered the healing powers of crystals, homeopathic medicines, and the channeled words of the Ascended Masters. Their friendship had, at first, delighted him. When Melinda began her serious study of the tarot, he had thought it little more than an amusing diversion. And when the two of them had flown down to Sedona for a weekend to attend a workshop on something called "synchronized harmonic attunement," he had thought of it as a women's version of a fishing trip.

But now, with Melinda becoming a stranger, their shared interest in alternative philosophies seemed to him to be a threat. They spoke a language he did not understand; they seemed able to communicate with each other but not with him. Melinda had once told him that she and Mary had discovered that they had been sisters in a former life. She'd speculated that her attraction to him was a resonance from that former life. "It's almost incestuous, us being married," she'd said.

It reached the point where Crow could not think of one without the other—the two women became welded in his mind, and he caught himself saying Mary when he meant Melinda, and vice versa. To avoid embarrassing mistakes, he took to calling them "my wife" and "my sister." Maybe Melinda was right. On some level he did not understand, they were the same.

The coffeemaker belched; a thin, dark stream flowed into the glass carafe.

"This is from Kenya," Mary said. "We joined a club where they send us a different kind of coffee every month. They roast it the same day they ship it."

"It smells good." It smelled great, especially after the gallons of Taster's Choice he'd chugged trying to stay warm on the Mille Lacs ice. Mary filled a blue mug, handed it to him.

"I made it," she said.

"I know," said Crow. "I watched you do it."

Mary's brow wrinkled. "I mean the mug."

"Oh!" He held up the mug and examined it: beautifully turned, with thin walls, a large, graceful handle, and a translucent glaze. "Nice. I heard you'd become a potter. Melinda mentioned it. I had dinner with Melinda a few nights ago, you know."

Mary shifted her eyes to the floor. "I know."

"Have you talked to her lately?"

Mary opened the cabinet under the sink, took a pink sponge from the wire rack on the inside of the door, moistened it, and wiped at an invisible spot on the tile floor. She nodded.

Crow said, "She's still using."

Mary attacked another spot. "She's having a hard time, Joe. She's out of balance." She rinsed the sponge, squeezed it dry, and replaced it in its rack.

"So am I."

"She told me you walked out on her in the middle of the night."

"Walked out on her? She was sitting at her kitchen table doing lines. What was I supposed to do, chop her coke for her?"

Mary touched her lips to the dark surface of her coffee. "So you went fishing."

"Are you trying to tell me something? What else did she say?"

Mary shook her head. "She said after you left, a policeman woke her up, pounding on her door, looking for you. Are you in some kind of trouble again, Joe? She said he was very threatening, looking for you. Can you imagine what that must have been like for her? The middle of the night? Are you in trouble again?"

"No more than usual. What policeman?"

"She said it was that man you used to work for."

"Johnson?" Crow sensed a wave of concern and protectiveness rolling in. He flattened it with a series of hard thoughts. She'd probably been sitting with her coke and her mirror, doing more lines. Probably scared the hell out of her. Served her right. He could see her sitting at the kitchen table, pale eyes challenging him. Challenging him to what? He made the image black and white, reduced it to wallet size.

"She'd better clean up her act," he said.

Mary did not reply.

Crow's fingers were wrapped around the coffee cup, squeezing it.

There was something here he didn't understand. She was his sister; she was Melinda's closest friend. He wanted to grab her, shake her, make her tell him what he had to do. Or tell him there was nothing he *could* do. Be straight with him for once. Inside this New Age crystal-head Stepford wife was his real sister, the old Mary Crow. He hadn't seen any sign of her in half a decade, but she was in there someplace.

He had to get off the subject of Melinda. Crow forced his mind to consider other issues. He'd been out of touch for three days. Had George Murphy gotten his kid back? Why was Orlan Johnson banging on Melinda's door? And where the hell was that doctor?

"I was just over at Dr. Bellweather's house," he said.

Mary's shoulders dropped back to their normal position, making him realize that she had been at least as tense as he. Her hands fluttered in a sudden release of energy. She sat down across the table from him.

"Oh?"

"There's a notice from the IRS on his front door. His property has been seized."

She tipped her head to the side, smiling, performing a slight brow crinkle. "I didn't know that," she said. She dropped her hands to her thighs.

"Has Dave said anything?"

She shook her head. "I was supposed to see him tomorrow. Maybe he'll be at his clinic."

"You were supposed to see Bellweather?"

"A follow-up appointment. He did a procedure on me a few weeks ago." She stood up and stepped back from the table, smoothed her slacks over her hips, unleashed a catalog smile. "Didn't you notice? I've lost ten pounds!"

The snowmobile bounced and ground its way through the storm, following a faint trail through the tangle of gray trees, fallen logs, windfalls, and brush. The gray sky descended and grew darker, spilling large clumps of snowflakes. Anderson buried his head behind George Murphy's wide back and waited out the ride, which turned out to be mercifully short. Less than five minutes from the lodge, the snowmobile stopped and Murphy shut down the engine.

"We'd best walk in from here," he said.

Anderson looked up. The snow was coming down harder. How were they supposed to find an elk in this kind of weather, let alone shoot one?

"Maybe we should try this tomorrow," Anderson said.

Murphy laughed. "Take my word for it, Steve, this is perfect weather for elk. I bet we can walk right up on the old bastard. Grab your gun and let's go!"

Anderson slung his Weatherby over his shoulder and trudged after Murphy, breaking through the crust, sinking knee high in the snow. He was thinking, Twenty thousand dollars? He followed Murphy's dark shape up the side of a tree-covered slope. When they reached the top, Murphy signaled a halt. The far side of the slope fell away quickly into a coulee, a narrow valley with sides so steep that areas of rock and naked earth showed through where the snow refused to settle.

Murphy pitched his voice low and said, "I think we got lucky, Steve. I think I see something." He pointed across the coulee toward the opposite slope. Anderson squinted into the snow. At first, all he could see was a mass of twisted, muted gray shapes. How far were they from the other side of the coulee? He guessed about fifty yards.

"There, on the far ridge, under that old oak."

Anderson looked harder and made out a shape that looked somewhat elk-like beneath the spreading limbs of a tree. He felt his heart start to pulse, felt the hairs moving on the back of his neck, felt his hands begin to shake.

"You see him now?" Murphy whispered.

Anderson nodded.

"You better take 'm. Might not get another shot like this one."

"You sure that's the one? I can hardly see him."

"That's him, all right."

Anderson lifted the rifle to his shoulder. He was shaking with buck fever, overloaded with primal hormones, breathing too quickly. He heard Murphy say, as if from miles away, "Take it easy, Steve. Take your time now. Squeeze it off, nice and easy. He's all yours. . . ."

He didn't even feel the kick of the rifle. The sound of the shot instantly melted into the thick snow. Nothing happened for a few silent seconds, then the elk shape collapsed like a puppet whose strings had been suddenly severed.

XVIII

'm sorry, Mr. Crow. Mr. Getter's busy at the moment."

"Really? Doing what?"

"I don't know. Would you like to wait?"

"No. Tell him I'm here."

Andrea, David Getter's receptionist/secretary/apologist, looked at her nails, conveying the message that the scarlet growths on the tips of her fingers were of far greater interest than the disreputable-looking, fishy-smelling Joe Crow. Andrea had been with Getter for over five years, long enough to strip her of any empathic inclinations. During those years she had insulated herself with an ever thicker layer of body fat, makeup, and attitude. She looked as though she had spent her entire life sitting behind that desk, growing thick, nylon-clad roots. Crow found it impossible to imagine her in any other setting.

"He asked not to be disturbed."

"I don't care." Crow hoisted a hip onto the edge of Andrea's desk and picked up her paperweight, a lump of fake crystal with a rosebud embedded in its center.

"Please don't sit on my desk," she said, leaning back. Her voice had a grating, nasal edge to it, a childhood whine evolved into something resembling a foghorn.

Crow lifted the phone receiver and handed it to her. "Call him."

Andrea sighed and took the phone with a sour expression, punched two buttons, then said, "Mr. Getter? Mr. Crow is here to see you."

She held the phone for a moment, then replaced it in its cradle.

"He's not in," she said.

"Oh, really? When did he leave?"

"I do not know. I believe he had an appointment."

Crow heard a door close.

"I think I'll just take a look in his office." Crow walked past Andrea's desk.

"You can't go in there," she honked. But she didn't move from her station.

Getter's office was empty. A suit jacket was draped over the back of his leather chair. Crow sat behind the desk. The chair molded itself to his body like a soft leather glove. It was still warm. Crow flipped through the Rolodex. All the cards were neatly typed.

Bellweather, Dr. Nelson. There was only one address—Bellweather's house—and two phone numbers—his home and office. Nothing Crow didn't have already.

There was no card for Nate Bellweather.

Flipping open Getter's desk calendar, he read through the day's entries. Getter's handwriting was excruciatingly neat. *9:30—haircut. 11:00—CPA. 4:30—Sinnamon.* It looked like an easy day.

Crow looked at the marble desk clock: 2:30 P.M. If Getter had stepped out to keep an appointment, it hadn't been important enough to note on his calendar. Not as important as a haircut, for instance. Or as important as Sinnamon, whoever or whatever that was.

He felt the pockets of the suit jacket that Getter had left hanging on his chair, extracted Getter's wallet—some exotic hide that Crow didn't recognize—and flipped through its contents. Eighty dollars in cash, an assortment of credit cards, business cards, and miscellaneous receipts. Crow was disappointed. He'd been hoping for something sordid and incriminating. The two side pockets had been left sewn shut to keep them from bagging out, as had the front breast pocket. The watch pocket, however, contained a business card from Myoka's Health Club.

"Ah," said Crow. He turned the card and read the girlish script on the back: *Sinnamon.* A little heart dotted the *i.* Crow smiled.

The fact that Getter had left without his coat or wallet indicated that he could not have gone far. There was a second door leading out of his office. Crow opened it and discovered a copier, several file cabinets, and another door, which led out into the hallway. It made sense that Getter would have two bolt-holes. Skunks employed a similar strategy. Crow walked down the hall and entered the men's room. He looked under the doors of the three stalls and discovered a pair of thin-soled, tasseled Italian loafers. The style was right. He entered the next stall, stood on the toilet, and looked over the divider at the thinning crown of David Getter's head.

The *Wall Street Journal* lay across his lap, covered by an open copy of a skin magazine, two bored-looking, big-chested blondes engaging in a bout of amateur gynecology.

"You forgot something," Crow said.

Getter twitched violently and ducked. He twisted his head to the side and looked up at Crow, scowling.

"What the hell, Joe?"

"You're supposed to take your pants down, Dave. You forgot that part."

Getter stood up, folded the paper around the magazine, tucked it under his arm, and exited the stall.

"What do you want, Joe?"

"Where's Bellweather?"

"I have no idea."

"I don't believe you. I thought you knew everything."

Getter turned on the faucet, soaped his hands, and rinsed them off. When he pulled a paper towel from the dispenser, the newspaper and its contents fell to the floor. *Hustler.* He didn't pick them up.

"Where is he?" Crow said.

"I told you, I don't know." Getter's voice was calm and matter-of-fact. If Crow didn't know him, he might have believed it.

"What's his status with the IRS?"

Getter smiled. "He's a client, Joe. I'm not free to discuss it."

"There's a notice pinned to his door," Crow said. "Something about his property being seized. The man owes me money, Dave. I'd like to see it."

"There's nothing I can do about that, Joe." Getter stood with his back to the sink, gripping it with both hands, slouching slightly in an effort to appear relaxed. He smiled, his lips pressed tight together.

Crow stared at the lawyer and thought about how it would feel to hurt him. He could feel his muscles loosening, his internal controls dissolving. To his own surprise, he realized that he was dangerously close to punching out his brother-in-law. He took a step back and looked away. As soon as his eyes left Getter's face, he felt better.

Getter bent over and picked up his *Journal/Hustler* taco. He folded his arms over the newspaper and tipped his head back a few degrees.

Crow imagined his fist striking the point of Getter's chin.

It would feel really, really good.

He would probably break his hand.

He turned woodenly and walked out of the rest room.

So far, Dave Getter, attorney-at-law, was having an uncomfortable afternoon. The club sandwich he'd eaten for lunch was clawing at his duodenum, and the confrontation he'd had with Mary's brother—the little prick jumping him in the can—had him all tensed up. On the other hand, he had won the encounter. Hadn't given the little prick a thing. Who did he think he was, demanding information that was none of his business? Getter derived a twist of pleasure from the power he'd wielded so effectively. Maybe if the little shit had asked nice, he would have told him something.

And then first thing he gets back to his desk, Andrea puts through a call from Bellweather, the other little prick in his life.

"Your bodyguard was just here," Getter said.

"Who? Crow? What did he want?"

"I think he wants his paycheck."

"Yeah, right. Did I tell you what he did? He went out to the ranch and talked to George. Came back and gave me a bunch of shit. You didn't tell him where I was, did you?"

"Are you still at Nate's?"

"For the moment."

"I didn't tell him anything. Where are you going?"

"I don't know yet, but we're out of here. David, how would you like to make some money?"

"Does this mean you're going to take care of your bill?"

"Of course I am. But I'm talking about something else. Something quick."

"I don't suppose this has anything to do with the Murphy kid, does it?"

"It might."

"I thought I told you to drop him off on a street corner someplace. Don't you have enough troubles?"

"Look, do you want to hear it or not? All I need is for you to make a few phone calls for me."

"Yeah, right."

"Are you listening?"

"I'm listening."

• • •

After hanging up the phone, Getter stared down at his desk blotter and tried to convince himself that this scheme of Bellweather's was worth the risk. He turned on his PC, logged onto his quotation service, and reviewed his diminished stock portfolio. Things had not improved in the past few hours. Alsace Technologies was still in the toilet, as was Eastwest Computer. Both stocks had been strongly recommended by Steve Anderson, Bellweather's ex-stockbroker. That had been back when Anderson was making tons of money for the doctor. After listening to Anderson's pitch, Getter had plunged all the cash he could get his hands on into the market. Fortunately, he reminded himself, he had backed away from investing in BioStellar GameTech. Unlike his client the doctor, he was only half broke.

Bellweather's idea—Getter refused to think of it as kidnapping or extortion—had come along at just the right time. If it worked. His role in the process would be that of mediator rather than participant. It wasn't as if he had planned it. Not like he had grabbed the kid himself. In fact, the kid had run away on his own. Getter's ethical position was that his client was in trouble and it was his job to help him out. Negotiate a settlement between the doctor and the Murphys. That was what lawyers did, wasn't it?

Nevertheless, he was not eager to talk to George Murphy. It would put him in a precarious legal position, to say the least. He would have to be careful. Get the message across to Murphy without coming right out and saying it. Take on the role of a disinterested third party. If the money didn't look so good, he'd flat out refuse to have any part of it. Getter made himself relax, dreaming about the money for a few minutes, spending it in his mind. Then he picked up the phone.

Anderson tossed back his fourth Scotch and soda and grinned. "By God," he said, "I did it!"

"You sure did," said George Murphy.

"I took the son-of-a-bitch!"

"With one shot," said Murphy. "An elk that size, that's not easy. Must've been a heart shot, the way he dropped."

"Christ, I don't even remember aiming. I was shaking in my pants."

"You looked pretty cool to me," Murphy said. This was not his favorite thing. But it was business. Sitting around watching one of his clients get drunk, reliving the hunt, shooting the damned thing over and over again, like working the remote on a VCR. You had to let them do it, have a few drinks, get the whole experience burned into their brains. It was always the same. He wished Anderson would hurry up and wind down.

"I can't wait to hang that sucker up. It's going right over the fireplace, no matter what Patty says."

George doubted that, but he said nothing. He was having trouble staying with Anderson's jubilant mood. Now that he'd taken care of the elk problem, Shawn's disappearance hung on him. Unpleasant imaginings buzzed gnatlike in his mind. He would brush them away, but they would gather strength and return. Flashes of Shawn and Bellweather. He was anxious to hear from Ricky, who had gone to pay Nate Bellweather a visit. With any luck, he would find both Bellweathers, and Shawn.

"You think it'll go over four hundred points?"

"I guaranteed it, didn't I?" In fact, he had measured Number One's antlers the day they'd found him dead in the north pasture. The rack had scored out at four hundred eighteen points. "Fact, I betcha it'll go over four fifteen."

Anderson gaped. "No shit? Four fifteen. That'll make the record book." He poured himself another slug of Scotch, this time skipping the soda water. "What a great hunt," he said.

George Murphy smiled, thinking back to that morning, when he and Ricky had spent two hours rigging the dead elk, hanging it in a jerry-rigged harness from the limb of the old oak. It had worked perfectly. The snowstorm had been a stroke of luck. In clear weather, even an idiot like Anderson might not have been fooled. He thought back to the first time Number One had been shot. Killed by a slug from a single-shot .22. That in itself was remarkable, that a fifteen-hundred-pound animal could be felled by a bit of soft lead no larger than a corn kernel. He felt an unexpected wave of pride for his son, the hunter.

Anderson was asking about the mount, wanting to know how long it would take.

"You tell Ollie I sent you," George said. "He'll give you the good service."

Amanda Murphy walked into the lodge, holding the cordless phone, a peculiar expression on her face. His heart jumped. Was it Ricky? So soon? He'd left only an hour and a half ago, but the way Ricky drove, anything was possible.

Mandy thrust the phone at him, antenna first. Murphy took it, smiled apologetically at Anderson, put the phone to his ear, and grunted a hello into the mouthpiece.

"George Murphy?"

"That's right," he admitted. Mandy was peering at him intently.

"This is David Getter. I'm an attorney."

"Yeah?" He gave Mandy a look. She crossed her arms and gave it right back to him. "What can I do for you?" he asked. "Somebody gonna sue me?"

"I understand your son ran away," Getter said.

Murphy sat up straight. "Yeah?" He stood, walked toward his office. He wasn't sure he knew where this conversation was going to go, but it would be better if Steve Anderson didn't hear it.

"I'm calling on behalf of a client who wishes to inquire about the reward."

"Reward? What reward?" He reached his office, closed the door.

"You aren't offering a reward for the safe return of your son?"

"How would you like to tell me who your client is?"

"He has asked to remain anonymous."

"But we both know which piece of dogshit we're talking about, don't we, Mr. Getter?"

"I'm sorry, but I can't discuss my client's identity."

Murphy sat in his chair, closed his eyes. "Tell me what you want, Mr. Getter."

"Ah, yes . . . My client has reason to believe that if you were to offer a reward of, say, three hundred thousand dollars, there would be a very good chance that he could locate your son."

Murphy couldn't believe it, but there it was. The son-of-a-bitch was asking for ransom. "Mind if I ask how you came up with that figure?"

"It's my client's suggestion. I'm simply passing it on to you."

"Are you sure you want to do this, Mr. Getter?"

"I don't understand."

George said, "Let me tell you something. If my son were to suddenly show up here on my doorstep, I would not be ungrateful. I might even pay over a small reward. But if I thought he had been kidnapped and if I was forced to ransom him . . . well, I might hold a grudge. You know what I mean."

Getter cleared his throat. "My client asked me to tell you that . . . ah . . . the matter is not open to negotiation."

"I see. I'm going to have to think about it. How can I get in touch with you?"

"I'll call you back." The line went dead.

Murphy opened his eyes. His mother was standing in the doorway to his office, her eyes crackling.

"I could feel him," she said. "I could smell the taint."

XIX

There are characters wearing hockey masks in low-budget teen-exploitation movies who show more care with sharp instruments. It sounded like a bunch of grade-school boys playing with Jell-O.

—A PHYSICIAN, AFTER VIEWING A LIPOSUCTION PROCEDURE

The receptionist at the West End Clinic wanted to know if he had an appointment.

"No, I don't," Crow told her. "It's a personal matter. I'm trying to locate Dr. Bellweather. It's important."

The receptionist pursed her collagen-inflated lips and asked him to have a seat. Crow had a seat. He picked up an *Architectural Digest* and flipped through the pages, looking at each photo. He saw little he liked and nothing he could afford. A moment later, a tired-looking man with tortoiseshell glasses entered the waiting room and approached him.

"I'm Dr. Neal. What can we do for you?"

Crow put down the magazine. "I'm looking for Dr. Bellweather."

"Are you one of his patients?"

"I've been doing some work for him."

"I'm sorry, but Dr. Bellweather is no longer associated with this clinic."

"Do you know where I can find him?"

Dr. Neal shook his head slowly. "I'm sorry, but I don't."

"Was there some problem?" Crow asked.

"I really can't say."

"I understand," said Crow, who didn't. Another thought occurred to him. "By the way, Dr. Bellweather told me I'd be paid through the clinic. Could you look and see whether there's a check here for me?" It was a long shot but worth asking.

Dr. Neal solemnly shook his head.

"You won't look, or there's no check?"

"Both," said the doctor. He clicked on a smile and held it until Crow turned and left the clinic.

Shawn climbed into the Jag and immediately started playing with the radio, while Dr. Bellweather stowed his bag in the trunk. Nate stood in the driveway, arms crossed over his flannel shirt, face expressionless.

"You gonna be okay?" he asked.

"I'll send you a postcard," Bellweather said.

The front door opened, and Ginny stuck her head out. "Nate, you get inside. You'll freeze to death without a coat."

Nate started back toward the house.

"She has you trained," the doctor said.

Nate said, "Fuck you, Nels." He entered the house without looking back. The doctor climbed into his car, put it in gear, backed out onto the street.

"You know what you should do?" Shawn asked.

"No, I don't."

"You should do like my dad does with his money."

Bellweather smiled indulgently, shifted to first, started toward the freeway. "Oh? And what does he do?"

"You should save your money. What my dad does is, when he gets a bunch of money he saves some of it. Then when he needs money he always has some."

Doc gave Shawn an appraising look. "Stuffs it in his mattress, I suppose."

Shawn knew he shouldn't be telling his dad's secrets, but Doc looked so interested and impressed, he couldn't stop himself. "He puts it in his safe," he said.

"George has a safe?"

Shawn nodded. He had the doctor's full attention now. "It's my secret 'heritance. I saw him put some money in it one time, and he made me promise not to tell my uncle or Grandy. I bet he has a million dollars. You know where it is?"

Bellweather shook his head.

"You know Louise, his pig? She's got this, like, little door in one side."

Doc took his foot off the gas. "Louise? Are you talking about that stuffed pig he has in his office?"

Shawn nodded. "You should do that. Get a safe for your money, so you don't run out. That would be the smart thing to do."

Andrea put through another call from Bellweather.

"Well?"

"I talked to him," Getter said. "He was upset."

"I bet he was." Bellweather laughed, hitting a high note that caused Getter to jerk the phone away from his ear. "So what did he say?"

"What do you think? He wants his boy back."

"And?"

"I told him what it would cost, and he said he'd have to think about it."

Bellweather did not reply. Getter let him hang for ten seconds, then said, "I called him back."

"Don't pull my chain, Dave."

"I'm not. He's agreed to our terms, with one exception."

"What would that be?"

"He wants to meet us at the ranch."

"That's funny. Did you laugh?"

"I said we'd get back to him."

"Good. Let him stew for a couple hours, then call him back and tell him you'll meet him halfway. Tell him you'll meet him at Birdy's."

"Meet him? Hey, I'm just handling the phone calls. I thought you understood that."

"I'm not paying this kind of money for phone work. You have to be there."

"I don't want to get within ten miles of that kid."

"Don't worry about it. You tell George to meet you at Birdy's. Tomorrow morning, ten o'clock. I'll be a few minutes away, at a phone. I'll call a little after ten. All you have to do is tell me if he's there and if he has the money. Then you tell him that I'm on my way. Then you leave."

"And what are you going to do?"

"Are you sure you want to know?"

"You're right. I don't want to know anything."

"That's very lawyerly of you."

"How do I get my share?"

"I'll get it to you."

"I don't know that I'm comfortable with that."

Bellweather laughed. "If you want, you can wait at Birdy's."

Getter cleared his throat. "I'll have to think about that."

"Fine. You think about it. In the meantime, set up the meeting." Bellweather broke the connection.

Getter sat behind his desk, staring at his diploma on the wall. Every few minutes, he checked his watch. At four-fifteen, he put on his suit jacket and overcoat. Forget Bellweather. He had more important things to do. Maybe he would make the call to Murphy later, if he felt like it.

"I'm gone for the day, Andrea," he said. "Stay with the phone till five, okay? If Mary calls again, tell her I'm in a meeting."

Andrea watched him leave without comment.

Thirty minutes later, Getter was beginning to feel much better, and shortly after four fifty-three he enjoyed five and one quarter seconds of genital-centered ecstasy. He was so pleased with himself he tipped Sinnamon an extra twenty bucks and didn't even bother to put his tie back on or button his overcoat when he walked out of the steamy confines of Myoka's Health Club and into the chilly winter predusk. A few flakes of snow drifted down, striking the black, salted surface of the street, melting on contact. He noticed a man standing directly in front of him, blocking his exit, holding a small yellow box in front of his face. Getter hesitated, not sure what he was seeing, when a tiny, bright light flashed in his eyes.

Crow said, "These are great. You walk into a store, pay them nine ninety-five plus tax, and you walk out with a cardboard camera all loaded up and ready to shoot. It's even got a flash." He grinned, looked through the camera, and snapped off another shot of Dave Getter standing in front of Myoka's Health Club. "Of course, I don't know about the quality. If they're any good, I'll make sure you and Mary get copies."

Getter slowly buttoned his overcoat. "This is low, even for you, Joe." He walked around Crow and headed down the sidewalk toward his Mercedes.

Crow put the disposable camera in his coat pocket and followed. "I agree," he said. "I've been feeling sort of low. So what?"

Getter stopped and turned around. "What do you want?"

"You know what I want. I want to know where Bellweather is. I want to know why his house is posted."

"I'm doing some legal work for Myoka. Those pictures you took, they don't mean a thing."

Crow smiled. The fact that Getter was bothering to tell him the photos weren't important meant that they were. "I know that, Dave. I probably won't even bother to get them developed."

"Good." Getter buried his hands in his coat pockets and walked away. The snow was coming down harder, dotting the shoulders of his overcoat.

Crow fell in beside him, saying, "This snow is supposed to get worse. I hear they're really getting hit out west of here."

"How awful." He stopped beside his Mercedes. "You know, I was thinking. Bellweather is your client too. We both have his interests at heart, right?"

"Of course," said Crow.

"I suppose a little shared information—just between us—maybe it would be a good thing."

"Do you think so?"

Getter nodded, as though considering a clever suggestion. "Look, I can't tell you where he is, because I don't know. As you know, he's having a little problem with the IRS."

"I gathered as much, seeing as they've seized his property."

"Yes. It's been an ongoing problem for him."

"You're telling me he's hiding from the IRS?"

"I don't know. I really don't. He's got three lawsuits pending against him, a half million owing in back taxes, and a number of creditors, including you and me. I wouldn't be in his shoes for anything."

"You're his attorney, right? Doesn't that sort of put you in his shoes?"

"Not really. A few months ago, he ran into a nasty lawsuit from one of his patients and asked me to handle it for him."

"I thought all these guys have insurance for that sort of thing."

"He didn't want to go to his insurance company with this one. He performed a routine lipectomy on a woman and caused her navel to migrate."

"What?" Crow wasn't sure he'd heard that one right.

"After the procedure, she claimed her belly button was two inches off center. It wouldn't have been a big deal, except that he'd had some other problems before and he was afraid his malpractice insurance wouldn't be renewed. I was able to negotiate a quick and quiet settlement for twenty thousand plus fees, which really impressed him. It could've cost him his practice if I hadn't been there. He liked the way I handled it so much, he told me about all the other problems he was having."

"More migrating belly buttons?"

"Nothing so cut-and-dried. He took a little fat off this one girl's thighs. No problem with the procedure, but when the girl wakes up she's got a hickey on her tit. Maybe she had the hickey going in, but that one cost him fifty grand. He's got two similar cases that I'm supposed to be working on, but I have to tell you, there's not a lot of incentive working for a guy whose assets are no longer under his control.

One of his patients claims she came out of the anesthesia and the doctor was performing an oral procedure on her private parts. That was how the complaint read. You'd think they'd just say he was giving her head, wouldn't you?"

"You think he was molesting the Murphy kid?"

Getter adjusted the collar of his coat. "The patients he was having trouble with were all young women. I don't think he goes for boys."

"Maybe the gender doesn't matter. Maybe he just likes them young and helpless."

Getter grinned. "So who doesn't?"

Crow looked away, felt the snowflakes striking his cheeks.

"Anything else I can help you with, Joe?"

"Does he have the Murphy kid?"

"I don't know. All I know for sure is that he has some serious financial problems. If he owes you money, I wouldn't count on seeing any of it. He owes me money too, you know. I had to take part of it in professional services."

"What do you mean?"

"Mary wanted some work done on her hips. Dr. Bellweather offered to do the work to reduce his legal fees."

"You sent Mary to have surgery performed by a guy who mislocates belly buttons? A guy who can't keep his mouth off his patients?"

"He didn't have the money."

"I don't believe it. She come home with any hickeys?"

Getter laughed. Crow didn't. The wind was picking up, the snow getting thicker. Crow was cold.

"What about his brother, Nate. You know where I can find him?"

Getter said, "You try the phone book?"

Crow didn't reply. The phone book? That was too easy. Besides, it hadn't occurred to him.

Getter held out a gloved hand. "You want to give me that camera now?"

Crow shook his head. "I've got a few more shots on the roll, Dave. I'll let you know when I get them developed."

Getter shook his head in disgust, climbed into his car, and drove off. When he was out of sight, Crow threw the camera into a trash can, walked to a nearby phone booth, and looked up Nate Bellweather's address.

*You think you know what you want. But what you have
to learn is how to want what you'll wish you'd wanted
once you finally get it.*

—*LAURA DEBROWSKI*

row locked and chained his apartment door, showered, and
changed into clean canvas pants and a wool sweater. He made himself
a meal of crackers and sardines, ate without tasting a thing, then sat
staring out the window.

He picked up the phone, dialed, let it ring.

He saw her again, sitting before the mirror with the bloodless face
and the bright, wasted eyes. As the image formed, he saw the corners
of her mouth curve up into a hollow smile. She reached out with one
pale hand and wiped a forefinger over the remains of a white powdery
line on the mirror's surface, put the finger in her mouth, and rubbed
the stray grains of coke onto her gum, still holding his eyes, still with
the ghastly smile. Crow felt the muscles of his abdomen contract, pressing his organs together. He thought about what Mary had told him. That
Orlan Johnson had been looking for him at Melinda's. Crow squirmed
in his chair. Why wasn't she answering her phone? The more he thought
about it, the more he had to know.

After thirty-five rings, he hung up, put on his coat, and let himself out
of the apartment.

Crow decided to drop by at Nate Bellweather's on the way
out of town, though he didn't expect to find Dr. Bellweather there. It
was worth a try; he didn't know where else to look. The address he'd
found in the phone book turned out to be a modest bungalow in

Nordeast Minneapolis, only a few miles from where Crow had grown up. The house was barely distinguishable from the other bungalows on the block, all of them cheaply built during the housing boom after World War II, now aging gracelessly. Nate's station wagon filled the short driveway. Crow pressed the doorbell, banged on the door with the side of his fist.

A few seconds later, the curtain over the door window moved an inch, fell back into place. Nate Bellweather opened the door about a foot.

"He's not here."

A fiftyish woman with artificially brown hair and a permanent-looking frown appeared at Nate's shoulder.

Crow asked, "Do you know where he is?"

"He's gone," the woman said.

"It's cold out here. Do you mind if I come in for a minute?"

The woman pushed Nate aside. "We don't know where he is. Go away."

"I'm concerned about him," Crow said, directing his words at Nate. "I think he's in trouble with the Murphys. Do you know how I can get in touch with him?"

"He's gone," the woman repeated.

"Shut up, Ginny."

"Don't you tell me to shut up."

Nate said, "He's not here, Crow. Your job is over."

"Where did he go?"

"He didn't tell me."

"You mind if I come in?" Crow pressed against the door. Nate resisted for a moment, then stepped back. Crow closed the door, looked around the neat, ordinary room. It looked a lot like the house in which he'd spent his childhood. Knickknacks, plates on the wall, a cheap throw over the shapeless couch, popular magazines—*Reader's Digest, People, Sports Afield*—fanned out on an oak-veneer coffee table.

Nate Bellweather crossed his arms and took a position in front of the couch. Ginny made a sour face and left the room.

"Nice place," Crow said.

Nate looked around the room, shook his head. "What do you want, Crow?"

"I'll be straight with you. Your brother never paid me for the time I put in. I'm just trying to collect my wages."

"One day's wages? You're kidding me."

"It's a matter of principle."

"Yeah, well, the principle here is that you're at the end of a long line of people that're going to be looking for their money." He sat on the couch, crossed his hands on his lap. "In any case, my brother's not here. He left about twenty minutes ago."

"Alone?"

Nate shrugged. "What my brother does is none of my business."

Ginny reentered the room, holding a shotgun, pointing it at Crow.

Nate said, "Aww, for crying out loud, Ginny. Would you put that thing away."

"I'm telling you what I told Nelson," she said to Crow, her voice shaking. "You get out of my house. You get out of here and don't you come back."

Crow held his hands out and backed toward the door. "Okay, I'm leaving," he said.

Nate sighed and sank deeper into the couch.

Crow opened the door, stepped outside. Ginny followed him to the doorway, keeping the shotgun trained on him, watched him walk to his car.

Crow hadn't been gone two minutes when somebody banged on the door again.

Ginny Bellweather said, "It's probably him again. Don't open it."

Nate glared at his wife. He was sick of it. He was sick of running interference for his brother, of getting involved in his crazy schemes. And he was sick of Ginny bitching, complaining, and ordering him around. Bringing out the shotgun was really too much. If it was Crow at the door, come back to ask about something he forgot the first time, he had half a mind to apologize to the guy.

"You hear me?" Ginny said.

Nate pushed his jaw out so far it hurt. *Screw you,* he thought but did not quite say. He pushed up off the couch, walked straight to the front door, and yanked it open.

It wasn't Crow. It was a skinny guy in a gray Stetson.

Nate opened his mouth. He didn't know what he was going to say but was saved from having to come up with something when the man on his doorstep planted the heel of his boot in Nate's belly, sending him stumbling back into the living room, crashing into the coffee table. Nate heard a shout from Ginny, then a thud and a squeal. He forced his eyes open, looked up, saw the cowboy holding the shotgun, saw Ginny slumped against the doorframe, holding her face. The cowboy turned his attention from Ginny back to Nate.

"How you doing?" He grinned. "You feel like telling me where that Nelly Bell's got hisself to?"

It was all Nate could do to breathe. He shook his head.

The cowboy's grin disappeared. He rested the barrel of the shotgun on Nate's chin.

"How 'bout now?" he asked.

Nate said, "I don't know. He left a little while ago with the kid. He didn't say where he was going."

The cowboy nodded, moved the barrel of the gun off to the side, brought it back, hard, slapping its length against Nate's temple.

"How 'bout now?" he said again.

Five minutes and several blows later, through the bright flashes obscuring his vision and the ringing in his ears, Nate heard the cowboy pick up the phone.

"He ain't here," he heard him say. "That's right. No, I talked to him and his wife both. They don't know shit. Okay."

Nate heard the cowboy hang up the phone, walk across the carpet, slam the door. He heard an engine start, then it was gone. He opened his eyes to look at his wife. She lay on her back a few feet away, her head turned toward him, a cut on her cheek, her nose and bottom lip bleeding. She gave him a look, daring him to say something.

He wasn't going to fall for that one.

After a few seconds she said it anyway. "I *told* you not to open the goddamn door."

The sun had set. Two inches of grainy snow covered the streets. Crow slipped and spun and skidded his way to Highway 12, turned west. The road crews had salted the highway. He brought the Rabbit up to sixty miles per hour. The fact that Melinda wasn't answering her phone could mean many things. He tried not to think about the worst of them, but no matter what direction he forced his thoughts, they would end with the vision of Melinda out of her mind, or dead on the floor. Or—another possibility—she had had some kind of run-in with Orlan Johnson, had wound up in jail. Eyes on the road surface, Crow began to construct an elaborate fantasy. Suppose that George Murphy, driven to an insane rage, was systematically kidnapping everyone who had ever had any connection to Dr. Nelson Bellweather. Suppose the Murphys were holding Melinda hostage. Soon they would approach him and threaten to feed his wife to the tiger.

On one level he knew such a scenario was absurd, but since no one was there to challenge it, he let it play, feeling his rage, imagining himself rescuing Melinda, shooting all the Murphys to get to her. He replayed the episode, trying a few variations, squeezing it for every last heady drop of adrenaline.

By the time he passed through Howard Lake, the salt was losing its battle with the gathering snow. A barking headache had settled low in the back of his skull. Drifts were building up on the roadway, and the snowflakes flashing in his headlights became bright bursts of pain. Crow hunched over the wheel, his jaw clamped tight, and held the speedometer at fifty. Ten miles later, he was down to thirty miles per hour, dodging drifts on the highway, straining to separate the road surface from the flat, white, featureless countryside. Thoughts of Melinda had lost focus and blended with the pain in his head, and he continued on propelled only by a sense of mission.

He arrived in Big River rolling slowly through four inches of blowing snow. Melinda's driveway was covered by a drift three feet high. Crow pulled over in front of the house and shut down the engine. He felt no relief at reaching his destination, though the pounding in his head receded somewhat. The house was dark, no sign of life. He slogged up to the front door, his shoes filling with ice. Snow had drifted against the door. He leaned on the doorbell and could hear it ring inside the house. He released the button. The house grew darker and quieter.

The mailbox was stuffed with three days' mail; Crow emptied the box and held the assorted envelopes in his hands like a bouquet or a box of candy. He listened for the sound of quiet footsteps, Melinda walking in her slippers, but heard nothing. Shifting the stack of mail to the crook of his elbow, he flipped through his keys, finally selecting the one that fit the dead-bolt lock he had installed a year ago. He opened the door. This time it wasn't chained. He stepped inside.

The air smelled stale. He dropped the mail on a chair and turned on a lamp. He let his breath out, realizing only as he exhaled that he had been holding it for some time. The living room was perfectly ordered, the furniture meticulously placed, the pictures hanging on the walls, the books aligned on their shelves, the magazines carefully arranged on the coffee table, every surface perpendicular or parallel to the walls of the room. The mirror hung in place, recently cleaned. The sense of Melinda's absence hit him low in the belly, and he sank down onto the sofa. Where had she gone?

On a trip? Crow experienced an image of Melinda on a beach in Cancún, drinking rum punch. I'm hallucinating, he thought.

Shadow creatures played at the periphery of his vision.

Another image: Melinda on her bed, her heart stopped, lying there dead for three days. Would the power of her copper pyramid preserve her body? More likely, it would be grotesquely swollen. He stood and walked slowly up the stairs, fighting the pictures in his mind. He had seen a few bodies during his years with the Big River police; the detail his mind retained was excruciating. Halfway up the stairs he struck an invisible, internal barrier and stopped, then was able to continue only by pretending that he was still a cop, that this was just another house, on another street, in another city. The bedroom door was closed. He pushed it open. The bed was made, there were no wrinkles of the bed-spread, no organic reek of decaying flesh. The pyramid was intact. There was no bloated body in the bathroom, or in the spare bedroom, or in any of the other rooms. He turned himself back into Joe Crow.

He called Felix, but Felix wasn't home either. His cat bowl sat empty on the kitchen floor.

She had made her bed and straightened the magazines, which meant that she was planning on leaving, planning on coming home. It wasn't like she had been raptured, or taken against her will. Crow looked at the sofa, remembering the times he had slept there, too loaded to climb the stairs to the bedroom. He took a step toward it, caught himself, then turned to the front door. He did not want to awaken in this silent, abandoned home.

Before he left, he shoveled the sidewalk and the driveway. Melinda hated the snow. As he shoveled, he began once again to wonder about Orlan Johnson. Although all the signs were that Melinda had left delib-erately and with some forethought, Orlan Johnson's grinning, cigar-impaled face continued to assault him. Was he responsible for Melinda's disappearance? Had his visit frightened her into leaving? Why was he driving all over the state, looking for Joe Crow? It had to be something to do with the Murphy kid. Did they still think he was involved in that?

Crow jammed the end of the shovel into the snowbank. Two facts stood out in his mind: The last person who had actually *seen* Melinda, so far as he knew, was Orlan Johnson. And Melinda was gone.

It would drive him crazy not to know.

Mary Getter mixed another Manhattan and brought it to her husband, who was slumped morosely in his leather club chair. This was number four, three more than he usually drank before dinner. He took the drink without looking up at her and tossed half of it down his throat. Mary sat across from him in her coordinating bone-colored leather armchair. She was getting these jangly vibes from David, and when she looked directly at him, then closed her eyes, she discovered the afterimage of an alarmingly blue aura—not David's color at all.

The eggless Caesar salad had been sitting on the dining room table for half an hour. The lamb roast with mustard sauce, prepared according to a recipe featured in the latest *Minnesota Monthly,* was slowly cooling, the fat congealing. David usually had a good appetite, but something was bothering him and tonight he had shown no interest in food. "Are you getting hungry?" she asked.

Getter shook his head.

Mary smiled and nodded, her brow knitted. A difficult case, she imagined. She considered eating her own dinner and leaving him to himself. But that wouldn't be right. Perhaps she could help him rechannel his thoughts. She thought back over her day, searching for a topic of conversation that might interest him.

"Joe stopped by today," she ventured.

A tremor shot up Getter's body, sending a globule of Manhattan arcing out of his glass onto his shirt. Uncharacteristically, he didn't seem to notice the spill. He kept his eyes locked on some distant landscape.

After a second, he said, "What did he want?"

Mary shrugged, looking at the spot on his shirtfront. "Nothing. He was asking about Melinda." She decided not to mention that Joe had also been asking about Dr. Bellweather. Whatever was bothering David, she didn't want to add to it.

"That's all?"

"Yes. He said he'd been fishing with that horrible old man."

Getter drained the remains of his cocktail.

"I hate to say it, Mary, but your brother is a sleazy little son-of-a-bitch," he said. "Not only that—he's a compulsive liar. Remember that, Mary. Nearly everything he says is untrue. I think he should be under the care of a psychiatrist. The guy's—what?—thirty-something? Look at the mess he's made of his life. Sticking his nose into other people's business. He's going to get himself killed. I can't say I'll be sorry."

Mary pressed her lips together but did not reply. She had never heard anything quite like this before. She knew that David didn't like Joe, but he usually wasn't so blunt about it. Besides, he was wrong in his assertions. Joe had had some troubles, and his mind was closed in many areas, but he had always been straight with her. In Mary's opinion, that was part of his problem. His honesty made people uncomfortable.

Getter stood up, weaving slightly.

"Do you want to eat now?" Mary asked hopefully.

Getter snapped his head back and forth. "I have to make a phone call," he said.

Amanda Murphy had no illusions about the quality of her cooking. Everything she made turned out dense, sticky, and powerful, like her sons. Her apple pie, for instance. The bottom crust was half an inch thick, charred on the bottom and slimy on top, covered with a loose layer of oversweet, mushy apples. The top crust was better, except for the lumps. Not the worst apple pie she had ever made and eaten, but darn near. Fortunately, George's sense of taste was not acute, and he'd been eating her pies since he was a kid. He didn't even complain about the raisins.

"Great pie, Mandy," he grunted through a gummy mouthful.

Anyway, it was nutritious. A pie that weighed that much had to have some good in it. Amanda cut herself a small slice, helped it along with a glass of bourbon-spiked Pepsi.

The late afternoon call from the lawyer had put George in one of his dangerous moods. Then when Ricky called to say that Nelly Bell wasn't hiding out at his brother Nate's, he got even worse. Threw his office phone right through the window, busted them both into smithereens. Amanda had been tiptoeing around him all evening. So far, the lawyer hadn't called back like he said he would, and with every passing minute George seemed to be getting shorter, darker, and wider, looking as if he was about to explode. She wished Ricky would get home, so George would have somebody to yell at.

When the phone on the kitchen wall rang, Amanda let George answer it.

"Murphy here."

He listened, grunted, listened some more.

"Okay," he said. "I'll be there." Pause. "Yes, I'll have your goddamn *reward* money. . . . Well, whosever it is, I'll have it. And you'd best have the boy. . . . Well, somebody sure as hell better have him." He hung up.

Amanda thought, Here it comes. His head is going to explode.

But George let out a long, whistling breath and returned to his seat at the kitchen table. "That was the lawyer," he said. "He wants me to bring the money to Birdy's tomorrow morning. He says Nelly Bell will be there with Shawn."

Amanda said, "How much money do they want you to bring?"

"Three hundred thousand dollars."

Amanda coughed into her Pepsi. "For a child?"

George shrugged. "What difference does it make?" he asked. "I don't have it anyways."

"Where are we going?" Shawn asked.

Doc Bellweather smiled. "Where do you want to go?" he asked.

Shawn thought about that. The adventure, hiding out with Doc and Nate and Ginny, had been getting old. He was glad to be going some-place instead of sitting around Nate's house watching TV, with Ginny always looking at him weird, like he was a dog going to bite her or something.

"The Mall of America," Shawn said. "Camp Snoopy. You can take me on the rides."

"You don't want to go there," Doc said.

"Yes I do."

"Well, we're headed the other direction. Don't you want to go home? See your dad?"

Shawn looked out the window. They were on the highway. He saw a sign: HWY 12 WEST. Did he want to go home? He thought about his room and about the animals. He thought about the tiger chained up in the lodge, the smell of Grandy's cooking. He thought about telling the kids at school about how he had run away.

"My dad's going to be mad," he said. "But I'd kinda like to see the animals."

"That's okay. I'll talk to him."

"He might be mad at you too."

"I think you can count on that," Doc said.

The man who has injured you will never forgive you.

—*Spanish Proverb*

ee Dee McCall was in deep shit. Working undercover as a hooker, she had infiltrated a gang of long-haired thrill-killing South African extortionists, and one of the bad guys, the albino, was trying to get her to shoot up a sample of a heroin shipment they had hijacked from a greasy-headed, bejeweled, sadistic dope peddler named Slash. Hunter was driving his beat-up green Plymouth, homing in on her concealed transmitter. Unfortunately for Dee Dee, the albino had discovered the transmitter while trying to feel her up and had attached it to the collar of a rabid German shepherd. Hunter stopped his Plymouth at the entrance to the alley, got out, and followed his hand-held homing device toward the looming shape of an overflowing Dumpster, behind which the shepherd was crouched, its mouth dripping with what looked like runny shaving cream.

Orlan Johnson was entranced. He could imagine himself in that situation.

The doorbell rang.

"Got-dammit!"

He kept his eyes on the television. He was perfectly comfortable, drink in hand, Hunter on the tube, sitting well back in his new oxblood-colored La-Z-Boy recliner with genuine leather on the seat and arms. No way was he going to move. The doorbell rang again, this time for several seconds, drowning out the growling rabid dog.

"Hill! You want to get the damn door?"

His wife didn't respond. She was way down in the basement, doing the laundry. The idiot on the doorbell wouldn't quit.

"Got-dammit, I'm coming," Johnson shouted. He set his drink on the side table, fumbled for the lever on the side of the chair, yanked at it until the footrest folded back into the chair, then heaved his abdomen up into a standing position. "I'm coming. Hold your got-damn horses, wouldja?"

He opened the door. "Aw, f'chrissake, Crow, what are you doing here?"

Crow pushed past him, walked right into his house.

"Hey!" Johnson said. "Who the hell invited you in?"

Crow said, "I heard you were looking for me." He pulled off his gloves, stuffed them in a coat pocket.

"Now who told you that?"

"What did you want?"

"Don't matter no more. I had some questions, but we don't need you no more, Crow." He turned his eyes to the television, attracted by the sound of gunfire. Hunter was doing his thing.

"Well, I have a question for you," Crow said. "What were you doing at Melinda's?"

"Who?" Johnson pulled his eyes from the set.

"My wife." Crow picked up the remote control and turned off the TV.

"What the hell? Are you drunk or something?" Johnson could feel his bile rising, a green mass crawling up his throat. He made a grab for the remote. Crow stepped back, holding it away.

"Just a simple question. I know you were there looking for me. What did you say to her? Did you threaten her?"

"I don't know what the hell you're talking about. Now give me that thing before I remote your ass in jail."

"Just tell me what you were doing there." Crow's voice was flat and quiet, each word delivered with equal emphasis, like a man trying to hold his breath and talk at the same time. "Just tell me if you know where she is."

Johnson squeezed his eyes down to where he could hardly see out of them, closed his fists and held them out to the side, a gunfighter ready to slap leather.

"You gimme that thing right now. The hell's wrong with you, Crow? You got some kind of death wish?" The words were coming out faster now. Johnson could hear the shrillness in his own voice, feel the tightness in his throat, the heat coloring his face. "Now get the hell before I haul your sorry ass down to city hall." He jabbed a shaking forefinger in Crow's face. "You mess with me—"

Crow slapped the forefinger aside as if it were an offensive insect. Johnson took an astonished step back, staring at his finger, his face finally hitting peak color.

"You just assaulted a police officer, Crow." Johnson took another step back, spread his arms wide, bent his knees, lowered his head, and charged.

To Joe Crow, the rapidly advancing bulk of Orlan Johnson embodied all the shit in his life—the Murphys, his missing wife, Bellweather, Dave Getter, and various other personal demons. He wanted to meet Johnson's charge head-on, but the undeniable fact that he was outweighed by more than a hundred pounds persuaded him to step aside like a matador.

He was almost quick enough. Johnson had the deceptive speed of a rhinoceros. His right fist flailed out and caught Crow on the ribs. Crow staggered back, hit the doorframe with his shoulder. The remote control flew from his hand; he twisted away just in time to avoid a second punch. Johnson's fist crashed into the wall, producing a depression in the wallboard and a grunt of pain.

Crow saw his opportunity and went for Johnson's belly, a hard, short jab, then followed up with a less successful blow that skidded off the top of the balding skull. Johnson responded with a wild backhand swing that just brushed Crow's chin. Crow backpedaled, giving himself room, not wanting to risk getting inside those surprisingly powerful arms. Johnson howled and charged again, but this time Crow was ready, dodging at the last moment, then coming back with a well-aimed foot to Johnson's well-padded rear, sending the big man crashing face-first into his recliner, which instantly reclined, the footrest snapping forward, the back thumping against the wall, followed immediately by the top of the chief's head.

Johnson lay stunned for a moment, his hands flapping against the leather arms of the chair. As he watched Johnson struggling, Crow had a moment of relative clarity, trying to figure out what to do next, now that he had attacked the chief of the local police in his own home. Perhaps coming here had not been one of his more brilliant moves.

A shiver ran up Johnson's corpulent body; he rotated, bringing his body into the more usual recliner position. His eyes fixed on Crow, his brow flexed. "You little bastard, I'll teach you, you little fuckhead—" He launched himself up out of the chair at Crow.

Crow did not mind being called a bastard, which he was, or even a fuckhead. It was the modifier *"little"* he objected to, so the moment Johnson's charge brought him within range, Crow threw his best punch, hard and straight as a steel bar, dead center on Johnson's ample gut. His fist buried itself deep—for an instant it felt as if it had gone right inside—then Johnson sagged to the carpet, breathless and paralyzed.

Crow was thinking how good that had felt. He was wishing Johnson would come at him again, when he heard a whisper of movement and turned in time to see what looked like a black hole rushing toward his head. He heard a loud sound, like a gong, and his legs gave way. He felt the texture of nylon carpet on his cheek.

All his effort went into forming a single coherent thought.

The answer to his problems was there, if only he could think of it.

Above him, far away, he could hear voices.

Something was thudding repeatedly into his side. He forced the roiling sludge that had been his brain to mold and form this remarkable idea that would fix everything. But when, as Orlan Johnson's slipper crashed repeatedly into his ribs, the thought finally bloomed and fell into focus, it turned out to be of no use at all. He was thinking, It's not fair—I still hurt from the last time I got the shit kicked out of me.

"Stop it, Orlan! That's enough." Hillary grabbed her husband's arm and pulled him away. "You don't want to kill him."

Orlan Johnson looked at his wife. "Why not?"

"It's not necessary. He doesn't matter anymore. Look at him." She gestured with the cast-iron frying pan. Crow was on his hands and knees, swaying, his head hanging loosely. "If he can leave, let him. You don't want to have to carry him out yourself, do you?"

"I want to throw his sorry ass in jail is what I want. The son-of-a-bitch hit me!"

Hillary shook her head. "You don't want to do that. Let him go. You put him in jail, you'll just have to deal with that lawyer again."

Johnson grimaced.

"What is he doing here?" Hillary asked.

"I don't know. He thought I knew where his wife was or something."

"Do you?"

"Now why the hell would I do something like that? I stopped by her house to see if this idiot was there, but she didn't know anything. Look at him—he's crawling like a got-damn animal."

Crow was moving toward the open front door. They watched as he used the doorknob to pull himself up. He looked back at them, blinking uncomprehendingly, his hands gripping the door as though it were a lone bit of flotsam in a raging sea.

Johnson grabbed the frying pan from his wife's hand and shouted, "You get the hell out of my house!"

Crow's eyes drifted, finally settling on the black iron pan. He shuddered, released his grip on the door, wavered, then toddled unsteadily out into the gathering snow.

Moments, minutes, or hours later, Crow regained consciousness in his car. He was sitting upright in the driver's seat. The windows were opaque with frost. He was cold. He searched his pockets for his keys, discovered them in the ignition. His head felt numb, as if it were coated with ice. He turned the key; the car started. He turned on the dome light and looked at himself in the mirror. A hillock the size, color, and shape of an overripened tomato had appeared above his left eyebrow. He remembered, with unwanted clarity, the bottom of the frying pan coming at him, but he could not remember how he had got back to his car.

"You look like shit," he observed aloud. The vibrations in his skull sent ripples of nausea down his body. He closed his eyes, breathed shallowly, and waited for it to pass. When he felt he could move without vomiting, he turned on the defroster and waited for the glaciated windows to clear. It would take several minutes for the thick layer of frost to disappear, but he was in no hurry. He wasn't sure he wanted to know where he was and, once he found out, had no idea where he wanted to go. Crow let his head settle back and observed disinterestedly as consciousness once again slipped away.

The Sea Breeze Motel, fifteen hundred miles from the nearest ocean, offered air-conditioning, phone, and HBO. Shawn watched from the car as Doc went into the office and got a key. When he climbed back into the car, Shawn asked him, "How come we're staying here?"

"Because it's only a few miles from here to Big River and because we can park out back," Doc said.

"I thought you were gonna take me home."

"It's snowing too hard. We'll stay here tonight. I'll take you back in the morning." Doc put the Jaguar in gear and, pulling around the office, drove back behind the long, low motel. "Here it is—number sixteen."

"It's not snowing so hard. You could probably call my dad. I bet he'd come pick me up."

"I bet he would. You know, they have cable TV here. I bet we can find a good movie to watch."

"Like what?"

"I don't know. Let's go inside and find out what's playing."

The eleven o'clock movie turned out to be something called *Daytona Dolls*.

"I never heard of it," Shawn said.

Bellweather was reading the program listing. " 'Mechanic and his three girlfriends foil Mafia plot to blow up racetrack, hard-driving brothers fall for twin beauty contest winners, a woman race car driver shows her stuff.' " He looked up. "Sounds like tits and tires to me, kiddo. Should we watch it?"

Shawn said, "Sure." He still wanted to go home, but the movie sounded pretty good. Doc picked up the phone and dialed.

"Hi, it's me. Did you call him?"

Shawn grabbed the remote and turned on the TV.

"Good! So we're all set, then. You'll meet them at ten tomorrow morning, right?"

Shawn flipped through the channels. A cooking show. *Hunter*. *Cheers*.

"Don't give me that shit, Dave. We have a deal. You'll be taken care of. You do your part, then you can leave, okay?"

Shopping channel. *Star Trek*. He paused and watched Mr. Spock for a moment, then continued to channel surf until he found a cartoon show.

"Don't be late." Doc hung up the phone. He grinned at Shawn. "He's a wimp," he said.

"Who?"

"The guy I was talking to."

"Oh." Shawn reached for the phone.

"What are you doing?" Doc clamped his hand down on the handset.

"I want to call my dad," Shawn said. He didn't like the expression on Doc's face. The smile was still there, but it looked wrong.

"You can talk to him in the morning."

Shawn didn't like that. "I wanna talk to him now."

Doc closed his eyes for a moment, shook his head. "Let's watch some TV."

"Why can't I call him?"

"I don't want to discuss it, Shawn."

Shawn was getting this really weird feeling. The urge to get away from Doc, to get home no matter what, was getting stronger.

"I changed my mind," he said. "I want to go home right now."

Doc shook his head.

Shawn rolled across the bed, stood up. "I'm gonna go," he said. He put on his jacket and started toward the door. What happened next completely surprised him. Just when he had his hand on the doorknob, Doc grabbed him by the wrist, gave him a slap across the cheek, threw him down on the bed, slapped him again, shook a finger in his face.

"You, you'll stay right here. You'll stay right here until I say you can go." Doc's face was all red, veins popping out on his forehead. "You understand me?"

Shawn was scared. His cheek stung, and his wrist hurt where Doc had grabbed him. Now Doc was digging in his bag. Shawn was afraid to move. Doc came up with a pair of handcuffs, grabbed his wrist again, clamped a manacle around it.

Shawn said, "Hey!"

"Just making sure you stay put," Doc said. He felt around the headboard and down along the side of the bed, looking for someplace to secure the other end of the cuffs, finally settled for clamping it around a leg at the foot of the bed, leaving Shawn facedown on the mattress, his right arm hanging over the side.

"There, that should hold you," Doc said. "Comfortable?"

Shawn didn't say anything. Doc asked him if he could see the TV. He could see it fine; it was only about three feet from his face. They sat and watched *Daytona Dolls,* which Shawn enjoyed despite his predicament. There were a couple of cool car crashes, a wet T-shirt contest, and this one part where one of the bad guys got run over by a steamroller. Just after the steamroller scene, Doc got off his bed and went into the bathroom. Shawn listened until he heard the sound of urine spilling into the toilet bowl, rolled off the mattress, lifted the corner of the bed, slipped the end of the cuff off the leg, opened the door, and ran.

When Bellweather heard the door open, he nearly collapsed. His knees actually buckled and hit the edge of the toilet bowl. He thought he was a dead man. He thought Ricky Murphy had found them. He didn't even care that he was pissing all over his leg. What difference did it make to a dead man? He forced himself to take a step back, to look out the bathroom door into the room. The door stood wide open. No Ricky Murphy. Nobody at all. Shawn was gone.

His relief was instantaneous but momentary. The kid had got loose. He started for the door, realized his penis was flopping around outside his pants, paused to zip up, caught himself. He stopped, frozen in the characteristic posture of a man in the thrall of his zipper, gritted his teeth, tore the zipper open. He almost didn't feel the pain.

At the open door he stopped. He didn't have his shoes on. The kid was already out of sight. He leaned from the doorway, called Shawn's name.

Silence.

A layer of sparkly snow, another six inches at least, had already coated the Jag. Shawn's deep footprints led toward the lobby, then veered toward the highway. What did he think he was going to do? There was nothing between the motel and the outskirts of Big River, five miles away, and Talking Lake Ranch was another ten miles out of town. The frigid air caused the fine hair on his legs to stand up, his scrotum to contract. Using greater care this time, Bellweather closed his zipper. He slipped his bare feet into his loafers, and threw his coat over his shoulders, and trudged out to his car, cursing the snow that immediately filled his shoes. It was deeper than he'd thought, all the way up to the bottom of the car door. He had to get the kid back before somebody picked him up. Before he got to a phone and called his dad. The Jag started immediately, but he couldn't see a thing. He jumped out and frantically brushed the blanket of snow off the windshield with his hands, got back behind the wheel, and dropped the gearshift into reverse. The car started to move, the back bumper pushing up a wall of snow. It slowed, wheels losing traction, then stopped completely as the wide performance tires spun impotently. He shut down the engine, climbed out, and took a good look at the mired Jag. Even if he got it moving, he'd never progress more than a few yards without once again becoming hopelessly stuck. He started walking across the parking lot, lifting his legs high, pushing through the knee-high snow, but stopped after only a few yards. There was no way he was going to get anywhere, especially in his loafers, already stuffed with snow. On the other hand, Shawn wouldn't get far either. He would almost certainly be back. Bellweather turned toward his room. He stopped at the Jaguar, opened the compartment in the back, and pulled out the aluminum gun case containing his shotgun. If the kid didn't return, if he somehow found his way home, it might come in handy.

XXII

I don't look for trouble. I look for balance.

—*JOE CROW*

T he Rabbit's windows were ninety percent clear the next time Crow regained consciousness. The engine was still running, the gas gauge hovering at a quarter tank. Last time he remembered, it had been half full. Christ, he thought, I'm lucky I'm not dead of carbon monoxide poisoning. The numbness that had filled his head before now felt like a rat-tail file embedded in his forehead, slowly rotating. Moving his head minimally, he examined the glittering, snow-covered neighborhood. He was still parked in front of Orlan Johnson's house. Snow had settled on every horizontal surface. Mailboxes wore six-inch caps of white, power lines bore fragile icy crests, trees and bushes sagged under their frozen load.

A few flakes still drifted down from the sky. Crow put the Rabbit in gear and slowly released the clutch. The front wheels gripped the new snow, and the car moved away from the curb, out onto the street. Crow held the wheel tightly, hardly able to believe that he was moving. He could hear the underbelly of the car dragging through the snow. He would have to keep rolling if he didn't want to get stuck.

Twenty minutes later, he turned onto the highway. The plows had been by, the surface scraped nearly clean. Crow let his shoulders drop to their normal setting and brought the car up to speed. The pain in his head subsided somewhat. The rat-tail file had withdrawn from his forebrain and been replaced by the repetitive pounding of a child's wooden hammer. As he passed beyond the outskirts of Big River, he allowed himself for the first time to reflect on his visit to the Johnson residence. He'd come away from his encounter with the Johnsons with two things: a possible concussion, and the memory of what he'd heard Johnson tell his wife as he staggered out the door: "I stopped by her house to see if this idiot was there, but she didn't know anything."

Wherever Melinda had gone, Orlan Johnson had not taken her there.

Five miles outside Big River, Crow drove past a boy running down the opposite lane of the highway. He thought, That's odd. The middle of the night, snow everywhere, cold as hell, and the kid wasn't wearing a hat. Crow drove another half mile, remembering what it felt like to be a child and to be cold. When he reached the Sea Breeze, a small motel, he turned around and went back. It would bother him for days if he didn't offer a cold kid a ride. When the headlights hit the running figure, the kid stopped, turned to face him, then took off into the ditch, sinking waist deep in the snow. Crow stopped and rolled down the passenger-side window.

"Hey, are you okay?" he shouted.

The kid stopped and looked back.

"You need a lift?"

The kid said, "I'm freezing."

"It's warm in the car," Crow said. "Hop in."

The kid hesitated, then slogged through the snow to the car, opened the door, climbed inside. It was a boy, ten or eleven years old, his face red with cold and effort, his eyes tearing. No gloves. He sat in the seat, shivering, hugging himself, breathing in gasps. Crow turned up the heater fan and directed the vents toward his passenger.

"Put your hands up next to the vent," he said. "Get them warmed up. And open up that jacket, let some heat in. What the hell were you doing out there?"

"Nothing." The boy, his hands against the heat vent, worked his fingers. A handcuff dangled from his wrist. He was a chubby kid, and his full cheeks looked frostbitten—red blotches encircled by a ring of pale skin.

"Just out for a stroll, huh?"

The boy shrugged, intent on absorbing all the available Btu's.

"Where'd you get the fancy bracelet?"

"I dunno."

"You got a key? You want me to get that off for you?"

"That's okay," the kid said.

Crow put the car in gear and pulled back onto the roadway, drove for a few minutes without speaking, waiting for his passenger to warm up. The pounding in his temples, which had temporarily receded, became louder, merged with the hissing of the heater fan.

"Where do you want to go?" he asked, hoping he could get the kid home before he passed out.

The boy turned his head and looked straight at Crow for the first time. "I don't know."

"Do you live around here? You want to go home?"

He drew his shoulders in. "I guess."

"Where do you live?" Crow heard the words coming out of his mouth, but he couldn't feel them. The pain in his head seemed to be migrating downward.

The boy pointed in the direction they were going. "It's up here a ways."

"How far?"

"I don't know. I know when to turn. Do you know where Talking Lake Ranch is?"

Crow took his foot off the gas and looked carefully at his passenger. "You're the kid," he said.

The boy drew back.

"You're the Murphy kid. What's your name?"

"Shawn."

Crow took a deep breath and brought the car back up to speed. This was too much for his pureed mind to deal with.

"What happened to your head?" Shawn asked.

"I ran into your aunt."

"You know my aunt?"

"Better than I'd like to."

Shawn said, "I know who you are. You're the guy."

"What guy?"

"The guy in Doc's car."

"You're thinking about somebody else. If you're talking about Dr. Bellweather, he's no friend of mine."

"It was you," Shawn said.

"Have it your way." Crow had no idea what the kid was talking about. It was hard to think and drive at the same time.

"You aren't going to take me back to him, are you?" Shawn asked.

"Back to who?"

"Doc."

Crow shook his head. "I'm taking you home," he said. "What were you doing with Bellweather? Did he put those cuffs on you?"

Shawn opened his mouth, closed it.

"You don't want to talk about it?"

"I don't care," Shawn said.

"Was Bellweather messing with you?"

"What d'you mean?"

"You know. Touching you and stuff?"

Shawn took a few moments to reply. "No," he said at last.

Crow nodded carefully, not wanting to jar anything loose in his skull. He kept the speedometer at forty, swerving occasionally to avoid the snowdrifts that were again invading the recently plowed highway. The car seemed to roll with unusual smoothness, as if it were floating a few inches above the icy road. The steering wheel felt thick, the pedals squishy. In a distant sort of way, Crow enjoyed the sensation of disconnectedness. They drove for what seemed like hours. He knew this highway, having driven it thousands of times during his stint with the Big River police, but now it looked different, a landscape white, black, silent, and surreal. He concentrated on steering. It was astonishingly difficult to keep the thing moving in a straight line.

"Hey, you're on the wrong side of the road."

Crow turned his head, which seemed to weigh thirty or forty pounds, and stared at the boy. For a moment, he had forgotten he had a passenger. He forced the steering wheel to turn, and the car edged back into the right lane.

His head was a watermelon, his fingers bratwursts. The road felt slick and spongy. The pain in his head had become a sound: whoosh, whoosh, whoosh. From time to time he looked at the speedometer. Sometimes it read fifty, sometimes it read twenty. It seemed to make no difference. Either way, the land rolled by.

Crow heard a voice.

"Hey, mister!"

He tried to think of a reply, one that would not take too much effort. The steering wheel evaporated.

"Hey! Look out!"

The roadway writhed.

Crow relaxed. He was too tired to care.

The landscape spun.

XXIII

A pig bought on credit is forever grunting.

—*SPANISH PROVERB*

ometime after three A.M., Bellweather fell asleep sitting up in bed, fully clothed, the shotgun resting in his lap. He slept for an hour or so—it was four-thirty when he woke with a start, rolled off the bed, sidled to the window, peeked through the curtains. Nothing. Just his snowbound Jaguar, and the few other vehicles that had been sitting there since he'd arrived. No Murphys, large or small. He went to the sink, threw a few handfuls of cold water in his face, dried himself, picked up the phone, and dialed.

After eight rings a thick voice answered. "Hello?"

"Rise and shine, Dave. This is your wake-up call."

"Jesus Christ. Who is this? Is that you, Bellweather?"

"*Doctor* Bellweather. Are you awake yet?"

"What is it, four-thirty in the morning?"

"Four thirty-five. Time to get up!"

"What are you talking about? I set up the meeting for ten."

"Big snowstorm out here, Dave. Better give yourself plenty of travel time. You're going to be there, right?"

"Don't worry about it," Getter said, and clicked off.

Bellweather hung up the phone and took another peek out the window. This was too nerve-racking, sitting in this motel room awaiting his fate. Besides, he had a serious transportation problem. He eyed a white 4 x 4 parked beside the motel office. Putting on his coat, he stepped outside. The snow had completely stopped, but the temperature had fallen. He could feel his nasal tissues freezing as he inhaled the subzero air. The lobby door was locked. Bellweather trudged through the snow around the motel office, to the back door of what looked like the manager's apartment, and he hammered on it until he saw the light go on. The door opened a crack, and an irritated male voice said, "Yes?"

"I'm Dr. Bellweather, staying in room sixteen?"

"Yes?"

"Are you the manager?"

"Maybe."

"Is this your vehicle?" He pointed at the 4 x 4. The door opened another few inches, and the man inside looked where Bellweather was pointing.

"That's my Isuzu. What's your problem?"

"It's quite serious. I've just been called on a medical emergency, and I have to get to Alexandria as quickly as possible. Unfortunately, my car—that Jaguar over there—isn't going anywhere in this weather."

"What sort of emergency you got? Can it wait?"

"I'm afraid not. It's an emergency multiple thoracic lipectomy. I'm the only surgeon in the state who is qualified to perform the procedure. I was scheduled for the surgery tomorrow, but the patient, a six-year-old girl, has had a serious prelapse."

The manager opened the door wider and turned on the light. "A prelapse, huh? You wanna come in, let me shut this door?"

Bellweather stepped inside. The small apartment, essentially another motel room, with a kitchenette squeezed into one of the corners, reeked of old perspiration, cigarettes, and intestinal gas.

"I'm Loyal Fitz," the manager said. "So you want me to drive you all the way into Alex?"

"Actually," said Bellweather, "I was hoping you would simply loan me your vehicle."

"My Isuzu?" Fitz scratched behind his ear. "Jeez, I just got the thing a couple months ago."

"I'm a very careful driver," Bellweather said. "And I'll be leaving my Jaguar here. I'll be back before noon." He smiled. "It would be much easier. You could go back to bed."

Fitz looked longingly at his rumpled bed.

"And of course, I'll pay for the use of your vehicle. Say two hundred dollars?"

Loyal Fitz nodded slowly.

Shortly after sunrise, the Murphys gathered in their kitchen. Amanda was making pancakes again. None of them had slept well.

Ricky wanted to leave early, get to Birdy's at nine or so, be there waiting for him, but George said there was no point to it.

"Best thing, Ricky, is just do what they say." He slurped a mouthful of coffee, set the cup carefully back on the table.

"You mean you're gonna give that son-of-a-bitch the money?"

"What money? What we do is, we go to Birdy's and we do whatever we have to do to get Shawn back. Except pay for him."

"How we gonna do that?"

"We just do it. You know what those guys are like. A couple of city boys. They think that because they're in a public place, nothing can happen to them. We just go in and make them give us Shawn. You want to do something useful, go get the Ford going and open up the driveway."

Ricky scowled. He finished his stack of cakes, then zipped up his parka and went out to plow the road.

"I still think you should call Orlan," Amanda said.

George rolled his eyes. "He'd just be in the way."

"I don't want you boys getting hurt."

"Hurt? By a chubby doctor and his weasely lawyer friend? Don't worry about it, Mandy. You just get lunch ready. That boy's gonna be hungry for some real food, he gets back here."

Although he always had his doors open by nine, Berdette Williams rarely made a sale until after eleven. The only reason he opened up so early was for the delivery guys and so that he could have a couple hours to himself. Arlene liked to sleep in, and that was fine by him. He had the whole rest of the day to put up with her. Sitting behind the bar, he sipped his third cup of coffee and let his mind slide. Used to be, he'd always been a nervous guy, always had to be doing something—cleaning up, repairing a broken something, watching television, talking on the phone, working the crossword puzzle. The last few years, since he had turned seventy-five, he didn't have to do that anymore. His energy had pretty much dissipated, and with it his anxiety. He could sit and drink his coffee, or just plain sit, and that was fine. He didn't feel things like he used to, didn't need to, and didn't mind a bit. The best of times, he had come to believe, were those times when a guy could let the time flow by without touching it, without feeling a thing.

He was surprised when the front door swung open a few minutes before ten o'clock. He was even more surprised—and irritated—to see George and Ricky Murphy enter his establishment. It took a lot to get him pissed off these days, but these two could do it.

Berdette put down his coffee.

"Morning, George," he said.

George inclined his big head.

Berdette shifted his eyes to Ricky. "Thought we had an understanding, Ricky."

"Oh, yeah? What was that?"

Berdette said, "Thought we agreed you were going to keep your scrawny ass out of here."

Ricky sat down at the far end of the bar. "Guess I forgot."

"Well, I'm reminding you."

"Now just take it easy, Berdette," George said. "Ricky, he's not going to do anything. Ain't even going to have a beer. Right, Ricky?"

Ricky shrugged.

"You're damn right he ain't gonna have a beer," Berdette said. "And if he ain't gonna have a beer, then there's no point in him being here, right?"

George sat down across from Berdette, put a hand on the old man's arm. "It's okay, Berdette. We're just here to meet a fellow. That's all. Ricky ain't gonna make any trouble."

"Still owes me for that stool."

Ricky laughed. "Hey, it was the guy's head broke it. I was just holding on to the legs."

Berdette glared, thinking about the old twelve-gauge he kept under the bar, wondering if the thing still worked. He'd had to wave it around a few times, but he hadn't shot it in years.

George seemed to read his thoughts and tightened his grip on Berdette's arm. "Now what's that stool worth, Berdette? Fifty bucks?" He released his grip, pulled out his wallet, and put two twenties and a ten on the bar. "Okay?"

Berdette looked down at the money sourly.

George said, "We'll be out of here in no time, Berdette. I promise."

Berdette stared back at him. He didn't have any quarrel with George, but Ricky was another matter, sitting down there with his shitty little grin. "You just make sure you keep a leash on that boy," Berdette said, picking up the money.

"I will, Berdette. Don't you worry about it, okay?"

Berdette turned away, found a clean bar towel, and started wiping down the schooners he had washed earlier. There wasn't a whole hell of a lot he could do except wait it out, whatever it was. There would always be unpleasant moments in this business, and they would always pass. George and Ricky sat silently, waiting.

•   •   •

At ten o'clock precisely, Dave Getter entered Birdy's. His eyes took a moment to adjust to the dim light. The bartender, an old man wearing a white shirt, stood behind the bar, polishing glasses. A big man wearing a baseball cap sat with his ass draped over a barstool, staring at him expressionlessly. That would be George Murphy. Getter looked around the room. At the opposite end of the bar, a gaunt young man glared at him from beneath the brim of a cowboy hat. Ricky. Getter pulled off his gloves, approached George.

"Good morning," he said. "George Murphy? I'm David Getter." His voice sounded pretty good. Hearty and confident. The first step was to put them at ease, impress them with his professionalism. He held out his hand.

George, unmoving, stared back at him.

"So." Getter clapped his hands together. "Here we are."

George said, "Oh? Seems to me somebody's missing."

Getter looked around. "Oh. You mean Dr. Bellweather. We should be hearing from him any minute now. Why don't we all have a cup of coffee and sit down?" He motioned at the man behind the bar. "Could we get some coffee here?"

The old man snorted but gave no other indication he had heard. Getter felt something behind him and turned around. Ricky was standing uncomfortably close. Getter took a half step back. "How's it going?" He gave Ricky a sharp nod, as if acknowledging an equal, looked down at the holstered revolver, looked at Ricky's hands, thumbs hooked into his belt on either side of an enormous brass buckle.

" 'Cowboys Do It in .45 Caliber,' " Getter read aloud. He laughed. "That's pretty good."

Ricky attached his unblinking gaze on Getter's forehead.

"Where's my son?" George rumbled.

The phone behind the bar rang.

"That's probably them now," Getter said. He leaned over the bar and raised his eyebrows at the bartender, who was answering the phone. "My name's Getter," he said. "Is that call for me?"

The bartender brought him the phone.

"Hello?"

"Are they there?" Bellweather's voice seemed strained.

"They're here. George and Ricky."

He could hear Bellweather's long exhalation. "Good. That's good. Anybody else?"

"Just the bartender."

"Good. Ask George if he brought the money."

Getter held the handset away from his mouth. "He wants to know if you brought the money."

"Sure I did," George said.

"He says he brought it."

"Does he have anything with him? A bag or a suitcase or anything?"

"I don't see anything."

"Okay. Here's what you do. Tell them I'm on my way. I'm bringing the boy with me. I'll be there in forty-five minutes. You stay with them, make sure they stay calm and reasonable."

"What? That's not what we talked about. I've done my part. I'm leaving."

"Fine. Leave, then, if they'll let you."

"If they *let* me? I—" The line went dead. Getter shook his head disgustedly.

"Where's my son?" George repeated.

"He's coming. Dr. Bellweather is bringing him. They'll be here in forty-five minutes."

"Forty-five minutes. That's a long time," George said.

Getter said, "It's not that long—"

A hand clamped on the back of his neck, he saw the top of the bar rushing toward him, he felt his nose explode on contact with the dark oak surface, heard George's deep voice say, "You're wrong, Dave. Forty-five minutes can be a very long time."

Six miles away, in the tiny office of Clint's Big River Amoco, Bellweather hung up the pay phone.

"Thanks," he said to Clint.

"Your quarter," Clint said, his cigarette bobbing up and down between his lips. "You gonna leave now?"

Bellweather had been waiting there for four hours, sitting in the smoky, oil-scented confines of the gas station office with Clint, the owner, checking his watch every five minutes. Clint had been friendly at first, glad to have company on this dead, snowbound morning, but for the past couple of hours he had become decidedly cool. Bellweather's hunting stories no longer held his attention.

"I'm leaving," Bellweather said. "Thanks for letting me wait inside."

Clint grunted and waved a hand laconically.

Bellweather ran out to the Isuzu, jumped in, took off. A mile up the highway, he turned into the road leading to Talking Lake Ranch, bounced and slid down the icy tracks. The dogs started barking as soon as he pulled up in front of the lodge. They could bark their little doggy heads off, so long as they stayed in their kennel. The door of the lodge was unlocked. As he stepped inside, he heard a clink of chain links. The tiger, reclined on her belly, had lifted her huge head and was staring at him. Keeping well beyond the perimeter defined by the chain, Bellweather crossed the room and entered the hallway leading to George's office. The door was open, the room dimly lit by the single window. He searched for the light switch, turned it on.

"There you are," he breathed. The mounted boar, which had never seemed particularly lovely before, now glowed with promise. Bellweather stroked the boar's bristly coat, probing with his fingers for the promised doorway.

A harsh voice sent his heart into a spasm.

"I smelled you."

Amanda Murphy was standing in the doorway, claws on her hips.

Bellweather clapped a hand to his chest. "Mrs. Murphy! You scared me half to death."

"I'm going to be doing worse than that."

Bellweather took a step toward the old woman, drawing his best bedside smile across his face. "George asked me to pick something up for him."

"Bull crap. I know what you are. Where's the boy?"

"He's with George and Ricky. I dropped him off with them at Birdy's. It was all a misunderstanding." He was only a few feet away now. Close enough to grab her and— "Whuff!"

Bellweather staggered back, clutching his crotch. The old bitch had planted a shoe right in his nuts, faster than he would have thought possible. He strained to overcome the pain, to go after her before she got to a phone, but she wasn't running. She was coming after him, claws held high. Bellweather lashed out with his foot, missed, and caught a cheek full of nails. He screeched and scrambled away from her, getting George's desk between them. She lunged at him, but her arms were too short. They circled the desk, Bellweather limping painfully, waves of nausea climbing from his testicles to his esophagus. He hadn't been hit in the balls like that since he was a kid—he couldn't believe how much it hurt. The old woman's face was contorted with fury. He didn't want to get anywhere near her. "I'm gonna rip your eyes out," she hissed. "I'm gonna cut your thing off and feed it to the animals."

In a burst of panic-induced strength, he picked up George's chair and hurled it across the desk. She was quick, but one of the chair legs caught her shoulder, knocking her off her feet. Bellweather ran around the desk, tried to get past her, but a wizened arm shot out and grabbed his leg, nails digging right through the fabric of his pants. Swinging wildly, he landed a series of punches on her head and arms, kept swinging until blood spouted from her mouth and nose and her grip loosened enough for him to shake her off. The old woman sank to the floor, moaning blood bubbles. Bellweather backed away through the doorway, horrified, his breath coming in loud, ragged gasps. All his instincts told him to get out of there, to run and never look back, but then his eyes once again caught sight of the boar. He hesitated, looked down at the old woman. She lay curled on her side, coughing weakly, a strand of bloody mucus connecting her mouth to the hardwood floor. She seemed to be out of it. He could still get what he'd come for. He started back into the room, giving her a wide berth, just in case. Sure enough, as soon as he got within a few feet of her she scrabbled after him, using all her limbs, like a tarantula after her prey. This time he was ready. The toe of his cowboy boot caught her on her temple; she went down as if she'd been sledgehammered.

Gasping, Bellweather watched her still body suspiciously. After thirty seconds had passed, he reached down and pushed up an eyelid. Her eyes were rolled up, a good sign that she wouldn't be coming around anytime soon. Her pulse was steady but faint.

"Okay, then," he said aloud. He returned his attention to the pig, feeling with his hands, seeking access. The boar's legs were permanently affixed to a heavy wooden base. Bellweather tried to slide the mount away from the wall. It weighed as much as a large sofa, but he was able to drag it out far enough to discover a flap on the wall side, revealing a metal door with a combination lock. It had been close to half an hour since his call to Birdy's. He wouldn't have time to remove the safe from the hog, let alone get it open. He looked over his shoulder at the unconscious Amanda Murphy, then at George's gun cabinet.

The cabinet was locked.

He used a chair to smash the glass front of the cabinet. Using his hands, he pulled away shattered bits of glass, then reached in and grabbed the metal box containing his old friend the MAC-10. He looked over his shoulder. Amanda hadn't moved. He opened the case, loaded the MAC, aimed it at the mounted hog, and let fly.

It took two clips to blow off all four legs. Bellweather's ears were howling from the repeated explosions. He loaded a fresh clip into the MAC, grabbed the quadruple amputee by its ears, and dragged it out of the office, through the lodge past an extremely alarmed tiger, and out to the waiting Isuzu.

XXIV

As I give thought to the matter, I find four causes for the apparent misery of old age; first, it withdraws us from active accomplishments; second, it renders the body less powerful; third, it deprives us of almost all forms of enjoyment; fourth, it stands not far from death.

—CICERO

Something reeks, Crow thought.

He was on his back, something lumpy pressed against his spine. He could hear breathing. His head hurt. A foul wind abraded his face.

Very close to his ear, a familiar cracked and ragged voice said, "He's coming round there, Puss. I told you he'd be okay. Look here, he's got his nose all squinched up."

A lighter, more distant voice replied, "That's on account of you blowin' your stink at 'im, H."

"My breath ain't that bad."

"Like my farts don't stink."

"Sheeit."

Crow hoped it was a dream. The last thing he remembered was driving down the highway, with Shawn Murphy sitting beside him. Or had that been a dream too? He opened his eyes a slit. As he suspected, the booze-and-time-ravaged visage of Harley Pike hovered a few inches above his nose.

"His eyes are open!" bellowed Harley, hitting Crow full force with the aroma of his diseased gums. Crow gasped and twisted away, grabbed the edge of the mattress beneath him, pulled himself into a seated position. Something banged around inside his head, showing him a few colorful flashes before subsiding to mere subvisual agony. He opened his eyes and took in his environment. He was sitting on a narrow bed at one end of a long, low, cluttered, dimly lit room. The air was warm, humid, and thick with cigarette smoke. Harley Pike, wearing nothing but a greasy, tattered black leather motorcycle jacket and stained gray briefs, stood over him, grinning.

At the other end of the room, Shawn Murphy sat at a narrow fold-out table, drinking an Old Milwaukee. Across from him, her long gray-blond hair hanging past her chin, sat one Gloria Schwep, better known as Puss. They were watching a small television. *Family Feud.*

Crow closed his eyes, counted to three, opened them. Nothing changed. He was still in Harley and Puss's dilapidated mobile home. Last time he remembered, it had been parked just off the highway on a piece of county land not far from the Murphys' ranch.

"You want a beer?" Harley bellowed.

Crow flinched at the renewed gas attack. "No, thanks," he croaked, reaching up to explore his forehead. The lump was tender, but smaller than he remembered.

"Best damn cure for a hangover."

He was right, of course, and Harley would know. His love of alcohol was local legend. Crow remembered his last encounter with Harley—was it only four days ago? Maybe longer. He had no idea how long he had been unconscious.

"You musta really been shit-faced, Crow. You won't believe where your car is."

"Where is it?" Crow asked.

Harley pointed out a smoke-yellowed window. Crow leaned forward and scanned the snow-covered panorama. His Rabbit was standing on its nose a few yards off the highway, its front end buried deep in a drift, the roof resting against a utility pole. He looked at Shawn.

"You okay?" It had always amazed him the way people could walk away from the worst-looking wrecks.

Shawn nodded. "I just got a little cut is all." He had a small piece of tape on his chin. Crow noticed that he no longer had the handcuffs hanging from his wrist.

"How'd you get those cuffs off?"

"H. got 'em off him," Puss said, firing a cloud of smoke through her nostrils. "I seen better locks on cheap luggage." Folks in Big River never quite understood how Gloria Schwep, a good local girl, had wound up with Harley Pike. To Crow, the answer was clear. Harley was the one who needed her, the one who made her feel sane. Puss had devoted her life to cleaning up Harley's messes, finding him odd jobs to keep him out of trouble for a few days at a time, bailing him out of jail when necessary. Her flat, grim expression never changed. She had a mission in life, which was more than most of them could say.

"I rolled a few cars myself," Harley said. "Never set one on its nose like that, though. I always knew you was no better'n me, Crow."

Crow moved his head, arms, and legs, testing them. Everything seemed to work. His head didn't feel so good, but it was better than it had been last night. At least he could think clearly.

"What happened?" he asked Shawn.

"I dunno. You passed out or something, and we ran off the road."

"Middle a the goddamn night, this kid comes banging on the door. Lucky I didn't shoot his ass." Harley squatted beside the small refrigerator and came out with a can of beer. "You sure you don't want one?"

"No, thank you." He looked at Shawn. "Aren't you a little young to be drinking beer for breakfast?"

"He was thirsty," Puss said with a defensive note. "We didn't have nothing else."

"Didn't know we was having company." Harley popped the top on his beer, took a long drink, belched. "Hadn't been for us, you'd a froze to death out there. Me and Puss, we had to drag you all the way back here. You was out cold."

"Yeah, well, thanks. I appreciate it."

Harley saluted Puss with his bottle. "Hear that, Puss? He fuckin' appreciates it. Sheeit. All the times he hauled my ass into jail, he's lucky I didn't leave his goddamn ass in the fuckin' snow."

Harley was starting to warm up.

Puss said, "Hey, H., you want to go knock the snow off the antenna? This reception is for shit."

Harley glared at her, breathing loudly through his nose. "Goddamn snow," he said. He grabbed a pair of filthy jeans from a pile next to the bed, pulled them over his hairy white legs, forced his bare feet into a pair of twisted, salt-rimed engineer boots. A minute later, they heard him thumping around on the aluminum roof, his muted curses raining down.

Crow turned to Puss. "How many beers has he had this morning?" He frowned. "It is morning, isn't it?"

"He's had a few," Puss replied. "He'll be okay for a while. He's mostly mouth these days."

"What time is it?"

"Ten or eleven, something like that." She looked at the television. "Whatever time *Family Feud* is on, that's what it is."

"I take it Harley doesn't have a job right now."

"He don't have no work today, that's for damn sure."

"Yeah. Listen, I've got to get this boy home. Have you got a car or something I can use?" Crow stood up. He was still wearing his shoes and his coat. His legs were shaky, but they seemed to be holding him up. That was good. "Or a phone?"

Puss lit another cigarette. "No phone. There's H.'s jeep back in the shed. The heater don't work so good, but it runs. Or if you want, we got this old Polaris. You're heading for the Murphy place, you might want to take the Polaris, go cross-country. It'd be a lot shorter. There's a trail runs along the river, you come right up in their backyard that way. If you take the road, you've got to go all the way around."

"I don't feel up to handling a snowmobile today, Puss. Mind if I give the jeep a try?"

"I don't mind, but H. might. You know how he gets."

"I suppose it won't hurt to ask."

Puss shrugged. "Mind if I ask you something, Crow? Why the hell you come back to Big River? You don't got enough grief already?"

"Business."

She snorted smoke. "I keep telling H. we should move, get him a real job, something with dental insurance so he could, you know, get his choppers worked on. He don't want to go."

Crow said nothing. A series of metallic booms announced Harley's descent from the roof. When he entered the trailer, Crow asked, "How's that jeep of yours running, Harley?"

"Runs fine," Harley said suspiciously. "Why?"

"I was wondering if I could borrow it to give this boy a ride home."

"I don't like nobody using my wheels."

"I won't need it long. Just an hour or so."

"Uh-uh."

"Harley," Puss said, "let the man use your goddamn jeep."

Harley twisted up his face and glowered at her. He raised a fist and worked it back and forth in the air between them.

Puss crossed her arms. "You touch me, you'll never be able to fall asleep again. You unnerstand me, H.?"

"Always taking the other side, ain'tcha."

"Only when you act like a shithead. Christamighty, H., you want these two hanging around for the rest of the day, or you want to make him a loan of the goddamn jeep?"

Harley scowled, then brightened. "How about I drive 'em into town myself."

"You ain't going nowhere, H."

"I'll go anywheres I damn please, bitch."

"You call me bitch again, I'm gonna piss in your goddamn beer next time you ain't lookin'. Now where you got those keys stashed?"

"Up my fuckin' ass. You wanna see?"

Fascinated by the display of interpersonal dynamics, Crow stood silently by as Puss negotiated the jeep for him. He tried to imagine having such a conversation with Melinda—down and dirty, no verbal holds barred. Maybe it would be good, if either of them survived it. It seemed to work for Harley and Puss—at least they were still living together.

The discussion went on for a few more minutes, getting louder and fouler all the time. Shawn, still sitting at the table gripping his half-empty beer, stared open-mouthed at the domestic drama. Crow wasn't sure what triggered it—perhaps they had run out of insults—but the discussion suddenly ended with Harley sitting back on the bed, sulking, while Puss dangled the keys to the jeep before Crow's nose.

"A couple things," she said. "You got to gas it up, and you got to pick us up a case of beer on your way back."

Crow took the keys.

"Hell with that," Harley snarled. "You get me a jug a that J.D. One a them big ones."

Puss said, "No way, H. I see you with a jug, I'm'n'a bust it over your thick skull. I had it with that shit. You stick with the beer."

"A case of beer it is. Let's go, kiddo," Crow said to Shawn.

After considerable hacking and groaning, the jeep, a veteran of the U.S. Postal Service, steering wheel on the wrong side, started. Crow put it in gear and lurched out of the tin garage, crawled through the snow toward the highway.

"So you think your dad will be happy to see you?"

"I dunno," said Shawn. "I think he might be kind of mad."

"Why? It wasn't your fault that Bellweather kidnapped you."

"I s'pose. Only he didn't, exactly."

"What d'you mean?"

"Well, I sort of ran away." Shawn wiped his nose on his jacket sleeve.

"Why'd you do that?"

Shawn shrugged. "I dunno."

"What did you do, hitchhike into town?"

"You took me."

"What? Me? I don't think so."

"I climbed in the back of Doc's car, and you drove me to Doc's house."

Crow said, "Tell me you're kidding."

"And then we went to stay at Nate and Ginny's. And then Doc said he was gonna take me home, only he didn't. He's really weird."

Crow was still working on the suggestion that he had taken Shawn Murphy. He remembered Bellweather showing him the large storage space in the Jaguar, a space big enough for a ten-year-old boy.

"You know what he likes to do?" Shawn asked.

Crow cleared his throat. "No. What?" He wasn't sure he wanted to hear this.

"He has this little machine. It's like a little thing that you put batteries in, you know?"

"Yeah?" Crow didn't, but he suspected the worst.

"He, like, he sticks it in his nose. He trims his nose hairs."

"He trims his nose hairs," Crow repeated.

"Yeah. Isn't that weird?"

"Hey, I told you no more of that," Berdette said.

Ricky shook out his fist. "Sorry, old man. I had a spasm."

Dave Getter wrapped his arms around his belly and coughed. His nose was swollen grotesquely from its encounter with the top of the bar. Ricky had been treating him to the occasional punch in the ribs, whenever it occurred to him.

"Long as you're in my place, you keep your damn hands off him. And don't call me 'old man.' "

"No problem, Bird."

"And don't call me Bird." Berdette didn't like having these three guys sitting at his bar, and he didn't like what was happening to the guy in the suit. It was a very strange situation. They would sit there and talk, then all of a sudden Ricky would give the guy a shot for no particular reason. Typical Ricky Murphy behavior.

George Murphy sat hunched over the bar, staring morosely into a glass of beer.

"Where is he?" he asked. "It's almost eleven, and I don't see my son."

"I don't know," said Getter miserably.

Ricky said, "I'm getting sick a waiting here."

The telephone rang. Getter's head lifted hopefully.

"That better be good news," George said.

Berdette answered the phone, listened for a moment. "No, sugar, there's nothing going on here. You come on in about noon, we'll be fine." He hung up. "Arlene," he said.

George scowled. Both George and Ricky looked at Getter, who drew back and squeaked, "What? What's wrong?"

Ricky's fist crashed into his cheek, knocked him off the stool.

"Hey!" Berdette shouted. This was getting way out of hand. They were going to kill the guy. He was getting all pumped up, feeling like he hadn't felt in years. "I'm talking to you, boy!"

Ricky ignored him.

"Let's go." George was up off his stool, headed out the door. "Bring him," he said over his shoulder. Ricky grabbed Getter's collar, jerked him to his feet, started dragging him toward the door. Getter screamed and tried to pull away. Ricky punched him again, in the belly, propelled him toward the exit. Getter dropped to the floor beside the bar, wrapped his arms around the foot rail. Ricky kicked him in the ribs. "Get up, damn you!"

"Hey!" Berdette shouted, coming around the end of the bar. "I mean it this time. Lay off him." He held the shotgun in front of his body, not exactly pointing it at anybody but letting them know it was there. "You hear me?" The shells were loaded with rock salt, a painful but nonlethal alternative to lead shot. Hadn't fired the thing for years, but he was ready to give Ricky Murphy a load any second now.

Ricky gave him a slit-eyed look, then grinned, helped Getter to his feet, brushed him off. "You okay?"

Getter nodded, wincing, wrapping his arms around his rib cage.

Ricky said to Berdette, "See? He's fine."

"Now you get your ass out of here, Ricky."

"No problem, Bird. Come on, Dave. You ready?"

Getter shook his head. "Please—"

Ricky gave him a jab, right on the tip of his swollen proboscis. Getter shrieked. Ricky said, "There, that'll give you something to cry about."

That did it. Berdette brought the shotgun up and around. A long-barreled revolver materialized in Ricky's right hand. Berdette heard a double explosion and suddenly found himself walking backward. The lawyer was screaming. Berdette wondered, Why am I walking backward? The shotgun fell from his hand. Ricky Murphy and his grin were getting smaller, racing away into the distance. Berdette thought, The son-of-a-bitch shot me. A moment before, he had been feeling his oats. Now he didn't feel a thing.

These guys you see walking down the street talking to themselves—they always seem to know what to say.

—JOE CROW

oyal Fitz, owner of the Sea Breeze Motel, was happy to have his Isuzu back but seemed somewhat alarmed by the legless hog.

"What is it?"

"What does it look like?" said Bellweather.

"A stuffed pig," said Fitz. "I thought you said you was going to save some little girl's life."

"I did," said Bellweather.

"So what's with the stuffed pig?"

"Just help me get it into my room," Bellweather snapped. He pulled on the pig's ears until it slid out of the Isuzu and landed with a crackling thud on the ice-coated asphalt.

"It's got no legs," Fitz said.

"I know that. I had to perform an emergency legectomy. You want to grab on there and give me a hand?" He grabbed the boar's snout with both hands.

Fitz grimaced but persuaded himself to grasp the curly tail and help the doctor carry the thing across the parking lot to room sixteen.

"Thanks," said Bellweather once they had lifted the pig onto the bed.

"What you gonna do with it?"

"Nothing."

Fitz frowned at the upside-down porker, his imagination straining but failing to grasp the significance of a stuffed, legless pig in one of his motel rooms. "You ain't some kind of cult weirdo, are you?"

"No, I am not," Bellweather said.

Fitz nodded slowly. "Checkin' out today?"

"Yes. Very soon. Now if you'll excuse me . . . ?"

Fitz nodded again, even more slowly, but did not leave.

"Would you please leave now?" Bellweather grasped Fitz's arm and guided him toward the door.

Fitz shook off his grip. "What about my two hundred bucks?"

Bellweather pulled out his wallet and gave him a handful of twenties. "For the room and the truck. Okay?"

Fitz accepted the money and said, "I got that pink car of yours all shoveled out. She's ready to go."

"I know, I saw. Thank you."

"What you gonna do with that pig?"

Bellweather gave him a final push out of the room. "I'm going to make bacon," he said as he slammed the door. He watched through the curtain as Fitz wandered back toward the motel office. He would have to move quickly. There was still the possibility that the kid had got home and spilled his guts. Bellweather opened his overnight bag and extracted a flat black vinyl case filled with medical paraphernalia. Using a scalpel, he began furiously to slice away at the boar, ripping through the tough, dry pigskin with the short steel blade, cutting around the small safe embedded in its side, stopping every few seconds to peer out the window. Within minutes, the bed was covered with shards of pigskin and musty-smelling excelsior, and Bellweather was holding a black metal safe that measured twelve inches on a side, frowning, wondering how the hell he was going to get the thing open.

"I don't think my dad's home," Shawn said. "Hummer's gone."

"He's probably out looking for you," Crow said.

"I bet Grandy's home. I'm really hungry."

"Grandy's your grandmother?"

"Uh-huh. I bet she's making lunch. You want to come in?"

Crow was hungry too, but not hungry enough to spend any longer than he had to on Talking Lake Ranch.

"No, thanks. I have to get going." He wanted nothing more to do with the Murphys. He would give George his kid back, and that was it. He wanted out.

"Okay," said Shawn. He opened the door and ran around the house to the kitchen door. Crow turned the jeep and headed back up the long driveway. He felt ill, whether from the beating he had taken, from the lack of good, quality sleep, or from the bouncing and swaying of Harley's jeep. His sense of purpose had deserted him. Not that it had been that strong in the first place, but he now felt as if he were falling in several directions at once. He needed desperately to land, to come to rest. Anywhere would do.

Bringing the jeep to a halt where the Murphys' private road intersected the highway, he sat there, engine idling. Puss hadn't been exaggerating about the heater not working so good. As near as he could tell, it didn't work at all.

"What am I doing here?" he said aloud.

"You're sitting in a damn jeep, freezing your ass off," he replied. He dropped the jeep into gear and pulled out onto the highway, turning left.

"Wrong way," he said.

"I know."

A camouflaged Hummer appeared, heading toward the ranch, George Murphy hunched over the steering wheel, staring straight ahead. As the Hummer passed, Crow caught a glimpse of a passenger who looked like . . . Dave Getter? Nah. He continued down the road, choosing not to waste any of his slim reserves of mental energy on a puzzle that could not possibly have anything whatsoever to do with Joe Crow.

"Old Joe Crow, he don't care," Crow muttered. A former idea bloomed again, sent a seductive surge of endorphins down his spinal column.

Crow drew a shaky breath.

"Okay, then," he said in a hoarse voice.

George climbed out of the Hummer and opened the door leading into the lodge. The tiger opened one eye.

"You all alone in here, gal?"

The tiger yawned.

George went back to the vehicle. "Take him inside. I'm going to go check my phone machine, see if that little son-of-a-bitch called here."

Ricky pulled Getter out of the Hummer and walked him into the lodge.

"What do you guys want? I keep telling you, I had nothing to do with it." Getter was limping from the blast of rock salt that had abraded his thigh.

"That's right, you keep telling us." Ricky shoved him into a chair. "Now shut the fuck up."

The tiger rose to her feet and walked toward them, her yellow eyes unblinking, until she was stopped by the chain. "You stay real still now," Ricky said. "She can snap that chain anytime she wants, you know?"

Getter closed his eyes and shuddered miserably.

Ricky followed George into the hallway. "I got to tell you, bro, I don't think he knows nothing."

George said, "Yeah, well, we got a whole 'nother problem now on account of he saw you center-shoot old Berdette. He starts screaming bloody murder, old Orlan ain't gonna be able to smooth things over."

"So we just feed him to the tiger."

George shook his head. "You'll make her sick. Keep an eye on him, would ya?" He opened the door leading into the kitchen.

"Well, I'll be goddamned."

Shawn Murphy, sitting at the kitchen table eating a bowl of Frosted Flakes, looked up.

"Well, I'll be goddamned to hell and back." A wide smile split George's face. "Where did you come from, boy?"

"I just got home," Shawn said. "That guy gave me a ride home."

"What guy?"

"He's gone now."

"Nelly Bell?"

Shawn shook his head. "A different guy. I think his name is Crow or something."

"Crow?"

"Something like that."

George let his head bob slowly, digesting this new bit of information. He reached out toward his son, let a hand fall on the boy's shoulder, covering it. "Crow," he muttered. "I'll be goddamned."

"He said for me to tell you he'd send you a bill."

Murphy nodded. "So where you been, boy?"

Shawn stirred his Frosted Flakes.

"Were you with that Nelly Bell?"

"I was for a while. Ow!"

George relaxed his grip, let his hand slide off the boy's shoulder.

"I got away from him," Shawn said. "He was gonna take me home, but then he didn't, and so I ran away. He's sort of weird, y'know?"

George pulled a chair away from the table, lowered himself into it. "Did he do anything to you? Like you were telling me before?"

Shawn shook his head.

George pushed his face forward, getting it between Shawn and the bowl of cereal. "He do anything to you?"

Shawn's face went blank. "He didn't do nothing."

George sat back. He wanted to ask more, but he could tell the kid was shutting down, and besides, he didn't really want to know. His son was back, and that would have to be enough for now. He filled his lungs with air, let it out, looked around the kitchen. Something was missing.

"Where's Mandy?" he asked.

Shawn shrugged. "I dunno. I don't think she's around."

Bronson's On/Off Sale Liquors had a sale on Old Milwaukee. Crow nodded to the woman at the cash register, walked through the store, grabbed a case of cans from the cooler. On his way back to the front of the store, he lifted a bottle of Old Crow from the shelf, set it alongside the beer on the front counter. The woman looked up from her *TV Guide,* smiled briefly, rang up his purchase. Eighteen ninety-two. Crow handed her his last twenty-dollar bill, wordlessly accepted his change, carried his new possessions out to the jeep, headed east. When he reached his upended Rabbit, he pulled over, unloaded the Old Milwaukee at the head of Harley and Puss's driveway, leaned on the horn. Harley opened the door to his house trailer a moment later. Crow waved and pulled back out onto the highway. He heard Harley shout something.

As he passed Birdy's, he noticed a silver Mercedes parked there. It looked a lot like Dave Getter's.

"Old Crow, he don't care," he muttered.

For the next seventy miles, Crow's mind stumbled through the wreckage of the past week. The days played back like a nightmare, a directionless, purposeless, painful journey. Melinda was missing? That was her problem. He no longer believed that Orlan Johnson or the Murphys had anything to do with it. Bellweather had skipped town? So what? It had been a lousy job anyway. Debrowski? Just another ex-doper in a motorcycle jacket. No matter how he diced and re-formed events, he was still broke and adrift. The nearest he would get to happiness lay within the unopened bottle between his legs. He could almost feel the promising burn of raw bourbon flowing over his tonsils. He rubbed his thumb on the smooth glass bottle, felt its square shape, picked with his fingernail at the edge of the label, gripped the knurled screw top, felt the hollowness inside his body grow. Unlike the people in his life, bourbon could be relied upon. He would drink it; he would feel better.

He kept going. The bottle remained sealed, but he was getting drunk, absorbing the alcohol right through the glass. The barrage of unwanted thoughts slowed; he had to concentrate to keep the jeep traveling in a straight line. His feet were getting numb. He hunched his shoulders to hold in the warmth and squeezed the steering wheel hard, forcing sensation through his gloves, into his fingers. The image of his apartment beckoned. He would let himself in, pour himself a civilized drink, sit down, and douse his mind. As the snowy countryside flashed by, he blotted recent memories with thoughts of anticipated pleasures. Passing through the small town of Clara City, he counted three liquor stores and seven bars. A nice little town. He could stop in at any one of those businesses, have a few drinks, talk about the Vikings, and see not a single familiar face. It would be warm, and friendly, and easy. Warmer and friendlier than his empty apartment—but not as easy. He continued on through the town.

By the time he reached the outer suburbs of Minneapolis, a new headache had formed at the base of his skull, and the bouncing and yawing of the jeep was making him acutely aware of his knotted, empty stomach. He frowned and swallowed. The Murphys appeared in his mind again. A smiling George, arm around his prodigal son. The ache rolled over the top of his head and began to throb in rhythm with the jeep's laboring engine.

"It's not fair." His words were sucked out of the jeep by the wind. It really wasn't fair. He hadn't even opened the bottle, and already he was suffering from a hangover. What kind of world is this, he wondered, where a man has to suffer for sins he has yet to commit? An angry impulse urged him to fling the bottle out onto the highway, but another voice told him that as long as he was already having the hangover, he might as well get loaded. A third Crow, the one driving the jeep, observed this dialogue with sour amusement.

"Too many Crows," he muttered.

"I agree."

A road sign became legible. CTY RD 40. For a moment, Crow rode alone in silence. That exit would lead him to Bellweather's house—actually, Bellweather's *former* house, since it now seemed to belong to the U.S. Government. It was not an exit he had any reason or desire to take, yet he found the jeep edging toward the ramp. Apparently, one Crow still cared about the whereabouts of the missing liposuctionist. The curious Crow. The one who was always getting him in trouble.

Another Crow retained control of the vehicle, passed the exit, and continued on toward his apartment, the bottle of Old Crow warm between his legs. The bottle was real. You could say a lot of bad things about alcohol, but one fact remained: It worked every time. Just thinking about it made him feel solid. He could fall apart again later.

XXVI

Nothing in his life became him like the leaving it.

—*WILLIAM SHAKESPEARE*

rlan Johnson was having a lousy day off. His belly ached where Crow had hit him, he'd tossed and turned all night, and first thing he gets up, the Hill wants him to go out and snowblow the driveway. He'd managed to stay in his bathrobe and grumble around the house all morning. All he really wanted to do was sit in front of the tube and have a few beers, let her bitch. It wasn't until she threatened not to cook him lunch that he put on his insulated bib overalls and fluorescent orange down vest, went out to the garage to fire up the Toro. He'd just gotten the snowblower moving, started his first sweep down the driveway, when Hillary started shouting and waving to him from the house.

Now what? He shut down the blower and glared at his wife.

"What's that?"

"You've got to get out to Birdy's, Orlan. Somebody's shot old Berdette."

Sure enough, when he arrived at Birdy's he found two of his officers—Nelson and Fleener—standing over old Berdette Williams. Arlene, who'd found her dead husband, was crumpled in one of the booths, looking about half her usual size. First thing he did, he took Nelson aside and asked him what in the got-damn hell was going on.

"Found him just like you see, Chief. His wife called it in."

"She shoot him?"

"I dunno. There's that Mercedes out front, and nobody to go with it.

Hasn't been there too long. Windows aren't even frosted up yet. And we found him with that old shotgun still in his hands, one shell fired. Looks to me like he took a shot at somebody and got his self shot instead."

"That don't mean she wasn't the one shot the poor bastard." The idea that a guy's wife would shoot him made sense to him.

"No, it don't," Nelson agreed. "Only I got a feeling it wasn't her that did it."

Johnson was disappointed. He liked crimes where he didn't have to go chasing people all over the countryside. He liked the ones where a guy knew right away who did it.

"Yeah, well, you and Fleener take her the hell out of there. Take her home. We can talk to her later. And run the plates on that krautmobile. You call the M.E. yet?"

"Just after we called you."

As soon as they left him alone with the dead man, Johnson got hit with a case of the creeps and figured out that what he needed was a good stiff drink. Even under such gruesome circumstances, he enjoyed playing bartender, figuring out where Berdette kept the limes and how to get tonic out of the soda shooter. He walked the drink back to his usual booth, slid in, put his Sorels up on the seat, took a look around the place.

It made him feel sad, like it was the end of an era. The Berdette Williams era. "Yeah, I knew old Berdette real well. Berdette was a friend of mine," he imagined himself saying.

Of course, Berdette might not've agreed with that.

The coroner finally showed up, asked a few stupid questions, took some notes. Johnson watched her go through her routine, which seemed to take forever. She and her assistant got the body on the gurney, raised it up, wheeled it toward the door.

Now that Berdette was gone, Johnson felt himself relaxing. He had never been all alone in a bar before. It was peaceful.

Feeling the need to do something coplike, Johnson considered the facts of the case.

One, Berdette was dead, shot in the chest.

Two, a mysterious Mercedes-Benz was parked outside.

Three, his glass was empty, and no one was there to fill it.

He slid out of the booth, walked around the end of the bar, made himself another v.t.—this one a double, for poor old Berdette.

• • •

Crow stood in the lobby of his apartment building, staring at the notice taped to the wall above the mailboxes. The illustration, done with felt-tip markers on a sheet of typewriter paper, looked a lot like Milo. Big and black, with yellow eyes. Above the illustration, large block letters spelled out LOST CAT. Below, in smaller print, it said: "Big black cat with yellow eyes. Answers to Milo." Two phone numbers were printed at the bottom of the page. One of them was his. The other one he didn't recognize.

He let himself into his apartment, put the bottle of bourbon on the kitchen counter, picked up the phone, and punched in the unfamiliar number. An answering machine picked up. He listened to twenty seconds of distorted rock and roll, then Debrowski's recorded voice instructed him to leave a message. He said, "This is Crow. Just calling to thank you for the sign." He hung up, feeling uncomfortable, as if he didn't deserve the favor, as if now that she had done this nice thing for him, he couldn't drink his bottle of bourbon.

He dropped his coat on a chair, turned up the thermostat, and stood over the heat register by the door. His hands were cold and stiff from gripping the steering wheel. The phone began to ring as he clenched and unclenched his hands, forcing fresh blood into the capillaries.

"Should I answer it?" he asked.

Okay, I'll answer it, he thought, and if it's not about Milo, I'll hang up and I'll pour myself a drink about eight inches deep.

He picked up the phone and listened.

"Officer Crow?"

Crow made an unpleasant sound in his throat.

"I want to thank you for returning my son to me." Murphy's voice sounded strained, as if he were talking with his jaw wired shut.

Crow shrugged. "No problem," he said.

"Do you know where I am, Crow?"

"I have no idea."

"I'm at the hospital in Alexandria."

"Oh?"

"I'm with my mother."

Crow waited.

"Someone hurt her, Crow. Beat her unconscious. Broke her ribs, beat her head, left her for dead."

"I'm sorry to hear that," Crow said. "I know how she feels."

"I doubt you do, Officer Crow. When you are nearly eighty years old, you do not take a beating as well as you do when you are a young man." Murphy was speaking oddly, spacing his words, holding himself back. "Do you know who did this thing to my mother?"

Crow said, "Are you asking, or are you going to tell me?"

"I am going to tell you. Your Dr. Bellweather did it."

Crow was surprised. It didn't seem like Bellweather's style.

"Yes, he did," said Murphy, answering the unspoken objection. "She is awake now, and she remembers."

"Why are you telling me this?" asked Crow.

"I want you to understand how serious I am. I want you to find that doctor, and I want you to bring him to me."

"Sorry. I already delivered your kid. That's it for me. Why don't you send your psychopathic brother after him?"

Crow listened to Murphy's breath whistling in and out of his nose. It took him several seconds to reply.

"I am being very serious with you now, Officer Crow. Ricky is like a duck on the ground when he gets in the city. He would not be able to find this doctor. You may not be able to find him either, but it would be best if you would. I am not the only person involved in this conversation to have a family member in danger. Are you listening?"

Crow's body began to tingle. Melinda.

He heard himself say, "I'm listening."

"Good. The doctor left here about three hours ago, shortly before you dropped off my son. He has a piece of property belonging to me, a mounted Russian boar about five feet long. Inside the boar is a small metal safe. I want you to find the doctor and the safe, and bring them both to me. Do you understand?"

Despite the horror he was feeling, Crow found himself thinking that Murphy sounded a lot like a *Mission Impossible* instruction tape.

"I understand," he said. "But I have no idea where Bellweather is."

"Find him."

"I want to talk to Melinda," Crow said.

Murphy hesitated. "Who is Melinda?" he asked.

Crow felt a pang of hope. "You said something about a family member."

"That's right. Your brother-in-law, the lawyer. He's with Ricky right now, but I don't think he's enjoying himself. Find the doctor, and I'll let you have the lawyer."

"Are you talking about Dave Getter? You think I care what happens to him?"

Murphy said, "I think you do."

Crow laughed and hung up the phone. He sat at the kitchen counter and waited for his insides to settle. So Bellweather had ripped off George Murphy. I should be enjoying this, he thought. He rotated the bottle, running his eyes across the words printed on the label without extracting any meaning from them. He was still sitting there when, ten minutes later, the phone rang again. He picked it up and listened.

"You're welcome," said Debrowski after a pause. "I just wanted to let you know—no one's called here yet."

"Here either."

"I stopped at the Humane Society. No yellow-eyed black cats."

"Thanks."

"You don't sound so good, Crow. What are you doing?"

"Sitting here." He cleared his throat. "You want to come over and help me get drunk?"

Pause. "Sure. What are you drinking?"

"I got a jug of fine Kentucky bourbon here."

"I'll be right over."

Debrowski arrived, replete with leathers and chains, fifteen minutes later. Her eyes scoured his face, then flicked to the bottle on the counter. The bottle was open. Beside it sat two glasses, each of them containing a carefully poured inch of amber fluid.

"Thanks for waiting," she said. "So what are we celebrating?"

"The end of sobriety," said Crow. He felt horrible. When he had poured the drinks, the smell of raw liquor had nearly made him vomit. Waiting for Debrowski, he'd managed to eat a few crackers. Now he was salivating uncontrollably, each swallow followed by a wave of nausea.

"You don't look so good," she said, perching on one of the stools. She picked up a glass, swirled the liquid, smelled it. "I used to drink this shit by the gallon."

Crow stared at her, horrified by the sight of her holding the glass so near her lips. "Are you . . . how long has it . . . how long have you been straight?" He was thinking of a matter of weeks.

Debrowski bit her lip and thought. "Four years," she said.

"Four *years?* Look, I don't like this. I don't want to—"

"Screw you, Crow." Debrowski raised the glass, swallowed the entire shot, slammed the glass back down on the counter. She squeezed her eyes shut, emptied her lungs, took a deep breath, opened her watering eyes.

Crow gaped at her, hardly able to believe what he had seen.

"See how easy it is?" she said, her voice lower by an octave. She poured herself another, larger drink.

"I don't want you to do that," Crow said.

"Why not? Isn't this why you invited me over here?"

Crow shook his head. He had no idea why he had invited her over.

"What's going on, Crow? Talk to me." She lifted her glass of bourbon.

"Please don't do that."

"Talk to me, Crow."

Crow took a breath. "What do you want?"

"You've got a problem, Crow. Tell me about it."

Crow turned and walked back and forth in front of the sofa. "It's sort of complicated," he said.

"Try me."

"My brother-in-law is the asshole of the world."

Debrowski set her glass gently on the counter.

"That's a start," she said.

She was a good listener. Crow wound his way through his story, giving it to her in bits and pieces, answering her questions, taking every opportunity to tell her what a jerk he had for a brother-in-law. He wanted to be sure she understood that part.

"So you don't like the guy."

"I never liked him."

"Why not?"

"I thought I explained that."

"What, he's a sleazy lawyer? Treats you like shit?"

"Basically."

"That doesn't sound so bad, Crow. You go around hating everybody that treats you like a dog, you wind up putting out a lot of negative energy. I mean, you act like a dog, people are going to treat you that way."

"Thanks a hell of a lot."

"What about your sister?"

"What about her?"

"Does she like him?"

"She hasn't divorced him."

"That's not the same."

Crow considered. "I think she cares about him," he said. "I don't know why, but she does."

"You like your sister?"

"She's a space cadet, but she's my sister."

"Do you think they'd actually hurt him?"

"Who? Getter? I think they'd hurt him a lot."

"But you think he deserves it."

"Oh, yeah." Crow sat on the sofa, crossed his arms, stared at his knees. "They'd hurt him good."

"So what are you going to do?"

"I'm not sure. What do you think?"

Debrowski shook her head. "Uh-uh, Crow, this one is all yours. Besides, you've already made up your mind." She picked up the two glasses, poured the bourbon into the sink.

Crow raised his head. "What are you doing?"

Debrowski tipped the bottle into the sink, let the liquor gurgle out. Crow watched, his eyes dull.

"I have to get going, Crow. I've got a meeting with one of my bands. Toesucker. You ever hear of them?"

Crow shook his head.

"Neither has anybody else." She opened the door. "Thanks for the drink, Crow."

XXVII

They want you to make it like it never bled and died,
like all they did was stop time. Like they snapped this
three-D photo, and you're the developer.

—OLLIE AAMOLD

llie Aamold sat in his workshop, surrounded by the body
parts of assorted animals, contemplating the head of a four-point buck.
He dipped the tip of a number-four sable brush into a jar of thinned
acrylic paint and carefully darkened the edges of the buck's eyelids.
Some taxidermists would use a marker for these final touches, but Ollie
was a perfectionist. The details were what made the difference. A good
mount looked alive—frozen in time, but alive.

Taxidermy was an art form, and Ollie Aamold was an artist.

He sat back and examined the shoulder mount. It was a pretty animal, had a nice inquiring tilt to its head, but no matter how good a job
he did, the animal would never make much of a trophy. He was repeatedly amazed by these so-called hunters who would plunk down hundreds of dollars to have their substandard kills immortalized. Buck like
that, he would maybe have shot it for meat, but more likely he'd have
let it walk.

What the hell. It was a living. He'd even mounted a few pet dogs in
his time. Once, he'd even done a gerbil for his nephew. Later, he
learned, the kid had used the thing to terrorize his little sister.

Thank God for the Murphys. At least they came up with some interesting animals. He'd done zebras, caribou, gemsbok, all sorts of creatures he'd never seen before. A few years back, they'd brought him a
white rhino—not a huge specimen, as rhinos went, but the biggest
thing he'd ever had a chance to work on. His favorite animals, though,

were the big cats. Beautiful. George had told him that the tiger would be coming his way soon. Ollie was really looking forward to that. He'd never done a tiger before.

The telephone rang. Ollie let it go for five rings, then picked it up.

"Ollie? Steve Anderson here."

"Yeah?" The name didn't do anything for him.

"You got my elk. I dropped it off a couple days ago?"

"Oh, yeah, the shoulder mount. You want it to be bugling, right? Nice rack." Another worthwhile trophy courtesy of the Murphys.

"Four hundred eighteen points."

"Is that right."

"I was wondering . . . I'm having a little party at my place in a couple weeks, some old buddies are going to be in town, and I'd like to, you know, show it off a little. I know it's kind of soon, but I was wondering if there was any way you could have it ready by then. A week from next Saturday, say?"

Ollie rolled his eyes up. He didn't trust himself to reply.

"Ollie? You there?"

"Yeah, I'm here." Always a mistake to pick up the damn phone.

"What do you think?"

"Negatory."

"Damn! Not even if I kick in a little extra money? Say an extra couple hundred?"

Assholes with money, think they can buy anything. "Negatory," Ollie repeated. "Haven't even sent your elk to the tannery yet, and that takes better'n a month."

"Jeez. I gotta tell you, I'm really disappointed. It would mean a lot to me."

Ollie gave the telephone the finger.

"Isn't there some way? I mean, suppose I was the President of the United States. Could you do it for the President?"

Ollie let out the breath he had been holding for the past thirty seconds. "Look," he said, keeping a tight leash on his voice. "This isn't like hammering together a birdhouse. Good work takes time. You bagged yourself a nice animal here. You don't want me to do a hack job on it, do you?"

"No, but—"

"But nothing. Even if you were the president of the goddamn universe I couldn't have it for you. A mount takes time—there's just no way."

"Suppose I—"

"Suppose nothing. Can't do it. Give me three, three and a half weeks, I could maybe pickle it here instead of sending it out, but it'd be losing hair inside a year. First you bring me a bison with its face all shot to hell, now this. If you were in such a damn hurry, you should have brought your elk in the day you shot it instead of letting it sit around. You think I like working with an elk that's been dead a week?"

"A week? But I—"

"Week, six days, whatever. You know when you shot it. All I know is I wouldn't want to have to eat the damn thing. Looked like it was froze, thawed, and froze all over again. Thing's already shedding hair like crazy. You shoot an animal like this, you got to get it caped and salted down right away. You had this big to-do planned, you should've brought it straight to me. Course, even if you had, I still couldn't a done 'er for you."

Anderson didn't reply for a moment, then he said, "I dropped it off the same day I shot it." It sounded as if he was holding the phone away from his mouth.

Ollie snorted. "Negatory. Let me tell you something, Mr. Anderson. I don't need your business. You can come and pick up your cape and antlers anytime you want. And let me tell you something else. I've seen a lot of dead animals, and if you brought this puppy in the day you shot it, then you must've shot yourself an elk that was already deader'n Elvis may-his-ass-rest-in-peace Presley."

Chief Orlan Johnson was faced with a dilemma. It was midafternoon, and he was already half drunk. Maybe more than half. What he wanted to do was go home, hit the recliner, and zone out, watch a football game or something. Problem was, Hill would kill him if he came home loaded again in the middle of the day. Probably come after him with the same frying pan she'd used on little Joe Crow. Way he saw it, he had two choices. He could start drinking coffee, get himself something to eat, and maybe get sober enough to fool Hill by, say, six or seven in the evening—in which case she'd be all over him for missing supper anyways. Or he could just keep on drinking and go home around five, plenty of time for supper, and let her ream his ass for being drunk.

Johnson fired up an El Producto, stared down at the bloody stain on the floor, and prodded the situation with his mind.

His radio buzzed. Maybe it would be Fleener or Nelson, calling to tell him that they'd caught the murderer or something.

"Yeah?"

"That you, Orlan?"

"George?"

"Yeah. Hey, I hear somebody shot old Berdette."

"Somebody shot him, all right. A guy in a Mercedes."

"No kidding. Listen . . . Orlan?"

"Yeah?"

"You know that Dr. Bellweather with the pink Jaguar?"

"Yeah?"

"Well, the good news is, Shawn's back home now. But I've still got to talk to that doctor. You tell your boys, okay? This is real important now, Orlan. Anybody sees him, you let me know right away, okay?"

"Sure thing."

"You sure you got that now?"

"I ain't stupid." Johnson turned off his handset. More orders from his brother-in-law. What the hell. He returned the full force of his mind to his previous dilemma. The solution was simple—either way, she was going to bust his balls. It would be a lot easier on both of them if he got himself shit-faced drunk for the occasion.

After breaking nine drill bits and pumping several ounces of perspiration onto his yellow suede rodeo shirt, Bellweather finally got enough holes drilled in the safe to knock the lock out with a hammer and chisel. Compared to liposuction, safecracking was a bitch. He looked through the ragged two-inch-diameter hole, expecting the worst, and was rewarded by the sight of a wad of banknotes. Yes! He congratulated himself on buying all these great tools and on pulling off the heist of a lifetime. His lifetime anyway.

Using the chisel, he tried to pry the safe door open. Nothing. He put the safe on the floor, wedged the chisel into the hole, and stomped on it. The shaft of the chisel snapped, producing a nasty gouge on his ankle. His face contorted with pain and anger, he kicked the safe, producing an explosion of pain in his big toe. Bellweather howled, but the safe remained impassively closed. He sat down on the floor, took off his shoe, and examined his throbbing, swelling digit. After a bit of painful prodding, he determined that he was suffering from a medical condition commonly referred to as a stubbed toe. He replaced his sock and shoe and renewed his attack on the safe, this time using a long-nosed pliers to reach in and extract the safe's contents a jawful at a time. The first wad of bills to come out were hundreds, three of them.

Working quickly, Bellweather yanked out bill after bill, keeping a rough count in his head as the pile of torn and crumpled bills formed a gray-green pile on the workshop floor. He quickly reached ten thousand, then twenty thousand. Most of the bills were hundreds, with a few twenties and fifties mixed in. No jewelry, bearer bonds, or other large-denomination negotiables appeared, but the banknotes kept coming. He continued to dig. The rough edges of the hole he had broken in the safe abraded his hands, but he kept at it, sitting on the floor, holding the safe under one arm, shaking it to redistribute the loose bills and bring them within range of the pliers' snapping jaws. There was something else in there, a book of some sort. After twenty minutes, he managed to fold it with the pliers, then pull it through the hole. A notebook. He held up the safe, shook it. Nothing.

Thirty thousand, give or take. That was all. He picked up the safe and threw it as hard as he could. It bounced on the concrete floor and tumbled to rest against the base of his never-used table saw.

He opened the notebook and read a scrawled entry: *When she's in there cooking, you got to keep your eye on the goddamn spoon.*

What did that mean? He looked at a few more pages. Ravings. He began to gather and stack the wrinkled bills. It would get him out of town, at least. He could catch his flight down to Costa Rica, get himself set up sucking fat for Guttmann. It would be work for hire. He'd have to talk Guttmann into putting up some pesos or whatever the hell it was they used for money down there—buying the equipment and renting him office space—but it would beat doing a few years in federal prison. He stacked the cash into four small bundles, amazed and a little disappointed by how little space thirty thousand dollars occupied.

A chime from upstairs—the doorbell—sent his heart into a spasm. Bellweather froze, listening intently. The doorbell chimed again. He grabbed two of the piles of money and tried to stuff them into the pockets of his Ralph Lauren dungarees. Too tight. He pulled up his left pant leg, crammed half the money into his cowboy boot, tugged the pant leg back down, filled his other boot with the other half of the money, picked up the MAC-10, hands shaking. Could he get up the stairs, through the kitchen, and out to the garage?

The sound of footsteps on the first floor stopped him. He took a position at the bottom of the steps, the MAC at his hip, its short barrel pointing up the stairwell, his feet sweating in each fifteen-thousand-dollar boot.

•   •   •

Crow's operating theory was based on a series of assumptions, any one of which might have been untrue. First, Bellweather, in possession of the locked safe, would wish to open it as soon as possible. Second, Bellweather would not want to share the contents of the safe with anyone, and in any case would have a difficult time finding a professional safecracker to assist him. Third, he would be willing to risk returning to his house, which contained, as Crow recalled, a well-equipped shop in the basement. And fourth, he was still there.

Crow had little confidence in this slapdash theory, but having no idea where else to look, he drove over to Bellweather's house. As he sat in his car, staring at the single set of tire tracks leading into the closed garage, he thought he might be onto something. The tire tracks were fresh, and Crow suspected that the pink Jag was sitting in there, with melting snow dripping on the heated garage floor. He pulled the jeep up to the garage door so that whatever was inside would be trapped there, then he high-stepped along the unshoveled walk to the front door, which still bore the seizure notice from the IRS.

He pressed the doorbell, waited, pressed the bell again.

Another twenty seconds passed. Bellweather would not be answering the door. Crow trudged across the front lawn to the window that had been broken. Someone had nailed a piece of plywood over it. He found the tire iron under a pile of beer cans in the back of Harley's jeep, used it to pry the plywood away from the window, climbed into another silent, empty house.

I'm doing too much of this, he thought. Walking into other people's homes.

He wished he hadn't left his gun in the glove compartment of his Rabbit.

He called out, "Hello?" and listened. The house had a hollow sound, an empty hiss. He stood motionless. Nothing. If Bellweather was here, he wasn't responding. He peeked into Bellweather's office, walked down the hallway, opened the door to the garage. As he had expected, the Jaguar was there.

He paused and listened again. No sounds of alertness, stealth, or panic. Nevertheless, he was convinced that he was not alone. The door leading into the basement stood slightly ajar. Crow considered his options. The smart thing to do, he thought, would be to sit and wait. He took a breath, let it out soundlessly, crossed his arms, and watched the basement door.

Several minutes passed. He began to wonder whether Bellweather was, in fact, present. Perhaps he had been there and gone, maybe taking a cab to the airport or getting a ride from his brother. Crow took a step, reconsidered, then picked up a chair and, standing to the side, used it to ease the basement door open.

The door exploded. A storm of wood splinters, a series of rapid, ear-hammering explosions. Crow threw himself back and landed hard, whacking both elbows on the kitchen tiles. The hammering noise erupted again, and a second line of ragged holes appeared in the shattered door, knocking it all the way open. Crow scuttled backward, his ass sliding across the floor, getting his body well away from the line of fire. He heard a click, the rattle of steel on steel—the sound of a second clip being slammed into place—heard footsteps climbing the stairs, the thumping of his heart over the ringing in his ears. Searching for a weapon, he scanned the kitchen. A copper sauté pan, hanging from a rack above the stove. He launched himself across the room, grabbed the pan, and twisted back toward the basement, hurling it as hard as he could at the open doorway just as Bellweather appeared at the top of the stairs.

Bellweather ducked, the pan sailed over his head and clattered down the stairs, but the tip of his right boot caught on the lip of the top step and he went down, his face hitting one of his two-hundred-year-old Spanish floor tiles. The MAC-10 flew from his grip, skidding noisily across the floor. Almost immediately he was on his hands and knees, scrabbling toward the MAC. Crow grabbed him by one foot and jerked him back. Nose spouting blood, Bellweather spun and kicked at Crow's wrist. Crow released his grip, stepped over the panicked doctor, scooped up the gun.

Bellweather rose to his knees. For a moment, Crow thought he might renew his attack, but the doctor suddenly deflated, his hands flapping weakly, his eyes losing focus. He moaned and sank into a pile, his nose pumping blood over his crushed lips, down his chin, onto his canary-yellow shirt. His encounter with the floor tile had left his face in poor condition. He groaned and spat out a piece of tooth, lifted his hands to his face. His eyes focused, searched, landed on Crow. "Joe?" he said, his voice muddy and perplexed. He tried to sit up straight. "My God. What did you do to me? What do I look like? My head hurts."

"Welcome to the club," Crow said. "It's the latest thing."

"What?"

"You're bleeding all over your nice yellow shirt."

Bellweather lowered his eyes to his stained shirt. "Oh. Do you think you could get me a tissue or something?" He put his hands on each side of his nose and pressed his nostrils together as if praying. He separated his palms, keeping his nostrils pressed together with his fingers, and, lifting his chin, said in a distorted voice, "What are you doing here?"

Crow pulled a roll of paper towels from its dispenser and tossed it down to Bellweather, who had to reach out with both hands to catch it. A string of gelatinous blood fell from his nose onto his shirt. He clamped a wad of paper to his face and scraped at the bloodied suede with the rest of the roll.

"Three hundred fifty dollars at Cedric's." He shrugged sadly. "You scared me. I thought you were Ricky Murphy."

"Yeah, right."

"I think my nose is broken."

"Too bad."

"What are you doing here?"

"I just got a call from your friend George."

"Oh?"

"He would like to talk to you."

"I suppose he's upset about his boy."

"I think he's more concerned with what happened to his mother."

Bellweather tried to purse his damaged lips, winced.

"He's also looking for his pig."

"I don't know what you're talking about."

Crow gestured with the MAC. "Let's go, then. Maybe George can explain it to you."

Bellweather pulled the paper toweling away from his nose, examined it. "I'd rather not." He looked up at Crow. "They'll kill me, you know." He touched his nose gingerly. "Do you think it's broken?"

"Not yet." It was true that Bellweather wouldn't survive another encounter with the Murphys. And it might not save Getter anyway.

"Why are you doing this?" Bellweather asked. "Is George paying you? I can pay you more."

"You still haven't paid me for the nights I worked," Crow pointed out. In fact, throughout this affair, he had yet to receive a dime from anyone, and so far he had lost a cat, a car, a wife, and almost his sobriety.

"I was planning to send you a check, Joe."

"Right."

"Look, Joe, I know this has been hard on you. I got you into it, and I want to make it right. What can I do?"

Crow considered. "Some back pay would be nice." He deserved *something*.

Bellweather nodded eagerly. "What do I owe you?"

Crow ticked off the items in his mind. There was the money owed him for his services as a bodyguard. The cost of replacing his Volkswagen. The value of time spent recovering from various beatings. Punitive fees for being forced to deal with particularly unpleasant individuals. It added up quickly.

"How about an even ten thousand," he said. It seemed fair. A nice round number.

Bellweather didn't agree. "I don't have *that* kind of money," he said. "I'm having a little problem with the IRS, as you may have heard."

"Didn't you get George's safe open?"

"What safe?"

Crow motioned with the MAC. "Let's go."

Bellweather didn't move.

"What was in the safe?" Crow asked.

"Not much. A few thousand dollars. Enough for me to get out of the country and start over."

"Where is it?"

Bellweather took a deep breath. "Look, it's all I've got. You take it, you might as well just shoot me. I need it. What I got from George is less than what he owes me. Really. All I want is what's mine. You let me go, I'll be out of your life forever."

Crow listened. He didn't want to be hauling the doctor all the way across the state, listening to him whine. He didn't want to commit murder by delivering him to the Murphys. He had no illusions about Bellweather's worth as a human being, but he didn't think he could kill him.

"I'll tell you what," Bellweather said. "Let me go, and you can have the Jag. I'll sign the title over to you."

"What would I want with a pink Jaguar?"

"I paid over sixty thousand for it, with all the work I had done. I can't take it with me. You might as well have it. Would that be fair?"

"Where are you planning to go?"

A hopeful look crossed Bellweather's face. "South," he said. "You'll never see me again."

Crow liked the idea of never seeing Bellweather again. He also liked the idea of owning a Jaguar, especially now that his Rabbit was out of commission.

"Let's have a look at that title," he said.

The title to the Jaguar was in his bedroom. Crow followed him up the carpeted stairs and into the master bedroom.

"Look what they did," said Bellweather, pointing at the hand-carved, bullet-riddled ebony headboard. "I paid twenty-five thousand dollars for that bed. It used to belong to Teddy Roosevelt. That's one of his safaris." An attaché case and a packed overnight bag were waiting on the mattress, ready to go. Bellweather opened the attaché case, riffled through the papers, came out with a green document. "All I have to do is sign it, and the car's yours."

"So sign it."

"I sign it and you'll let me go, right? We have a deal?"

Crow hesitated, then nodded. He'd made his point with Bellweather. He wanted out.

"You'll have to drive me to the airport," Bellweather said.

"Take a cab."

Bellweather shook his head sadly. "Joe, I really don't understand why you're giving me such a hard time."

"Maybe because I don't like what you were doing with that kid."

"Shawn? I don't know what you're talking about. What did he say? It's not true."

"I don't want to discuss it." The problem was, Shawn hadn't really come out and said that the doctor had molested him. In fact, he had more or less denied it. "Look, sign over the title and I'll give you a lift. Okay?"

Bellweather signed, handed the title to Crow.

"Let's get going," Crow said. "Before I change my mind."

Bellweather reached for the overnight bag, hesitated.

"I have to change my shirt," he said.

"So change."

Bellweather stripped the stained yellow shirt from his soft body. He opened his closet and selected a pale-pink version of the same shirt.

"What do you think?"

"Very nice," said Crow. "Now let's go."

"I have to go to the bathroom."

"So go."

Bellweather went into the adjoining bathroom, closed the door. Crow thought, could he really let this sleazy little child-molesting surgeon leave town? It didn't seem fair. The thought of Bellweather roaming free gave him a queasy feeling. Maybe he should simply hand the doctor over to the police. The IRS had seized his property, so the cops must want him for *something*. Crow frowned, staring at the bathroom door. That wasn't necessarily true. Bellweather's offenses of record were probably civil, not criminal. In any case, a deal was a deal.

Crow shifted his eyes to Bellweather's black nylon overnight bag. He unzipped the bag. It was packed full of clothing. Summer shirts, shorts, sandals, socks, underwear. What did he expect to find? Pictures of naked children?

He shifted the MAC-10 in his hand, heard the toilet flush, then the sound of Bellweather washing his hands. A new idea took form in his mind, and as he had no time to evaluate and rationalize, he simply acted. Folding the wire stock of the small machine gun, he inserted it between Bellweather's khaki shorts and a Hawaiian-print silk shirt, then zipped the nylon bag shut.

XXVIII

Honest differences are often a healthy sign of progress.
—MAHATMA GANDHI

etter sat bent forward in a chair, his hands tied to his feet, looking thoroughly miserable. The tiger lay stretched on the floor, her eyes nearly closed, one paw resting atop the remains of an elk's foreleg. Ricky was sitting at the card table, playing spin-the-Ruger.

During his first few hours as a guest of the Murphys, David Getter had been more concerned with the possibility of being maimed than with the unthinkable prospect of dying. Even after seeing Berdette Williams shot, Getter still considered himself too important a person for the Murphys to outright murder. He would be missed, and besides, now that George had his son back, there was no reason for them to continue holding him hostage. They were only making their legal position more precarious. If they would just untie his hands and feet, he could help them. If he could just make a few phone calls, everything could be smoothed over. He had tried to explain this both to George—who simply ignored him—and to Ricky, who slapped, punched, or kicked him. His face now felt thick and numb, like a slab of meat hanging off the front of his skull. Nevertheless, he kept trying, convinced that he could argue his way out of anything.

"I' look like selp-depense to me," he said, the sweet voice of lawyerly reason undermined by a pair of painfully swollen lips. "He wa twying to shoo us. You din ha any choice. I'd ha no prob'm tedifying to tha in court."

Ricky spun his gun on the table. The Ruger stopped with the barrel pointing at the tiger. Ricky reached out a long forefinger and rotated the barrel until it pointed at Getter, who continued to speak.

"I' wa a hones mistake, right? I mean, you know now I din do anyting. No hard feelings, okay?"

"You think you're so smart," Ricky said. "Hell, I knew old Berdette had a gun full of salt. It weren't self de-fense—I just wanted to shoot the old bastard. There you go. Now you can say I kilt the old man on purpose, you ever get a chance to say anything. How you like them apples?"

Getter did not like them apples at all. He was formulating an argument, but before he could speak, Ricky pulled a grimy red paisley bandanna from his back pocket and stuffed it into Getter's gaping mouth.

"Steve Anderson. Can I help you?"

"Mr. Anderson?"

Anderson expelled a silent groan. Mrs. Franklin Pilhoffer, flakiest rich widow in the western hemisphere. Every week, the same damn thing.

"Yes, Mrs. Pilhoffer."

"Could you please tell me how much my 3M stock is worth today, Mr. Anderson?"

"That would be at eighty-seven and a quarter per share, ma'am. You have—let me look—three thousand forty shares."

"And is that one going up or going down?"

"It's down a quarter point from yesterday."

"Oh, my. Is that a lot?"

"It's a normal daily fluctuation, ma'am. I wouldn't worry about it." Why didn't she just look up the prices in the paper? It wasn't like she was going to be buying or selling anything today.

"I see."

Knowing it was hopeless, Anderson made a halfhearted pitch.

"3M is a good, solid stock, Mrs. Pilhoffer. Of course, you've made a lot of money on it since your husband bought it back in the 1960s. It might be a good time to take your profit and get into something even safer. T-bills, for instance."

"That's a very good suggestion, Mr. Anderson. I'll talk to Franklin and see what he says. He doesn't like to sell his stocks, you know."

"So I've heard," Anderson grumbled. Why did he bother? Every week, the old fool made him go over her entire portfolio. Every week, he tried to get her to do something, anything to generate some account activity. And every week she told him she would have to consult with her husband, who had been dead and quit of her for thirteen years. Old dead Franklin Pilhoffer, unfortunately, was of the buy-and-hold-for-all-eternity school of investment. Anderson was in no mood for this today. All he could think about was that damned elk.

"Now let's see," continued Mrs. Pilhoffer. "What about my Coca-Cola? How many shares do I have?"

He knew that one by heart. When Wicky had given him the Pilhoffer account two years ago, Anderson thought he'd hit the big time. He remembered staring goggle-eyed at the numbers. Three thousand shares of 3M, fifteen thousand of NSP, twenty thousand of Dayton Hudson, a collection of lesser quantities of lesser stocks, and then the biggie.

"One hundred thousand exactly." Every week, he told her the same damn thing. The Pilhoffer account was as static as it was enormous— she hadn't made a trade since her husband died. "Just like always, Mrs. P.," he added, his mind drifting. He could just have the elk mounted, and no one would know that he hadn't really killed it, but he would never be able to look at it again without getting all twisted up inside. He kept seeing George Murphy, grinning, slapping him on the back, telling him what a great shot he'd made.

"Excuse me?" Mrs. Pilhoffer's voice had gone all frosty.

"Sorry, did I say something?" Anderson was momentarily confused.

"My name is Mrs. *Pilhoffer. Not* 'Mrs. P.' "

Anderson blinked. Had he actually called her Mrs. P.?

"Now please tell me, Mr. Anderson, what is my Coca-Cola stock worth today?"

Anderson cleared his throat. "That would be at forty-three even. One hundred thousand shares at forty-three. Do you want me to multiply that out for you, or can you handle it yourself?" He'd had enough of Mrs. Pilhoffer for today, and they weren't even a quarter done with her weekly portfolio review.

"*Excuse* me?"

She sounded angrier than ever, but he couldn't bring himself to care. All he could think about was George Murphy, laughing at him.

"I'm sorry, Mrs. Pilhoffer. What was that? We've been having some trouble with our phones. Listen, if you can hear me, here's what you should do. You should go buy yourself a newspaper and learn to read the stock tables, okay? Oops, I'm getting this buzzing in my—" He hung up. The best way to hang up on somebody is to do it while you are talking. Hang up on yourself, and they'd blame it on the phone company.

If he was lucky, she'd be too upset to call back. He had this elk problem to think about. He was in no mood to deal with Mrs. Pilhoffer.

His phone buzzed, an internal call. Anderson picked up.

"Stevie, you want to come in here, please?"

It was Rich Wicky, his boss.

He sounded pissed.

"She's gonna be okay, then?" Ricky asked.

"Quit asking me that," George said, taking off his coat. "The doctors say she'll be fine. She was sleeping when I left."

"So how come you never told me about you had that pig stuffed with money? I wanted some cash, you always give me that song and dance about having to sell some of our stocks, about how our money was out there working for us. Christ, getting a few hundred bucks was like a major production or something, and here you was sitting on a stack of cash all the time."

George raised his eyebrows. "You knew about it, you'd've been out there spending it."

"Damn right I would've. I work hard around this place."

"So do we all," said George.

"Well, I don't like it. How much you say was in there?"

"A few thousand. Not enough to get all bent up over."

"Yeah, well, as far as I'm concerned, whatever that doctor took, it's coming out of your share of our profits."

George blinked. "Oh really?"

"You might be my big brother, that don't mean you can cut me out."

"You think I was trying to cut you out?"

"I'm just saying it ain't right. You got no right to be holding out on me that way."

George sat down at the table, gathered up a deck of cards, shuffled.

"You hear me, bro?"

George closed his eyes and took a full breath. "You want to run this ranch, Ricky?"

"I damn well could, and that's for sure."

"Well, you ain't never going to. It's in my name, and you're here on my say-so. I make all the executive decisions. You understand that?"

Ricky squeezed his eyes into two hyphens. "I'll tell you what I understand, Mister Ex-ek-you-tive. Our deal is I get a third. That's what me and you and Mandy agreed. You're in charge, but we each get a third."

"That's right. I'm in charge. And you get your share of the profits as long as you're working here. But it's *my* goddamn business. *I* say what's profit and what gets plowed back in. You don't like that way I run it, you got two choices. You can like it or you can leave."

"We'll see what Mandy has to say about it," Ricky said.

"Mandy don't got nothing to say about it. What do you think, she's gonna spank me?"

"Wouldn't be the first time."

They heard the door from the house open and close. Both men turned toward the entrance. Shawn, his eyes still half closed, stood sleepily in the doorway.

George said, "Morning there, sleepyhead."

"Morning," Shawn said. He blinked and dragged the back of a hand across his eyes. "Is it morning?"

George laughed and stood up, walked over to his son, tousled his hair. "It's about six o'clock at night, boy. You sure conked out there!"

"I'm sort of hungry."

"Well, go get yourself a snack out of the fridge. We'll cook up a little something later on."

"How's Grandy?"

"She's not feeling so good. We can go visit her tomorrow, okay?"

Shawn nodded, then noticed the trussed lawyer.

"How come he's sitting like that?"

"He's negotiating."

"What does that mean?"

George looked uncomfortable. "It's business, Shawn. Go get yourself a snack, then watch TV or something, okay?"

Shawn said, "Okay," and wandered back toward the house. After he had gone, Ricky opened his mouth to say something, but George cut him off with a hand motion.

"I don't want to hear no more, Ricky."

Ricky glared at him but got no response. He aimed his gun at Getter, said, "Bang, you're fucking dead." Getter, his head bowed, did not respond. Ricky cocked the revolver. "I'm gonna shoot you dead, you piece of shit." A tremor swept Getter's body, but he wouldn't look up.

"Cut it out, Ricky," said George. "Leave the poor son-of-a-bitch alone."

Ricky sighted carefully along the long barrel and fired, blowing a sizable hole in the floor a few inches to the left of Getter's tasseled loafer. The sound of the explosion sent both George and Getter straight up into the air, with Getter achieving the greater altitude despite his bound and gagged condition. George landed on his feet and swung, hitting the gun aside with one paw and delivering a powerful backhand to Ricky's cheek, knocking him off his chair.

"What the hell you think you're doing? Look what you did to the floor!"

Ricky was sitting on his butt, laughing. Getter had landed on his side and was trying to worm-walk his way out of the room, his eyes wide with terror, his pants leg dark with moisture.

"Sorry, bro." Ricky grinned. "I thought he was trying to escape. I had to make an ex-ek-you-tive de-cision."

When Shawn came running into the room to see what the shooting was all about, he found his father and his uncle red-faced and glaring at each other. The bound man was on the floor on his side, trying to wriggle his way out of the room like a snake. The tiger sat watching, a ridge of fur erect on her back, eyes wide and dilated to solid black orbs, nostrils flared at the scent of fresh human urine.

XXIX

Always do right; this will gratify some people and astonish the rest.

—MARK TWAIN

Mary Getter answered the door wordlessly. The chunk of quartz hanging from a silver chain around her neck must have weighed close to a pound. She turned and walked back into the house. Crow stepped inside, closed the door, followed her to the kitchen. She sat down, her crystal thudding against the edge of the small kitchen table. Knotting her hands in her lap, she looked up at her brother, the skin on her face transparent, fine blue and red veins showing through.

"Have you heard from Dave?" Crow asked.

She lifted her knotted hands to the table. White knuckles, more blue veins. She shook her head. "He was supposed to be home hours ago. His secretary won't tell me anything. He's been so tense, and then he didn't come home. I'm getting a bad connection here, Joe. I can't feel him."

"He's out at Talking Lake Ranch."

"That hunting club? David doesn't hunt."

"I know."

"But he's all right?" She looked hard at him, afraid to believe but begging to be lied to.

Crow felt her plea knot his intestines. After dropping Bellweather at the airport, Crow had driven his new Jag back across town, arguing with himself. David Getter's plight was none of his affair, he told himself. The guy had dug his own hole and slimed his way into it. Mary would be better off without him. He'd tried to go home, back to his apartment, but found himself drawn to his sister. He needed her permission to bow out. Now, as he stood before her, he realized that it was a futile hope. His sister actually loved the guy.

"I'm sure he's all right," he said. The lie left his throat raw.

"I don't believe you. What's he doing out there? He left this morning dressed for the office. He left at six this morning. David never gets up that early." She leaned toward him, breasts pressing the quartz bauble against her clasped hands. "What's going on, Joe? I want you to tell me what's going on. You are holding something inside. I can feel it."

Crow looked away, focused on an embroidered serenity prayer hanging on the wall near the refrigerator, a bit of mystical detritus more suited to their mother's generation.

"Dave has got himself in some trouble."

Mary sat back in her chair, crossed her arms, made her face into a waxen mask. "Tell me."

He took a breath, then told her as much as he thought she could absorb. He told her how Shawn Murphy had run away and how the doctor had, according to George Murphy, tried to ransom the kid by using Dave as a go-between. He told her that the doctor was now attempting to flee the country, leaving Dave at the mercy, such as it was, of the Murphys. Mary had her fist pressed against her teeth. Was she hearing him?

When he had finished his story, she said, "David wouldn't do that."

"I'll admit it seems strange, but you're wrong. David *did* do that." Why did he want to convince her that her husband deserved whatever was about to happen to him? Would that make it okay? Mary was shaking her head, but he thought he could see something in her eyes, in the set of her lips. She knew it was true, but that didn't matter. It was true, but not true. Mary was good at that. Hot, but cold. In, but out. Red, but blue. It had served her well as an artist, and it now made it possible for her to love Dave Getter.

She said, "We have to call the police."

Crow shook his head. "George Murphy owns the Big River police."

"We have to get him back. You can get him, can't you, Joe?" Her eyes accused. "You can if you want to."

"I don't owe him a thing, certainly not enough to justify risking my life for him."

Mary sat back in her chair, her eyes shrinking. "Melinda was right about you."

"What?" Where was *that* coming from? Her voice sounded different. Deeper, and stronger.

"You really are a narcissist, aren't you? You don't care about anybody but Joe Crow, do you?"

"That's not true." He stared at her face, which had come into hard focus. Her eyes glittered with life and anger.

"Bullshit," she snapped. "All you care about is being right. Fuck you."

He hadn't heard her talk like that in years. "That's not true," he repeated, watching her carefully.

Mary leaned across the table, getting her face inches from his. "I want my husband. I want him back. If you aren't going to help me I'll go get him myself, goddammit."

Crow said, "Look, if I wasn't going to go after the son-of-a-bitch, I wouldn't be here." His lips formed a wry smile. He remembered this woman. This was his big sister, Mary Crow, back for a visit. "I knew you were in there somewhere," he said.

Mary sat back, her shoulders rigid, holding him with hard eyes.

"Tell me something. Is it really you, or is the other Mary channeling you?"

She raised an eyebrow. "Is that supposed to be funny?"

"Yes."

"Are you going to help me?"

"I said I was. But tell me something else. Where is Melinda?"

Mary's eyes shifted to his chin. "In what sense?"

"The physical. As in: Where has she gone? You know where she is, don't you?"

She remained motionless.

"Is she all right?"

After a pause, Mary nodded.

"Where is she?"

Mary shook her head. "First you bring me back my man."

Crow said, "It's good to see you again."

The phone rang twice before George's voice answered.

"This is Crow. How's it going, George?"

"We're still waiting here, Officer Crow."

"Let me talk to him."

"He doesn't feel like talking right now."

"You want Bellweather, you put Getter on the line."

"He's doing fine."

"Put him on."

Crow heard an exasperated exhalation, then the sound of cloth on cloth, then heavy breathing, then George's distant voice: "Heads up, Counselor. I've got Officer Crow on the line. You want to talk to him?"

Ragged breathing, a cough.

"Joe?"

Crow looked over at Mary, gave her a thumbs-up. She nodded. The hope in her eyes was painful to see.

"That you, Dave? How's it going?"

"Tell him I'm making calamari risotto for dinner," Mary said.

"Dey're goding do *gill* be! Dey shod thad old ban in da ba. I saw id do it. You god do ged me oud a here, Joe."

"You're having squid for dinner," Crow said. They'd shot Berdette? He wished Getter hadn't mentioned that in front of the Murphys. It sort of limited his options for negotiation.

"Let me talk to him." Mary grabbed the phone. "David?" Her face fell. She looked at Crow, stricken, handed him the phone.

George Murphy was back on the line. "You satisfied?"

"He doesn't sound so good."

"I told you he didn't feel like talking. So you know where Nelly Bell is?"

Crow smiled into the phone. "I know exactly where he is."

Drinking Black Russians in the middle of a weekday afternoon made Steve Anderson feel dark and dangerous. He had claimed a booth for himself way in the back of Myron's Pub and was playing videos in his mind. Some of the tapes were pleasant fantasies, like the one where he got to shoot George Murphy with his Weatherby. Other tapes were recent memories, like the one where he'd walked into Rich Wicky's office and been told to take off.

Anderson's heart had about stopped.

"I don't understand," he'd said. "Am I being fired?"

Dickie said, "I just want you to take a few days off, Stevie."

"What for? What's going on here?"

"I just listened in on your conversation with Mrs. Pilhoffer, Steve."

"Oh. You listened?"

"You know I do that, Steve. It's part of my job. Now all I'm doing is asking you to take a few days—a week, say—and get it together."

"I've got it together. Who was your top performer last month?"

"I was, Steve. But you did good. You're a hell of a salesman, Steve. That's why I'm suspending you instead of firing you. Understand?"

"For one bad phone call?"

"One bad phone call on a three-million-dollar account."

"Yeah, a three-million-dollar pile of dogshit."

Dickie had said, "Go home, Steve. Come back to work a week from Monday."

Ouch. Bad video. Anderson took another sip. A black river of vodka and Kahlúa cascaded down his throat. He hit his mental remote control. Dickie Wicky running across a snowy field, tie flapping over the shoulder of his Brooks Brothers suit. Taking careful aim, going for the knee shot.

"Kapow," he said.

"Kapow? What's he talking about, 'Kapow'?"

"Damned if I know." Rich Wicky leaned over the table. "Stevie? Who are you talking to?"

Anderson blinked, momentarily confused. Rich Wicky and Jack Mitchell, another broker. He hadn't seen them come up. He was torn between wanting to punch Dickie in the nose and throwing the remains of his drink in his face.

Wicky, who could read facial expressions the way most people can read a menu, quickly said, "I can't tell you how goddamned sorry I am about what happened this afternoon, Stevie."

"You didn't look very sorry," Anderson said. He dipped a forefinger into his drink, examined his wet digit, licked it off. "What're you guys doing here?"

Wicky looked at Mitchell, made a wide-eyed face. "It's ten minutes past the bell, Stevie. Quittin' time. Mind if we join you? How 'bout I buy you a drink?"

"I don't care."

Wicky signaled a waitress. He and Mitchell slid into the booth across from Anderson.

"So tell me, Stevie, what got into you with Mrs. Pilhoffer anyways? I gotta tell you, I just about bust a gut when I heard you call her 'Mrs. P.' "

Anderson hiccuped, then laughed. Wicky laughed too, then Mitchell joined in. The waitress brought their drinks.

"You know," Wicky said, "if I hadn't been afraid that old man Litten might be listening in too, I'd have let it slide. Hell, everybody's gotta blow off a little steam now and then. So tell me, Stevie, what's on your mind? It isn't like you to go off on a client that way, no matter how much she deserved it."

It took two more drinks and a lot of prodding by Wicky, but Anderson eventually spilled it, what had been bothering him. He told them how he'd been tricked into shooting a dead elk.

"Let me see if I got this right," Wicky said. "You paid this guy twenty K to let you shoot an elk."

"Record-book elk," Anderson clarified. "Boone and Crockett."

"Right. This huge mother. And so you went out and you shot it, and then later you found out it had been dead a week. And you couldn't get it off your mind, so you told Mrs. P. to take a flying fuck."

"That's right," Anderson said.

Mitchell and Wicky looked at each other, then broke out laughing.

Anderson was not amused.

Mitchell was the first to stop laughing. He donned a serious expression and asked Anderson what he planned to do.

"Get drunk," Anderson said. "Can't go home. Can't tell Patty I got suspended."

"I mean about the elk," Mitchell said. "You gonna let those guys get away with it?"

Anderson squeezed his eyes closed, opened them wide. "Whad'ya mean?"

"I mean, if somebody sold me a piece of bad meat, I sure as hell know what I'd do. I'd send it back to the kitchen."

*Extensive interviews show that not one alcoholic has
ever actually seen a pink elephant.*

—CENTER OF ALCOHOL STUDIES, YALE UNIVERSITY

row contemplated his upended Volkswagen. The sun had
nearly set, and the car's shadow stretched far to the east, fading out
after several car lengths. Both doors hung wide open; the front end
remained buried deep in a snowdrift. He was sorry he couldn't remember the accident; it must have been quite an experience. He closed and
locked the Jaguar, trudged through the drift toward the snowbound
Rabbit.

For once, he was perfectly warm and comfortable.

He was wearing Getter's waterproof Sorels, and he liked it. They
were a size too large, but they kept his feet warm and dry. He felt as if
he could walk through anything. The quilted parka, a high-tech affair
with dozens of Velcro'd pockets and zip-out layers, enveloped his
body like warm armor. A matching Thinsulate hat with earflaps, and a
pair of fur-lined gloves, completed his borrowed outfit. One thing
about Dave Getter—when it came to clothing, he bought the good
stuff.

Thinking he might have to walk in on the Murphys, Crow had
asked Mary if she had a parka he could use, something with a bit more
warmth than his cheap trench coat. She had shown him a closet
packed with Dave's outdoor clothing, most of it looking as if it
had never been worn. After he'd dressed himself, turning up three
inches of pant cuffs and a couple inches of sleeve at each wrist, his
sister had nodded approvingly. Now that Crow had agreed to try to get

her husband back, she seemed calmer, as if his success were preordained.

To his surprise, as he left, she had told him to be careful.

Crow leaned into the upended Rabbit, opened the glove compartment, and recovered his Taurus. He put it in one of the many pockets. Now he was completely dressed.

Armed and suitably clad, he still needed a way to get to his destination. A few minutes earlier, he had driven past the entrance to Talking Lake Ranch. The county plows had made another, wider pass down Highway 7, throwing up a ridge of dirt-gray ice and snow three feet high, blocking access to the ranch. No problem for a jeep, but he'd left Harley's vehicle at Bellweather's, and there was no way the Jag would be able to mount that barrier. Short of walking in, only one other possibility occurred to him.

Fifty yards away, the door to the trailer opened, and Harley Pike stepped out.

"Hey!" Harley shouted, staggering forward. "What the hell you doing?"

"It's just me, Harley," Crow called. "Crow."

"Crow? Where the goddamn hell are my wheels?"

Crow walked to meet him. "How's it going, Harley?"

"It's going fine. Where the goddamn hell is my jeep? You took my goddamn jeep. You were gonna bring it right back."

"Your jeep is fine, Harley." Crow looked past Harley at the trailer. "Is Puss around?"

"Why?" He held his bare fists clenched at his hips; his bloodshot eyes glared from beneath a shelf of wild eyebrow.

Crow said, "You get that beer I left off here?"

"Yeah, I got it." Harley's eyes misted, and his face went soft, all the anger flooding out of him at the memory of the free case of beer. "You want a cool one?"

"No, thanks," Crow said. "I need to ask you for a favor."

Harley frowned. "What's a matter, you don't want to have a drink with me?"

"I need to borrow your snowmobile, Harley."

Harley's mouth went slack, then closed with a click. "You already got my wheels—now you want my skis?" He looked Crow up and down. "What the hell you got on there, Crow? You look like some guy in a catalog picture."

"The thing is," Crow persisted, "I need to get over to the Murphys' place, and I don't think my Jag's got the clearance to handle that road of theirs."

Harley's eyes hunted for, then landed on, the pink Jaguar. "Some-body oughta shoot that thing," he said.

"Somebody has. Where's your woman, Harley?"

"She's watching one a her soaps. You want a beer?"

"I want to borrow your skis, Harley. Tell you what, you loan 'em to me for an hour, I'll buy you a bottle of J.D."

Harley's eyes went small and greedy. "One a the big ones?"

"I'll get you a whole liter. How's that?"

Harley looked over his shoulder. "You won't tell Puss?"

"I won't say a word."

"I can hide 'er in the snow," he said, thinking out loud. "Keep 'er nice and cool."

The door opened, and Puss stuck her head out.

"What's going on out here?"

Harley grinned at her. "Ol' Crow here wants to borrow the Po-laris, Puss. I told him it was fine with me. I'm gonna go get 'er fired up right now." Harley slogged through the snow around the trailer.

Puss frowned at Crow. "Where's his jeep?"

"I'll get it back to you tomorrow."

Puss brushed a shank of long gray hair away from one eye, squinted at him. The sputtering of a snowmobile engine rattled the aluminum walls of the trailer. Her thin lips formed a short arch. "I'm surprised he's letting you take his skis, Crow. I just hope you didn't promise him a jug."

Harley Pike's ancient Polaris was no improvement over his dilapidated jeep. It rode rough and slow, and every time Crow hit a dip in the trail, the fiberglass hood popped up, blocking his vision. He headed due west from Harley and Puss's snowbound trailer toward the bluffs along the river, following a faint snowmobile track. The ten inches of new snow covering the trail made it difficult to follow. Twice, he went off the edge and became mired in soft drifts. Up to his waist in unpacked virgin snow, he'd had to muscle the heavy old machine back up onto the path. The trail zigzagged down the coulee toward the river. By the time he reached the wider, more recently traveled trail that fol-lowed the east bank, he was drenched with sweat.

As he crossed the southern border of Talking Lake Ranch, moving faster now that the trail was clearly visible, the confidence and resolve that had brought him that far started to waver. The wind clawed at his face and his perspiration-soaked undergarments began to cool. He tucked his head between his shoulders and squeezed the throttle, telling himself that so far everything was going according to plan. Boiled down to its essentials, the plan had been to pick up the gun he'd left in his Volkswagen, get to Talking Lake Ranch, and save Dave Getter's miserable life. It would serve as a kind of penance, a selfless act, an act of pure, courageous altruism. Melinda would hear about it, and she would be proud.

Crow sat erect on the speeding snowmobile. Imagining that she was watching him, he concentrated on driving the snowmobile perfectly, his jaw set, guiding the machine flawlessly across the winter landscape.

"Well, I'll be got-damned." Orlan Johnson gripped the doorframe and swayed, muttering to himself. "Dark out. How'd that happen?" Cold air swept past him into Birdy's, rustling the empty potato chip bags that represented the remains of his dinner. His squad car, windows opaque with frost, sat parked a few yards away. Johnson felt his pockets, found a set of keys, and launched himself toward the car. His chosen trajectory was off by about twenty degrees, but by closing one eye he was able to make a midcourse correction and arrive safely at the driver's-side door. He fumbled with the door handle, came to the conclusion it was locked, made several stabs at it with the key. "Slippery bugger," he growled, breathing loudly through his nose. He finally succeeded in opening the door, inserted his bulky torso into the car, got the right key into the ignition, started the engine.

He was ready to go, but he couldn't see a got-damn thing. He grabbed an ice scraper off the seat, got out, scraped a saucer-size hole in the ice-covered windshield. A minute later, the Big River police's flagship squad car, a Ford Crown Victoria with all the performance goodies, fishtailed out onto Highway 7, headlights sweeping the road from side to side to side, Orlan Johnson driving with his chin on the steering wheel, peering out through the hole he had scraped in the frost. He was not looking forward to seeing his wife. The woman had a mouth that wouldn't quit. He imagined himself giving her a good one, right on the kisser. One a these got-damn days he was gonna do it. Maybe tonight, if she gave him a hard time. Wasn't for those brothers a hers, he'd a done it a long time ago.

Something pink appeared in his headlights.

"Whoa there," Johnson said. He moved his foot to the brake pedal, pushed it down. Even with the ABS, the big Ford slewed sideways, came to a stop perpendicular to the highway.

Couldn't see a thing. Johnson rolled down his window, stuck his head out, looked back down the road. There it was, that pink car George was looking for.

Johnson got the car turned around. At least he wouldn't have to worry about taking on a load of shit from his wife tonight. He found that doctor for her brother George, he'd be King of the Hill for a week at least.

XXXI

That was the phrase for it when a safari went bad. You ran into another white hunter and you asked, "How is everything going?" and he answered, "Oh, I'm still drinking their whisky," and you knew everything had gone to pot.

—ERNEST HEMINGWAY, "THE SHORT HAPPY LIFE OF FRANCIS MACOMBER"

he Murphys' lodge first appeared as a ghostly glow, its lights filtered up through the tree branches, spilling down the coulee toward the frozen river. Crow throttled down the Polaris, rolled to a stop, turned off the engine. He figured he was about a quarter of a mile away. He would walk in, come at them silently from below.

Beyond that, his plan remained in development.

Crow got off the machine and followed the icy zigzag track up the bluff toward the lodge, his boots squeaking on the packed trail, one hand in his pocket warming the grip of the Taurus. He didn't know how he was going to play this, but something would occur to him. According to Sam, when you're playing with a short stack, you've got to go with your instincts, and you can't afford to wait for the cards to come to you. "You get dealt deuces, you'd best play 'em like they's aces."

In other words, there was no percentage in computing the odds.

He reached the back of the lodge building, stood looking up at the bank of picture windows. The room was lit up, and from his angle he could see the big log beam running the length of the ceiling, the top of the fieldstone fireplace, the tip of the mounted rhino's horn. He would have liked to see who was in the room, but the bottom sill was six feet above his head.

Crow explored the perimeter of the buildings, considering each window and door as a candidate for clandestine entry. He continued around the house. A door on the east side, where he had met Amanda

Murphy on his first visit, led into the kitchen. Crow looked through the window, saw Shawn Murphy at the kitchen table, eating a bowl of cereal.

One strategy would be simply to wait. Sooner or later one of them would come outside. He'd be much better off if he could separate George and Ricky. The problem was, even in Getter's high-tech regalia he was getting colder by the minute, and besides, he was tired of waiting for things to happen to him.

He heard a sound coming from behind him, a low woof.

Oh, shit, he thought. The dogs.

He turned and looked at them in their chain-link enclosure, at which point they exploded into a series of howls, barks, and growls. So much for stealth.

Having no other options, he decided to take the direct approach. He walked up to the lodge door. George Murphy was standing there, holding it open, looking to see what had his dogs all upset.

"Officer Crow!" said George Murphy. He looked past Crow and frowned. "Where is he?"

Crow ignored the question. "Is Getter here?"

"Sure he is. Where's your friend?"

"Right here," said Crow, planting the barrel of the Taurus in George Murphy's ample gut.

George looked down, his face collapsing into a sorrowful expression. "Not a good idea," he said, shaking his head. "Somebody's been giving you bad advice."

Crow pushed the gun deeper, forcing George to step back into the lodge. As more of the room became visible, he saw Ricky sitting at one of the tables. A few inches from his left hand, a long-barreled revolver lay on its side on the tabletop.

"Tell him to move his hand away from the gun," Crow said.

George took another step back, turned his head. "You hear what the man said, Ricky?"

Ricky nodded his head a scant centimeter. His hand did not move.

George said, "He's mad at me, Crow. Besides, he never listens to me anyways. You gonna shoot me now?" The lower half of George's face stretched into a grin, but his eyes remained opaque.

Crow examined the rest of the room as best he could without letting Ricky out of his peripheral vision. Dave Getter lay curled up on the floor beside one of the club chairs, staring up at him with eyes the size of hen's eggs. A piece of red cloth had been stuffed into his mouth.

Crow prodded George's abdomen again with the gun, moving him farther into the room. He wanted to keep as much of George as possible between him and Ricky.

"You okay?" he asked Getter.

Getter shook his head frantically. Crow saw that his hands were attached to his ankles with bright-yellow nylon cord. George was standing very still, his head turned to the side, looking back at Crow.

"What are you going to do now, Officer Crow?"

A very good question.

George stood directly in front of him, his belly inches from the end of the gun barrel. Ricky sat about twenty feet away, his hand inches from his revolver, tendons and veins popping, eyes slitted.

At the far end of the room, Crow detected a fifth presence. The tiger yawned and blinked, watching the humans with the mild curiosity of a well-fed though never entirely sated carnivore. It stood and stretched, long claws digging through the straw into the wooden floor, muscles writhing beneath its striped coat. This is just great, thought Crow.

"Do you know what I'd do if I were you?" George asked.

"Please tell me," said Crow. "I'm open to suggestions."

"I would go home," said George.

"I plan to do that." He did not like the motionless Ricky Murphy. He wanted a blink, or a facial tic—anything other than the reptilian resolution he was seeing. He had no idea how Ricky would move, or when. Nevertheless, he was convinced that the man wouldn't remain motionless for long. There was no way he would be able to untie Getter without getting both of them shot.

He would have to convince George to do it.

"I think you should go now," said George, "before somebody gets hurt."

"Soon. First let's get Mr. Getter untied. You think you can handle that?"

"You want me to untie the man? Why would I do that? Ricky went to a lot of trouble to get those knots just right. Besides, I don't see Nelly Bell. I thought we had a deal."

Crow shook his head.

Again George displayed his capacious, mirthless grin. "You know what you could do? You could shoot me and Ricky both. How would you like that, Crow? Then you could go in the house and shoot my boy. Then you would have your kidnapping lawyer back. You think that'd be a good idea, Officer Crow?"

It sounded good to Crow. He was trying so hard to watch George and Ricky at the same time, his eyes felt as if they were protruding from their sockets. He had to make a decision. He visualized himself taking a step to the side, aiming, and firing at Ricky. The problem with that was that Ricky was almost certainly faster and more deadly with a handgun. Crow didn't think his marksmanship would stand up, and even if it did, George would be on him before he got off a second shot.

"The other thing you could do would be to back slowly toward the door, close it behind you, and go find me that doctor."

"The doctor is out," Crow said. "He's gone."

"Oh?" George's eyebrows ascended. "Where's he run to?"

"I don't know."

"I think you do."

"I want you to untie him."

George shrugged but did not otherwise move. "It's not going to happen, Officer Crow."

For several seconds, the four men and the tiger formed a tableau.

Am I going to have to kill somebody? Crow wondered, less disturbed by the concept than by its flip side: Am I going to have to die?

The sound of tires rolling over snow crackled through the open door. George's eyes narrowed and jerked past Crow. The sound of a car door opening, slamming. Crow backed up, getting farther away from George, holding the Taurus in both hands, the barrel now pointed more at Ricky than at George. Ricky's hand had somehow moved an inch closer to the revolver grip, but his eyes were on the doorway. Crow thought, I could do it now, swing the gun a few degrees to the right, pull the trigger, pull it again for good measure, then deal with George and whoever was outside. He heard footsteps, something being dragged toward the door. The back of his body prickled.

George's expression dissolved into a look of utter astonishment.

Crow couldn't help it. He had to look. He turned his head.

It took his mind a moment to identify what he was seeing. A man in a business suit backing in through the doorway, dragging an enormous set of antlers. The antlers were too wide for the opening; the man had to twist them sideways to get them through the door. The remains of an elk's head, neck, and shoulders—or rather the empty hide that had once contained them—was attached to the antlers.

Crow snapped his attention back to Ricky, whose mouth was hanging slightly open. Entranced by the arrival of the man with the dead elk, he had missed his opportunity.

The man dropped the antlers and turned on George.

"I want my money back," he gasped.

George said, "Stevie? What's the matter?" He tried a friendly grin.

Both George and Ricky seemed to have forgotten Joe Crow. Even Getter had his eyes focused on the elk man. Crow now recognized him. He'd seen him once before, at Birdy's. One of the Murphys' customers, though apparently no longer a happy one.

"You know what's the matter, you son-of-a-bitch—you had me shoot a dead elk!" Anderson shrieked, his voice cracking as it hit the word "elk."

George cleared his throat. "Uh, Steve, you think we could talk about this some other time? I think you've somehow gotten the wrong idea here—"

"You think I'm stupid?" Anderson beat a fist on his chest, staggered to the side from the force of his own blow. Crow realized he was not only furious; he was also besotted. "You think I'm a fool?" He took a step toward George, jabbing a forefinger at his sternum.

George stood his ground and let Anderson thump him. His smile showed too many teeth, and his cheeks were visibly heating up.

Ricky had moved slightly. He was still seated, but his shoulders had shifted. His eyes remained fixed on Anderson.

Behind him, the tiger sat on its haunches, alert, its golden eyes following whatever moved. The black tip of the tail twitched. Its mouth parted slightly, revealing a creamy length of fang.

"You think I'm some kind of sucker? You think I'm stupid? This thing'd been dead a week when I shot him. What do you take me for?"

Crow thought, A guy that shoots a dead elk, then comes back shit-faced to complain about it. What does he expect to be taken for? He noticed that Getter was moving, performing a sidewinder-like motion that was carrying him away from Ricky Murphy an inch at a time. If no one else noticed him for twenty or thirty minutes, he might get somewhere.

"I want my money back, Murphy. Now!" Anderson raised his chin triumphantly, as if he had scored a fatal thrust of logic. To follow it up, he made another jab at George's chest, but this time his finger ended up locked in George's fist, George standing solid as a ton of scrap iron, Anderson swaying slightly, his extremities twitching with anger, staring with bewildered fury at his captured finger.

George growled, "Take it easy now, Stevie."

Anderson squeezed his lips together, inflated his cheeks, and jerked his finger from George's grasp. They could hear the soft pop of a knuckle dislocating. Anderson gasped and hunched over his injured hand, then lifted his head and launched himself at George with an unintelligible cry. George stepped aside to avoid him.

At that point, Crow realized that he had made a mistake. It had seemed that the Murphys had been totally focused on their unhappy elk hunter, but George had not forgotten Joe Crow at all. As he twisted back, away from Anderson's charge, one arm shot out and up and struck the underside of Crow's forearm. The Taurus flew from his grasp. George reversed direction, whirling like a fat dervish, and struck again, this time hammering Crow's chest with a four-pound fist. Crow staggered back, registering as he did that Anderson's drunken charge had taken him past George's position and toward Ricky, who was now on his feet, bringing up his revolver, eyes on Crow.

Crow dropped to the floor, rolled behind one of the heavy leather sofas, thinking only of getting something solid between himself and Ricky's gun. George was coming at him again, fast. Where had his Taurus landed? There, ten feet past the end of the sofa. Too far. He heard Anderson shout something, heard Ricky yell at him to get the fuck out of the way. Crow was on his hands and knees, speed-crawling toward his lost gun, expecting George's weight to come crashing down on him at any moment. He dove out into the open, his hand landed on the gun, its taped grip feeling like the only solid thing in the universe. He twisted, looking back just in time to see George descending on him, his body filling Crow's field of vision. Crow swung the gun in a short, hard arc and caught George on the jaw as he twisted his body away. George's momentum carried him past Crow into the poker table, sending the table and several chairs crashing down as he landed hard on his belly.

Crow rolled into a crouch, gun in both hands, looking for Ricky.

At first, he didn't know what he was seeing.

Steve Anderson had his arms wrapped around Ricky, wrestling with him. It looked like the last drunken dance of the night, but there was no music, and Ricky was squirming frantically. Crow saw Ricky's hand come around with the gun, slap it against the side of Anderson's head. An explosion. Anderson screamed, grabbed his ear. Ricky stepped back, locked his eyes on Crow, and raised his revolver.

Crow fired. The lead slug flattened against Ricky's oversize brass belt buckle, sent him staggering back toward the corner. He seemed to recover, raised his gun. Crow was about to fire again when an orange-and-white shape rose up behind Ricky. In a gesture that looked like love, the tiger reached out with a plate-size paw, wrapped it around Ricky's waist, drew him back. It seemed to happen slowly, Ricky rotating in the tiger's embrace as if to return it, narrow eyes widened to almonds, then going rigid as the tiger tipped its head to the side, gently kissed the base of Ricky's throat, and released him.

A jet of bright crimson arced across the room, spattering the windows.

Ricky dropped his gun, clapped both hands to his neck, and spun, hosing down a ten-foot-diameter semicircle with arterial blood. He staggered away from the tiger as it stood watching, its instinct telling it that the food would soon stop moving and could be more conveniently devoured at a later time. Ricky dropped to his knees, his eyes rolled up, and he fell facefirst into a gathering pool of red.

Anderson had fallen to his side, both hands cupped over his left ear. A high-pitched gasping, keening sound came from his mouth, providing an eerie sound track for the scene.

George Murphy climbed to his feet. He made a low sound in his throat and started toward Ricky, his eyes on the revolver still gripped in his brother's hand. Crow watched, wondering whether the tiger was about to kill two Murphys in one day. George stopped himself before reaching the perimeter of the tiger's territory. He looked back at Crow, his face gone slack.

Crow shrugged as if to say, Hey, this wasn't what I had in mind.

He heard a muffled, frantic sound. Getter, who had managed to worm his way almost to the door, was staring wide-eyed at something behind Crow, trying to shout through the gag in his mouth. Crow spun and found himself facing Shawn Murphy, who was armed with a small-caliber rifle, pointing it at Crow's midsection from six feet away. His face was dead white but for two red disks glowing on his cheeks. The boy's entire body shook, the end of the rifle barrel moving an inch or more with each tremor of his arms, but at six feet he could shake all he wanted and still make a hole in Joe Crow.

Crow looked back at George. "If he shoots that gun, I'll kill him," he said.

"You put that gun down, Shawn," George Murphy said. Shawn looked at his father, breathing fast and hard. "Now!" George said.

The rifle fell from the boy's hands, hit the rug with a dull thud. Shawn sidled away from Crow, then broke and ran to his father. George wrapped his arms around his son. He looked at Getter, then at Crow, then at Anderson.

Still making the strange throat noises, Anderson had managed to stand up. He brought his hands down, looked at them. No blood.

Crow said, "Are you okay?"

"What?"

"Are you hurt?"

Anderson shook his head. "I can't hear you." He started toward the door, hesitated, grabbed the unfinished elk mount, and dragged it after him. They watched him leave.

"What was that about?" Crow asked.

George Murphy just shook his head. Getter was squirming again, trying to talk. Regretfully, Crow bent over and slowly pulled the red kerchief from Getter's distended mouth.

Getter worked his swollen lips. "Ah dose my clothes?" he said to Crow.

Crow looked at the slimy piece of cloth in his hand and briefly considered putting it back where he'd found it. He looked over at George.

"I still want that Nelly Bell," George said.

"Get in line," Crow said.

George Murphy scowled. "What the hell's that supposed to mean?"

G. Wayne Zizzi, eight-year veteran of airport security at Hubert H. Humphrey International Terminal, was having one of his best days ever. He'd started out, ten o'clock that morning, by spotting a flick knife in a teenager's carry-on. A lot of guys wouldn't have spotted it on account of it was sitting at this weird angle in the kid's bag, but stuff like that didn't get past Zizzi. They'd finally let the kid go after confiscating the blade. Zizzi got to add the knife to his personal collection. Then an hour later, he'd got a joker, one of these guys that says some dumb-ass thing like, "You better take a good look in there. I might be the mad bomber of Minneapolis."

Guy like that, Zizzi took personal pleasure in helping him miss his flight.

Early afternoon, he'd spotted another knife. Turned out it was a kitchen knife, a present for this guy's sister in Toronto. Couldn't let it on the plane, though. The guy was pissed. They made him check it through baggage.

Days like this, Zizzi really loved his job. Felt like he was doing some good. Protecting people.

Mostly, though, it had been a pretty boring eight years. Looking at X-rays of people's luggage, it got so you knew what you were going to see just about every time. People were predictable.

Another thirty-five minutes until his next break.

He stared at the screen, at the ghosts of disposable razors, lipstick, car keys, compacts, belt buckles. . . . He'd gotten so good at it, he didn't really have to think about what he was seeing. Another bag moved into view.

Zizzi stopped the belt, backed it up.

He could feel the hair rising on his neck.

Here was something he had never seen before. Except in training films.

Zizzi looked up at the man standing at the end of the belt, waiting patiently for his bag. Not a big man, not particularly dangerous looking in that prissy leather cowboy shirt. Reminded him of Roy Rogers, only his nose was all swollen and he had a bandage over his upper lip. Could be a disguise.

Zizzi looked back at the screen, at what appeared to be a machine pistol with a full clip. A TEC-9, or maybe a MAC. One of those little machine pistols.

This is a biggie, thought Zizzi as he flipped on the silent alarm switch on his belt radio. This one's gonna make my day.

XXXII

I like outlaws better'n in-laws.

—ORLAN JOHNSON

O rlan Johnson tipped back a beer, swallowed, belched. He waved his cigar in the air.

"Y'know something," he said. "I always thought you was an all right guy, H."

Harley Pike's head flopped forward, then back. "Me too," he said, sucking on one of Johnson's El Productos. He was having trouble keeping it lit. He reached for his beer, found it already in his hand, poured another ounce into his mouth.

Johnson slapped his hand on his thigh. "Is jus' too got-damn bad we wound up on opposi' sides a th' law, y'know?"

"Uh," said Harley. He would have passed out a long time ago if it were not for the novelty of playing host to Big River's number one cop. He was having trouble keeping his eyes pointed in the same direction.

"I got to tell you, you folks, you know how t' live. Got-damn Hill, she won't even let me smoke in my own got-damn house, you know what I mean?"

Puss turned up the TV.

Harley said, "Uh?"

"I mean, you know what I mean?"

Harley opened his mouth, but no sound came out.

"Got-damn right," said Johnson.

. . .

"I want to talk to my lawyer," repeated Dr. Nelson Bellweather. "I don't know where that gun came from. I don't know anything. I want to call my lawyer."

He was sitting in a white room, about the same size as one of the examination rooms at his clinic. Correction. His former clinic. With the two airport security guards, each of them weighing as much as a razorback hog, the room felt very small. So far, they hadn't gone for the rubber hoses, but they weren't exactly looking out for his rights.

The dumb-looking one with the cold sore on his lip, the one named Zizzi, was enjoying himself. His phlegmatic partner, Al, watched disinterestedly.

"Please remove your shirt and pants, sir," said Zizzi.

"I want my lawyer. I'm not doing anything until I talk to my lawyer," Bellweather said, thinking that the thirty thousand dollars in his boots wouldn't do anything to improve his situation.

"Please remove your shirt and pants, sir," repeated Zizzi.

Or maybe, he thought, it will get me out of here.

"Just a second," he said. "Let me ask you guys something. How much money do you take home every month?"

Zizzi and Al looked at each other.

"What are you trying to say, sir?" asked Zizzi.

Bellweather took a deep breath. There was simply no elegant way to do this.

"I'd like to offer you boys a bonus. Say five thousand apiece?"

Zizzi ran his tongue over his teeth. "Let's see it," he said.

Bellweather hiked up his pant leg, reached into his boot.

Five minutes later, he was standing bare-ass naked before the two uniformed men, the money stacked neatly in a metal basket along with his watch, wallet, neck chain, and passport. He couldn't believe they were doing this to him, and said as much to Zizzi, who shrugged and pointed his thumb toward the corner of the room, where, Bellweather noticed for the first time, a wide-angle video camera was pointed directly at them. Bellweather felt sick. No wonder they hadn't gone for the bribe.

"And what else do you have to show us, Mr. Bellweather?" Zizzi inquired politely.

Bellweather, caught between fury and despair, could only goggle at him.

"Mr. Bellweather?"

"What? What more do you want? Do you think I have a bomb up my asshole or something?"

Zizzi smiled, pulled a disposable rubber glove from a dispenser on the wall, turned to his partner, Al. "You hear that, Al? He said something about a bomb up his asshole."

XXXIII

*I figure H. is good for another three, four years before
something blows out on him. Most likely, his brain'll go
before his liver or heart. It's, like, his weakest link, you
know what I mean?*

—GLORIA SCHWEP

Gloria Schwep, aka Puss, wearing leather chaps and a down
vest, was standing outside the trailer, smoking a cigarette, when Crow
and Getter bounced across the field on the sputtering Polaris. Crow
parked the snowmobile, waved at Puss, then noticed Orlan Johnson's
squad car parked on the highway behind his Jaguar.

"Uh-oh," he said.

A shivering, blue-lipped Dave Getter, dressed only in his torn and
bloodied suit, looked up from his seat on the snowmobile.

"Whad's a madder?"

"It seems like we've got some company." He looked at Puss, pointed
at the cop car, raised his eyebrows. She jerked a thumb toward the
trailer. Crow walked over to her. Getter stood up and followed, looking
hopefully toward the mobile home.

"I'm code," he said.

"What's going on?" Crow asked.

"It's a mite close in there, but you can take a look," Puss said. "You
won't believe it."

Crow opened the door and stepped into the trailer. The warm
air was palpable with alcohol, cigarette smoke, and a mélange of
unpleasant human excretions. Getter crowded past him and put
his hands over the propane heater. Harley was passed out, propped
up in the corner of the built-in bed. Orlan Johnson had achieved
a similar state, his corpulent body laid out across Harley's legs.

Both men were snoring heroically, lips flapping visibly with each expelled breath.

"I just wish I had a camera," said Puss.

The man with the bloody dish towel wrapped around his right hand wanted to talk. His name, he said, was Bott. He grinned and knocked himself on the forehead with a knuckle. It made a hollow sound, something like *bott!*

"Messed up my hand," Bott said with a forced laugh. Bott was a tough guy. Only his dead-white face and the sweat beading on his forehead gave him away.

Crow nodded sympathetically.

"The wife dumped another fork down the In-sink-erator."

Crow wasn't sure what an "Insinkerator" was, but he nodded.

"I hadda dig for it. Get my feelers down in there, the bitch hits the goddamn switch." He pushed out his jaw. "I been sitting here half an hour, waitin' to get it looked at."

"That's rough."

"So what're you in for?" Bott asked.

"Brother-in-law," Crow said. "He's in there getting his nose fixed."

"Yeah? Car accident?"

"Not exactly," Crow replied.

"You punch him? I got a brother-in-law I'd sure as hell like to bust his nose." Bott looked at his In-sink-erated hand. "Only maybe not just now."

Crow saw Mary enter the emergency room, coat unbuttoned, hair roughly and badly combed, purse dangling carelessly from one hand. He stood and waved, grateful for the interruption. She stopped in the middle of the lobby, feet spread too far apart, and waited for him to approach.

Crow put a hand on her shoulder. She leaned into it, and he embraced her awkwardly.

"He's all right, Mary," he said, wondering which Mary he was embracing. "They're taking care of him now, getting his nose packed and taped, cleaning the salt out of his thigh."

"Salt?" She pulled away, touched her hair with a shaking hand.

"He was shot, but the gun was only loaded with rock salt."

"He was *shot?*"

"It was just salt. He's fine. Let's sit down."

"My God, he was *shot?*"

Crow led her to a pair of empty plastic chairs near the television. Mary's eyes drifted, then locked onto the TV screen.

"I've seen this show," she said.

"What is it?"

"I have no idea."

"Do you want to know what happened?"

She shook her head. They sat for a few minutes, watching the figures move across the screen. Mary looked at her watch. "How long do you think they'll be?"

"I don't know." He waited. "Are you going to tell me where she is?"

"Who?"

"Melinda."

Mary bit her lip, keeping her eyes on the television. "She doesn't want to see you right now."

"You talked to her? Did you tell her I've been trying to get hold of her?"

Mary nodded slowly.

"Tell me."

Mary turned and looked at him, her eyes searching his face. She nodded sadly, then shook her head. "She's checked herself into the program at Southridge Center, Joe. She's trying to get clean."

"She went into treatment? That's great! Nothing could make me happier. It's what I've wanted for her all along. Why wouldn't she want me to know?" He stood and paced, clapped his hands together. "How long? When will she get out? I want to see her."

"She'll be in the program for another three weeks, Joe. But I think you'd better leave her alone for a while, even after she gets out."

"Why? This is our chance to rebuild. We can start over—get clean and start over fresh and new. Two clean machines. We can make it work."

Mary was shaking her head. "Joe, I don't think Melinda feels the same positive energy you do. She might not want to try again."

"Wait till she gets straight. You'll see. It was the coke and the booze that was wrecking our marriage. All she wanted to do was get high."

"Maybe. But you have to remember that you're the one who got her started. She never used to do coke. She never even drank that much until she met you."

"I was a different person then."

"So was she. You took her there and then you left her."

"I quit! I quit using, and she kicked me out!"

Mary's voice hardened. "That's not the point. You took her. . . . It's like you took her to a really bad play with no ending in sight and you were sitting together in the front row and then she turned to you to tell you what a rotten time she was having and you were gone. You got in your car and left."

"That's not what happened."

"Don't you get it? It doesn't matter what happened on the physical plane. What matters is what Melinda's soul is experiencing."

"You mean, what matters is what she thinks happened. What really happened doesn't matter."

"Just because *you* can't see it doesn't mean it's not real."

Crow hugged himself. "Anyway, she's okay, then," he said. He looked at his sister. "Which Mary am I talking to?"

Mary shrugged, nodded, looked away, picked at a bit of lint on her coat. She smiled, the corners of her mouth pulled back, her eyes dull. "There's only one of us, Joe," she said.

Crow sat down and deflated. I can handle this, he thought, looking at his sister. But I sure do wish she'd stop smiling like that. He looked for the man with the bloody hand, but he had disappeared, gone to get his digits repaired.

"She'll feel different when she gets out," Crow predicted, convincing no one.

"That's great, Crow."

"I just wanted to call and let you know how things turned out."

"Right. That's good. I was wondering."

"And I wanted to thank you for coming over yesterday."

"No problem. Thanks again for the bump. So do you know where she is? I mean, do you know which program she's in?"

"Southridge Center. It's supposed to be a pretty nice place."

"It's nice, considering that most of the people there are dopers."

"You've been there?"

"I did my time. Hey, Crow?"

"Yeah?"

"I gotta go."

PART FOUR

XXXIV

Querent: Do our light bodies dwell within us as well as somewhere else?
Ashtar: They are dwelling multidimensionally. That is why you have to call them down in your meditations and feel them reemerging within you. There are light vehicles, your merkabah vehicles, waiting for you to reconnect so you can use them to travel throughout the universe.

— *"Ascension, Final Instructions," a channeled interview with the extraterrestrial master Ashtar (Ashtar is currently serving as commander of the Confederation Fleet in our sector of the universe)*

cheduled free time, an hour to read and reflect. Melinda had started by reviewing the twelve steps but quickly became bored. For nearly a month she'd been studying that same book, from front to back. She reread a chapter in *The Celestine Prophecy,* searching for substance, finding empty words. She wished she had brought a deck of tarot cards. She would ask Mary to bring some next time she visited.

Free time was the worst.

She sat on the edge of her mattress and gazed at her reflection in the full-length mirror beside the door, breathing consciously, deeply, regularly. She concentrated on gathering the positive energy. Today's center was high, a few inches above her sternum, between her breasts. Her eyes were clear. The lines that had appeared on her forehead were fading. She could feel every part of her body; the numb spots had returned to life, humming with electromagnetic energy. She almost looked like an athlete, in the purple-and-green silk warm-ups she had borrowed from Mary. She felt better than she had in years. And more bored.

And fatter. Four weeks' clean living with unlimited access to Southridge Center's vending machines had added ten pounds, most of it going to her already burgeoning thighs. She stood up, dropped her warm-ups, looked at her legs. Big, white, and a bit bumpy, like Tonya Harding gone soft and curdled.

But she was drug free. Soon she'd be going home, back to Big River, back to her cat and her looms. Then she could get her thighs fixed. She'd heard from Mary that Dr. Bellweather was no longer in business, that he'd been arrested or something, but he wasn't the only liposuctionist in town.

The door opened. Melinda yanked up her warm-ups.

"I think you have the wrong room," she said coldly. That was one of the things she didn't like about Southridge. It was supposed to be the best chemical dependency treatment facility in the state, but they didn't even put locks on the doors.

The woman standing in the open doorway crossed her arms and let her shoulder rest against the doorjamb. Chains swung across black leather. Sunglasses with tiny purple oval lenses. Red lipstick. Slim thighs tightly wrapped in black leather jeans.

"You're Melinda Crow, aren't you?" the woman said.

"What do you want?" Melinda asked.

The woman smiled humorlessly, red lips stretching across her face, showing a set of neat white teeth.

"I just wanted to have a look," she said. "See what we're dealing with here." She turned, chains scraping the doorjamb, and walked back down the hall toward the exit.

Melinda shivered. She sat on the bed, tucked her legs into a half lotus, concentrated on her breathing. Ten minutes later, she began to wonder whether the visitor in black leather had been real or a noncorporeal manifestation of her fears and desires. She wished again that she had her tarot cards. A quick consultation with the Empress, and she would know for sure.

Laura Debrowski spun out of the Southridge Center lot, winding the engine out in second gear before slamming the gearshift into third. She jammed a random cassette into the tape player, cranked up the volume to the distortion point, then beyond. Iggy and the Stooges. Debrowski blew through the traffic control light on the entrance ramp and hit the freeway at eighty, her jaw pulsing.

"Why do I do this shit?" she shouted over the roar of the music.

Iggy Pop answered, "Now-I-wanna, be your dog."

She pulled up in front of her duplex, shut down the abused Honda, banged into her apartment, threw herself on the sofa.

Silence, but for the buzzing of the refrigerator and a faint ringing in her ears.

She lit a cigarette.

A minute later, a soft thump. A black cat, yellow eyes, came padding out from the bedroom, jumped onto her lap, looked intently at the tip of her nose, purring. Debrowski raised a hand, brought it gently down onto the cat's back, stroked.

"God damn your fuzzy face," she said.

XXXV

When I play with my cat, who knows whether she is not amusing herself with me more than I with her.

—MICHEL DE MONTAIGNE

One of the first things Crow learned about serving paper was that above all he must not look like a guy who earns his living by serving paper.

He had tried several looks before arriving at what he called "The Coach."

The Coach was an athletic fellow, usually dressed in a University of Minnesota sweatshirt and sweat pants, with a beat-up letter jacket he'd picked up at a vintage-clothing store. He was clean shaven, his hair was cut short, and he was always smiling, as if remembering his last victory. He had a Nike athletic bag slung over his shoulder. The Coach did not look like a process server. He looked like a guy who was trying to find his softball team. Also, it helped to be driving a pink Jaguar, which tended to confuse people and to make them curious about him.

Another thing he had learned was that Saturday morning was prime time for catching his targets at home. They were usually muzzy enough to answer the door, usually a little hung over, usually with only one thought in mind, which was to tell the doorbell ringer to stick his doorbell-ringing finger up his ass and fuck off.

Crow liked to make his calls early. Five or six in the morning was about right.

By eight o'clock on Saturday morning Crow had served three residents of South Minneapolis and one Saint Paulite. He'd been serving papers for three weeks now, trying to get his head above financial waters, and had quickly picked up enough clients to keep him busy two or three days a week. It wasn't a bad way to make a buck. Better than working for a plastic surgeon.

Contrary to the usual midwinter deep freeze, the first week in January turned out to be mild, almost balmy, the weather going from sub-zero to blustery sunshine, with highs reaching the mid-forties. Banks of snow receded, exposing their black, greasy cores. Oily rivers ran in the gutters. People walking around with their coats flapping wide open, smiling, telling anyone who would listen what a nice day it was. Pseudo springtime in Minnesota. It wouldn't last long.

Crow had heard nothing from George Murphy since he left Talking Lake Ranch with Dave Getter on the back of Harley's snowmobile. Murphy no doubt had his hands full, now that Ricky was gone. The more time passed, the more Crow was inclined to think that George wasn't really such a bad guy. Just another dumb bastard caught up in a series of unpleasant events. At least you knew where he stood.

Dr. Nelson Bellweather, the last Crow had heard, had made bail by convincing his brother Nate to take out a second mortgage, after which the doctor had promptly disappeared. Nate had been quite upset. He had even called Crow and tried to hire him to fly down to Costa Rica and find his brother.

Crow had turned down the job.

Today he was going to call Melinda. Her course of treatment at Southridge Center would be complete. She was probably home already. He felt his heart lift in his chest, hammering too quickly. Was it excitement or fear? He rolled down the window and took several slow, deep breaths. Did he really want to see her? He no longer knew who she was, this woman he had married. The thought of living with her again, should she agree to it, was as terrifying as the prospect of life without her. The problem, he feared, was that he really didn't like her anymore. The thought that he might have fallen out of love with his wife came with an ocean of guilt.

He hadn't seen Debrowski in almost two weeks. Their last contact, a lunch at Emily's Lebanese Deli, had been horribly uncomfortable. Crow had been distracted, his mind ping-ponging from the memory of Ricky Murphy's death to the imagined image of Melinda sitting in a small white room, hugging herself and hating Joe Crow. He'd picked at his cabbage roll and said hardly a word. After a while, Debrowski had stopped talking too. They'd sat eating in silence. Finally, like a jerk, he'd started to talk about Melinda, the way she used to be. He had failed to keep the hope out of his voice. Debrowski had paid the check.

She'd said, "Give me a call when you get your shit together, Crow."
She'd walked out of the restaurant, climbed into her little yellow
Honda, spun the wheels making a U-turn, headed back up University
Avenue.

Crow had felt as if he'd just eaten a bowl of warm concrete.

But he hadn't called her.

He pulled the Jag to the curb in front of his building. A man in a blue
Dodge Aries parked behind him and got out of his car.

The man was wearing a gray suit with highlights on the knees and elbows. The suit looked like it might have fit him forty pounds ago, but
now the waistband was buried between rolls of flesh. Eight inches of
yellow shirt protruded from between the left and right lapels. He wasn't
wearing a tie, having opted instead to bury a gold-plated chain in the
abundance of chest hair sprouting from the open collar of his shirt. On
his head, the hair was locked in place by some shiny chemical substance, was combed straight back, not quite covering the pink scalp on
top, and did a sort of loop-de-loop over a pair of excessive ears. The
man was holding a sheaf of papers in his ringed fist.

Now that, Crow thought, looks like a process server. In fact, he
looked so much like a process server that it was almost inconceivable
that he could actually be one. I mean, Crow asked himself, what kind
of idiot would answer the door?

The man looked at the paper in his hand, then looked at Crow's
building, then walked into the lobby and buzzed Crow's apartment.
Crow followed him, trying to guess what he was doing there. Building
inspector? Salesman? Wrong address? He walked up the steps behind
the man.

"Good morning," he said. The man turned and fixed him with a
matched set of tiny red eyes.

"You Joseph M. Crow?"

"That's right."

"Here." The man jammed the sheaf of papers at Crow's chest and let
go, then walked back to his Dodge, made a note on a clipboard, and
drove off.

Crow stared at the paper in his hand, reading:

. . . you are hereby summoned and required to serve upon Petitioner's
attorneys a response to the Petition for Dissolution of Marriage which is
herewith served upon you within thirty (30) days after service of this
summons upon you . . .

What? He flipped through the pages. Legal gobbledygook. On the
last page he read, beneath a scrawled signature,

David A. Getter, Attorney for the Petitioner.

He licked his lips and said it out loud: "She's divorcing me." The words seemed to melt into the air as he spoke them. He climbed the steps to his apartment, picked up the morning newspaper that was lying in front of his door, went to the telephone, and dialed Melinda's number.

"Hello?"

"This is Joe."

Silence.

"I just got served papers."

"Oh."

"Is that all you've got to say? *'Oh'?*"

Crow did not hear a click, but after some time had passed, the telephone produced a dial tone. He replaced the handset, crossed his arms, and sat motionless for nearly an hour, waiting for the anguish to strike him down, wondering at the peculiar lightness in his chest. Oddly, he did not feel bad at all. He felt as if someone had relieved him of a great weight, almost as if he could fly. It was a familiar sensation, but he couldn't remember when he had last felt this way.

A bittersweet taste coated his tongue.

He remembered now.

The flavor of green Chartreuse.

"Take your time, boy. Rest it right here, alongside this branch. Hold it right there. She's not going anywhere—you just get yourself settled there and take your time now."

George Murphy squatted beside his son in the melting snow.

Shawn wiped his nose on the thumb of his glove, lowered his head, peered through the scope. The .270 Winchester felt heavy, much heavier than his .22. He pressed his cheek to the smooth stock.

"She's right there, son. Just go easy, relax, let me know when you see 'er."

The image in the scope wavered. Shawn repositioned his hands, concentrated on holding the rifle steady. He found the crest of the hill, moved the rifle slowly to the right, looking for the tree, the big white pine.

There. He gradually brought the tip of the rifle down.

There. Sitting at the base of the pine, looking right back at him, its white-orange-and-black body bright against the dark tree trunk.

He couldn't even see the chain.

"You got 'er?"

Shawn said, "Uh-huh."

"Then you take 'er, boy. You squeeze it off nice and easy. Take your time."

Shawn took a deep breath, held it, focused on his target, waited for the crosshairs to settle on the tiger's white breast, on the point of the V formed by two black stripes. He could feel his father standing behind him. The tiger yawned. He squeezed the trigger.

The recoil knocked his shoulder back six inches, but Shawn didn't even feel it. The tiger staggered, regained its balance for a moment, then toppled.

George let his breath hiss out through his nose. He said, "That was a good shot, son. You'll make a damn fine hunter."

"Has it affected your ability to do your job?"

"Well, I have to hold the phone with my right hand now, since I can't hear very well out of my left ear. That means I have to take notes and enter commands into my terminal with my left hand. It definitely slows me down."

"That's good. That's excellent. So you aren't able to handle as many calls. What do you think, it slows you down fifty, sixty percent?"

"Maybe ten percent."

"Are you sure?" David Getter's pen made circles in the air above his notepad. "I think we could go higher."

Steve Anderson, catching on, nodded. "Sixty percent. Also, the time I lost at work, all the doctors I had to see."

"Good. We'll argue that you've lost sixty percent of your earning capacity, which is . . . what did you make last year?"

"About two twenty."

"So your injury is worth a hundred thirty-two thousand a year. We figure you've got another forty years to retirement and that your earning ability will increase by, say, ten percent a year—I think they'll go for that. Where's that put us? Say fifteen million?"

Anderson's eyes widened. "Really? You think we can get it?"

"Depends on how much money George has and whether he's carrying a good liability policy."

"It sounds like a lot of money."

Getter smiled. "We're just getting started, Steve. Let's talk about how your injury has affected your sex life."

"Well, it really hasn't—"

"You sure? No problems obtaining and maintaining an erection? You're in bed with Patty, you maybe think about that tiger, and you all of a sudden lose it? Think carefully now—we might not have another shot at this."

Anderson looked away. "Well, maybe I do have a little trouble. What would it be worth if I did?"

Crow sat on his sofa bed, reading the newspaper. Starting with the front page, he read every article, enjoying them all. The newspaper was really quite interesting when you read it carefully. On page 2A he read about a local politician who had been arrested for solicitation of a minor. The editorial page provided him with some interesting perspectives on the impact of free trade with Mexico, and the comic section, which he read in its entirety without smiling, was highly amusing.

He was as happy as he had been in years, but he didn't know what to do with it. An odd sensation, to be happy in a vacuum.

Someone knocked on his door. Crow looked up from his paper. The security door downstairs had been broken for weeks. People he did not want to see—bill collectors, sales professionals, Mormons—would come right up to his apartment door and pound on it.

Crow set down the paper and opened the door. A black, furry, yellow-eyed shadow banged into his leg, trotted past him. He felt a bubbling in his abdomen, as if a bottle of Dom Perignon had been uncorked in his chest cavity. Milo, fat, sleek, and energetic, made a beeline for his food bowl. The cat rounded his bowl, which had been empty for weeks, and came back to bump his head insistently against Crow's shin. Crow felt a well of tears mount his lower lashes. He picked up Milo and buried his face in the cat's fur, wiping away the wetness, feeling the bass vibrations of his purring.

Milo's fur smelled like tobacco smoke.

He put the cat back on the floor, then looked out into the hallway. Debrowski was leaning against the wall, smoking a cigarette.

"How you doing, Crow-like-the-bird?"

Crow felt himself smile, using all the muscles in his face. "Much better," he said. "I'm doing okay. I really am."

ABOUT THE AUTHOR

Pete Hautman's first novel, *Drawing Dead,* was selected as one of *The New York Times* notable books of 1993. He lives in Minneapolis with mystery writer/poet Mary Logue, an unfriendly but honorable cat named Ubik, and Réné the dog.